CRASH & BURN

LENNY'S BARTENDERS BOOK #2

KATY MICHELE

To the readers who got butterflies…

*Thank you for loving a story
about a teacher and a bar owner.*

NOTE TO READER

Crash & Burn is book #2 of the Lenny's Bartenders series. This book is made up of two parts.

Part 1 takes place a few months after book one of the series, *Giving Me Butterflies*, ends. Part 2 takes place during and after the epilogue of *Giving Me Butterflies*.

Characters and various plot elements from *Giving Me Butterflies* will also be found in *Crash & Burn*. It is recommended but not necessary to read *Giving Me Butterflies* before reading this book.

Crash & Burn contains topics that may be triggering to some readers. These topics include explicit sexual content, panic attacks, grief, death of a significant other, suicide, domestic abuse, anxiety, and brief mentions of a school shooting.

If any of these topics are triggering to you,
please do what you need to protect your peace.

PLAYLIST

"AT LEAST WE'LL BE TOGETHER WHEN THIS ALL CRASHES AND BURNS"

The Tide by Niall Horan
She Looks So Perfect by 5 Seconds of Summer
Wrapped Around Your Finger by Post Malone
When I'm Alone by Post Malone
Paper Rings by Taylor Swift
How Do You Love... by Why Don't We
Music Again by Adam Lambert
Uncomfortably Numb by Arrows in Action
Kinda Into You by Victoria Anthony
Perfect by One Direction
If I Can't Have You by Shawn Mendes
Act Like That by State Champs
LANGUAGE by BOYS LIKE GIRLS
Falling by Trevor Daniel
The Better Me by Beartooth
679 (feat. Remy Boyz) by Fetty Wap
It Wasn't Me by Shaggy
(You Drive Me) Crazy by Britney Spears

PART ONE

CHAPTER 1
MIA

"YOU DID WHAT?!" Mateo barks into my ear, the sound ringing loud and clear over the hustle and bustle of Water Street on a Saturday night. My older brother doesn't raise his voice often, aside from when he's on stage hyping up a crowd.

Or, when I've done something to piss him off.

"Where. Are. You?" he bites out over the phone, taking a pause after each word. He's trying to intimidate me, but I just punched a grown man in the face.

Intimidation doesn't stand a chance against my adrenaline right now.

"Camila, I swear to—"

"Why are you calling me that?" I interrupt. "You're not my dad. Don't call me that." Mateo may be the closest thing to a father, but I cannot stand when he uses it against me.

I hear Mateo's scoff in my ear as I continue my walk towards my apartment. Lucky for me, I'm not like the dozens of people around me trying to find an Uber. It's 1 a.m., but you would think it was just after dinner with the number of people out.

My apartment is a few blocks away from the bar I just

walked out of, and the June night is cool enough to subside the anger boiling just under my skin.

I came out tonight to catch up with two of my college roommates because they have been asking me for weeks. I was tempted to decline again—for no reason other than how I'd rather be home—but they are some of the few friends I have left.

We graduated college a little over a year ago, and yet I'm still trying to figure out what to do with my life.

I was hoping that seeing them, asking what they were up to and how they were using *their* marketing degrees, would kick my ass into gear.

My marketing degree is being used as a full-time nanny because my brother didn't want me go to school for photography like I wanted when I finished high school.

By the time the three of us were done with catching up on life—filling each other in on jobs, travels, and love—I was barely able to keep a smile on my face. After being reminded that I've been working the same job since freshman year of college, don't have the money to travel, and my love life is an off-limits conversation piece, I wanted nothing more than to go home and forget the night happened.

The conversation did nothing but confirm that the last year and a half of college, where I was supposed to figure out what to do with my life, ended up being a blur of therapy sessions, funeral planning, and refusing to leave my bed.

It also confirmed that I'm much better off using my free time to stay at home and avoid everything that comes with leaving the comfort of my apartment.

I was lucky to finish college in the first place, but all I'm left with is a degree I can't imagine putting to use and all the plans for my life thrown out the window.

Who knew one night would change everything?

I was already on edge being in such a crowded space, feeling way too close to the people surrounding us by the high-top table we were standing at. The music I used to blast in my car, dorm, or anywhere with speakers now makes me anxious, and it didn't help that my skin felt prickly with the shame of not sharing anything as exciting as my old room-mates shared.

Then, I felt my mouth go dry, despite the drink in my hand, when I felt a hand slide down my back and across my backside. I felt the room close in on me, and all that came to my mind was that I needed to claw my way out.

I felt like a volcano about to explode, and that's exactly what I did.

I punched him in the face without even thinking. Twice.

Madness erupted, and I slithered my way out of the waves of people, trying my best to avoid any more contact. I made my way out of the bar to the street, and I sent a text to my friends—with the hand that wasn't throbbing—letting them know I was heading home.

"I'm the closest thing you have to one, so watch it," Mateo replies, bringing me back to the present moment. "You have three seconds to tell me where you are."

It's just like him to hold our ten-year age difference over my head.

"I'm twenty-three years old, Mateo. Don't talk to me like a child."

Our parents died in a car accident when I was eight, so I've lived life longer without them than with them. Mateo was eighteen at the time, and he became my legal guardian. He's the one who had to deal with puberty, the sex talk, and all the teenage angst. I'm forever grateful that he stepped up, not having any other relatives that could take me in.

And he's lucky I never gave him much trouble.

At least not until recently.

"One . . ." Mateo says through his teeth. I can picture him seething with his phone in his hand.

"Quit it," I complain a little too loudly, causing a few

heads to turn my way. This isn't going to work. I am an adult, and he can't treat me like I'm still ten years old. "I'm leaving the bar now."

"Two . . ."

"I don't even know what the big deal is, I'm on my way home to m—"

"I'll see you in ten minutes, Camila."

And with that, I hear the *beep* of the call ending, and I question why I even called him in the first place.

My initial intent was to let off some steam, to vent a little, and to hear him say how his little sister is a badass. Instead, he's pissed at me and on his way to my apartment to lecture me on what he will most likely call another "overreaction" even though he knows that leaving my apartment makes me anxious and jumpy.

With a huff, I stick my phone in the back pocket of my faux leather skirt and pick up my pace.

The closer I get to my apartment, the more the sidewalks clear out, and the breeze from the Milwaukee River helps level my head. With less people and less music, my thoughts start coming in more coherently.

Sure, maybe I didn't need to punch the guy in the face, but I didn't know what else to do. My options were to be nice or be a bitch, and both routes would have left me feeling either unheard, uncomfortable, or pissed . . . or all three.

It was a lose-lose situation no matter how you look at it.

There's no way the guy was going to back off, and he didn't need to put his grimy hand on my ass. He *definitely* didn't need to take my elbow to his chest as an invite to continue his advances. The drink I threw in his face should have been his second clue.

I should have known going to a crowded bar blasting music was going to make my anxiety skyrocket, and I'm lucky I got out of there without having a full-blown panic attack.

It's been a few months since my last one, and I've been fine as long as I avoid my triggers, but I was overconfident tonight. I was stupid to think I could focus on the conversation and ignore the music playing. After years of therapy for managing my anxiety and grief, I can usually calm myself down. But tonight, there was way too much going on for me to do anything but act out of instinct.

I see my apartment building come into view, but I'm barely able to grab my keys from my purse because I am starting to shake so badly. My thoughts started out clear and calm, but now I'm seeing red and want to go back to the bar, find that asshole, and use my foot instead of my hand to target a much lower region.

Stop, I tell myself.

I freeze just outside the doors of my building, trying to see through the red clouds blurring my vision.

Breathe.

I inhale, then exhale, trying to push the memories that are threatening to come to the surface away, and I keep my eyes wide open.

Too afraid that I'll see *him* if I close them.

I take one more deep breath before heading into the building.

My therapist will have her job cut out for her on Thursday.

I wave at the security officer manning the lobby and round the corner to head to my place. Having an apartment on the first floor is convenient, especially because I can avoid the elevators.

I hate those things.

As I turn the corner, not one, but two faces come into view. One is Mateo, standing with his arms crossed in the middle of the hallway just outside my apartment door. He has one of his hoodies on with the familiar logo of a heart on fire with his band's name, Cross My Heart, written across it.

Mateo is the lead singer of a rock band with three of his

friends. I've known the three of them since I was fifteen, and they were all in their mid-twenties. The band started off as a side thing for them—all four guys have day jobs and spend their free time practicing. Over the past two years, Cross My Heart has been playing more gigs around the state which helped them land a spot opening for some bigger names across the Midwest. They're hoping in the next year some of those bands will offer them a spot on a U.S. tour.

Mateo never let me come around the band when they were practicing. Theo, the guitarist, and Silas, the bassist, were friends Mateo had in high school, but their current drummer joined the band when Mateo met him in his first year of college.

And, to my surprise . . . there he is.

The other face that greets me is Cross My Heart's drummer: Eddie Ramirez.

Eddie is leaning against my apartment door, with one foot on the ground and one foot on the door behind him. His arms are crossed, and he looks rather bored to be here. Eddie has jet black hair that isn't too long or too short, wavy but not curly, and attractive features.

Wait, attractive? No. They're just features.

I walk towards my brother and Eddie, wishing I was coming home to my couch *alone,* but my brother, and Eddie, apparently, aren't going to let that happen.

As I get closer, my eyes dart between the two of them, noticing how unimpressed they both look to be here. I'm only a few steps away from my door when I notice a pair of drumsticks in Eddie's back pocket.

They must have been at a band practice, and since the two of them are also roommates, I assume Mateo had to bring him.

Great.

With important shows coming up, I am not at all surprised

that my perfectionist of a brother has the band practicing at every waking moment to prepare.

But now, not only do I have to hear my brother's lecture about what I did at the bar, I will also have to hear him lecture me about how I interrupted a band practice this close to the Midwest shows starting.

I stop in front of my brother who has yet to say a word.

"You didn't have to come," is all I say to him before turning to face Eddie whose eyes find mine immediately.

I'm ready to tell him to move out of the way, so I can get into my apartment, but the words are caught in my throat. I'm too distracted by the green of Eddie's eyes—so light and striking against his tan skin. I try to tear my eyes away from his when I notice a scar across his left eyebrow down to the center of his cheek. I've never noticed it in the dozens of times I have met him or gone to one of Cross My Heart's shows, not that I've been to one in a while.

I've also never been this close to him before.

Mateo's hand on my shoulder startles me slightly and snaps me back to reality, and Eddie's face disappears from view as my brother turns me around to face him. I'm not short, standing at about five-nine with my three-inch wedges, but my brother still towers a good five inches over me. I shrink back into myself, remembering how it feels to have my brother disappointed in me.

"What the hell were you thinking?" he barks, not caring that it's now after one in the morning, and we are in the middle of my building's hallway.

"What's the big deal?" I whisper-yell as I try to shrug off his hand, that is still on my shoulders, not wanting my neighbors to witness the embarrassment of my brother yelling at me like a kid who got caught breaking curfew. His grip doesn't let up, so I reach up to remove his hold on my shoulder but wince when pain shoots up my right hand.

Mateo grabs my wrist and sees the few cuts on my knuckles as well as some swelling on my pinky.

"I'm fine," I hiss, but he doesn't seem to care.

"You're not fine, Camila. You're an adult. You can't go around punching guys in the face for looking at you the wrong way!"

I rip my arm away from him, not letting my face show another quick rush of pain in my hand. "I told you not to call me that." I close my eyes and huff out some air. My brother is the only one who ever uses my full name, and he only does it when he's mad. "He didn't just look at me, Mateo. And, I know how to punch."

Mateo lets out a humorless laugh before wiping his hand down his face. "I know you know how to punch, Mia. Because I taught you." He steps around me towards my door, and I spin around to be reminded that Eddie is still here, watching this all go down.

I avert my gaze to my hands and slowly find my door fob on my keychain, being careful not to irritate my hand that will most likely be bruised tomorrow.

"Now, get inside." Mateo's voice is sharp, disapproving, and exactly what I would expect from my overprotective, older brother. "You are going to tell me exactly what happened this time."

I roll my eyes as I unlock the door.

Of course, he had to add "this time" because he just *had* to clarify that this isn't the first time I have, in his opinion, over-reacted in a situation where my anxiety skyrockets, and my brain tricks me into thinking something is very wrong.

Mateo follows me inside, and Eddie is directly behind him. I hear the door close behind Eddie as I walk into my living room. My apartment is small, just big enough for me, so it feels crowded with my brother, who looks like he just walked into a dollhouse, and his equally-large friend.

I kick off my shoes and sit down on my couch while Mateo grabs a bag of frozen fruit from my freezer, and Eddie stands at my kitchen island. I can feel Mateo trying to get a hold of his frustration as he wraps the frozen bag in a paper towel, but Eddie just looks like he's ready to hear the story as he leans on the island, looking between Mateo and me.

He doesn't look uncomfortable or out of place.

He looks . . . *interested*.

I shake the thought away as I grab the blanket I keep folded on the couch and wrap it around me.

"I'm not going to tell you if you just keep yelling at me."

"Okay," Mateo responds as he walks towards me. "I won't, but I'm worried about you. Ever since Ni—"

"Don't." I refuse to let him finish that sentence because I'm not talking about *that* right now, and this doesn't have anything to do with *him*.

I notice Eddie stiffens at my tone, and Mateo freezes mid-step.

I close my eyes and lay my head back on the couch cushion behind me. I feel the couch next to me dip as a rush of cold lands on my fingers and shoots up my arm, burning for a few seconds. I let out a hiss just before my hand slowly becomes numb.

I turn my head and open my eyes to find Mateo looking at me.

His anger and frustration has faded.

What is left hurts me more.

Pity.

I shake my head to push the tears I feel prickling at the back of my eyes away.

"He didn't just look at me," I repeat my previous statement as I take over holding the makeshift ice pack over my hand.

"Okay," Mateo responds. He stands back up and sits

down on one of the stools I have at my kitchen island, next to where Eddie is standing. "Start from the beginning. What happened?"

CHAPTER 2
EDDIE

HOW THE HELL did I get caught in the middle of this siblings' quarrel?

When I agreed to give Mateo a ride to band practice earlier today, I knew it was going to be a late night. With the first night of our Midwest series coming up in just two weeks, and Mateo being such a perfectionist, I wasn't expecting to be home any time before 1 a.m., but I didn't think *this* is where we would end up.

At his little sister's apartment.

His little sister who is *definitely* not so little anymore.

And who apparently punches guys.

In the face.

In her free time.

I should've stayed in the car because I have absolutely no business being here.

I almost headed back to the car to wait for Mateo, but Mia got here before I could escape, and when I saw her it was like she froze me in place.

All I know now is I'm invested.

Not in her.

In this situation.

Right?

I haven't seen Mateo this pissed off since he almost kicked Theo out of the band three years ago when he caught him looking at Mia's ass a little too long.

She had come to one of our shows at a bar near her college campus with a group of her friends, and the night ended with me having to hold back Mateo from kicking Theo's ass.

And it's not like I've never sneaked a peak over the years, especially right now, in her leather skirt, but hearing what happened to the last guy who paid too much attention to her ass, and being best friends with her older brother, I will keep my wandering glances to myself.

I've known Mia for seven years, but I have exchanged maybe fifteen words with her. I haven't physically seen her since that show three years ago, and I could not tell you anything about her aside from what Mateo said in passing.

I know she graduated college last year, nannies for a living, and I remember Mateo saying something about her liking photography.

He keeps her completely off-limits to Theo and Silas, due to their roaming eyes and womanizing ways, and I am assuming the same goes for me because he refuses to let her around us unless he's there too.

Mateo is protective over her; he always has been.

When I met him my freshman year of college, he had just been granted sole guardianship, and I respected him for taking on the role of her older brother *and* parental figure. I know what it's like to have to step up and take care of the women in your life, so I've always kept my distance from Mia, out of respect for him.

I don't see her as anything besides Mateo's little sister, and, even if I wanted to, I wouldn't live long enough to enjoy it.

As we walk into her apartment, the smell of lavender and

coconut wash over me. I close the door behind me and try to be a fly on the wall.

Resting my elbows on her kitchen island, I watch Mia as she sits down on her couch and uses one arm to cover herself with a blanket.

"I'm not going to tell you if you're going to keep yelling at me," Mia tells Mateo as he gets something to ice her hand, and I can't help but be a little impressed that she knows how to punch and isn't afraid to. Otherwise, we probably would have met her at the emergency room with a few broken fingers.

Badass, if you ask me.

"Okay," Mateo responds as he walks into the living room where Mia is seated. Her blonde hair is in loose curls, displayed along her shoulders and the back of the couch. Her brown eyes look worn and tired, and not just from the night.

When we saw each other in the hallway, I couldn't help but notice the golden flakes that pepper her dark irises. Her cheeks had a pink to them, and I can't believe I never noticed how beautiful she is until now.

Whoa, absolutely not.

These thoughts about Mateo's little sister cannot happen.

Not now.

Not ever.

"I won't, but I'm worried about you, Mia," I hear Mateo say as he walks over to her. "Ever since Ni—"

"Don't," Mia interrupts before he can finish the thought.

I freeze at the iciness in her voice, feeling the tension settle in the air as Mateo stops mid step.

He hit a nerve, and I suddenly feel like I really am a fly on the wall. Something is exchanged between the two of them, unspoken but loud and clear to Mateo, who sits down and places the makeshift ice pack on her hand as Mia closes her eyes. Her chest slowly rises and falls.

After a few moments, Mateo walks back into the kitchen

to sit down and asks her to start the story from the beginning. Mia lets out a breath before explaining how she went out to meet a few friends at the bar. Mateo and I listen carefully as she explains that she was already a little on edge because of how crowded it was and how loud the music was.

She doesn't like loud music and her brother is in a rock band?

An observation I file in my brain for later.

"There was a group of guys about my age standing near us, and I didn't think much of them, aside from how I wished they would move. I thought they were harmless, just standing too close," she explains. Her shoulders are tense, and I can hear in her voice that reliving this moment is not a pleasant experience for her.

"Why didn't you guys move?" Mateo asks.

"There was no other place to go. The place was getting more and more crowded by the minute, plus I was planning on finishing my drink and then leaving," she tells him.

"Then what? Did one of the guys say something to you?" he asks her.

I feel my fingernails dig into my palms and a slight pressure in my chest as I picture Mia in a bar with a bunch of guys around her making her feel uncomfortable.

She may be Mateo's little sister, but something about this story is not sitting well with me.

"I tried to ignore the people around us and focus on Becca and Jess." A shiver runs down her spine. I can see the visceral reaction to the memory. I can almost feel the shiver myself.

"What?" Mateo asks through his teeth, and I think if I were to talk right now, I'd sound the same.

"I felt a hand slide down my lower back and down to my butt, so I sent my elbow back into his chest thinking that would make him stop. But he wouldn't take his hand off me, and then he squeezed his hand around my ass, and I felt like the room was shrinking in size by the second." Her voice is calm, but her body language is anything but. She is relaying the story clearly with an even tone, but there's a bite to her words.

As she continues, she starts to rip at the paper towel around the frozen bag of fruit on her hurt hand. "I had my drink in my hand, and there wasn't much left. It was my first reaction to turn and throw it in his face, so that's what I did. I thought it would be enough to send the message that he had no right to put his hands on me. But then, he wiped his face, looked me up and down with this disgusting smirk, and winked at me."

I feel myself breathing a little heavy, and I can't unclench my fists. The more she says, the more pissed off I am that this guy got out of this with *just* a punch to the face.

"So I threw the punch," she concludes.

Mateo nods his head as if he's putting all the pieces together.

He's the type of guy to have a solution for a problem or a way to fix something, even if it isn't broken. From what I understand, this has happened before. I don't know to what extent, but it has happened. And I doubt he's going to let it happen again.

While I think it is awesome that Mia stood up for herself, you also never know what someone is capable of, and she's lucky she didn't get hurt even more.

Even though she shouldn't have been hurt at all in the first place.

Physically or emotionally.

And I only care about her like that because she is my buddy's little sister.

"Look, Mia," Mateo starts, "I see why you did it, but this can't happen again. You could get seriously hurt."

I can't help but chime in, "You never know what could happen. I'm a bartender, and I've watched fights, that don't seem too big, escalate into full-on brawls, and believe me, shitty people don't care who's in the crossfire."

There have been so many times where it takes two or three of us to break up fights, and the guys working at Lenny's aren't exactly the type who let bullshit slide. Lenny's is a dive bar with a series of regulars ranging from all suitable drinking ages, and the owner, Emmett, has zero tolerance for violence in his bar. People don't care though, and fights still break out over the stupidest shit with alcohol running through everyone's system. Luke, the other male bartender, and I are constantly having to keep an eye on things. We try to avoid and stop those shitty situations, like what happened to Mia, but those things can slide under the radar.

"I can handle myself. It's not like this will happen again. I barely go anywhere besides work anyway," Mia explains.

"Yeah, but every time you do go out, it doesn't end well," Mateo counters. "You're either the center of some sort of conflict, or you hole yourself up at home and refuse to go anywhere."

"I said I can handle myself. I don't need you telling me what to do," Mia argues, her voice raising in volume, the skin on her chest exposed by her top is slowly reddening. She stands, the ice pack and blanket now on the floor. Mateo stands too and walks over to her in the living room.

This conversation no longer seems to just be about what happened tonight.

"Apparently, you do." Mateo pinches the bridge of his nose and lets out an exhale before continuing. "You're right, that asshole never should have touched you, but the way you reacted is not okay!" His volume now matches Mia's.

"What am I supposed to do?" she cries. "Ignore him? Say thank you? Wait for someone to intervene? That's not going to happen!"

"No, that's not what I'm saying. What does your therapist

say? Is it normal how you go from zero to a hundred when you're uncomfortable?"

She scoffs, "That's none of your business."

"Actually it is. I am your guardian, and I am responsible for you. Do you even tell her how bad your anxiety has gotten?"

"First of all, I am an adult. Second of all, what are you talking about? I'm fine! I haven't had a panic attack in months. I'm going to my weekly sessions and taking my meds. Anxiety or not, that asshole at the bar deserved it."

"Mia, you're not fine! What kind of brother would I be if I just stopped caring about what you did when you turned eighteen. When I agreed to be your guardian, it was for life." He looks down, shaking his head, before looking back at Mia. "You're acting out. You're losing friends. You're not even using your degree. You refuse to pick up your camera. You won't even talk about—"

"I said, I'm fine!" she counters, ignoring all of Mateo's accusations and not letting him get to his last one.

"You're not the one who died that night, yet I feel like I lost you all the same!" Mateo's raised voice causes my skin to tingle with discomfort because he always keeps his cool. I can tell that another nerve of Mia's has been hit.

And this was a bad one.

Is he talking about his parents? I know they died when she was young.

I step into the living room, not wanting to get between them because it's none of my business, but I don't want this to escalate any more than it already has. I feel my own protective instincts take over, the same way they would when my father would raise his voice at my mom.

I am positive that Mateo would *never* hurt Mia, but I don't want either of them to say or do something they might regret.

"Mia, Mateo," I say softly, yet sternly, stepping between them. Mia looks like she was shot right through the chest.

"It's late," I continue, "you guys are tired. Mateo, I think it's time to go. Mia needs some rest. You guys can continue this conversation tomorrow."

I place a firm hand on Mateo's shoulder, and I can feel the frustration radiating off him. I turn to see Mia's hurt all over her face. The two of them are stuck in a staring match, and I'm not even sure they heard me.

After a few seconds, Mateo turns and heads to the door without another word.

I have the urge to say something to Mia because I feel the need to take that hurt look off her face, but I tamp the ridiculous thought down.

I am her brother's friend, not hers.

I barely know the girl.

I steal one more glance at her face, wishing the tension in the air would ease, knowing I can't do anything about it. She doesn't meet my eyes as she continues to stare at her brother's back as he grabs the doorknob.

I can tell there are words on the tip of her tongue that are not coming out.

I follow Mateo, who turns around before opening the door to leave, looking right past me and directly at Mia. "Nico is gone, Mia. He isn't coming back."

And with that, he opens the door and storms out of the place. I turn around to see those pretty brown eyes cloud before I follow Mateo and close the door shut behind me, wishing I had just stayed in the car.

CHAPTER 3

MIA

THE DOOR quietly closes as Mateo and Eddie leave, and I feel like my entire body is frozen in place. I can't feel the pain in my hand, or the embarrassment in my cheeks from Eddie watching Mateo and I go at each other. All I feel is a familiar numbness in my chest as my mind takes me back to the memories I try so hard to keep in a special place in my brain that I only visit in my dreams or in therapy.

Nico.

The name that haunts my nightmares but brightens my dreams.

The name that brings so much happiness and so much sadness all at once.

My eyes flutter close, and before I can stop them, the memories start flooding in. It is almost like I can feel Nico's arms wrapping around me—the feeling I miss every waking moment—as I replay all the moments I share with him in my head like a beautifully tragic montage of the best and worst moments of my life.

No.

My eyes snap open, and the warm embrace I felt is gone as quickly as it came, almost as if it was never actually there.

I need to go to bed.

No more thinking of tonight, or Mateo, or *Nico*.

But, not thinking of something is much easier said than done when you're someone with anxiety.

I constantly struggle with taking back power over my thoughts, and I feel like I'm always stuck in a spiral that prevents my brain from shutting off, especially before bed. Before therapy, I could barely sleep. I would stay up, staring at the ceiling, feeling like the thoughts inside my head were shouting at me as they moved a million miles per hour.

Therapy and the right medication have helped me take back some of my power, but there is no fix-all solution. Some nights, I feel normal. I feel like my thoughts are my own and in my control. Other nights, like tonight, it feels impossible to shut my brain off.

I walk over to my bathroom and strip off my clothes before getting in the shower to wash the mess of tonight off my skin. The only sound around me is the water falling in streams.

If this were high school, or even the first few years of college, music would have been blasting while I showered. It didn't matter what time of day or who could hear, it used to be my favorite part of taking a shower. There was nothing like finding a playlist to match whatever mood I was in and singing like my life depended on it. It didn't sound good because Mateo was the one who got all the singing talent, but it *felt* good.

These days, music reminds me of the song I can't get out of my head.

The song that reminds me of the worst day of my life.

The song that my memory can't quite place, but it gets stuck in my head anyway.

So, I avoid music—as much as I can.

My lavender body wash feels like a breath of fresh air as I lather the soapy bubbles all over my body. I can feel the notes of the unnamed song form in my brain, tempting me to hum the melody, but I refuse.

I turn the shower off and put on my robe, wishing for the kind of warmth that I will never feel again.

I moisturize my body with my coconut-scented lotion, and then head into my bedroom before putting on my silk pajamas that keep me cool on these summer nights in an apartment with no central air. The building is old, and it has been redone to look more modern with new appliances and updated décor—but still no AC.

These pajamas also come in handy because most nights, I wake up with a layer of sweat over my body from trying to chase a memory in my dreams, or run away from one in a nightmare.

My therapist has suggested sleeping aids, but I'm not interested. The self-loathing side of me thinks I deserve chasing the dreams, and running from the nightmares because I'm alive to do it. The healthy side of me knows that they are a part of healing, and they will eventually fade.

All of me just hopes that one night, I'll finally get the song out of my head.

———

"No!"

My eyes snap open as I scream into a dark room. My blackout curtains only let a sliver of light shine through. I feel my hair sticking to my forehead, and my arms are slick with sweat. My comforter somehow landed on the floor, and my sheets are twisted up at the bottom of my bed, yet I still feel like I'm boiling.

I sit up to gather myself, trying to catch my breath.

After a few seconds, I lay back down and close my eyes, trying to remember the memory that played out in my dream tonight.

"How was it?" I ask.

"Fine," Nico says, but he doesn't seem fine.

There's something off about him.

Before I can ask what's wrong, he looks at me. His brown hair shines almost blonde under the afternoon sun, and his bright blue eyes look conspicuous, as if he knows something I don't know.

"I almost finished the song," he explains. "But, I can't quite figure out the last part."

"Can I hear it?" I ask, hopeful this will be one of those times he says yes.

He smirks at me, an all-knowingness in his features, before he leads me to a bench in the middle of the sand and takes his guitar out.

"Well, it is for you," he says before he starts playing a few chords—chords I have heard in many dreams before this—but before I can recognize the tune, his fingers continue moving along the strings, his mouth singing the lyrics, but I could no longer hear it.

I try to tell him I can't hear, but it's like he can't hear me.

The louder I screamed, the further away I got from him, as if he was being pulled into the dream, and I was being pulled out.

I open my eyes, frustrated that this dream-turned-nightmare always ends like this. It's one of the few I have in cycles—all ending before I'm ready for them to.

I've had them so many times since Nico died, I've lost count. I'm always so close to hearing the song he wrote for me, or convincing him to stay the night, or telling him I didn't mean what I said, but he always gets pulled away.

If only I could play an instrument, something to figure out the song that haunts me. I can almost hear it in the melodies that play on the radio and the lyrics on my old Spotify playlists, but I can never find *the* song.

I pull my knees into my chest and close my eyes, trying to remember anything else from the dream that I can, but I already feel it fading away.

As I open my eyes, the dream is overshadowed by last night's events as they all come flooding back.

Talking with Becca and Jess in the crowded bar.

Punching that guy in the face.

Mateo coming over.

Mateo yelling at me.

Mateo bringing Eddie.

Eddie's green eyes.

Eddie's worried expression.

Eddie's clenched fists as I told Mateo what happened at the bar.

Eddie, my brother's bandmate, roommate, and best friend.

Eddie who probably thinks I'm as fucked up as Mateo makes me out to be.

Without another thought, I put on a pair of leggings, a sports bra, and sneakers, careful to avoid irritating my right hand. It doesn't hurt half as bad as I thought it would this morning, but I will need to be careful with it over the next few days so it can heal. Once I've brushed my teeth and pulled back my hair, I'm out the door to blow off some steam on this lovely Sunday morning that Mateo will inevitably ruin when he calls me to rehash last night's fight.

Running is a form of self-care I try to implement, and it helps me get out of the house, which my therapist noted I should do more of. Just like I predicted, Mateo called me on my run, but I ignored the vibrating and kept going, telling myself I will call him when I get back to my apartment.

My true crime podcast isn't as motivating as my old running playlists, but the voices retelling a case where an abused woman cuts off the penis of her abuser keeps my mind from spiraling.

When I get home, I shower and make a smoothie for breakfast before I sit down to call Mateo back. Sundays are the only days he doesn't start band practice until ten, so I know this next hour is going to be a lot of listening to him tell me I need to clean up my act.

I know he's frustrated with me, and I can understand he feels like I've changed, but I don't know what else to tell him.

I sit on the couch right as my phone rings again. For a moment, I consider ignoring my brother for a second time, but I ultimately decide that I should just get this over with.

I put the phone to my ear. "Hello?"

"Hey," Mateo responds.

"I'm assuming you're calling to continue our conversation from last night?"

"Yeah, about that," he pauses for a moment, trying to put together the words he wants to say next. "I'm sorry for bringing up Nico. I couldn't sleep last night knowing I threw that at you, but I can't help but think how you have been acting lately roots back to him."

I let out a shaky sigh.

Hearing Nico's name always sends a shock through my system. Mateo is the only one, aside from Nico's family, who knows what happened *that* night, but it's never gotten easier to talk about him. Not with my therapist, not with Mateo, not with anyone.

"I don't know what you want me to say."

"Mia, I can't say I know what you're going through because I don't. The closest thing I can relate to is when Mom and Dad died, but I know it isn't the same." Mateo had to deal with the grief of losing our parents while he was learning how to parent an eight-year old, and I know it wasn't easy for him. "I remember there were daily aspects of my life that became hard for me after they died because it reminded me of them, but I didn't let it take over my whole life."

I half-listen as Mateo goes on about how there are certain smells that bring back memories or certain foods he can't eat without wanting to cry, but I just can't relate. His thoughts and feelings about our parents' death are completely valid, but they belong to him.

He continues, "I'm just trying to understand what you're going through, but I can't unless you explain it to me."

Mateo has absolutely no idea about how music has become a trigger for me. When I listen to music, my thoughts start racing trying to remember Nico's song, pulling me back into memories that can send me into a panic attack if I let them. And how the hell am I going to explain that to him without making him worry about me any more than he already does?

Through therapy, I've learned to cope because it's impossible to avoid music all together, especially with a lead singer of a rock band for a brother. I can usually tolerate music just fine when I'm distracted by something else. I can let the music fall into the background.

When I don't respond to his earlier sentiment, he redirects the conversation in the most unexpected way. "You're going to come work for me."

"Um, what? What the hell are you talking about?" I ask, defensiveness lining my words.

"I'm hiring you as our band photographer."

"Absolutely not," I assert.

"Yes, you are."

"No, I'm not. You can't just make up a job for me, so you can keep a better eye on me," I explain. "I haven't taken pictures since—" I pause because I don't know how to finish that sentence. I can't even remember the last time I picked up my camera.

"Exactly," Mateo responds, keeping his voice calm and even, as if he's approaching a wounded animal. "You need to dive back into it. You love photography, and you're good at it. Plus, we need someone to take pictures for our social media. If we want to get onto a U.S. tour, we really have to impress the scene with these Midwest shows."

There is, no doubt, that he is choosing to ignore the ulterior motives I accused him of, but I'm too stunned to articulate a response.

"I'm sure the Davidson's won't mind if you take some time off or let them know you've found another job. They've cut back your hours with the boys getting older anyway. Plus, you're going to need to open your schedule. You'll be coming to our practices, our social events, our shows, everything."

"Whoa, hold on. I did not agree to this. Why are you acting like I already said yes? I don't want to work for you."

"You don't have a choice, Mia. Either you let me help you, or I'm cutting you off, and I don't want to do that. But, I will if I have to."

My brother works as a computer scientist during the day and he makes enough money to comfortably take care of the both of us. He helps me pay for my rent, car, insurance, school loans, and pretty much everything else. My job as a nanny doesn't cover even half of my expenses, so I need his help financially.

"You can't hold money over my head," I argue, the defensiveness now taking over my words.

"I don't want to, but this has gone too far. I can't keep watching you throw away your life while you still have one to live."

I let out a gasp as if the words physically touched my skin. "That's not fair." My voice is small, but he keeps hitting me where it hurts.

"Nico wouldn't want this," Mateo reassures softly, knowing that this is a truth I don't want to hear. Tears threaten to fall, but I don't let them. That has always been his tactic, and it works because he knows me better than anyone.

I want to tell Mateo he has no idea what Nico would have wanted. I want to tell him how all Nico wanted was to be happy, but he couldn't overcome the demons in his head no matter how hard he tried.

But, I keep my mouth shut and ponder how the hell I'm going to get out of this.

I don't want to be a band photographer for Cross My Heart.

The last thing I want to do is be surrounded by music, and I haven't picked up my camera in years. It has been in a box I keep in the back of one of my dresser drawers since Nico's funeral, and that is where it's going to stay.

"I can't," I manage to say, and my brother somehow knows the thoughts going through my head.

"You can," he responds, and I can't argue with that because he adds, "and you will. I'm on my way over. You're coming with me to practice."

CHAPTER 4
MIA

I THOUGHT I would be able to convince Mateo I needed some time to think about what we talked about, and how I would come to band practice when I was ready, but he didn't want to hear any of it. He refused any answer that wasn't, "Okay, I'm coming."

The guys practice in an empty warehouse next-door to one of the bars they frequent, both as customers and as performers—Lenny's. It's also the bar Eddie works at when he isn't practicing.

Cross My Heart used to practice in Theo's garage, but after too many noise complaints, they were forced to find a different space. Luckily, Eddie is close friends with the owner of Lenny's who also owns the empty warehouse.

The warehouse is made up of a concrete floor and gray walls, and despite it being summer, the inside is cold, not to mention small and bare. The guys each have their instruments, and there are amps set up with a microphone stand for all four of them. There is a table with a few chairs that fill up one of the corners of the space and gives me somewhere to sit while they practice.

When we got here, I could tell Mateo had already warned

Theo, Silas, and Eddie that I would be coming because there was not a hint of surprise on their faces when I walked in behind Mateo. Mateo and Eddie usually drive together for practice, but I'm sure Mateo asked Eddie to meet him here since he wanted to drive me. I can also safely assume Eddie got more than enough of Mateo and me last night.

I can also tell that Mateo told all three guys to leave me alone because all I got was a wink from Theo, a smile from Silas, and a small wave from Eddie.

I've always noticed that all three guys are insanely attractive in their own way. Watching them from afar, for so many years, allowed me to appreciate their looks the same way you do a celebrity's, knowing you can look but nothing will ever happen.

Theo, the guitarist, has always turned heads with his dark hair and eyes so brown they almost seem black. Silas, on the other hand, reminds me of someone you would see in a country band rather than a rock band—always in a flannel, with blond, shaggy hair that peeks out from his backwards trucker hat. Both are the type of guys that break-up songs are about—heartbreakers through and through.

Neither of them measure up to Eddie, though, whose green eyes would haunt my dreams in far more exciting ways than I'm used to. That is, if my mind wasn't so occupied with the grief and trauma that dictates my life.

Mateo has always made it clear that all three of these guys are extremely off-limits, and has told me, since I was fifteen, to "not even think about it."

Not that they have any interest in me anyway.

I have much more important things to deal with anyway, so my brother's friends are the absolute last thing on my mind.

I have my camera bag with me, but I have yet to take it out. It's been about half an hour since we got here, and, so far, I've heard a bunch of random chords, beats, microphone frequency, and, "Test 1, 2, 3," as they get everything ready to start practicing their five-song set-list for the opening set they will play at each of their six Midwest shows.

Which I, *apparently,* will be at.

Standing at crowded venues.

With blasting music.

Taking pictures.

"You good?" Mateo asks me.

I nod. "Yeah, I'm fine. Just going to watch for now."

His look is questioning, but he lets it go. "Remember, we need pictures of everything. Feel it out for a bit, and then you're going to need to pull that camera out."

Exactly what I don't want to do, but I keep that to myself and give him another nod.

"We ready?" Mateo asks the other three, who did a good job of pretending not to listen to Mateo and my conversation. Since the warehouse isn't very big, the five of us are going to become *very* comfortable with each other over the next few weeks.

Eddie responds with a few hits on the bass drum, and then clicks his drumsticks together three times to signal for Theo to start with his opening riff.

Before he can use his tattooed fingers to swipe his guitar pic over the strings, I take a deep breath in.

I can do this, I tell myself. *It's just music.*

I've heard these five songs dozens of times, but it's been a while.

As I exhale, the song begins, and Mateo's vocals start.

His voice has a rasp to it that makes it unique, and the lyrics always seem like they were made for him to sing. He and Silas used to do most of the writing, but ever since Eddie joined the band, he has taken on writing the lyrics.

The five songs in their set are made up of three older songs, their rock cover of "When I'm Alone" by Post Malone, and one song they are still working on and will debut at the first show they do for their mini tour.

Their cover of Post Malone is Mateo's tribute to me because he's my favorite artist, and I used to listen to his albums religiously.

As the guys practice their opening song, I can't help but close my eyes and try to find a familiar beat that may help me figure out the song from my dream that I can't get out of my head.

Just as I start to feel like the song is coming to me through the melody playing, my heart starts beating faster, and my mind takes over.

"Nico?" I call out as I knock on his bedroom door. He was supposed to meet me at a restaurant near campus, but he didn't show. His place is only a few blocks away, so I decide to go check on him when he didn't answer my texts.

We got into a fight the night before. I was stressed about finishing a paper because my grades would impact finding an internship for next year. Nico was frustrated I wasn't paying attention to what he came over to show me. It was the February of my sophomore year and things were picking up, so we fought.

I was mad.

He was mad.

We both said things we didn't mean.

But I love him. I will always love him. I don't know why I let my anger get the best of me and tell him otherwise. I didn't mean it when I said loving him was becoming a burden.

That couldn't be anything further from the truth.

"Nico," I call out again as I twist the doorknob of his bedroom door.

"STOP!" Mateo's bark tears me out of my thoughts. Luckily, I was pulled out before I could spiral with no hope of getting myself out of it. I am, however, left with a familiar feeling of defeat—the need for a release that never comes.

Like the frustration of not being able to place why something seems familiar, but being constantly reminded of it.

This is why I do not let myself listen to music, why it shouldn't be anything more than background noise. Whenever I feel like I'm beginning to place the melody that I only hear in my memories and dreams, the song changes or stops or my thoughts take over.

I buried the memory too deep and I can't uncover it no matter how hard I try.

"Eddie, you're a half beat behind. That can't happen, man." Mateo sounds annoyed but not angry. He's a perfectionist, and these upcoming shows mean a lot to him.

"Sorry, just a little distracted," Eddie responds. "Let's do it again."

Before Mateo can say anything else, Eddie is tapping his drumsticks together and the song is starting again.

After thirteen do-overs and half an hour of me messing with the settings on my camera just to focus my mind elsewhere, the guys finally get through the first song without needing to stop, and the song now just sounds like static to me.

"Alright, five minutes and then we're doing it again and playing right into the next one," Mateo directs as he walks over to me. "What did you think?" he asks me.

It has been just about three years since I went to one of his shows, and it wasn't until I saw the shine in his eyes, or heard the hopefulness in his voice that I realized he's happy I'm here sharing this with him.

"Great!" I respond with a little too much fake-enthusiasm. I take a sip of water from my emotional support water bottle to take a second to think through what I should say next. Before I get the chance to speak, Eddie comes over to us, and I magically forget how to formulate words.

"How's your hand?" he asks with a friendly grin on his face, but I'm taken aback by the concern in his voice.

"Oh yeah, we heard you were throwing punches last night," Theo says as he finds a spot standing next to Eddie. "Mateo, you didn't tell us your little sister was such a badass."

"Don't encourage her," Mateo replies.

"You teach her how to punch?" Silas asks as he walks over to join us.

Mateo nods as he snatches my water bottle from me and takes a sip.

"Hell yeah," Theo beams as he holds up his hand for a high-five, and I can't fight the wash of pride I feel being acknowledged by my brother's friends as I reach up from where I'm sitting to clap my non-punching hand to his.

"Alright, Rocky. Tell us what happened," Silas says as he sits down on the chair opposite of me.

"Rocky?" I can't hide the confusion as to how Silas has known me for almost a decade and still doesn't know my name.

"Or do you prefer 'The Italian Stallion'?" Theo asks with a chuckle. I turn to Mateo for clarification because we're not even Italian, but when I see him chuckling too, I catch on to the Rocky Balboa references. Before I can say anything else, Mateo interjects and tells them to stop talking to me and get back to practice.

The three of them begin walking back to their instruments and mic stands, and I see Mateo swat Silas on the back of the head with one hand and then he delivers a similar swat to Theo with the other. The resemblance between Mateo, Theo, and Silas is that of a paternal figure condoning his two sons. I can't hear what was exchanged, but I'm sure it was something along the lines of, "Leave Mia alone."

I can't help but feel a little boost in confidence that Theo thought what I did was badass, and that Silas sounded impressed that I knew how to punch.

"You sure you're okay?" Eddie asks. I didn't notice he was

still leaning on the wall next to my table. He's dressed in a white Cross My Heart T-shirt with black jeans. His eyes should be dulled by the lack of bright lights in the warehouse, but they are still as striking as ever. His arms are crossed, revealing his toned forearms and making his biceps strain against the fabric of his t-shirt.

"Mia?" he says again, and I refocus on his face when I'm greeted with a hint of what would be the sexiest smile I've ever seen . . . if it wasn't my older brother's friend delivering it. I feel my chest heat up at the fact that he just caught me checking him out, so I stand up and grab my camera from the table just to do something with my hands before saying, "Yeah, totally fine. Not even bruised."

The words come out forced and rushed, but at least I was able to form the words while also looking at his face. That is an improvement.

For some reason, being the center of his attention caused a weird alteration in my brain chemistry because I never had an issue with him when he was kept at a safe distance.

Stop it, Mia.

Before he can respond, I rush out another string of words with no spaces between them that I *hope* makes a coherent sentence.

I never used to be someone who struggled to keep up with comebacks or shy away from a smartass comment, so the fact that I feel all the blood bubbling just under the skin on my chest is embarrassing. Not because I care what Eddie thinks about me checking him out, but because of the fact that I can't hold my own anymore.

Holding my camera, I walk towards where the rest of the band is.

Apparently, I'm going to take some pictures.

CHAPTER 5
EDDIE

I THOUGHT I was distracted at the beginning of practice with Mia being here, but after watching her check me out, I don't know how I'm going to focus on something as trivial as staying on beat.

And that right there is a problem, because my music is the *most* important thing to me, aside from my mom and sisters.

When Mia and Mateo got here, I thought I was prepared to see her again, convincing myself that last night's overprotective thoughts about wanting to make sure she was okay were merely a fluke. But now, seeing her again in her jean shorts and an oversized Cross My Heart crewneck, there's a pressure in my chest that has never been there before.

Her blonde hair is up in a high ponytail and her face is bare of any makeup unlike last night. Her pretty brown eyes, high cheekbones, and heart-shaped lips are definitely distracting enough, but when her attention is directed at me I had to remind myself that she was Mateo's little sister.

I couldn't help but watch her as we started playing because I was so confused by her expression. The second Mateo started singing, it was like her mind went to a completely different place. It wasn't until he yelled at me that she snapped out of it.

When I take a seat behind my drum set, Mia is still awkwardly clutching her camera as if it's holding all the secrets of the world. I barely understood her when she ran away from me just now, but I'm surprised to see her here with a camera at all after what I witnessed last night.

But I am glad to hear her hand is okay . . . that *she* is okay.

Mateo told me and the other guys this morning that Mia was going to be hanging around taking pictures of us for the band's social media, while he also reminded us that she is off-limits, aside from polite conversation and respectful banter which is already an upgrade from the usual.

It was nice to see her talking with Mateo, Theo, and Silas with a shy, soft smile on her face. It was a drastic contrast to what I saw last night.

Now that I've seen what she looks like when she is content, I hope she stays that way.

Because she's Mateo's sister.

No other reason.

I'm surprised to find that she's shy and soft-spoken, though. A girl who punches grown men in the face doesn't seem like she would have those character traits.

"Eddie!" Mateo shouting my name takes me out of my thoughts.

"What?" I ask, confused.

"Didn't you hear me? I asked you three times if you were ready." Mateo doesn't sound mad, just stern. When he's like this, he reminds me of a high school teacher who scolded you for being late to class.

"Oh, sorry. Yeah, ready." I count the guys in as I hit my drumsticks together three times, and then start the song.

Damn, I think to myself as Silas starts the bass line and Theo comes in with his electric guitar. *Why is she so damn distracting?*

My question is quickly answered when I find those two pretty brown eyes staring right at me as I play. Mia is still clutching her camera, but she is watching me. It's taking everything in me to play the song I know by heart when those eyes are on me.

"Stop!" Mateo shouts over the music. I see him look directly at Mia and follow her gaze to turn to me. "You're behind again," he says, but there's more to his words. He caught her staring at me, and I'm being scolded. Again.

He turns back to Mia. "Why don't you take a few pics?" He poses it as a question, but it was an order.

Mia doesn't say anything but nods her head and loops the strap connected to her camera around her neck.

"Busted," I hear Silas say under his breath. I ignore him and the glare I'm getting from Mateo, and I count them back in to start the song over.

———

I manage to get through the rest of practice without getting distracted by Mia, even though I couldn't help but follow her in my peripheral vision as she walked around with her camera at her eye, snapping pictures of us.

She started out slow, looking at every picture right after she took it, but then I watched as she got more comfortable.

I don't know much about photography, but I can imagine it's all about finding the right shot and angle, the same way that writing a song is about finding the right feelings and memories to convey something people can identify with.

Taking photos must be like riding a bike because Mateo had said something about her not doing this a lot lately, but she jumped back into it as if she never stopped.

We pack up our stuff and decide to go next door to Lenny's for a drink. Mateo usually ends practice early on

Sunday nights because we all have jobs to go back to on Monday.

The four of us are regulars there in addition to being their recurring performers. The owner, Emmett, finally let his girl-friend, Drew, convince him that live music was a perfect addition to his bar. I've been working for him ever since we graduated college, and when I'm not with the band, I'm there. Especially since Drew and Emmett started dating earlier this year. I spend a lot of time there because Emmett has *finally* given himself hours that allow him a social life outside of Lenny's.

Mateo and I met in college, and Emmett was my best friend and roommate. The two of them became good friends too, especially now that we practice next door to his bar.

As I cover up my drums, Mateo finishes wrapping up the microphone cords. Theo and Silas already headed over to the bar. Mia is sitting at the table looking through the photos she took, her brows furrowed and her bottom lip is between her teeth. She looks very invested in whatever is on that little screen on the camera. I watch her as I twirl one of my drum-sticks between my fingers.

My line of sight is blocked by snapping fingers in front of my face. I take a step back and drop my drumstick.

"What the hell?" I smack Mateo's hand from my face.

"What do you mean 'what the hell?' Why are you staring at Mia?" he whisper-yells to remain out of Mia's earshot. Not that anything could grab her attention right now. She's down-right mesmerized with whatever she's looking at on her camera.

"I wasn't staring," I whisper back, not even trying to hide the annoyance in my voice.

"What don't you get about 'off-limits?' She is in no place to deal with *you*. She has enough going on."

I bend down to pick up my drumstick that I dropped, and I put both in my back pocket. I try to ignore that insinuation of how me, of all people, would be the worst thing for Mia. I can hear it in Mateo's voice, and I can't help but clench my now-empty fists.

Mateo is one of the few to know about my *complicated* history, but he has no right to throw it back in my face.

Even though I just put them in my pocket, I grab my drumsticks again and start twirling one in my fingers just to do something with my hands.

"Don't worry. I'm not interested in your little sister." He should be way more worried about Theo and Silas than me. The two of them are perfect examples of men you don't want anywhere near your little sister. I, on the other hand, have never been interested in charming the random girls who come to our shows into one-night stands, like the other two are.

"Good, because she isn't going anywhere. I need to keep an eye on her. That means she's going to be around a lot, and I can't have you getting distracted, especially over her. Like I said, she has enough going on."

"Yeah," I manage to say because I'm not about to admit to Mateo that his little sister is the most distracting person I've come across in years, and I've spent less than twenty-four hours with her.

"I mean it, Eddie. I barely got her to agree to take pictures for us, when all she used to do was beg for me to get her new camera equipment."

This grabs my attention more than it should. "Why did she stop?" I ask.

Mateo lets out a sigh and glances over to Mia who is still clicking through her camera. "It's not my story to tell."

While I want to know about the unspoken words I witnessed last night, and why she stopped coming to our shows, I can appreciate the way he prioritizes her privacy.

"She's been through a lot," he continues. "She's trying to cope with what happened to her, but she needs a little help.

She gave up something she loved because she lost someone. I'm hoping that if I remind her how much she loves photography, she will start seeing that she has her own life to live for."

Damn.

There is so much going through my head at this revelation about Mia.

Losing someone?

Giving up what she loves?

Living her *own* life?

I shake my head and steal a glance at Mia. She finally turned off her camera and started packing up her stuff. "Like I said"—I tear my eyes away from her to look back at her brother—"she's your little sister. I wouldn't do that."

"Thanks, man." Mateo slaps his hands down on my shoulder before turning to walk over to Mia. He says something to her before they head out the door of the warehouse to walk over to Lenny's.

No more being distracted by this girl.

Whatever she's dealing with is enough.

And just like Mateo said, I'm the last thing she needs.

CHAPTER 6
MIA

LENNY'S IS EXACTLY what I would expect for a dive bar in a small town outside of Milwaukee. The lights are dim with neon signs lining the wall. There aren't a lot of windows, so it almost feels like you're in someone's basement.

And right now, it's quiet and empty, aside from Theo and Silas, and the two guys standing behind the bar.

"Hey, Mateo," the blond guy behind the bar says. He's handsome with a chiseled jaw and wide smile that feels inviting and genuine. He reminds me of a golden retriever.

"Hi, Luke. No Annie tonight?" my brother asks.

The man next to Luke lets out a bark of a laugh—deep and gruff. He's dressed in a black T-shirt with tattoos covering the visible skin on his arms and hands, and he has his dark hair pulled back into a loose bun on the crown on his head.

"Yeah, Luke. Tell Mateo where Annie is," Tattooed Guy says as he slaps Luke on the back.

"Shut up, Emmett," Luke says, but there isn't much strength behind the words. He gives Tattooed Guy—or Emmett, apparently—a shove, but Emmett doesn't even budge. "Annie and I had a little spat about a guy getting a little too friendly with her last weekend. I intervened and told the guy to back off, but she didn't like that."

Theo, Silas, Emmett, and even Mateo are trying to hide their smirks as Luke continues. He lets out a sigh, before adding, "So now, she doesn't want to work shifts with me because she thinks that I think she can't handle herself."

"And that's why I'm here on a Sunday night instead of between my girlfriend's thighs."

"Emmett," Mateo says sharply through clenched teeth, and I don't have to look at him to know he's trying to communicate to Emmett with his eyes that *I'm* here.

My cheeks heat at Emmett's comment, and I feel like my eyes are about to pop out of my head. I'm not a prude by any means. I pride myself for being sex-positive and not having hang-ups about sex, even though it's been years since sex has even come to the forefront of my mind, but I can't help but feel a little flustered.

Lucky for me, I'm not someone who shows my emotions on my face, but I'm sure everyone can see the redness blooming on my chest with the tank top I'm wearing.

"Oh, sorry," Emmett says, not sounding sorry at all. "Didn't know you brought a guest."

Mateo just shakes his head before introducing me as his little sister to Luke and Emmett. He explains that I'll be taking pictures for them during their Midwest shows.

"Nice to meet you," Luke says with that swoon-worthy smile as he reaches his hand out to me, and the blush on my chest deepens.

What is it about this bar and men that seem to be written for the female gaze?

Luke's fingers wrap around my hand, and a spark of pain shoots up my wrist. With all the craziness of the day, I totally forgot my hand is still a little sore from last night.

"Sorry," I say quickly before letting go of his hand. "I hurt my hand last night."

"Yeah," Silas chimes in. "Rocky here punched a guy in the face," he tells Emmett and Luke. He turns to me before adding, "You still owe us that story."

All six guys' eyes are on me, and I suddenly feel like I'm two feet tall. "Um . . . yeah. So . . ." Words are completely escaping me, and then I mentally slap myself in my face for, once again, turning into this shy girl who doesn't know how to hold a conversation.

Before I show my internal self-loathing on my face and embarrass myself even more, Mateo chimes in and fills Luke, Emmett, Theo, and Silas in on what happened. With the attention on him, I make a break for the corner of the bar with the restroom sign.

Once the bathroom door shuts behind me, I lock the door and rest my back against it. I lean my head back and close my eyes as I take what feels like my first deep breath since my run this morning.

The day went much better than I thought it would. Focusing on taking pictures helped me keep my mind occupied, and I forgot how fun it is to lose yourself in the moments around you. I've always loved photography because I love finding the stillness in the chaos, capturing natural moments of someone doing what they love.

I didn't truly fall in love with photography until I started taking pictures of Nico. When he played guitar, he had this look of bliss on his face that I rarely ever got to see. His features were soft, his eyes were focused, and the demons that invaded his mind were nowhere to be found.

I thought picking up a camera would be hard, but Mateo was right. I do love photography, and today helped me remember that.

The pictures I took weren't my best, but it felt like riding a bike. After the first few shots, I felt like I had never stopped. It will take me a little bit to find the right angles and lighting for each of the guys, but I captured a few good shots today.

My brother is easy because I've been taking photos of him forever, so that won't be an issue. He's used to being in the spotlight as the lead singer of Cross My Heart, and his confidence always shows when he's in his element—someone who radiates confidence like him makes for an easy subject. That confidence is something we used to have in common, and seeing how good it looked on him today, I realize that I want mine back.

Just like Mateo, it also helps that Theo and Silas are so photogenic. As I continue going to their practices and eventually their shows, I'll get the hang of how to use that to my advantage.

Eddie, on the other hand, I figured out right away.

My skin heats at the thought of Eddie's pictures on my camera. I couldn't stop looking at them after I took them. I barely even noticed him and my brother talking in the warehouse before we came over here because I couldn't focus on anything but what was conveyed in each photo of him.

There's something about the photos of Eddie that were seamless. No matter the expression, gesture, timing, or lighting, every shot of him told a story and drew me in.

I could feel his love for the music and his attachment to his sound. I could see the pride of being part of the band. And I could almost hear his voice in the music that was playing.

I walk over to the sink and splash some water on my face to cool down, bringing my hands down my neck and chest, hoping to ease the heat that bloomed there.

It's been years since I thought about music in a way that wasn't defeating or degrading, and I don't know what to do with all the feelings I'm having.

Photography, music, my confidence, and *feeling* in general —these are all things I gave up on when I lost Nico, and I never planned on getting any of them back.

Knock, knock.

"One second!" I say before giving myself a quick once-over in the mirror, and then heading back out to the bar.

I open the door expecting my brother, but I end up finding a face I am getting all too familiar with.

"Hey," Eddie says with a small smile that leans towards one side of his face. He has to look down to account for our height difference, and our eyes lock, my feet glued to the floor. At this angle, I can see the scar on his face more clearly.

"Hi," I manage to reply, not being able to hide where my eyes follow the lighter, slightly raised skin, starting at his forehead and leading down across his eye to the middle of his cheek where a tiny dimple threatens to show.

A few beats pass before either of us say anything, and I feel the air get heavier with every second that ticks by.

"Um," he starts before ripping his eyes from me and looking over my head. "Your brother was looking for you," he says to the wall behind me.

"Oh, right. Sorry." I unglue my feet from the floor and walk around Eddie who seems like he's in no hurry to move, and I make my way back out to the bar where the rest of the guys are.

"There you are," my brother says. "Do you want something to drink?"

"Oh, sure." I turn to Emmett and Luke who are still behind the bar. "Do you guys have White Claw?"

Emmett lets out a chuckle at a joke only he is in on before he says, "Yes, we do." He pulls out a lime White Claw and pops the tab for me as I take a seat at the bar next to Theo who is turned the other way talking to Silas and my brother who is standing between them.

"So, Mia," Luke begins, and I turn my attention from Emmett to him. "What's your story? Mateo mentioned you're going to be taking pictures for them. Are you a photographer?"

There's something about how Luke talks that makes you

feel like you're the only one in the room. His blue eyes are focused on me, and I start to feel a little exposed. I've dealt with guys like him before, harmless flirts that still manage to make you feel like they want to know every inch of you. Even though he's not my type, I feel my body warm at the attention. As I'm about to tell him that I just got back into photography after taking a little break from it, I feel a familiar presence behind me.

"Beer, please."

I see Luke's eyes move from mine to the ones behind me, and a smirk graces his lips. It's the kind of smirk that hints that he knows something I don't know. I look over my shoulder to find Eddie standing just behind my chair. His usual smile and friendly demeanor is gone, and he's staring daggers at Luke as if he just walked into something he didn't like.

"Sure thing," Luke says before finding my eyes again and giving me a wink. He turns and pulls out a beer before uncapping it and handing it to Eddie.

The rest of the night is relatively uneventful. I find myself on the outside of conversations, and I don't mind. Usually, with this many people, it feels crowded, but there's something about this group that feels *normal*. At one point, the conversation moves towards the band and the upcoming shows. Mateo, Silas, and Theo fill Luke and Emmett in on where the shows are and what days, so they can try to make it to the venues nearby.

I notice Eddie is quiet, standing next to Mateo. He follows the conversation, and it's interesting how he easily falls into the background. It seems deliberate, like he's making sure that everyone gets their turn for his undivided attention.

"Mia, do you play any instruments?" Luke asks me, pulling me back to the moment and into the conversation.

"No, piano lessons didn't stick with me like they did with Mateo."

Luke turns to Mateo. "Wait, I thought you sang."

Mateo takes a sip of his beer before explaining, "Yeah, singing is my main focus, but I started with piano before taking voice lessons when I was young and then I learned to play bass."

"What about you?" Luke asks Eddie. "Do you only play drums?"

"I play guitar, just acoustic though."

"Wait, you play guitar?" I turn to Eddie. I have to twist in my chair to face where he's standing next to my brother.

He looks down at me and nods his head as he takes a sip of his beer.

I'm not sure why I'm surprised. The drums seem so different than the guitar, especially an acoustic one, so it's hard to picture Eddie going from one to the other.

"It's usually what I use to write the songs. Playing helps the lyrics flow once I find a melody that fits our sound."

I turn to Theo. "Do you only play electric guitar?" I ask.

"I started off learning on the acoustic, but I switched to electric after learning the basics. The two are super similar, but there is a big adjustment to how you play and how it sounds. I haven't picked up an acoustic in years."

The conversations continue with more questions, answers, and tangents, but I sit back and listen while I ponder this new information.

Something Eddie said keeps replaying in my brain, and I'm not sure if it is the roller coaster of feelings and new things today brought or if it's the alcohol, but the words slip out of my mouth before I can think much about them.

I turn to Eddie. "Will you teach me how to play guitar?"

All conversations cease, and all eyes are on us.

Eddie is frozen in place with his beer bottle at his lips and his eyes wide. I feel my brother's harsh stare going back and forth between us, but I don't care. I have one thing on my mind right now, and it's learning how to play the guitar.

If Eddie can use the guitar to *find a melody*, so can I.

What feels like an eternity passes of him and I locked in a starting match, but finally Eddie brings his beer bottle from his lips and says, "Sure."

A moment passes before Emmett claps his hands and announces, "Alright, on that note, everybody out. I want to go home." Emmett has the type of demeanor that makes you feel like you have to listen, but there's also something about him that makes him approachable. "I want to see my girl-friend before she falls asleep."

Feeling more comfortable by the moment with these people, which is something I don't want to think too much about right now, I ask, "Your girlfriend goes to sleep at 10 p.m.?"

Emmett lets out another chuckle, and I can't help but be a little surprised that a guy who looks like such a grump can be so smiley when it comes to his girlfriend. "She's a sixth-grade teacher. Her last day for the school year was this past Friday, but she's definitely struggling with residual exhaustion from the year."

"Sixth grade? Wow, I can't believe people willingly go back to that grade," I say. I have such respect for teachers, especially with everything they deal with. There's no way I could do it.

"It's been a rough year, but she made it through," he adds before turning to the rest of the group, a shadow briefly coming over his face, and then it disappears as if it never happened. I wonder what he means by a *rough year*. "And that's why you all have to leave. I want to be home with her."

He swipes my empty can from the bar in front of me before wiping it off with the towel that was hanging over his shoulder. Luke grabs the rest of the glasses and bottles before rounding the corner and turning off the lights.

"See you tomorrow?" Emmett asks Eddie as we all start heading towards the door.

"Yeah, see you then," Eddie answers, but he seems distracted.

"Good," I hear Emmett respond, "because we have a lot to catch up on."

I wonder what it is they have to catch up on, but as I turn to see the exchange, Emmett looks amused and Eddie's usual grin has a slight discomfort to it, so I decide it's none of my business and follow Mateo to his car.

"So," Mateo starts as we make the drive home. The first few minutes were a comfortable silence as I reflected on how positive I feel after a day that had the possibility of being horrible. "You want to learn how to play guitar?" He's staring at the dark road ahead of us as we make the drive back to my apartment.

"Yes." I cross my arms. "Why?"

"No reason. I was just . . . surprised."

"Why?"

We stop at a red light, and he turns to look at me. "You've never shown interest before."

"I thought you wanted me to branch out? You know, find things to live for or whatever," I say, throwing his words from this morning back at him.

"Don't get me wrong, I'm happy to hear it. But like I said, I'm just surprised." The light turns green, and he turns back to the road to continue driving and ignoring my attempt to be a smartass. "I didn't think you still had an interest in music."

I internally cringe. *Why does he have to be so damn perceptive?*

I should have known he would pick up on it.

I try to think of an excuse, but I decide to go with a half-truth instead. "Today reminded me how much I love photography. I figured maybe I'd see if I forgot how much I loved music."

It isn't a lie, but it definitely isn't the whole truth. I don't want to tell him I want Eddie to teach me how to play guitar, so I can try to figure out this damn song that invades my mind to the point of wanting to claw my own brain out of my head.

I've never told Mateo about the song Nico was writing for me, or how every time I think I'm remembering it, it disappears out of my grasp, or sends me into a panic attack. It might make sense to tell my brother, especially with how musically inclined he is, but it's something I want to figure out myself.

I owe it to Nico.

Out of the corner of my eye, I see Mateo nodding his head. He either believes me or he is trying to figure out the holes in my explanation.

If he knows I'm avoiding telling the entire truth, he doesn't show it. "Okay, I'll find someone to teach you."

"What?" My voice raises a few octaves. I clear my throat before continuing, "What do you mean? Eddie agreed to teach me."

"Yeah, I don't know about that."

I let out a dramatic groan. "Ugh, don't worry, Mateo. I don't want to bang your friend."

"Um, ew. No. No. There will be no banging *anyone*." He shivers before adding, "And absolutely no talk of banging." I can't help but laugh at my brother's discomfort at my statement. Like I said, I don't have any hang-ups talking about sex because I think it is important to talk about it to negate the societal stigma that comes with it. Apparently, my brother has his own hang-ups. Or maybe because it's his little sister who is the one talking about it.

"Then what's the big deal if Eddie teaches me?" Sure, there's attraction there, but him teaching me how to play guitar will be a professional relationship. He's my brother's friend and he's just doing me a favor, and I'm sure he doesn't even think of me like that anyway. I have enough going on in my mind to catch feelings for Eddie, no matter how hot he is, so there's nothing for any of us to worry about.

Right?

Mateo thinks on this for a few minutes before concluding, "Fine, but you can't be taking up his time this close to our shows. You guys can have your lessons in the warehouse during breaks at our practices or when we have down time between shows."

That reminds me. "How are we getting from show to show?"

"Theo and Silas will be driving the van with all of our equipment, which means you will be driving with Eddie and me."

I nod my head as I absorb this.

So, in two weeks, I will be road-tripping around the Midwest with my brother and my brother's best friend who is teaching me how to play guitar so I can uncover the memory of a song my dead boyfriend wrote for me.

Cool. What could possibly go wrong?

CHAPTER 7
EDDIE

WHAT THE HELL am I doing? Why did I agree to help Mia learn how to play guitar? I told Mateo I would keep my distance and not put anything else on her already-full plate, yet here I am, on my way to practice with my drumsticks in one hand and my guitar case in the other.

I thought Mia didn't even like music, so what made her want to learn?

Isn't photography her thing?

Doesn't she hate music?

Shut up, Eddie, I tell myself.

Honestly, how bad will it be? A few teaching sessions in between practicing our setlist, and she will have it down in no time.

Mia is a smart girl, and the guitar isn't that hard to learn. I learned when I was in elementary school, and if I can do it, so can she. I'll just teach her the basics, and she can learn the rest on her own.

I haven't seen Mia in almost a week ago because she hasn't been at our weekday band practices. When I asked about her, Mateo first accused me of caring too much about where she was and told me to fuck off. He eventually told me that she was finishing up the last week of her nannying job when I assured him I was only asking because I needed to know when I had to bring my guitar to practice.

That seemed to settle him down.

Even though, in all honesty, I wasn't even thinking about the lessons when I asked.

With Mia not being around this week, my mind has been solely on the setlist and making sure our sound is exactly where it needs to be for the upcoming shows. Our first show for this run is the first Saturday of July which is already in exactly one week. We aren't "officially" on tour with these bands, but they are letting us play before the openers for the shows near our home base. If all goes well, we are hoping they will bring us on tour as openers for their U.S. tour which is happening next summer.

Now that we are a week away, I'm a little nervous these guitar lessons I agreed to are going to occupy my mind more than they should.

Maybe Mia will tell me *why* she wanted to learn how to play guitar all of a sudden, and then I won't have to wonder anymore and I can teach her without being distracted.

But why does that feel like it isn't a possibility?

Either way, I have no idea how the hell someone could say no to her when she looks at them with those big brown eyes.

I shake my head at myself as I open the door to the warehouse where Theo and Silas are waiting. They haven't caught me alone all week, and I'm 99 percent sure they are about to use this moment as an opportunity to ask me what my interest is in our buddy's little sister since Mateo isn't here yet.

"There he is," Silas says as I walk into the warehouse. He's messing with his bass as Theo plugs his electric guitar into his amp.

"Long time, no talk, lover boy." Theo teases as he loops his guitar around his neck. "I see your lessons start today. Tell me, besides guitar, what else will you be teaching *our* little Mia?"

Theo and Silas laughing like hyenas at 8 AM on a Saturday morning is the work of nightmares, and there is something about the way he says "our" that makes my blood heat up a few degrees.

"Just remember to be careful," Silas adds. "Rocky and her brother aren't scared to throw a punch when assholes get a little too comfortable."

I want to remind Silas that *he* is one of those assholes who learned that the hard way, but I ignore them as I set my guitar case by the table in the corner where Mia will be sitting when she isn't taking pictures.

I asked Mateo if he needed me to bring Mia another one of my older guitars, but he said she had her own. I didn't think much of it, but now I can't help but wonder why she has a guitar when neither she nor Mateo play.

"Seriously, Ramirez. Do you have a death wish or do you just enjoy pain?" Theo asks.

"Am I supposed to know what that means?" I walk over to my drum set and sit down before tapping the bass drum a few times and adjusting my cymbal stands.

"What about Mateo's warning of any of us even *looking* at his sister with questionable intentions makes you think that giving her private guitar lessons is a good idea?" he asks.

"It's not like that," I clarify, not even trying to hide the annoyance in my voice.

"Ha, of course it isn't." Theo laughs. "Are you going to have her sit on your lap as you wrap your arms around her?"

"And will you interlock your fingers as you help her find the right chords," Silas adds like the hopeless romantic he pretends to be to get laid.

I'm holding on to my drum sticks so hard that they are about to snap, and it's taking everything in me to not walk over there and shove one down each of their throats.

"She'll be begging you to keep her your dirty little secret in no time." Theo laughs, and that does it.

I'm going to kill him.

I push off my stool and march over to him as he and Silas snicker like little girls.

I grab him by the collar of his T-shirt and bring his face to mine.

I usually don't have a problem with Theo, or Silas for that matter. They are two of my closest friends, right behind Mateo, Emmett, and Luke. But in this moment, I don't care who the fuck he is. Growing up as the oldest in my family, my protective instincts have always been strong. That's why I always admired Mateo's protectiveness over Mia. With the anger I try to keep buried starting to cloud my vision, Theo looks less like my friend and more like a man with no respect for women.

And I've dealt with enough of those in my life.

"Don't talk about Mia like that," I spit. "Ever."

Theo's face shows nothing but surprise with a lick of fear, but it quickly contorts to a smirk when he realizes that he pushed a button I didn't even know was there.

"Noted," he says before stepping out of my grip. He's lucky he's my friend; otherwise, his ass would be on the floor right now. Silas watches with a smirk of his own, and as my anger subsides, I know I fucked up.

I just gave them one more reason to believe that agreeing to these guitar lessons had more to do with *who* I would be teaching over anything else.

"What's going on?" I hear as the warehouse door closes behind Mateo and Mia who, luckily, got here a few seconds after the situation that just played out calmed down. "Everything okay here?" Mateo asks when the three of us stay quiet.

I clear my throat. "Yeah, all good," I say, but I don't know how convincing I sound.

We're halfway through practicing a run-through of our entire setlist, and we are sounding good, all things considered.

Mia has her camera around her neck and holds it up to her face. Her bronzed skin shines against her light pink tank top and half of her blonde hair is pulled up into a small messy bun at the top of her head, revealing her devastatingly full lips and the brown eyes that make my knees feel weak.

The memory of her looking up at me from her chair at Lenny's last week is burned into my brain. The way she looked at me . . . I would have given her the world if she asked me for it. Luckily, it was just guitar lessons.

As we play, Mia walks around finding every and all angles to get a good shot of the four of us. There's more motive in her movements today versus the first time she came to our practice. There's a confidence in her that I didn't see last weekend.

We finish the first run-though, and Mateo gives us each a few notes before we take a break. Theo and Silas leave to do a coffee run after getting all of our orders while Mateo stays back to, I assume, keep an eye on Mia's first guitar lesson.

"You ready?" I ask as I walk over to the table Mia is sitting at as she looks at the pictures she took. She has her laptop today with her camera plugged in. She must have not heard me because she keeps clicking the arrow buttons on her laptop, pictures flashing across the screen.

I take a few steps closer with my guitar in one hand, but before I can ask again if she's ready, I notice the pictures on the screen, and I freeze.

On her laptop, a photo of me is taking up the entirety of the screen, but I don't even recognize myself. My arms are up with a drumstick in each hand, capturing the moment right before I'm about to hit them back down. My face shows concentration, but there's something else there that I didn't know I was capable of feeling anymore: pride.

It's subtle but noticeable in the brightness of my eyes and determination in my features. It's been years since I've felt any sense of pride after feeling like there was nothing in my life I could be proud of.

My horrible excuse for a father never failed to remind me that I would never amount to much, even though I spent my entire childhood trying to be everything he wasn't for my mom and three younger sisters. Getting the four of them away from my dad is the only thing in my life I am truly proud of. No diploma or degree measures up to finally being able to see the bruises on your mom go away.

"You ready?" I say again, this time a little louder to get both Mia's attention and mine back on the present moment.

She turns to see me and quickly shuts her laptop before standing up. "Ready!"

There is a pink hue to her chest, but I don't let her know that I could sense the fake enthusiasm trying to hide her embarrassment—as if I caught her watching porn. And it was just a picture of me.

I act like I don't notice and replace the slightly awkward moment with a question. "So, Mateo said you had a guitar to use?"

She nods before reaching under the table and pulling out a guitar case just like mine, only this one has stickers covering the hard case.

"Yours?" I ask.

She bends down to open it up and pulls out an acoustic guitar that looks used and a little weathered, and she shakes her head.

"A friend's," she answers, and I think that's the only answer I'm going to get—at least for now. She doesn't look at all interested in explaining. Instead, her eyes are glued to the guitar sitting in the case. I watch as she carefully pulls it out by the neck. The warehouse is completely silent, and I'm not going to be the one to interfere with this moment. Mia doesn't say a word as she sits down on the ground and brings the guitar to her lap.

I guess the floor is as good a place as ever for her first lesson.

Turning around, I see Mateo scrolling on his phone before I sit down next to Mia, leaving more than enough room between us, and pull out my own acoustic, definitely more worn and weathered than the one she has. I can't help but look at her face, and I find that her pretty brown eyes look cloudy, and I would bet my left arm that her mind is somewhere far away from here.

She comes back to this moment and must feel me staring because her body language completely shifts. Her face no longer has a trace of sadness as she straightens her shoulders and loosens her grip on the neck of the guitar.

"So," she says with a small smile, "will you teach me how to play?"

––––––––

Remember when I said that Mia was a smart girl, and she would pick this up in no time? I was wrong about that.

Like *completely* wrong.

I've taught two of my three sisters how to play, and they picked it up in a matter of weeks with consistent daily practice. With how this first lesson is going, I don't think that will be the case for Mia.

A big part of learning a new instrument, or a new skill in general, is allowing the student to be creative and help them gain confidence while also guiding them in getting to know the parts of the instrument.

Mia is acting as if the guitar is going to bite her.

I started with showing her how to tune the guitar, letting

her know that learning how to do that would come with time. Then I moved on to showing her how to properly hold the guitar and I couldn't help but notice how uncomfortable she looked holding it.

After a couple adjustments, the discomfort faded slightly from her body, so we moved on to looking at the numbering of the fingers and the individual notes. I figured once we did that she would gain some confidence and then we would move on to strumming and maybe even get to a few chords.

That was *not* the case.

Her tiny fingers had trouble fretting the strings, and we spent most of the hour we had having her practice moving up and down the fretboard with enough pressure to play the notes.

I hate to say it, but she sucks.

The confidence I noticed she had today while strutting around the warehouse with her camera was nowhere to be found when she was holding the guitar.

I could tell she was trying, and she didn't give up, but we didn't get as far as I thought we would. With practice and drive, it's possible she will get there, but I can't help but notice her *distance* from what she's doing. Almost as if she's being forced to learn how to play rather than doing it because she wants to.

Which is none of my business.

And I shouldn't care.

I *don't* care.

But regardless of why she wants to learn, it's going to take much longer than I thought it would.

We didn't have much conversation aside from my directives and her questions, which is fine with me. The last thing I need is Mateo thinking I'm using these lessons for getting to know Mia.

Or worse, *falling* for her.

Or even worse than that, *her* falling for *me*.

"Okay," I finally say. "That's enough for today."

"Hold on," she responds. She bites her bottom lip as she tries to press her finger down in the right place while simultaneously strumming, but I don't know how many more times I can hear her dull and empty notes today.

Before she can strum her pick down the strings, I lightly touch her arm without even thinking, feeling the warmth from the way her soft skin feels under my calloused hands shooting up my arm.

Even with the slightest touch, for the briefest moment, I feel a spark in the air and a flutter in my chest, and I don't know what to think of it.

Before my mind can catch up to what my body is feeling, Mia freezes, her body going rigid as a small gasp leaves her lips.

I rip my hand away as if her skin was boiling hot and run my fingers through my hair.

"Sorry," I murmur because I don't know what else to say, and I start packing up my guitar to get back to band practice. Mateo is going to stop pretending to look at his phone any minute to tell me it's time to run through the set again, and Theo and Silas will be back soon.

"For what?" she asks, and I barely hear her. If I wasn't becoming so attuned to her voice, I probably wouldn't have even noticed it.

"Lesson's over!" Mateo yells as he walks back up to his mic stand. "Time to get back to practice."

Theo and Silas get back from their coffee run right as Mateo announces, so I quickly finish packing up my guitar, never giving Mia an answer.

"Well, thanks for the lesson," she says, but I avoid looking at her as I murmur that it was no problem and practically run over to my drum set.

When I'm in my stool and absently listening to Mateo remind us of the slight change in our opening song, I watch

Mia from the corner of my eye. I see her stand up from where we were sitting on the floor, and she sits back down at the table with her laptop and camera, but she doesn't open her laptop or grab her camera to take more photos. Instead, she puts her elbows on the table in front of her and sets her head down in her hands. Her shoulders slump, and her chest moves up and down as if she is taking deep breaths.

Noted, I think to myself.

Mia, without a doubt, doesn't want me touching her in *any* way.

The rest of practice is a blur as I try to figure out how I am going to get out of these guitar lessons.

CHAPTER 8

MIA

GUITAR LESSONS WERE A BAD IDEA. I don't know what I was thinking when I asked Eddie to teach me, and I *definitely* wasn't thinking when I grabbed Nico's old guitar from under my bed to use for the lessons.

If I *was* thinking, I would have reminded myself that the last time I saw that guitar out of its case was when Nico was playing me the song he wrote the night before he died.

I got overly confident with how well it went bringing out my camera, thinking that bringing out the guitar and learning how to play would be the same, thinking that Eddie teaching me how to play *Nico's* guitar would work.

I could barely even hold on to the guitar, let alone play it. I must have looked ridiculous trying to mimic Eddie's seamless movements, trying to stay calm when all I wanted to do was scream in frustration with every strum.

I used to love music and appreciate every instrument for the way it contributed to the overall sound of a song. I loved connecting to the lyrics and finding the different ways they spoke to me.

But I have always been a *listener*.

Mateo was the one who wanted to make music, not me.

Nico too, he loved making music.

I rinse off the face mask I put on after I got home, but a Saturday night with white wine and a purifying face mask is not enough self-care to make me feel any better about how today went.

After the guitar lesson, I tried to convince myself that I could do this because I was doing the guitar lessons for Nico. That I was honoring his memory by trying to figure out his song. I tried to forget the complexities of how I used to love music, and how it now makes me uncomfortable. I wanted to ignore that I never had an interest in playing guitar, but it would help me find the song.

But now that I'm thinking about it, it felt like a forced and cheapened way to feel close to Nico. I was tricking myself into doing something he loved because I thought it might help me deal with the loss of him.

This will be fun to unpack in therapy later this week.

In the end, the whole thing just made me look like an idiot in front of Eddie who had to waste an hour of his time teaching me how to do something I have no interest in learning how to do.

Eddie.

And what am I supposed to think regarding the feeling of Eddie's fingertips grazing my arm? There was a moment I thought he felt the same spark I did—the same magnetic pull between us. But it must have been this stupid, unreciprocated interest that is forming for him because he pulled his hand away as if touching me physically burned him.

Guitar lessons were a stupid idea.

I'll have to figure out the song another way.

I take off my robe before climbing into bed, not caring that it's still light out. Practice ended early because the guys wanted to celebrate at Lenny's for running through the setlist twice without any mistakes, but I asked Mateo to drop me off at home.

I didn't have the energy to put on a face that everything is fine.

Because everything *isn't* fine.

Only a week left of band practices and then six shows over the course of three months to go to.

Then I'll be done being Cross My Heart's photographer.

And I'll never have to be around Eddie again.

Eddie, who was just trying to be nice to his best friend's little sister. The shy little sister with no confidence who causes issues and wastes everyone's time, and who can't even control the thoughts in her own fucking brain.

"I think I finally got it," Nico says. It's the summer before my sophomore year of college and we're sitting across from each other on his bed, his guitar is in his lap. I've been listening to him play the song he's been working on over and over again.

I don't think I'll ever get sick of it.

I find myself humming it whenever I'm not with him.

"Okay, I'm ready," I say with a smile. He always says he thinks he has it, but then he plays it and stops midway through, or even almost to the end, and says it's missing something.

Maybe this will be the time.

He begins to strum the familiar chords, and I fall in love with him all over again. His eyes are closed as he plays each note and his voice envelopes me. I watch as any sign of internal struggle or doubt melts away from his features. But they never come. He looks like he's at peace. Nico never looks like he's free from the demons in his head, except for when he's playing.

He makes it to the first chorus without stopping, which is a good sign, but we've been here before. My heart begins to race as he gets closer and closer to the end of the song, the look of bliss still outlining his features. I begin to pay more attention to him than the sound of the song, but I don't care. In this moment, I never want to forget what he looks like when he isn't fighting with himself.

He plays the last chord and pauses before opening his eyes and finding mine. Before I can say anything, I notice there are tears in my eyes because I feel so proud of him.

He drops his pick and sets down his guitar before his hands find the sides of my face.

His forehead lightly presses against mine, and I hear him let out a laugh before I close my eyes, waiting to feel his lips on mine, but they never come.

"Nico!" I scream into a dark, empty room. I glance at my bedside table to see it's just after 3 a.m. I've had this dream so many times, you would think it would lose its effect. But somehow, waking up always takes my breath away.

I'm able to fall asleep for a few more *dreamless* hours, but I wake up with an uneasiness in my stomach that, I know, stemmed from having that dream again.

Maybe it's time to let go of this.

Mateo's right.

Nico's gone and I can't keep centering my life around this nameless song that I'll never remember. I don't want to be led down this road that heads straight to disappointment, regret, and frustration every time I think of him.

It's been three years.

If I haven't remembered the song now, I probably never will.

With the shows starting in less than a week, Mateo and the guys decided they could skip today's practice, so I have all day to myself. Most of my time will be used to sort through, edit, and organize the pictures I took at the past two band practices so I can start figuring out which I should use to update their website, but that's about all I have on my plate.

I also have to figure out how I'm going to tell Eddie I don't need guitar lessons anymore before the next time I see him.

I peel myself out of bed and head into the kitchen as I hear my phone begin to ring. I know who it is without even having to look. Only two people ever call me—the mom of the boys I nanny for or my brother. Since I quit my nanny job to focus on the photography for Cross My Heart, I answer with barely a glance at the screen, assuming it is Mateo.

"What's up?" I say as I hug my phone between my cheek and shoulder to open my freezer. I see the bag of frozen fruit that was used as my ice pack two weeks ago, and I have a hard time believing how much has changed since that night.

No life-altering changes, I know that. But, for me, I have had virtually no changes in three years, and after two weeks, I have a new job and spend most of my time with people I barely even knew two weeks ago.

I wouldn't really consider Theo, Silas, and Eddie friends, but I am gravely lacking in that department, so anything even remotely close to a friend is something.

I open and close the hand I used as a fist two weeks ago, and I think back to the concern Eddie had when I saw him the day after that night I punched the asshole at the bar. Maybe he could be a *friend* . . .

"Mia?" I hear on the other end of the phone as I grab the frozen bag of fruit, but it is not the voice I was expecting. I set the cold plastic bag on the counter and pull my phone from my shoulder to check the Caller ID. Mateo's name is there, but it's definitely not his voice.

I put the phone back to my ear. "Who is this?" I ask.

"It's Eddie," I hear, and my phone almost ends up on the floor.

Eddie?

Why the hell is he calling me from Mateo's phone? What happened? Is everything okay? Where's Mateo?

My mind begins to spiral, my anxiety taking control like it always does.

"Sorry for calling you from Mateo's phone, but he wouldn't

give me your number," Eddie says, completely unaware of my heart beginning to beat faster as I assume the absolute worst. "He's home with me, by the way, and knows I'm calling."

"Um . . . Okay," I manage to say, beginning to calm down. Mateo is fine. Nothing is wrong. *I'm fine.*

"So, I'm sure you're confused why I'm calling." He lets out an awkward chuckle, and I'm not sure what to say so I stay quiet. Eddie clears his throat before continuing, "I was actually wondering if you had some time to meet up today? I wanted to talk to you about your guitar lessons."

Of course, it's about the lessons. I shake away the initial shock I had about why he was calling and then the shock that he *was* calling, and now I'm left with a feeling that can only be explained as strange.

"I thought our next lesson would be Friday during the band's last practice before the tour," I answer, relieved that my voice is even.

"Yeah about that," he starts, but then I hear him say something to, who I assume is, my brother, but I can't make out what it is.

"Can I stop by?" he asks me.

Definitely not what I was expecting him to say.

I know my brain is telling me this isn't a good idea and that we can have this conversation on the phone, but the word, "yes," flies out of my mouth along with a flip in my stomach at the thought of seeing him.

Well, that's not good.

"Okay, I'm on my way," he responds.

Before the phone hangs up, I hear a muffled interaction between Eddie and Mateo as Eddie gives Mateo's phone back to him without hanging up.

"You're going over there?" Mateo asks Eddie.

"Yeah, just to talk to her about the lessons."

"I'm going with you."

Eddie brushes him off. "No, that's weird. We don't need a chaperone."

"What do you have to tell her that you can't say in front of me," Mateo retorts, and this piques my interest because now I have the same question.

"Relax, Dad," Eddie says instead of an answer to the question. "I already told you. She's your little sister. I'm not interested."

Ouch.

I hang up the phone, wishing I had before I overheard their conversation. It's not that what Eddie said isn't true, or that I don't agree with what he's saying, but why did it make that strange feeling come back? I shouldn't have *any* type of feelings about Eddie *just* wanting to talk to me about the guitar lessons or saying he's not interested in "Mateo's little sister."

That is *exactly* what he should be saying.

But it makes me feel like shit.

CHAPTER 9
MIA

WHEN I OPEN my apartment door, not only do beautiful green eyes and toned biceps greet me, but my eyes immediately find that mysterious scar that I wish I knew the story behind.

"Hey," Eddie says, and I can't fight the urge to drop my eyes to his lips, curved in a crooked smile that shows off the dimple I noticed that night at Lenny's. Eddie is the kind of guy who is always smiling, and his smiles range from soft to brighter than the sun. I've caught glimpses of all of Eddie smiles during my time at band practice and my down time with the guys, but I tell myself that's only because I'm his band's photographer, and it's my job to notice.

I want to divert my eyes from his face, remembering the slight betrayal I felt when I heard him inform Mateo that he wasn't interested in me, but I can't. Now that he's up close, I can see how *this* smile doesn't quite reach his eyes.

"Thanks for letting me stop by."

"Oh, sure," I say, shaking away the thoughts, remembering that it's not appropriate to stare at my brother's best friend and admire his facial features. I don't need him thinking that I'm interested in him, especially after he's made it perfectly clear that I'm of no interest to him. I move out of the doorway, so he can come in and, because of his height, he almost has to duck under the door frame.

I follow close behind not only noticing how his muscular thighs stretch his jeans as he walks, but also noticing the stark difference between today and the last time he was here, the two visions almost giving me whiplash.

That night him and Mateo came over, it felt so crowded in here, especially because it is always just me. But today, having Eddie here now, it feels more *full*—but not in a bad way.

I don't really know how to explain it.

The first time Eddie was here, my priorities were so different. No, my *life* was so different. I was concerned about hiding from my feelings and avoiding my triggers, just trying to get through each day. Now, just two weeks later, I feel like my priorities are the band and my photography, and that makes the days easier to get through.

"Oh, here," Eddie says just before he reaches the counter in my kitchen. I quickly bring my eyes up to his face, hoping he didn't catch me checking out his backside as I lost myself in my thoughts for a moment, but the slight raise of his eyebrows say otherwise.

I didn't even notice he was holding two coffees in his hand until now, and I mentally slap myself in the face for how distracted I am when I'm in his presence.

Even though I've known Eddie for years, I haven't spent as much time with him as I have in the past two weeks. Some younger sisters develop harmless crushes on their older brother's friends, almost as if it's a rite of passage or a part of the teenage experience. I can honestly say that I missed out on that part of growing up, thanks to never being allowed near Theo, Silas, or Eddie. This is actually the first time I've ever been alone with one of them, and I quickly become intimately aware of that as Eddie stretches out an arm towards me, holding an iced coffee from a local place down the street from me.

"Earth to Mia?" he prompts, as I just stare down at the plastic cup as if I've never seen one before.

"Oh, um, sorry," I stammer before reaching to grab the coffee from him, and I wish I had a better comeback than a half-assed apology. As I do, our fingertips brush, sending sparks up my arm despite the cold condensation on the cup. I almost let go but can't help but lean into the feeling. A moment passes before Eddie lets go, reminding me these stupid sparks are all in my head.

Really, Mia? You touched his hand. Relax.

"Thanks," I say as I avoid his eyes and step around him to take a seat at my kitchen island. I take a sip from the straw as I sit down to stop myself from saying anything stupid.

Along with the familiar taste of creamy coffee with a hint of vanilla, confusion coats my tongue as I ask, "How'd you know my coffee order?" A more acceptable response to the coffee would be "thank you" or, "you shouldn't have," but I can't stop the question from leaving my lips.

Eddie looks confused before answering. "You gave it to Silas yesterday," he states as if the answer was obvious.

"I did?"

He nods.

"And you remembered?" I ask, a slight smile gracing my lips.

It's an iced latte.

With oat milk.

And vanilla.

My favorite.

And he *remembered.*

He lets out a dry chuckle as he shakes his head, and I must have imagined the slight red in his cheeks because his voice takes on a stern tone, one I've heard from Mateo so many times. "It's just a coffee, Mia. It's not a big deal."

I nod and take another sip, embarrassed at the thoughts I was having just a second ago, not letting the unwarranted disappointment show on my face at the way he brushed me off.

I don't even know why I am disappointed, but I do know that thinking this gesture was anything but polite is pathetic. Reading into it, like I am, is proving that I am just Mateo's little sister, with the confidence of a deflated balloon.

Letting Eddie come over, being alone with him, was a bad idea.

"So," I begin, "what did you want to talk about?" The quicker we get whatever *this* is over with, the better.

A flicker of *something* flashes across his face, but I don't let myself read into it.

"Right. So, I don't think guitar lessons are going to work out."

I should have seen this coming.

"Yeah, me either." I knew this. I knew they weren't going to work out. Just last night I was thinking about how they were a bad idea. The petty side of me wishes *I* was the one to broach this topic first. The self-deprecating side of me wants to know why *he* doesn't think they were going to work out.

Guitar lessons were never going to work because I don't even want to learn how to play. Making music has always been Mateo's thing; it *was* Nico's thing. It was never something I wanted to do.

For me, it was always about listening, enjoying, appreciating. Wanting to learn how to play in an effort to try and find the song Nico wrote was stupid.

But Eddie doesn't know about Nico. Eddie doesn't know about any of this, so why does he think the lessons won't work out?

And why do I care what he thinks?

"It's just," he starts. His hands are now resting on the counter across the island where he's standing. His last few sips of black iced coffee sitting next to one of his hands, and I have a perfect view of his corded arms and strong shoulders.

He looks down and shakes his head, making me notice his dark hair, the strands damp like he just got out of the shower. He looks up at me, a few strands just above his eyes, contrasting with the green in them. "It didn't seem like you were into it. You won't learn anything if you aren't interested."

That confuses me, and I'm learning that confusion is something that comes with every interaction I have with Eddie.

"What made you think I wasn't interested?" I ask as I trace the water droplets on my iced coffee, so I have something other than green eyes framed with dark hair to look at.

"It just seemed like your mind was elsewhere, and you looked uncomfortable with the guitar."

I looked uncomfortable with the guitar.

That shouldn't come as a surprise. I had an inkling I wasn't hiding my discomfort well, but I didn't think Eddie would care enough to notice. Holding Nico's guitar for the first time since he died sent grief through my body at a moment I should have expected.

I'm making progress with how I'm dealing with the grief, which is growth for me after not dealing with it properly over the last few years, but I know the work isn't linear. I also know that grief will always be a shock to my system, ranging in intensity, coming whenever it feels like it.

But I don't even recognize myself anymore.

I'm the broken girl who needs her older brother to swoop in and make everything better.

The broken girl who won't let herself heal.

The broken girl who can't move on.

Losing a loved one, especially your partner, is impossible. The pain never completely goes away, and you never really *get over it*. Time continues to pass. Life continues to happen, and you're forced to keep moving forward because it's all you can do.

I know this. I know this in my heart and soul. It's been almost three years since Nico died. He would want me to be happy, and he wouldn't want me to feel guilty for trying to live.

I'm in a good place for the first time in what feels like forever. I'm in a place that doesn't make me feel broken. These past two weeks have shown me that I can move forward, but not without acknowledging what broke me in the first place.

I'm coping. I'm becoming stronger. I want to wake up from my dreams and let them hurt for a moment, but I want to keep moving forward. I want to be able to look back at my time with Nico and smile. I want to share his memory, not replace it.

And I don't want to feel guilty for doing so.

"It was my boyfriend's guitar." The wind is knocked out of me as the words leave my lips, but in a way that feels like a release rather than a punch. Words I have never spoken out loud, aside from within the safe walls of my therapist's office, but it is as if the sentence had been on the tip of my tongue for years and rushed out in a moment of weakness, a moment I wasn't trying to hold it in and bury it deep inside me.

I take a few more sips of my coffee, uneasiness filling my chest at the realization that this is a conversation Eddie was most likely not expecting when he asked to stop by.

Eddie doesn't say anything, so I lift my eyes to see he's looking at me in a way I don't know what to make of.

Curiosity is glazed all over his face, a look I am getting all-too used to, and I can almost see the questions forming in his brain. His eyes are soft and his mouth is slightly open, his hands are still on the counter but he's leaned in more towards me.

"Did he get a new one?"

"Who?"

"Your boyfriend."

"I don't have a boyfriend."

"But you just said it was your boyfriend's guitar."

That is when I realize my statement may have been unclear and does prompt an explanation, so I simply clarify, "It was. When he died, his mom gave it to me."

The words came out so easily, I almost don't realize I said them. I haven't talked about Nico this seamlessly in . . . *ever*. And, now that I have, I realize I should have never tried to keep my memory of him hidden.

"He was a guitar player for a band that he and his friends started in high school. We started dating our sophomore year and were together until he died during my junior year of college."

A few weeks after Nico's funeral, his mom called me asking if I would come over. I almost said no, but I had already declined her invitation to help her go through his things. The memory of driving over there and her hugging me at their front door is a blur, as if it was someone else going through the motions as I watched from afar. I'm thankful she didn't invite me in, whether it was for her benefit or mine. Instead, after she let go of me, she handed me the black guitar case that I had seen Nico hold so many times.

I remember thinking Nico would be wondering where it was until reality set in and reminded me that he was gone. After taking it from her, I went to my car and cried in their driveway until it got dark. And I was thankful his mom didn't come out to check on me, whether it was for her benefit or mine.

"I'm sorry for your loss," Eddie says. "I didn't realize," he pauses and shakes his head. I can't blame him for not knowing what to say. Death isn't exactly the easiest conversation piece. "Your brother mentioned to me that you were going through something, but I didn't realize . . ." he doesn't finish the sentence.

"Wait, what?" Mateo said something to him? Why would he bring this up to Eddie of all people? It's not his business. It's mine. "Why would he tell you about Nico?"

"Oh, no. No. He didn't tell me about him. He just mentioned that *I* shouldn't, I mean, *we* shouldn't bother you." He runs his fingers through his hair before pushing his hands into the front pockets of his jeans. "You know, because you're our band photographer now, and he doesn't want me, Theo, or Silas to screw that up."

Something about his answer leaves me uneasy, but I can't quite place it.

"Oh, got it," is all I can say, trying not to make it obvious that I doubt Mateo would go into detail about why the guys shouldn't bother me because he's never given a reason before. Not since I was a teenager and labeled off-limits to the guys. "Well, I'm fine. Grieving isn't linear. I've been in a bad spot for a while, but I'm starting to feel like myself again."

"How did he die?"

My last sip of coffee burns like acid in my throat as a swallow. I've hit my limit for talking about Nico today, and am left with the residual anger of finding out that Mateo equates me to a wounded puppy. So now Eddie, and probably the other guys too, feel like they have to walk on eggshells around me.

"Is this why you came over? Did Mateo put you up to this?"

"What? No, of course not. Look, I'm sorry for asking."

"Then why are you here? You could've just told me the next time I saw you that you didn't want to teach me. Which, by the way, I felt the same way."

"No, it's not that I don't want to teach you. It's just that you don't seem interested."

I pause, not at all understanding why he feels the need to clarify, and I'm not sure if I'm imagining this tension building under my skin. I take a breath, hoping to release it when I exhale. "Whatever. It doesn't matter."

"You can tell me."

"Tell you what?"

"Why you asked for guitar lessons in the first place, even though you weren't interested in learning."

The way he looks at me threatens me with the idea that he *actually* cares. His brows are furrowed causing his forehead to crease. His eyes are deep set, and there is an intensity in his gaze that makes me want to give in and tell him my deepest, darkest secrets.

"It's nothing," I reply, unsure why I have this urge to tell him the truth.

"Then why are you keeping it a secret?" He playfully challenges, but the intensity remains, almost covering up the sadness that seems to be permanently laced in his irises.

I want to pretend I never let this encounter with Eddie happen, but, at the same time, I have to fight the urge to prolong this moment.

"I'm not. It's just none of your business," I say in a tone that says *this* is where this conversation will end before I unload my grief and trauma on my brother's best friend who will most likely just report back to Mateo.

I stand up to throw out my now-finished coffee and grab Eddie's almost-finished cup too, holding them against my stomach.

"Enough about me," I say as I step past him to open up the cabinet under the sink where my trash can is. "Don't worry about the lessons. I was going to let you know I didn't need them anymore tomorrow at practice, so no big deal." I close the cabinet and turn around, instantly feeling like the walls of the room are closing in on me, but not in a bad way.

Eddie was positioned at my kitchen island but right in front of my sink. When I went to throw out our cups, I thought I had enough room to avoid any and all contact, actually keeping a safe distance between us, but I was sorely mistaken.

Since he's no longer resting against the island, when I turn around, I'm met with a broad chest and smooth, tan skin peeking out of a black V-neck. The smell of him, vanilla with a hint of spice, envelops me as I trace my eyes up Eddie's throat, watching as his Adam's apple bobs as he swallows, before my eyes find his lips in a shape I've never seen before.

Eddie Ramirez is smirking at me.

And I know that because my eyes are inches away from his lips.

I thought I've seen all of Eddie's smiles. The soft ones, the wide ones, the bright ones, the dull ones, even the fake ones, but I have never seen *this*.

I'm absolutely frozen as I follow the outline of his perfect lips to the dimple that has no business being on this chiseled of a face.

It should be illegal to have that strong of jaw line and that adorable of a dimple.

It isn't fair.

My heart is beating in a way it hasn't since high school, and I feel a flutter in my stomach as Eddie's smirk widens to a wicked grin that makes my knees weak. Any tension that was growing in my shoulders is gone, and all traces of anger have subsided. My brain must be short-circuiting because I'm no longer thinking of guitar lessons. My mind is clouding with thoughts of how Eddie and I would be a match made in hell.

With each moment that passes, my thoughts begin to clear, and I'm left with the sole question of how did I go this long not noticing how sad Eddie's eyes are up close.

A door slamming shut out in the hallway snaps me back into reality.

MIA, WHAT THE HELL?

On instinct, I drop my eyes to the floor as if I just saw

Eddie naked, and side-step him, rounding the island to not only put distance between us, but a whole counter because *what. Was. That*?

One second, I'm getting pissed at his inability to mind his own business, and the next I am basically melting at his feet. Lucky for me, I've never been one to show my emotions on my face, and I am incredibly thankful that I put on a hoodie before he came over because I feel heat creep up my chest, and even my neck, proving to myself that Eddie has an influence over me that I must get under control.

I avoid his gaze because I can feel his eyes on me, and I don't know what will happen if I look at him again.

"Anyway," I fake nonchalance even though it's quite possible my heartbeat can be heard across the kitchen as I let out an exhale.

Breathe, Mia.

This is just an intense physical reaction to a situation that is out of my control. My body is reacting to an unprecedented circumstance, like a panic attack. My body is just reacting to the environment.

Breathe.

"Like I said," I continue as I idly mess with my sweatshirt strings, "don't worry about the lessons. Thanks for agreeing to do them in the first place, but I don't need them."

I tie the string in a bow before looking up to find Eddie watching me, leaning back against the sink with his arm crossed. His smirk is still painted on his handsome face, but I'm not as affected by it from afar apparently.

He doesn't say anything, just continues to look at me, so I fill the silence. "I'm sure Mateo appreciates having a friend like you who is willing to help out his sister."

"You know, I can be *your* friend, too."

What?

Is this a joke?

This must be a game to him.

But joke's on him, because I don't want to play.

"That's okay, you don't have to pretend I'm anything but Mateo's *little* sister." I emphasize the word "little" making it clear that I overheard him earlier this morning.

Eddie's smirk slightly fades from his face. "Mia, I didn't mean anything by that. You're going to be spending a lot of time with the band as the photographer, and I'm here if you need a friend."

I do need a friend, but I also know that it isn't a good idea to be friends with Eddie.

But, against my better judgment, instead of saying "no thanks," I find myself saying, "okay," even if I am still apprehensive about his motives.

"Great. So, because we're friends, I feel like I can ask you something I've wanted to ask you for a while now."

I knew this was a bad idea. Is he going to circle back to the guitar lessons thing? Why does he care so much about why I asked for lessons? Maybe it wouldn't be such a bad idea to tell him about Nico's song. Eddie's a musician, maybe he could help. He writes songs, so maybe he could help me figure out the song that is permanently stuck in my head and makes music unbearable.

"Okay."

"Did you know you spilled coffee on your sweatshirt?"

I look down, and sure enough. My favorite white hoodie has three brown splotches across the front of it.

"Ugh, this is my favorite sweatshirt, and you waited until right now to tell me." Slightly annoyed for more reasons than one, I pull the sweatshirt off over my head because I don't want the stain to set.

I have no idea how long I've been sitting with an embarrassingly large stain across my stomach, and now I am left in just a tank top. "When did this even happen?" I rhetorically ask as I walk back over to the sink to run the stain under water.

Eddie is standing in my way, but he looks like he has no intention of getting out of my way.

I'm about to ask him to move when he deadpans, "Probably when you were checking me out."

My jaw drops, and there is no hiding the redness that covers my chest. "Wh-what are you talking about?!" I stammer as I bring the sweatshirt up to cover myself, not letting him see the embarrassment creeping all the way up to my neck. "I was *not* checking you out."

Instead of prolonging my humiliation, Eddie breaks out into the biggest grin that I think I could get used to seeing for the rest of my life. There's not even a single trace of anything but pure enjoyment shimmering in his eyes as he looks at me.

It is in this moment I realize, even if it is at my expense, I never want to see anything but happiness on this boy's face.

One of my hands lets go of my sweatshirt, and I bring it up so it is eye-level with Eddie before I flip him off and push him out of my way, not being able to contain my own smile. He lets me shove him aside, so I can turn the faucet on.

"You know what? You're right," I say. "It probably did happen when I was checking you out, but which time? When I was looking at your ass or your lips?" I turn to face him, grinning bigger than I have in months, and my heart stops.

Eddie Ramirez is *blushing*.

When I said I wanted to see happiness on his face, that was before I saw him blush. The combination of his grin and his rosy cheeks, I don't think I will ever be the same.

"What's the matter, Eddie?" I tease. "I thought we were friends?" I flick my wet fingers in his direction, getting a few water droplets on him, my cheeks already sore from the amount of genuine smiling I've done in the past five minutes. And, what does that say about me that my facial muscles are so not used to smiling that they are *already* sore?

He pretends the few drops hit him harder than actually possible. "Friends don't do that, Mia," he teases back before dipping a hand under the running water and flicking me back, "But you do look like you could use a cool down after all that drooling you did over me."

I respond with a combination of a fake gasp and a laugh, and then he hits me with the trifecta and gives me a wink.

Now, I know for a *fact* I will never be the same.

"Two can play at this game," is all he gives me before he taps my nose with his finger and walks out my door.

CHAPTER 10
EDDIE

THERE IS a pep in my step that I haven't had in years, and I refuse to believe it's because of a friendship I formed with a certain blonde with devastatingly full lips that bloom into the most beautiful smile I have ever seen.

It has been a week since I went over to Mia's to bring her coffee and talk about guitar lessons, but I've been seeing her at band practice for the past five days. We have one more practice tonight before our first show of the Midwest tour tomorrow night, and we have never been more ready.

I don't know if it is the excitement of the tour starting—or something else—but I've been on top of my game this week and so have the rest of the guys.

Mia has a new spark to her too, and it looks good on her.

I still don't know exactly what to think about those moments in her kitchen last week, and I'm trying not to think too hard about them, aside from the sight of her flustered in her little pink tank top and the glimmer in her eyes when her face was inches away from mine.

I'm also trying not to think much about how selfish it was telling her I would be her friend.

When she opened up to me about her boyfriend's death,

I couldn't help the protective instincts that took over. It was the same instinct I've had my entire life for my mom and my younger sisters. Only, there was nothing *sisterly* about the selfishness of wanting to keep Mia close in any way I could.

Letting myself be selfish, for once in my life, is something I'll happily go to Hell for, if it means I get to see that smile on Mia's face, and that *I'm* the one putting it there.

Part of me knows it's a bad idea, but the other part wants to be right alongside her when it all crashes and burns.

My curiosity also got the better of me. I almost blew it with my questions and prying, but I can't help but hope she continues to open up to me. I recognize the sadness in her eyes because it mirrors my own. But there's no helping me; I'm a lost cause. Mia on the other hand, she's a fighter; I can tell.

I knew Mateo would not be thrilled about her and I becoming friends, especially because he made it clear that any relationship the other guys or I had with Mia was to be strictly professional, but when I told him what she said about the guitar belonging to Nico, he seemed slightly okay with our newly-developed friendship.

I made sure not to tell him more than that though. I wanted to prove that she could trust me.

Besides, I'm sure he's just happy she's actually talking about something she kept buried for so long. And I'm happy if he's happy.

Practices are busy with playing our setlist, beginning to end, almost non-stop, so I haven't had a ton of time to talk to Mia. I use any open time to sit with her at what has become her table at the warehouse, asking her questions about what she's doing, messing with her camera, and asking to see the pictures she took.

She pretends to be annoyed about it or says that I'm bothering her, but I've come to realize our friendship is growing from the foundation of giving each other a hard time and seeing who cracks first.

And, it's usually me.

I don't know what I was expecting when I accused Mia of checking me out that day in her kitchen, but it definitely wasn't what she gave me. It was a risk outwardly saying something *that* flirtatious in nature, but Mia did not back down. I can't even remember the last time I blushed like a teenager, or smiled so stupidly wide, but she managed to make me do it.

Theo and Silas have thankfully kept their mouths shut about Mia and me, only sneaking in two or three smartass comments, and I can tell by their glances that they think something besides friendship is going on, which there *isn't*.

Nothing can *ever* happen between Mia and me, and I think we both know that.

They did ask what happened to the guitar lessons, but I just brushed them off saying that we decided we didn't have time for them. What I didn't tell them is I'm still trying to figure out what happened to them myself.

With my drumsticks in my back pocket and a cardboard tray of coffee in one hand, I open the door to the warehouse. With it being a Friday afternoon, we're planning on doing two or three run-throughs and then heading over to Lenny's for a celebratory drink to kick off our first tour.

It won't be a late night because we have to be up early tomorrow to drive the few hours to La Crosse, but Emmett, Drew, Luke, and Annie wanted to send us off.

When I walk in, Mateo is on the phone and Theo and Silas are setting up their instruments while Mia is setting up the mics. Her hair is up in a ponytail, and she's wearing jeans and a red Cross My Heart t-shirt that she cropped, giving me a perfect view of her ass as she bends over to grab the cord on the ground.

My hands would fit perfectly in those back pockets.

I shake the thought away before I can think too much about it.

"Thanks for gracing us with your presence, Ramirez," Theo announces, taking me out of my head, as I walk over to Mia's table

"You're late," Mateo states, but I know it is only two minutes after 1 p.m.

Ignoring them both, I set Mia's iced vanilla latte with oat milk at her table knowing she will see it when she's done with the microphones and head over to my drum set.

We run through the setlist once, and I am feeling super confident. The setlist showcases our sound perfectly, and we created it with the intent to compliment the bands we are opening for, hoping the crowd likes what they hear from us.

There's a lot riding on the six upcoming shows. These next three months are vital for Cross My Heart's growth, and the hope is if we work our asses off, we will be getting ready to *actually* tour with these bands by this time next year.

"Let's take five and then clean up the ending of the third song before we run it all again," Mateo announces before going back to his phone. He mentioned he was in contact with the tour manager for the bands we are opening for.

Mateo isn't just our lead vocalist; he does all the administrative stuff too since we aren't in a position to hire a band manager to take that on for us.

I stand up from the stool behind my drum set and put my drumsticks in my back pocket before heading over to Mia's table. Earlier this week, she decided she had enough practice photos, and she now spends her time editing the pictures and updating our social media.

I've learned a lot about Mia in the past week, both through conversations with her and just from watching her. I've learned that she doesn't like to wear shoes because, after about ten minutes of her getting to practice, she takes off her shoes and walks around in her socks. I have also learned that she's someone who doesn't feel uncomfortable with silence, and she likes the color pink. Her water bottle, nails, laptop case, and the anklet she wears are all pink.

She also started this new habit where she hums when she's editing photos, and it is always the same tune. I don't recognize the song, but I've never asked her about it because I don't think she even realizes she is doing it.

The coffee I got her is now empty next to her laptop, and her eyes are focused on the screen in front of her as I approach her table. I grab the empty cup and toss it in the trash can near the table before I sneak a peek at her screen to see what she is doing.

With her background in marketing, she has been updating our social media to get our followers hyped for the upcoming shows. Right now, she is currently typing a caption for a photo she is posting of us practicing, most likely something about us prepping for our show tomorrow. As I get closer, I hear her humming that tune, and I still can't place what song it is.

"Working hard or hardly working?" I ask as I slump down on the chair across from her.

"You just can't get enough of me, huh?" She teases, not even looking up from her screen. "Thanks for the coffee by the way," she adds on a more sincere note.

I give her a nod before asking, "Are you coming to Lenny's with us after practice?"

"Probably not. I think I'm just going to head home when I finish scheduling some of these social media posts." She is still looking at her screen rather than me, and I don't like it. I reach across the table and slowly tilt her laptop screen down, so she has no choice but to look at me, rolling her eyes first.

"Come for a drink. You can finally meet Drew."

"Emmett's girlfriend?"

"Yeah, you'll like her. And Annie will be there too."

"She finally forgave Luke for standing up for her at the bar?"

I chuckle because I totally forgot Luke told us about that when we brought Mia to Lenny's after her first practice with us.

Because of our upbringings, both Luke and I had to take on the protector role for our families, me for my mom and sisters and him for his younger brother, and it has definitely shaped us into the kind of men we are. We both have the tendency to let our protective, borderline-primal, instincts take over in certain situations, and it can most definitely be taken as an insult to women who don't need it.

Annie, being one of those women who can handle herself, but Luke can't help but try and take care of her, even though she wants no part in it.

I have been a witness to Annie and Luke's turbulent relationship for months now because they both bartend at Lenny's with me, and I have only just recently found out that they actually knew each other growing up. It makes a ton of sense now based on the way they treat each other, but there is a history there they both refuse to talk about.

"Sort of. With me needing more time off from bartending to be with the band, Emmett needed her to pick up some of my shifts, so she has had no choice but to be around Luke again."

"So they will all be at Lenny's tonight?"

"Yep, to kick off the first show tomorrow night. They won't see a show until the last one here in town, but they still wanted to celebrate." Life for the next three months won't be too different with only being invited to play the six Midwest shows, but the shows are arguably the most important shows we've played because we have to make a good impression.

"Yeah, I think I'll probably just head home."

"Come on, Mia. What could be more fun than hanging out with your friends?"

She laughs at this but it is dry of humor. "They're my brother's friends, not mine."

"They could be your friends too. I mean, look at me. I'm friends with both of you." I smile at her, hoping to myself that my fake confidence isn't too obvious.

It isn't like I'm a prize of a friend to Mateo or Mia.

I think I'm actually the opposite.

"That's still up for debate," she deadpans, but her lips twitch when she says it, threatening to smile.

"It'll be fun. You can meet Drew and Annie. They'll love you. I'm sure they're dying to have another girl around, especially one that can hold her own with Mateo, Theo, and Silas." This past week, not only have I gotten to know Mia more, but she has come more out of her shell. The first two weeks she was coming to practice, she was soft-spoken and kept to herself.

Now, not only does she give me a hard time any chance she gets, but she does the same with Theo and Silas, and I can tell Mateo isn't as worried about her. He gave up on the whole guard dog thing because it is obvious Mia doesn't need one.

I mean, when I saw her three weeks ago, she did just punch a grown man in the face.

"I'll think about it. Now, leave me alone," she opens her laptop back up and her attention goes back to what she was doing before I distracted her. "Time to practice," she says before shooing me away.

"Yeah, Ramirez! Quit flirting with Mia, or Mateo will kick you in the balls!" I hear Theo yell from where he, Mateo, and Silas are standing by their mics. "We're waiting for you."

Before I can say something back, Mia yells to him, "Aw, Theo. Don't be jealous, you know you're my favorite." I learned Mia knows exactly how to get what she wants from Theo, and that is playing up his ego. Yesterday, she convinced him to give her his phone charger by telling him he was her favorite. The dumbass did too, even though his phone was at 2 percent and hers was above 30 percent.

"Hey! I thought I was your favorite!" Silas says, playing into this ridiculous exchange, and obviously also under Mia's spell. She called him her favorite on Tuesday because he got her sweatshirt from Mateo's car when it was raining.

"You are both idiots. Mia, stop distracting my band," Mateo retorts as I walk back over to my drum set. He's pretending to not be enjoying this, but I can tell his usual seriousness is absent from his voice. And I will be the first to admit, it's absurdly entertaining to watch these two self-proclaimed womanizers be completely whipped by Mia.

But not in a romantic way.

Mateo would not let *that* happen.

And I wouldn't either.

"Actually," Mia says, "I hate you all. Eddie is my favorite."

Pride blooms in my chest when it shouldn't, knowing this is all just messing around, but loving when her spark comes out.

Atta girl.

CHAPTER 11
MIA

I DECIDE to go to Lenny's with the guys because the rest of practice was fun. Actually the past *week* of practices have been fun. Each day, I've felt part of something for the first time in a while, and I'm grateful to Mateo for giving me that.

Not only that, Mateo has taken a step back and left me alone to take care of myself with the guys. He doesn't try to keep me away from them like he used to, and I think he can see that they are becoming my friends too. Which is something I definitely didn't expect to happen, but I am forever thankful for. I forgot how nice it is to be around people who make you laugh and who laugh along with you.

I will admit, with Theo and Silas, it is different. I still think it is hilarious they will do what I want as long as I bat my eyes and smile at them, but it is similar to how Mateo would too. I play the *younger sister* role with them.

With Eddie, it isn't like that.

And I would rather not think too much about it.

After we stopped arguing over who was my favorite, the guys played the setlist one more time before packing up the equipment so Theo and Silas could take it to the venue tomorrow.

As a band, they ended up deciding their final song would be one of their older, more popular songs, and they would debut the new song on their last show of the tour because Eddie is still working on it.

While they played through the setlist, I finished scheduling some social media posts for them and editing the practice photos I had. I also made some plans for what shots I wanted to get during their first show tomorrow night, knowing it would be a little different being at the concert versus in the warehouse.

I let myself worry for a few minutes about what it would feel like being at my first concert in years. Something I used to do frequently now made my palms sweaty. The last concert I went to was a small show Nico's band played at near my college campus. Before that, it was when Nico, me, and our friends saw Cross My Heart at one of the new bars on campus.

That was over three years ago.

"You ready?" I hear behind me. I'm sitting in front of my laptop, but the screen has gone black since I have been sitting in my own thoughts for who knows how long.

"Yeah, sorry. Just got to pack up my stuff," I tell my brother. Eddie, Theo, and Silas must have finished packing up everything and headed to Lenny's because it's just me and Mateo left in the warehouse.

"Before we head over, there's something I wanted to talk to you about."

The nine words that will always set my anxiety off.

What could he possibly need to talk to me about? Did something bad happen? Is he mad at me? Did I do something wrong? Is he firing me?

No, he wouldn't fire me.

I must have messed something up.

Instead of asking him any of these questions firing in my brain, I ask, "What is it?"

Mateo walks over to sit in the chair across from me. The one Eddie has been frequenting all week.

"So," he begins, "I've noticed that you're . . . *different*."

"Um, okay."

"I don't know what it is, but this week," he pauses and lets out a little laugh to himself. "It's like you're finally you again." I can hear the emotion in his voice, not at all where I thought this conversation was headed.

Mateo clears his throat before continuing, "I haven't seen you smile this much in years, and your sense of humor, your sass, your wit, it's all back. I didn't think I'd ever see it again."

When I told Eddie last weekend that I was starting to feel like myself, it was more than just feeling motivated to do something with my life again. It was like my personality had been muted, and someone finally turned the volume back on.

It has all come back more and more because of how good it feels to see in color again after seeing only in black and white since losing Nico. I know I will never fully get over what happened, but I finally feel like standing still isn't my only option anymore.

I actually feel myself putting one foot in front of the other.

"And I wanted to apologize for being so protective of you when you first started coming around. I can tell the guys like you, and you get along with all of them well. I think they see you like I do, which means I have nothing to worry about."

"Yeah, nothing at all," is the only thing I can say because I have a vague feeling of disappointment in my stomach at the thought of *all* of the guys seeing me like Mateo does, but I decide, instead of burying the feeling, to let it go.

I'm in a good place, or at least heading towards one. I'm making friends. I have people who care about me. I'm doing something I enjoy. That's all I need right now.

"Are you ready for tomorrow?" He asks.

"Yep. Got my new ear plugs too, so I don't have to listen to your songs for the millionth and one time."

Mateo chuckles at my joke before asking, "But seriously, are you going to be okay?"

At this moment, I have two choices.

One, settle his concerns and tell him he has nothing to worry about.

Two, be honest and tell him how I'm nervous, but ready.

I decide to go with option two.

"I'm nervous. The last time I was at anything even resembling a concert was when I saw Nico's band play. It was the last show before he died."

"I know."

"But I'm ready."

"I know."

He stands up, and I follow suit. He wraps me in a hug and kisses the top of my head. This is the first time in I don't know how long that Mateo has made me feel capable rather than someone he has to take care of.

"Mateo?" I take a step back from his embrace. "Thank you."

He looks down at me, confused. "For what?"

"For always taking care of me."

"It's my job."

"But you know I can take care of myself, right?"

He smiles and shakes his head before wrapping his arms around my shoulders and resting his chin on the top of my head. "I do now."

Mateo and I walk over to Lenny's after we both make some sort of joke about how we both had enough emotional chatting for one day.

When we get there, Theo and Silas are standing at the bar. Across from them, on the other side, has to be the most gorgeous person I have ever seen. She has long dark brown hair, so silky and smooth I swear it is shining. Her prominent cheekbones and big brown eyes make it hard to look anywhere else. She is leaning up on the bar, and Theo and

Silas are both competing for her attention as they order a drink, but she didn't look the least bit affected. It's not just her looks that make her so compelling, but she carries herself in a way that you feel like you would do anything to impress her.

To her left, I see the familiar blonde hair and blue eyes of Luke, but his normal golden retriever-like demeanor is nowhere to be found. Instead, he's watching the brown-haired girl and every move she makes as she got Theo and Silas each a drink.

Next to Luke is Emmett who is wiping down the bar, as he looks like he would rather be anywhere else, which was not surprising.

The few times I have been around Emmett, I have learned that he's grumpy 90 percent of the time and is as intimidating as he looks with his freakishly large frame, semi-permanent scowl, and tattoos. Unless he is talking about his girlfriend, Drew, who must not be here yet.

I walk up and take the seat next to where Silas is sitting when Eddie comes out from the Employees Only door with two drinks in his hand, a beer and a White Claw. I watch as he scans the room until his green eyes find mine, and I feel a swoop in my stomach when he smiles.

"There you guys are," he says as he looks between me and Mateo, who sat down next to me, from the opposite side of the bar. He sets the beer down in front of Mateo and the White Claw in front of me before popping the tab on the white can and pushing it towards me.

The brown-eyed girl comes over to us before I have a chance to thank him. "Eddie, thank goodness you're here. Now, *you* can serve the drinks while I talk to your new friend." She turns to me. "Hi, I'm Annie. Mia, right?"

"That's me." I take a sip of my drink. "Nice to meet you."

"Likewise." She turns to Mateo, "Your two yahoos are making bets as to who can get the drunkest tonight."

"Theo! Silas!" my brother barks. "You two have to be up at

6 a.m. tomorrow. Neither of you are getting drunk." With that, he stands up from the chair to wedge himself in the middle of them, so he can play dad for the night.

Annie turns to me and smiles. "He's so easy to work up." She grabs my drink and circles around the bar gesturing for me to follow. I look at Eddie who gives me a wink before walking over to Luke and Emmett who have joined the other three guys.

I follow Annie over the high-top table she sat down at.

"I'm so happy to finally meet you," she says, and there is something about her that is so genuine that I can't help but smile. It has been a while since I spent time with other girls, aside from when I saw my old college roommates a few weeks ago, but that did not end well. Just as I suspected, I haven't heard from either of them since.

"You too," I reply. "I've heard a lot about you."

She laughs, and I finally understand what people mean when they say some smiles are contagious. "Well, if it was from any of those guys over there," she gestures to six guys talking and laughing about something at the bar, "it is probably far from the truth."

I can't help but hover my eyes over one of the guys in particular. Eddie is standing between Luke and Emmett behind the bar, and, while all three guys are incredibly handsome, there is something about Eddie that makes him stand out. His dark hair is getting long and perfectly frames his eyes that are roaming between the guys around him as he follows the conversation. His face is lit with a smile, and he just listens to each of the guys, laughing when they laugh, smiling when they do.

Eddie has the type of smile that shows all of his teeth and makes the skin next to his eyes crinkle but stops there. On the surface, it looks like a genuine smile, but, as I have gotten to know him more, there is something about it that seems to be more of a mask than anything else.

As if feeling my gaze, Eddie turns his head to catch me staring. I quickly look back at Annie who has an all-knowing look on her face that makes my chest feel hot with embarrassment.

I clear my throat and take a sip of my drink in an attempt to cool down, "So," I begin, "You've known them all a while then?"

"Um, no," she responds.

"No, you haven't?"

"Um, no. As in, you are not about to act like *that* didn't just happen."

I fake confusion, but it is not at all convincing, "What?"

"Don't 'what' me. You were *totally* checking Eddie out."

"Shh!" I hush her even though she wasn't talking all that loud. "I was *not*."

"You so were, and he's doing the same to you now."

"What?" I turn to look at Eddie. "No, he is not."

"Yeah, but damn you wanted him to be, huh?" She leans back in her chair and crosses her arm, her face amused at my humiliation. *How is it that I just met this girl, and she saw through me in mere seconds?*

"It's a gift," she explains as if she read my mind.

"What's a gift?" I hear from behind me. I whip my head around to see hair the color of red wine and jade eyes. "Hi," she says with a smile on her beautiful face, "I'm Drew."

A few inches shorter than me, she hops up on the empty chair at our table, before adding, "You must be Mia. Emmett told me you would be here with the band tonight. Sorry I'm late. Dinner with a friend of mine ran late."

"Who'd you have dinner with?" Annie asks her.

"Just Lacey," she says to Annie before turning to me, "A friend from home," she clarifies before adding, "I'm happy to finally meet you. I barely ever get to come around when the band is here because I'm always too tired from school, but I'm excited to be around more now that it is summer and get to know you and your brother, and the other two."

I don't even have time to reply because, as if he appeared out of thin air, Emmett appears behind her, wrapping his arms around upper body from behind and nuzzling into her neck.

"Finally," I hear him whisper, and Drew's cheeks turn the same shade as her hair.

"You get used to it," Annie says to me, reading my mind again. "He's only in a good mood when she's around."

"You're fired," Emmett says, still wrapped around Drew.

"No, I'm not," Annie replies. She is apparently immune to Emmett's grumpiness. "Anyway," she continues, stretching out the word. Her attention is back to me, "You and Eddie, huh?"

I bury my face in my hands because I just met these people and now they think that I have a crush on their friend, who is also my friend.

And *only* my friend.

"Annie, leave the girl alone," Drew says, and I immediately fall in love with her. But, I'll keep that to myself because Emmett doesn't seem like the type to share. "I'm sure they are just friends. How do you like being their photographer, Mia?"

I look up from my hands to see Emmett give Drew a kiss on the cheek and walk back over to the bar, and her cheeks finally start fading to their natural color.

"It's been a lot of fun. I used to be into photography in high school, but I gave it up for a while. Mateo needing a band photographer helped me rediscover my love for it."

"And how is it working with your brother?" Annie asks.

"It was a little difficult at first because Mateo can be a little bit of a helicopter parent, but things have been good since we found our footing."

"A helicopter parent?"

"Ha! I use that term all the time at work," Drew adds. "It's when a parent or guardian pays super close attention to their child—always getting involved and asking questions."

This makes me laugh because it is the *perfect* way to describe Mateo. "Mateo has been raising me since I was eight, so the line between older brother and parent has been blurred for most of our lives."

"Mateo mentioned before that you two lost your parents," Drew says.

"Car accident."

"I'm sorry for your loss."

"No worries. It was a long time ago."

"This crew does better without parents anyway," Annie adds, bringing an obscure light into a dark conversation.

"What do you mean?" Not that I'm offended, but it is an odd thing to say with no context.

"You fit right in. Drew doesn't talk to her parents, Emmett barely sees his, you and Mateo lost yours, Luke and I can't stand ours, and Eddie—"

"Eddie what?" I felt him before I even heard his voice behind me.

Drew and Annie exchange a quick look before Drew answers. "Annie was just telling Mia about how this group has an interesting track record when it comes to our parents. How we do just fine without them." I can tell Drew is trying to explain without *actually* explaining.

I turn and look up to see Eddie's usual easy-going grin contort in frustration, obviously not happy about the conversation. I have yet to see anything but interest, happiness, or pure focus on his face, so I am taken aback by the frustration and borderline anger. His hand is resting on the back of my chair, and I feel my chair move in the slightest as his grip on the wood tightens. He is close enough that I can smell the spice of his cologne, and I am momentarily struck silent by the tension radiating off him.

I didn't hear what Annie was going to say about Eddie's

parents, but I can imagine it isn't something good based on his reactions.

"Okay, changing the subject," Annie continues, barely skipping a beat. "Eddie, are you excited for the upcoming shows?" Apparently, Emmett's grumpiness isn't the only thing she's immune to. Pissing off Eddie doesn't even faze her. I guess it could be expected working with both of them, but I can't help but be a little impressed because I feel like Eddie is about to break the back of my chair.

"Um, yeah," he says. I watch as any sign of negative emotions melts from his face and goes back to normal. "Anyway, sorry to interrupt. I just came over to see if Mia needed another drink."

He looks down at me from where he is standing next to my chair, and I file away the questions I have because something tells me now would not be a good time to do anything but keep that smile on his face. "I'm good," I answer, and he gives me a nod before walking back to the bar.

"And I thought Emmett was territorial," Annie says under her breath, but I don't have the capacity to process it. The sadness in Eddie's eyes, the reason why his smile only occasionally ever reaches past his lips, why he is always more concerned about those around him than himself . . . So many thoughts circling in my head, all centering around wanting to understand the complexities of who *exactly* Eddie is.

Not only are his parents a sore subject, not only is there something that is making it impossible for him to put on a genuine happy face, but he has some serious anger bubbling right under the surface.

It seems like it could come out at any moment.

I want to ask Drew and Annie to find out more about these questions circling my head, but that wouldn't be fair to Eddie. Even though there is no way keeping that hidden away can be good for him, I know better than anyone that no one can force you to heal.

I watch as he settles back in his spot between Luke and Emmett, and I can't help but wonder what secrets he's holding, what feelings he's burying, what memories he's trying to forget.

And my gut tells me it has something to do with what Annie was about to say.

CHAPTER 12
MIA

THE REST of last night consisted of getting to know Annie and Drew more, and we wrapped up around 9 p.m., so the guys and I could all get some rest before having to drive the four and half hours to the venue for the first show for Cross My Heart.

Theo and Silas were disappointed that Mateo put a damper on their "who could get drunker" contest, but I was thankful to be home after such a whirlwind of a night.

I kept my mind off what happened with Eddie at the bar before going to bed because I started thinking about how I was going to spend my time over the next three months.

Since the guys won't be practicing as much and only have five more shows after the one this weekend, I'm going to have a lot of free time on my hands but not a lot to fill it with during the next three months.

I was scrolling through jobs that coincided with my yet-to-be-used marketing degree when I noticed that the Cross My Heart social media pages were getting a lot more traction since I started posting on there more frequently.

There were some comments and direct messages asking

about the photography and the social media campaigns, and the follower count was consistently growing. I started playing around with the idea of focusing on my photography as a career.

I felt an excitement about the possibility of a job that brought together what I went to school for and something I love, so I started putting together elements for a website that could launch my freelance services. With Mateo coding websites for his nine-to-five, I could launch the site sooner rather than later with his help.

I didn't fall asleep until 3 a.m., so I plan on avoiding the awkwardness of this road trip with Mateo and Eddie by sleeping in the backseat.

We are staying the night at a hotel near the venue and driving back Sunday, so I pack an overnight bag with some jeans to wear to the concert and clothes to sleep in. Mateo wants me to wear Cross My Heart merch to the show (in addition to the band member badge I'll have around my neck), so I don't get confused with someone in the crowd, but I'm still waiting to pull it out of the dryer.

Because I'll be spending the night in a hotel by myself, I also decide to pack everything I need for a perfect night: a face mask, a bottle of wine, and my laptop. I plan on watching my reality TV show reruns, uninterrupted and alone, which I'll need after being at a crowded concert venue for three hours.

I also grab my favorite hoodie that is now permanently stained with three splotches of coffee, but no one will be seeing me once I'm locked in my hotel room, so it doesn't matter.

The perfect night, in my opinion.

It is about 7:30 a.m. when Mateo texts me that he and Eddie are parked outside my apartment complex, so I lock up my place, grab my overnight bag and my camera bag to head to the lobby.

"You ready?" I hear Mateo ask as I climb into the backseat.

"As I'll ever be," I reply as I pull out my headphones from my backpack to listen to a podcast to pass the time.

"Any song requests?" Eddie asks, and it isn't until I see the reflection of Mateo's eyes on me in his rearview mirror that I realize the question was directed at me. I can tell by the way my brother is looking at me that he wants to know how I'll answer.

"Oh, don't worry about me. I have a podcast to listen to," I say as I awkwardly hold up my headphones to show him as if he has never seen a pair before.

I'm suddenly feeling flustered, and I don't know if it is because the absolute last thing I have is a song request or if it is because the memories of last night come rushing back when I take a second to notice Eddie's side profile.

His elbow is resting on the center console with his phone in his hand. His dark hair has a slight curl at the end that makes me notice the tan skin lining his neck. He's wearing a white hoodie that looks similar to the one of mine I ruined, only his looks so much more comfortable. I notice for the first time a gold chain around his neck, simple and small.

He turns around more, so his eyes find mine.

"What kind of podcast?" Eddie asks, a hint of a smile on his face.

"True crime."

"You don't listen to music when you drive?"

"I don't drive much. I walk most places." I avoid the true nature of the question, but it doesn't matter because he follows-up.

"So you're not a music person?"

I don't really know how to answer this question because I am.

Or I was.

I used to be.

But not anymore. Now, I'm a person who usually drives, runs, walks, or sits in silence until my thoughts become too loud. Then, I became a podcast person.

My face must reflect the spiral my mind is going in because Eddie lifts an eyebrow at me, and our eyes are locked. Something passes between us, and I forget that Mateo is in the car. For a few moments, it is just me and Eddie, and I want to tell him everything. There is something in his eyes, in his gaze, that knocks down the walls I have built up. I feel like he can sense it too because he lets his usual mask slip.

In the time I have gotten to know Eddie more, I've noticed that he never lets his guard down completely, and his form of a defense is a happy face. I feel like he lets me see slightly past it every so often, and that is when the sadness deep in his eyes becomes more prominent.

I don't know if I recognize the sadness because it is the same kind I see in my reflection, or maybe, just maybe, I have the same effect he has on me.

"Not anymore," I tell him.

I feel more words form in my mouth, but I watch as the mask slips back on and the knowing gaze I thought I saw turns back into a wide smile.

"Your loss, sunshine," he says before turning back to face the front.

Sunshine.

The nickname is less than fitting, especially when the one calling me that wears one of the brightest smiles I have ever seen.

Even though there is something dark about it too.

"Not my loss, actually," I say as he scrolls on Spotify. "Wouldn't want to spend the next four and a half hours listening to whatever shit you like." I give him a playful scoff, resorting back to our usual banter because it is comfortable. More comfortable than what was happening before.

"Ouch," Eddie says, bringing a hand to his heart as if my words physically hurt him. "Careful there. Friends don't call other friend's music taste shit."

I see Mateo in the rearview mirror pretending not to be amused by us, but he also has no trace of interest in joining the conversation.

"No friend of mine has shitty music taste," I argue, as if I have any platform to make this argument, but Eddie doesn't need to know that.

"You don't even know what I listen to."

"Yeah, but I know what you write."

"Hey!" Mateo intervenes, no doubt only because the band was alluded to. "Our music is anything but shit."

"Yeah, listen to your brother," Eddie retorts, looking over his shoulder. They're ganging up on me, but it is nothing I can't take.

I'm also glad Eddie can take a joke about his music.

I actually really like Cross My Heart's music, and Eddie writes the majority of it. It is a little harder than stuff I usually listen to, but I can definitely appreciate it.

Not that I would ever give Mateo, or Eddie, the satisfaction.

I stick my tongue out at him before putting my headphones on.

He winks at me before turning around again.

I ignore the flip in my stomach and hover my thumb over the play icon to start my podcast episode as I hear the beginning notes of "Wrapped Around Your Finger" by Post Malone. I would recognize any of the songs on that album within the first two seconds, even if it has been months since I listened to a full song aside from Cross My Heart's.

The verse continues, and my temptation gets the best of me. I take my headphones off and rest my head against the window. I listen to the words, feel the subtle beat of the bass, and I turn my head to watch out the window as we drive. We are cruising on the highway now, and it is early enough that we have no traffic to worry about.

For a moment, I forget why I ever stopped listening to music, especially in the car, where it is the most fun to sing along. Where it is the most fun to find a song that fits whatever I'm feeling and then embrace those feelings.

Then, my mind wanders as the chorus begins to play. My lips threaten to sync up with the song as I wonder if these lyrics would fit with the song Nico wrote.

And, just like that, my mind brings me back to those last few memories of him. The memories I want to keep away and hold close at the same time.

If I could only remember those chords, the ones hidden so deep in my mind.

I need this song out of my head.

My eyes find Mateo's in the rearview mirror again, but I look back out the window as I put my headphones back on and distract myself with a true crime case I already know but will drown out the music the guys will be playing.

It isn't until we are an hour into the drive, and I'm on my second podcast episode, that I begin to feel my eyelids get heavy.

Just before I drift to sleep, I realize I forgot to grab my Cross My Heart T-shirt out of the dryer.

———

Nico and I finally are spending some time together after not seeing each other for a few weeks. Classes have been kicking my ass, and he's been working on finding venues that will let him and his band play to get some visibility.

Right now, he's playing me the song he's been working his ass off on. The one he's been working on for weeks and wants to be perfect.

The one he is writing for me.

"Hold on, let me just finish this last paragraph."

We're sitting on the floor of my dorm room, our backs up against the side of my bed. His guitar is on his lap, and my laptop is on mine. I'm working on a paper that is due at midnight because I didn't have time to do it when the boys I nanny for were at their swim lesson. "Babe, are you even listening?"

"No. I mean, yes. But wait, let me finish before I forget what I want to say."

He lets out a harsh sigh and the music that was playing in the background stops as he lets go of his guitar and leans his head back on the bed. I can tell this is going to be another argument, but I have to finish this paper within the next half an hour, or it'll be late.

Nico and I have been arguing a lot about our priorities, mainly him feeling like I'm not making him one. I hate that I'm making him feel like I don't have time for him, but my priorities have shifted since the second semester of my sophomore year started.

"Nico, stop. This is important."

"What, and my song isn't?"

I let out a sigh of my own and close my laptop before turning to him. "Don't put words in my mouth. Yes, it's important."

"You have a funny way of showing it. You can't even listen to it for two minutes." He puts his guitar in the case sitting on the ground next to him before closing it and standing up. He has been quicker and quicker to anger lately, as if his patience evaporates faster and faster with every fight we have. He walks over to where his jacket is hanging on my desk chair. February is a snowy, cold month in Wisconsin, but all he has is his black denim jacket.

"Where are you going?" I ask, standing up and putting my laptop on my bed.

"You have better things to do, so I'm just gonna go." He slides his arms into his jacket before walking past me to pick up his guitar case. His tone is harsh, but I don't like leaving him alone when he gets like this.

"I'm almost done, just wait." I grab his arm, trying to make him look at me.

"I don't want to wait, Mia." He rips his arm away from me. "I've been waiting weeks for you to have time for me, and I'm sick of it." His voice is rising in volume, and I hate when he gets like this. I know his emotions are hard for him to control, but I just need him to be patient.

"Stop, please don't leave angry."

"No, Mia. I'm done!" He's yelling now and stomping towards the door. He opens the door before stepping out of my room and slamming the door behind him.

"Come back!" I scream, but I'm no longer looking at my dorm room door closing. Instead, I'm in the backseat of my brother's car, but it isn't moving. And I'm alone.

It's been months since I've had *this* dream, and it's the one that hits the hardest. It's the one that's the closest to reality. The one that reminds me of our last night together. The night that represents the biggest regret of my life.

It takes me a second to register that we're stopped at a gas station, so Mateo and Eddie must have gone in and didn't want to wake me up.

I take my headphones off that are no longer playing anything and sit up. I rub my eyes before I reach for the handle of the door, and my whole body freezes.

Outside the window, Eddie is staring at me. One of his hands is in a tight fist at his side and the other is on the gas pump that happens to be on the side of the car I am on.

He looks like he just saw a ghost.

My brother must still be inside, leaving Eddie to fill up the tank. This means he most likely heard me scream into an empty car after being completely passed out, and I don't know if it is the remnants of the dream I just had or the embarrassment of Eddie seeing me, but I can't move.

Eddie is watching me, and I can tell he doesn't know what to do.

My mind finally remembers how to move my body, and I slowly open the car door. My one and only priority is getting out of this interaction with my dignity still intact. I don't even have time to think about the dream itself, so I push down the feelings that threaten to boil over and the thoughts that will send me into a spiral.

As the car door opens, Eddie has to take a few steps to the side to get out of the way. He doesn't take his eyes off me.

"Take a picture, it'll last longer," I tease, figuring that our usual, *comfortable* exchanges will extract the tension in the air, but the usual cadence of my teasing isn't coming through.

"You don't have to do that," Eddie responds, surprising me.

"Do what?" I ask.

"Pretend."

"Pretend what?"

"Pretend that I didn't just see what happened."

So, it looks like I'm not getting out of this with any dignity.

"I don't know what you're talking about," is what I decide to go with, hoping that he drops it.

"Does that happen a lot?"

I wrap my arms around myself, not because I'm cold, being that it is the middle of the summer, but because maybe it'll protect me from this conversation.

"Like I said, I don't know what you're talking about."

"The dream seemed pretty intense."

"What do you mean?" I ask. He only saw me when I woke up. There is no way he could know that I was having an out-of-the-ordinary dream. "It was just a dream."

"You were moving around a lot, and you looked uncomfortable."

"I looked uncomfortable?" I ask, not even hiding the annoyance in my voice that he is, in fact, not letting me out of this conversation.

"Your face was all scrunched up. Like you were in pain."

"So you were watching me while I slept? Pretty creepy if

you ask me." I try to ease the tension again, and it works for a moment because I see a tiny crack in his serious demeanor, so I play into it. "Forget what I said. Taking pictures of sleeping girls is frowned upon."

"Is that what they say in your crime podcasts?" I'm thankful that he plays along, hoping my eyes tell him the words my mouth doesn't. His features soften, so I know I have my in, but I also have a feeling this is just a temporary pause on the conversation.

"They actually specifically warn against drummers of rock bands," I tease.

"I warn against those for you too, sunshine." My stomach flips, not only because of the use of that nickname again but because even though his words are warning me, his smirk is doing anything but.

"Why do you keep calling me that?"

"What?"

"That's the second time you've called me 'sunshine' today."

"Every rainy day needs some sunshine."

I roll my eyes because this has to be the opening for a punchline or something, and I am in a fragile headspace after all this whiplash. "Ha Ha. Well, then what does that make you? The rainy day?" I tease.

"Not when I'm with you."

My jaw drops, and I think I'm still asleep because there's no way my brother's best friend just said that to me.

My feet are glued to the concrete, and I can't do anything but watch Eddie take the gas nozzle from the car and put it back on the pump as he smiles to himself. I hear him let out a chuckle, and I know that this round just went to him.

I see him glance towards the door of the gas station shop before looking back at me. He lowers his face, so he is just a few inches from my face, and I know for a fact that I'm still asleep because I think Eddie Ramirez is about to kiss me.

Alarms go off in my head, but I ignore them all because, for some reason, I want this to happen. It is a bad idea in every single way, but nothing sounds better than saying "fuck it, it's fine" and leaning in.

Eddie takes my chin between his fingers, and a bad idea has never looked so good. "Take a picture, sunshine," he whispers. "It'll last longer." He lightly lifts my chin to close my still-opened mouth and turns around to walk back to the passenger seat.

"Mia?" I hear from behind me.

I whip around to see my brother with a plastic bag in one hand and a bottle of Diet Coke in the other, and I slam back into reality.

What the fuck did I almost do?

No, not even that. I didn't *almost* do anything.

What the fuck did I just *want* to happen?

I just melted in the hands of my brother's best friend while my brother was inside the gas station getting us snacks.

And the best part, it was all a game.

A game where Eddie is the winner, and I am the absolute loser.

But this game is far from over, and the tables are about to turn.

CHAPTER 13

EDDIE

IT ISN'T until the last hour of the four and a half hour drive that I feel like I can relax. Mia stays awake for the rest of the ride, her headphones on listening to her true crime podcast. We have light conversation here and there for the rest of the ride, but the three of us stay mostly in our own minds until we pull up to the venue around noon.

Mateo wanted to scope everything out before our sound check at 1 p.m., and then we will head over to our hotel to prepare for tonight. We go on at six tonight, so we will have a few hours before we have to head back over here.

Even though Mia took a little nap, she looks even more tired than before her eyes closed. I can't explain the feeling I had watching Mia sleep. I have never seen someone look so tense when they were sleeping in my entire life. I find it hard to believe that her body could even relax enough to fall asleep with how strained her face looked.

I know Mateo noticed too, but he didn't say anything. He was gripping the steering wheel much harder than he needed to, and I couldn't blame him. My fist clenched with every small gasp or whimper Mia made.

When we stopped for gas, I wanted to ask Mateo if he

thinks we should wake her up, brushing it off as she might want a snack or need to go to the bathroom, but instead I told Mateo I would fill up the tank while he went in to grab what he needed.

I wanted to make enough noise to wake her up, but I don't think there was any noise loud enough that would have woken her up from the state she was in. I watched through the window as her brows furrowed and her eyes squeezed tightly shut, even though they were already closed. Her hands were in fists and seeing that made mine do the same as I filled up the car.

Then, when her eyes shot open, and she yelled out, I had to stop myself from opening the car door and telling her everything would be okay.

If I was a better man, I wouldn't have let myself be her distraction when she got out of the car. I would have urged her to talk to someone, *anyone*, about it, but I am so selfish when it comes to her, only wanting her to feel as light and free from worry.

When she looked at me with those pretty brown eyes, telling me without the words that she wasn't ready to talk about whatever happened in that dream of hers, I knew that what I initially thought was wrong.

I couldn't give her the world if she asked for it, but I could burn it down if it meant that nothing would ever hurt her again.

I know it isn't fair, and I know it isn't healthy.

But I never said I was good for her.

She may not believe me, but she really is my sunshine.

And I'm too broken to be anything but her rainy day.

When we get through security and into the concert hall, I can't help but feel the kick of excitement in my stomach at the thought of this venue being packed with people in a few hours. I have my drumsticks in my back pocket and my guitar case over my shoulder.

With our down time between sound check and the show, I plan on finishing up the song we will be debuting at the last show of this mini tour. I decided to scratch everything I initially had written after *a certain tune* got stuck in my head.

I look around and see Theo and Silas chatting with some of the band members from the other two openers. They arrived about fifteen minutes ahead of us; they had already brought in all our equipment. The members of the headlining band are set for sound check any minute, and then it is our turn.

I'm never one to get nervous, but I feel some uneasiness at the thought of not knowing how tonight will go. We knew the first show of this six-show series was going to be the hardest because first impressions are important.

The headlining band and the tour managers are going to be watching how the crowd reacts to us, if they like us, hate us, don't care about us, and now that the show we have been prepping for is finally here, I can't help but feel the nerves kick in.

"You good?" I hear Mia ask. I turn to see her standing next to me in her coffee-stained white hoodie that she put on when Mateo refused to turn off the AC during the last thirty minutes of our ride.

"That's a good look," I tease, gesturing to the stain on her stomach. "A good memory too. Haven't caught you checking me out in a while," I tease, alluding to the day she got the stain and when this whole mess of her and me began. Even though it is a complete lie because I caught her this morning. I tried to pretend I didn't notice because it is almost unfair how often I go unnoticed watching her.

Every time I look at her, I wish there was someone who would take *her* picture. She's always the one behind the camera, but, if it were up to me, she would be the one at the center of everyone's attention because she's always at the center of mine.

"You wish, Ramirez," she retorts before setting her camera bag down at her feet to pull her hoodie off over her head. I try to ignore the stupid grin on my face at how cute she looks with her hair all messed up, and I can't help myself from reaching out and fixing it for her, lightly flattening some strands and brushing a piece behind her ear.

She looks up at me with her pretty brown eyes, and it is the same look she gave me at the gas station right before Mateo came out. If I didn't know any better, I would have thought she wanted me to kiss her. I am constantly reminding myself that we are just friends, and this reaction I have to her is platonic, but I don't think there is anything platonic about that look.

Before I can do or say anything that further shows that she has got me in the palm of her hand, I hear Mateo call for her from behind me.

"What?" she asks, looking past me as she picks her camera bag back up and hangs her sweatshirt over her arm.

"Where's your band tee?" Mateo asks.

"Oh," Mia says, looking down at her T-shirt that does not have the Cross My Heart logo on it, "I may have accidentally left it in my dryer."

Mateo runs his fingers through his hair before telling her he'll get her one from the boxes of merch we have.

"No need," she says. "Eddie said I can wear his."

"What?" I say, and I find her looking at me as if she knows that I can't say no to her.

"He did?" Mateo says, and he has a slight tone of annoyance. "Okay, well make sure you have one tonight."

"Yes, sir," Mia says, giving him a two-finger salute. He turns around and she flips off his back with the same hand.

"When did I say I was lending you my shirt?" I ask.

"When you said two could play at this game," she explains, and my puzzled look gives away that I have no idea what her angle is. I left our last exchange thinking I had the upper hand, but I am starting to understand Mia has a way of making me question my own reality. "Come on, raindrop. Just think about how good I'll look in your T-shirt." She adds.

I don't even register the nickname. Instead, my breath hitches, and my mind goes to dirty places that should most definitely not involve my best friend's little sister in nothing but my T-shirt.

Now, I know her angle.

And she knows exactly how to kill me.

I clear my throat and find the chain around my neck. I lightly pull it from where it is resting around my neck as if it is what is making it hard for me to breathe. Mia is smirking up at me, looking at me with a challenge that I just can't resist.

"You're right, sunshine. I've only ever seen that in my dreams." I give her a wink before the mention of dreams reminds me of earlier today. "Speaking of dreams," I add.

Her smile briefly fades before she recovers, and I assume I got her where I want her, regretting provoking me. "Are you ready to tell me about the one you had today?" I add.

It isn't until the smirk fades and the light in her face disappears that I realize I ruined the good thing we had going, and I crossed a line.

Before I can try to apologize or change the subject, she says, "I'm going to look around. Need to plan my shots, so I'm ready for tonight. Good luck with sound check."

With that, she hurries away, and I wish the ground would swallow me whole.

I don't get a moment with Mia for the rest of the day. I keep an eye on her as she walks around the venue, does some practice shots, and messes with the settings on the camera, and not one time did she look at me.

Sound check went fine, and we took some time to introduce ourselves to all the bands. It finally hits me how we will be playing with bands we look up to, but there is still a pit in my stomach at the way I left things with Mia.

When it is time to head back to the hotel, I ask Mateo where Mia is with the excuse that I need to get my T-shirt to her, and he says she had already gone back to the hotel. I don't know how to ask what room she is in without setting off alarms with Mateo, so when he and I get to the hotel room we are sharing, I give him the T-shirt so he could get it to Mia.

I went the rest of the afternoon without seeing her but being able to perfectly picture the look on her face when I pushed her too far.

We're friends, but we're still getting to know each other. I don't even know what kind of friend she sees me as. Sometimes I feel like I'm just someone for her to mess with, maybe flirt a little with, and sometimes I feel like we know each other on a deeper level. Moments pass between us where I feel like she gets me, without me even having to open up. I don't feel like my smiles are fake around her, and she makes me *feel* in ways I didn't think I was capable of anymore.

I'm backstage with Theo and Silas, and we go on in about ten minutes. The nerves have *fully* taken over. Even though I'm still upset that I haven't been able to talk to Mia, my mind starts to focus on the fact that we are about to do our first official show opening for the openers of a headlining band.

I begin to pace, listening to the random conversations happening backstage. We have already talked to the audio and visual teams to make sure the lights and other effects are taken care of for our set. We made sure all the sounds were balanced during sound check and already had our ear monitors on when we got here, so now we just wait until we get the signal that it is time to go on. Mateo walked Mia out into the crowd to make sure she had everything she needed.

She has a photo pass around her neck that identifies her as the band photographer, so she can get past security and venue staff. She has my Cross My Heart T-shirt, but I can't help but share Mateo's concern that she is all alone in the crowd.

We get the two-minute warning, and I take a second to collect myself because, if I don't, this is going to be a disaster. I tell myself that I'll talk to Mia afterwards, but for now, I have to focus on doing my absolute best for this show. Mateo, Theo, and Silas are counting on me, and I refuse to let the people who depend on me down, no matter what. I take a breath before rejoining Theo and Silas who don't have a nervous bone in their body.

Mateo comes up beside us just before the lights go down, and we get the signal.

It's time.

CHAPTER 14

MIA

I WATCH from the outskirts of the crowd as the lights go down. In the dark, I can see the silhouettes of Mateo, Theo, Silas, and Eddie make their way to their spots on stage, Mateo in the middle, Theo to his right, Silas to his left, and Eddie at his drum set in the back center.

The crowd is small because the doors just opened thirty minutes ago, but I know it will grow. Right now, it is good because it gives me room to find where I can get some good angles. My plan is to start out here, get some photos, then get some from the area that is sectioned off for security and other venue staff. I'll get some up-close shots and shots of the crowd there. Then, I'll end back out here for the last song.

I don't have time to think about anything else because the lights are about to go up, and Eddie is about to hit his drumsticks three times.

Eddie.

He probably thinks I'm crazy, closing off after he asked about my dream.

It just caught me off guard.

Not because I was reminded of Nico, but because I *had* to be reminded of him.

After I had the dream in the car, I was able to distract myself, and Eddie is the perfect distraction.

It wasn't until Eddie asked about it again before sound check that I realized how easily the dream drifted from my mind.

I've spent three years waking up from my dreams and longing for them to be reality, telling myself I would do anything to make them one. I've also spent the last three years having those dreams remind me of a time in my life that I barely made it out of.

Today was the first day that the dream was just that, a dream. And I didn't know how to feel.

I still don't.

So, I was caught off guard.

It wasn't until I was alone in my hotel room, getting ready for tonight's show, that I realized there is still sadness at the memory of Nico, but there is a new-found happiness too.

There was also no guilt.

I made a note in my phone to talk about this in therapy next week because it is the first time in a long time I felt there was movement forward in my healing process.

My hands find my camera hung around my neck, and I take a deep breath because I will be okay, and it is the first time I tell myself that and actually believe it.

———

The guys are killing it.

With every song, the crowd grows larger, and I can't even see open space in the back of the venue anymore. It is obvious not everyone is here for them, and the venue is in no way at capacity, but the consistent growth of the crowd is definitely hyping the guys up, and they are doing amazing.

Mateo is doing an awesome job of keeping the crowd engaged, and Theo and Silas are in perfect rhythm with each other, their background vocals perfectly complimenting Mateo's lead vocals.

And I've never seen Eddie so in his element. I thought he looked good when he was practicing, but that's nothing compared to watching him on stage. He does not miss a beat and looks like he is having the time of his life.

Watching him reminds me of how it felt to watch Nico. Every doubt, every trace of sadness, has melted away. All that is left is peace and love for what he is doing.

I thought it would be challenging to find the shots, but it's seamless, and I'm having so much fun. I find myself singing along to the songs, and I forgot how good it feels to listen to music and just enjoy it.

Their second-to-last song is finishing up, and I got all the shots of the crowd I wanted, so I show my photo pass to security to get back into the crowd. The venue is standing-room only, so it is basically just a big hall with a stage and a bar lining the back. Now that the crowd is significantly bigger than it was at the beginning of their setlist, I have to squeeze through more people to get to where I need to be.

My skin begins to prickle at the closeness of the people around me, but I try to ignore it and focus on my task.

As I politely push my way through, saying, "Excuse me," and trying not to make anyone think I am stealing their spot, I am stopped by a group of guys that are either ignoring my attempts to get past them or they are too invested in Cross My Heart's show to notice me.

I try to give them the benefit of the doubt and assume the latter, but with each step I try to take forward, they won't budge.

No, it is almost as if the guy closest to me widens his stance to make it harder for me to get through.

I'm trying to go the opposite direction of the stage, so most people are letting me through with no problem because I'm not trying to make my way to the front, but this group of guys, or maybe just *this* guy, keeps blocking my way.

The song ends, and Mateo starts announcing that this is their last and most popular song, and they can't wait to sing it for everyone. I'm bummed that I'm missing this shot of him talking to the crowd as Theo and Silas move to the center to stand next to him, so I get a little less polite as I try to make my way through.

"Excuse me," I say as I take a step forward, but the guy in front of me just looks down at me and then back up at the stage.

"I said excuse me," I try again, a little more stern this time and try to step forward, but Mr. Doesn't Want To Let Me Through actually takes a step in my direction to stop me from getting through.

Now, I'm pissed because the band is about to start the last song, and I do *not* want to miss these shots. This is their first big show as an opener, and I don't want to miss their last song.

"Dude, I'm not trying to steal your spot," I start to step and feel him tense rather than move out of the way, but I don't back down. Instead, I use some strength to push past him. He is bigger than me, but only a few inches taller, but he staggers a little off balance. Luckily, I'm out of there before he can say anything.

I hear him yell to one of his friends, "What a bitch," as Theo's opening riff starts, but I'm able to get to the outskirts of the crowd in no time for the shots of the guys.

The last song finishes, and I put my camera down to join the clapping and yelling for them as Mateo says, "Thank you! If you're interested in Cross My Heart merch, please see our booth in the back. Can't wait to see you all soon!" The flannel he was wearing at the beginning of the set is now around his waist, and his brown hair is sticking to his forehead. Theo throws his guitar pick to the crowd before joining Mateo in the middle of the stage as Silas throws his Cross My Heart trucker hat to a girl he was probably eyeing the entire show.

Eddie stands from his drums and comes up to join the other three. He took off his T-shirt after the second song, and I can't blame him. It is fucking hot in this venue, and he did the whole crowd a favor playing the drums in nothing but his black jeans and gold chain.

I snap a couple pictures of the four of them as they wave to the crowd and then hug in a quick huddle as the lights on stage go out and the bar lights go on.

People start moving towards the back of the place for drinks before the next opener, and I can't wait to sneak a peek at the shots I just got.

I click the display button on my camera and instantly feel a rush of emotion as I see the last picture I took. The four guys all have their arms around each other in their huddle, and I can see the proud smiles on their faces. It is a moment I am so grateful I got to capture.

I'm overly eager to see the other shots I got, so instead of meeting Mateo and the other guys by their merch booth like we agreed on, I find an empty spot against the wall near the restrooms where I won't be in anybody's way and start to click through the other pictures.

I'm completely distracted by the genuine happiness on their faces as I click through the pictures that I don't feel a presence approaching. And when I finally do, it is not one I recognize.

"Cute, a groupie," a voice says, and I look up to see the guy who wouldn't let me past him in the crowd. He is just under six foot with a stocky build, and he is wearing blue jeans and tennis shoes with a T-shirt of the headlining band. His blonde hair is receding in a direction that makes me think he is at least fifteen years older than me.

I am used to being around Eddie, Theo, and Silas who are all around ten years older than me like Mateo, but none of them have ever looked at me in the predatory way this man is looking at me right now, and I feel my heart start to beat faster.

Before I can say anything, he walks a few steps closer to me, and I look around to see that I am near the men's restroom that never seems to be as crowded as the women's, so it is basically just me and him.

The merch booth the guys are waiting for me at is on the *other* side of the crowd, and I am regretting my decision to find a quiet corner in a venue that is made up of mostly men.

"So which one of those shitty musicians are you fucking, groupie?" he says with a disgusting smirk on his face. People are walking by, but there is no way an outsider's perspective would think anything is wrong with just a quick glance.

My mind begins to race as I feel the room close in on me. I feel myself go into fight or flight, but I refuse to back down from this asshole.

"First of all, I'm the photographer. Second of all, it is my brother's band," I let my camera drop, the strap still around my neck, and I push off the wall I was leaning on and begin to take a step past him. "And who I fuck is none of your business," I add for good measure.

He intercepts my step, and his sweaty hand wraps around my upper arm. I freeze as he brings his face closer to mine, and I can smell the stale scent of beer on his breath. "Unless it's me," he says as if anything about my face, voice, or demeanor leads him to believe that would be something I want. "Come on, honey. Let's get out of here."

"Fuck off," I spit, but that only pisses him off. His sleazy grin contorts, and I know I said the wrong thing.

"Don't be such a bitch," his grip on my arm tightens as I try to pull away and I am wishing I went straight to the booth after the show ended.

I look around, but no one's close enough to be in earshot

with music playing while the next band gets ready to perform.

He uses his grip on my arm to push me back to the wall, and I am no match against him. I feel like I'm sinking further and further underwater, but I will not let myself drown. He is grabbing my left arm, so I fist my right hand, hoping it is recovered enough to be used again, and I move to swing just before I hear a familiar boom of a voice. But, this time it isn't thanking the crowd for coming.

"Hey! What the fuck are you doing?!" Mateo yells, bringing all the attention in the surrounding vicinity to us. I see him running up to where the guy is holding me, and I see Theo and Silas running behind him, but there is no sign of Eddie.

I know Mateo, and his tactic will be to deescalate the situation, but I don't know if a guy like this is going to back down easily.

"Mind your fucking business, pretty boy. You should be more concerned about your shitty music than your groupies," the asshole gripes, still not letting go of my arm.

I watch Mateo's nostrils flare, and Theo and Silas both look like they are about to snap, but all three of them know they have to stay calm. The last thing they need is to make a scene at their first show and earn the reputation of hotheads who beat up people in the crowd.

"Watch it," Mateo barks, "that's my sister, and you're going to take your hand off of her. Now."

The asshole has the audacity to laugh, but he is smart enough to let go of me. "Whatever, she's not even—"

Eddie's fist meets the side of the guy's face before he can even finish that sentence. I didn't even see where he came from.

"Fuck," I hear Theo say under his breath before him and Silas grab Eddie before he can swing again.

Mateo rushes up to me while the asshole cups the side of

his face, red-faced and looking like he is about to cry. Mateo wraps an arm around me as he turns to Eddie and points right in his face. "Don't you dare," he growls, and I can tell by Eddie's face that he has no intention of stopping there. It takes me a moment to register that Mateo, Theo, and Silas all acted in quick unison the second Eddie threw the punch.

Theo has Eddie by the right arm, and Silas has him by the left. Mateo put himself right in the middle of Eddie and the guy with no hesitation.

Has something like this happened before?

I take this moment to look at Eddie. He has the same look of anger he had at the bar with Annie and Drew, only this is ten times worse.

If I didn't know any better, I would think that Eddie has every intention of killing this guy.

I don't know what comes over me, but I instantly feel responsible. "Eddie, hey. Eddie, look at me," I say from under Mateo's arm.

Eddie's eyes meet mine, and there is an instant look of relief. The anger momentarily fades, and he rips his arms away from Theo and Silas before joining me grabbing the arm that the guy was gripping and looking it over.

Mateo watches him before he turns back to me, "Are you okay?"

"He left a fucking *handprint* around her arm," Eddie growls, and before any of us can do anything, Eddie is stomping over to the guy who finally found his footing and started walking away.

"You're dead," Eddie bellows. "You're *dead*, asshole."

Luckily, security caught on to what was happening and two of them were already heading over to grab the guy.

"We got it," one of them says to Eddie, holding out his hands. Eddie sees enough through his anger to stop charging at the guy.

"Get him out of here!" he yells at the security guard. "Now!"

The security guard nods and joins the other, and the two of them escort the guy out.

Eddie turns around and comes back over to us, and I can see Mateo's wheels are turning, and he does not like the conclusion he is coming to.

Eddie looks at me one more time before heading in the direction of backstage, the crowd around us quickly dissipating, and Theo and Silas follow him.

"Mia, are you okay?" Mateo asks again.

I nod because I'm not sure I trust my voice right now.

Mateo and I head backstage to where Theo and Silas are, but Eddie isn't with them. My heartbeat has evened out, and my adrenaline is wearing off. There is a dull pain on my arm, and I know I'll have a bruise tomorrow, but that isn't important right now.

I need to find Eddie.

"You good?" Theo asks when Mateo and I walk up to him and Silas.

"Yeah, thanks," I reply.

"No right hooks today, Rocky?" Silas asks, trying to brighten the mood.

"Almost," I manage to say, letting out a dry laugh, but my mind is elsewhere. I was ready to throw a punch, and I would have if Mateo didn't yell out when he did.

"He's outside," Theo says, reading my mind, jutting his chin towards the door that leads to the back parking lot.

I glance at my brother to find him looking at me. I've always been able to read his face like a book, but today I see a look I don't recognize. I turn away before he can say anything and nod a thanks to Theo before heading straight out the back door.

A rush of cool air meets me as I push the heavy door open. It leads to a private gated lot where our car, a few others, and all the bands' equipment vans are parked. It is still light outside and I find Eddie pacing. There's no one else out here, but I'm not sure he notices me.

The door slamming behind me pulls him out of his head and his eyes immediately lock with mine. In no more than a second, he is standing right in front of me, his hands gripping my shoulders.

"Why didn't you meet us by the booth?" he asks, but he doesn't sound angry. He sounds like he is in pain.

"I was looking at the pictures I took," I answer because, for some reason, I feel like I owe him an explanation. I gave my camera to Mateo before I came out here; otherwise, I would show Eddie what photos I was looking at to distract him from whatever battle is happening in his head.

With his hands still gripping my shoulders, he pulls me in and wraps his arms around me, one hand on my lower back, one hand holding the back of my head, and I instantly feel any tension in my body dissolve. My arms wrap around his waist and my head rests against his chest.

With my head resting there, I can hear Eddie's heartbeat. It starts out fast, beating loud against the side of my head, but the longer we stay like this, the slower it gets.

I don't know how long we stay like this, but I think I could have stayed in his arms forever. There is something about his embrace that makes me feel safe and protected, which I never thought could be a feeling I would long for after so many years of feeling suffocated by Mateo treating me like I would fall apart at any moment.

With Eddie, it's different. I don't feel like he's trying to keep me from breaking into pieces. It feels like he is reminding me these pieces of me mean something.

Like they mean something to *him*.

"I was going to kill him," he says into my hair. "When I saw his hand on you, I knew at that moment I was capable of killing him." His voice is just above a whisper, but it is heavy with pain. Pain like when he asked me why I didn't meet them at the booth.

Until today, I've never heard his voice sound like this.

I tighten my arms around his waist. "You're not capable of hurting a fly, raindrop." I whisper into his chest, adding the silly nickname I made for him in hopes to alleviate the weight I hear in his voice.

He loosens his grip around me and leans back to look down at me. The hand behind my head slowly finds the side of my cheek.

"I don't think you know what I'm capable of, sunshine."

Dark, long lashes contrast with the green of his eyes. The green that is drowning in a mix of the familiar sadness and *something else*. His gaze is locked on me, pulling me in with every second that goes by.

The longer I stare into his eyes, the more I want to destroy everything and anything that puts this sadness there.

And that thought scares me. It means I'm at risk for caring about him in ways that I shouldn't.

My eyes find his scar and follow it from where it starts in the middle of his forehead, down to where it ends where his dimple would be if he was smiling.

I act out of instinct not completely thinking about what I'm doing, as I run a hand up his chest until I find his cheek, swiping my thumb along where that dimple would be, as if my touch would magically make it appear, magically make him smile.

As I do this, his eyes never leave mine, and his body is completely still aside from the slight movement of his head as he leans into my touch.

I move my gaze down to his lips, slightly parted, and my heartbeat quickens.

And so does Eddie's. With my body still pressed against his, I can feel the effect I have on him, and he can feel the same from me.

We are entering a dangerous zone, one I don't know if we could come back from. One that I don't know if I could handle.

I lift my gaze back to his eyes, and all traces of that sadness are gone. Replaced with that *something else* I saw mixed in before.

Before I can figure out what it is, Eddie's lips crash into mine, and time stands still.

With every move of his lips on mine, I fall into another world.

A world where we can pretend the broken parts of us are healed.

A world where we are deserving of the happiness we chase.

A world where we don't have to paint smiles on our faces or bury our feelings.

A world where it is just us.

Butterflies explode in my stomach, and my body feels like it is a million degrees as the kiss deepens and moves with a gentle urgency that tells me he doesn't want this to end either.

That he doesn't care that we are falling headfirst to the point of no return.

I hear the push of the metal door behind me, and I slam back into reality as Eddie pulls away from me and steps around me as if to block me from whoever is coming outside.

"Everything okay?" I hear my brother ask, and I hope that Eddie has a better poker face than me because if Mateo saw me right now, he would see right through me.

"Yeah, Mia and I were just talking," Eddie replies, turning over his shoulder to look at me. I find his eyes and nod, picking up on his subtle *play along* glance.

I let out an exhale before pretending I didn't just kiss my brother's best friend and that I'm not about to lie right to his face. "All good. Just talking."

Mateo gives a curt nod before saying, "Well, I need to talk to Eddie."

I don't know how to tell him that we need a few more minutes to *talk* because not only am I currently dealing with the residual shock of what just happened, but *I* need to talk to Eddie about what the fuck just happened.

"Yeah, of course, man," I watch as Eddie flips a switch and resorts right back into his usual, carefree self. "Mia was just heading back in," Eddie answers for me, and I try to ignore my uneasiness with how easy it was for him to switch gears so fast.

"Right," I say before sneaking a glance at Eddie as I walk past him to head back inside. He meets my eyes and gives me a small smile. "We'll talk later. Okay, sunshine?"

I nod, not wanting Mateo to have any idea of *what* exactly Eddie and I have to talk about, but when I head to the door where Mateo is standing, he does not look happy.

CHAPTER 15

EDDIE

MATEO LETS the door shut behind Mia, and my chest instantly tightens when she is out of my sight.

Before she came outside, I felt myself losing control. From the second I spotted that asshole grabbing her, there was no way I was going to be able to stay calm.

Getting away, coming out here, this is what I needed.

I needed to be alone.

If I hadn't, I don't know what would have happened.

I hate that she saw me like that, and I hate that I kissed her.

Watching her walk out here was watching a dream come true. Her hair flew back as she pushed open the door leading to the lot, and her face was flushed, whether it was from how hot it was inside or from the adrenaline, I don't know, but it was the most beautiful shade of pink I have ever seen.

She had on my T-shirt and a possessiveness I never felt before bloomed in my chest. And now, I don't think it will ever go away. I'm tempted to stoop as low as burning all her clothes, so the only choice she has is to wear mine.

When I rushed towards her, my anger was gone. It had completely evaporated with my first step in her direction. All that was left was a magnetic pull, the need to get to her and figure out why she wasn't at the booth in the first place.

I grabbed her shoulders as if I was making sure she was *actually* there because seeing her walking towards me honestly felt like it could only happen in my imagination.

I felt the heat of her skin through the cotton of my t-shirt she was wearing, and it was like I was set on fire.

But not in the way I'm used to.

I'm used to a constant, dull burn from burying parts of my life I never had time to deal with.

By the time I got my mom and my sisters out of that house and made sure my father would never be able to get to them again, it was too late. The anger, frustration, and sadness was buried so deep, it was easier to keep it there.

But with Mia, it was like something inside of me came to life. A part of me that lost its light was brought to life again, so I couldn't help it.

Pulling her in felt like the most natural thing to do—like she belonged there.

More right than anything has felt in years.

And her lips.

Fuck.

I have thought of those lips for weeks, convincing myself that I'll only ever be able to look, not touch.

Yet here I am, selfishly giving in to my desires to be close to her because she makes me feel like I am capable of being whole again.

And that's fucking scary.

She looked at me with those pretty brown eyes, and I was ready to fall to my knees.

"What the fuck was that about?" Mateo barks, taking a few steps towards me. He is careful not to raise his voice too loud, keeping his usual-cool demeanor in case someone was to overhear us in the gated lot.

I can tell he is not very happy with me.

"What was what?" I ask, playing dumb and trying to keep my defensiveness in check.

I had a bad feeling when we got to the merch booth after we finished our set, slightly coming down from the high of how amazing the show went, and Mia wasn't there. I had my eye on her the entire show, watching as she weaved through the crowd with her camera in her hands. I was still able to focus on the show, proving that I am somewhat getting ahold of the distraction she is to me, and we fucking killed it.

The first show of this six-show series couldn't have gone any better, until it all went to shit because I took my eye off of her for one second and some dickhead who couldn't keep his hands to himself got a hold of her.

"You know *exactly* what I'm talking about," Mateo says. "Since when are you so protective of Mia?" I was already on edge when it came to Mia because of how our last conversation ended, but then seeing the look on her face when that guy wouldn't let go of her, I couldn't keep my anger down. I honestly thought I was going to murder the guy.

"It is no different than you." Mateo and I both have younger sisters and grew up basically raising them, so I have no idea why he would be pissed about how I handled the situation. Mateo has never been one to let his temper get the best of him, but I don't mind being the one to throw the punch. "Or Theo. Or Silas. You three were pissed too seeing how that guy was all over her when she didn't want anything to do with him."

"It is completely different. None of us threw a fucking punch, Eddie!" Mateo's cool is dissolving fast. "I haven't seen you get mad like that in years, and I can't help but think it has something to do with your feelings towards my sister."

I open my mouth and immediately close it.

My feelings towards *his* sister.

That same sister he almost caught me kissing two minutes ago.

What the hell am I doing?

"It wasn't like that." Even though that is *exactly* how it was.

I can't be having these feelings about Mia, and tonight proved that I am headed in the *wrong* direction with her. The direction that leads to me arguing with my best friend.

The kiss was a mistake.

I should have never given in to those feelings.

I don't deserve them.

I deserve the anger. The frustration. The *rage*.

That is what I am good at.

Tonight proved it.

Mateo blows out a breath he has been holding and takes a few steps closer to me. My hands are in my pockets, but I feel my nails dig into my palms.

I get why he is accusing me of caring too much about Mia. I have cooled down enough, in more ways than one, to see it clearly too.

I do care about her, and it isn't the way that Mateo, Theo, or Silas care.

And it can't happen.

"When you get mad, Eddie, you turn into a different person. You can't lose it like that. Not if we want to be asked to come back. You are lucky security stepped in when they did, and that the guy was too scared to do anything but listen to them."

He is right.

If I had punched someone else, someone who came looking for a fight, it could have turned into a brawl in there. The same way I have seen it happened so many times before at Lenny's.

I just couldn't control myself.

When I saw that asshole's hand wrapped around Mia's arm tightly, it was like I was transported back to my child-hood, watching my dad put his hands on my mom, threatening her to stay quiet or he would grab one of Lucia, Carmen, or Isa to take his anger out on.

I was eight the first time I watched it happen, and I remember closing my eyes and praying like my mom taught me. Praying to a god that was allowing my father to take my mom by the arm and throw her into the wall with all his strength. My mom, who put on a happy face the next day, despite wincing every time she picked up one of my sisters. That night, and every night after, I prayed to be like the big, strong characters with superhuman strength in the cartoons we watched every morning before school, the cartoons that drowned out my mom crying in her bedroom after my dad left for work.

But I didn't grow big or strong enough until I was eighteen.

"Don't worry," I reassure Mateo, burying the memories and feelings deep down like I always do. "I got heated. I don't know why you're reading into it so much."

I try my hardest to be nonchalant, but I don't know if it comes off as believable. Talking about Mia as if she isn't my number one priority is much harder on me than it should be.

But for now, what Mateo doesn't know won't hurt him.

Mia and I are friends.

Who kissed *once*.

And it will never happen again. It *can't* ever happen again.

"I would've done it for any girl in that situation," I explain to further convince him, and I watch as Mateo ponders this. I think he believes it.

"So it wasn't just because it was Mia?" he asks.

Motherfucker.

How do I explain that I only noticed the situation because it was Mia?

And what does that say about me that I was so concerned about where she was that I couldn't think straight?

"I would have done it for any girl in that situation," I repeat.

But Mia isn't just *any* girl, and I hate myself for pretending that she is.

Mateo nods his head, and I think I'm in the clear. "Look, I'm happy to hear you're looking out for her as a friend, but just make sure it *stays* that way. I'm barely on board with this friendship of yours, but I know it's good for her to have friends. And I do feel better now knowing you want to protect her the same way I do."

If he only knew.

Mateo is right. I want nothing but to protect her.

What he doesn't know is that it isn't because she's like a sister to me. It is because she's the first person to make me feel *something* after being numb for so long.

"You both are hotheads though," he laughs. "I'm starting a Punching Jar. Anytime either of you throws a punch, you put a dollar in the jar." Mateo slaps my back with a smile on his face. "And you both owe me a dollar."

I laugh along with my best friend, knowing it comes off as genuine because of years of practice. I'm good at faking the smiles–except to a certain pair of pretty brown eyes that see right through them.

There is no way I am ever forgiving myself for lying straight to Mateo's face.

CHAPTER 16
MIA

NOT ONLY IS my body tired from the long day, but my brain feels like it has been on overdrive for the past twelve hours–more so than usual. It has been working hard, but it doesn't seem to be slowing down anytime soon.

I keep replaying the day in my head, trying to pinpoint where my combination of feelings is coming from while trying to keep them all straight.

My stomach has a pit in it, and I have a feeling of uneasiness floating in the air around me about leaving things with Eddie unfinished.

I feel so incredibly proud with how the first show went, but I'm also pissed that it was ruined by some asshole who was looking for trouble. I'm happy to feel a part of something for the first time in so long, and it feels good to have people in my corner, but I also know that nothing good lasts forever.

I try to focus on the reality stars on my laptop screen trying to find love on some island, but it's hard to stay engaged after seeing this episode two times before. Watching TV show reruns is usually therapeutic to me in a way I don't want to read too much into, but it isn't cutting it tonight.

I exit out of the Netflix tab before closing my laptop. I

glance at the clock on the side table and see it's just after eleven. I reach to turn on the lamp next to it to get some light into the dark hotel room because there's no way I will be falling asleep anytime soon.

I lay back and close my eyes, taking advantage of the silence.

My ears still have a slight buzz to them after being around such loud music and crowds cheering, and the remnants of adrenaline from earlier are still moving through my veins making me restless.

After Mateo came to talk to Eddie, I went back inside and found Theo and Silas who stayed within two feet of me everywhere I went for the rest of the night. Mateo came back in after a few minutes saying Eddie was going to head back to the hotel for the night, and the four of us watched the rest of the bands from backstage.

I tried to hide my concern for Eddie not staying for the rest of the show while also trying to ignore the disappointment I felt with him not being around.

As I lay in the king-sized hotel room, my mind drifts to what happened in the lot before Mateo came out. I try to ignore the butterflies in my stomach at the thought of the stolen moment.

Eddie and I didn't get a chance to talk about what happened, and it seems like our list of *stuff we really should talk about* is getting longer with every passing hour. There was his concern for the dream I had on the car ride here, and his reaction to what happened after their show.

And the kiss.

I've thought about kissing Eddie—more times than I'd like to admit—and I can't help but think Eddie has thought about kissing *me*. I didn't even have time to register it until it happened, and now I can't stop thinking about it.

I thought my friendship with Eddie would be simple. Simple, harmless, maybe even fun, but my mind spirals with all the hot and cold, and I am starting to see that nothing about our friendship—*relationship?*—is simple.

I try to untangle everything going through my head, remembering what my therapist says about *me* being the one to have control of my thoughts.

Do I want to talk to him about my dream? *Kind of.*

Do I think we need to talk about what happened at the show? *Yes.*

Do I think we need to talk about the kiss? *Definitely.*

Friends don't kiss each other.

And if they do, they talk about it.

Right?

It was just the adrenaline because of the show and what happened, and we weren't thinking in the heat of the moment. I have to keep telling myself that—the truth—or I think I'll go crazy.

Kissing Eddie was soul-altering in the most terrifying, exhilarating way.

The thoughts, always so tangled in my brain, ceased, and I didn't have to focus on anything besides the taste of his lips, the warmth of his breath, the feel of his body pressed against mine.

The kiss was like a promise.

A promise that he understands me in a way neither of us fully understand.

A promise that he will protect me, even from the thoughts in my own brain.

And that makes my mind spiral even more because he is the one person I should *not* be kissing.

My thoughts are interrupted by a knock on the door.

I sit up and glance at the door. I'm not expecting anyone.

My brother walked me to my room an hour ago before heading down the hall to the room he's sharing with Eddie. He didn't say anything about coming to check on me, but I wouldn't put it past him to do so.

I get up from my bed and look through the peephole, and my heart skips a beat at who I see on the other side.

All my coherent thoughts fly out of my brain, and my body moves on its own to open the door.

And because I didn't take a second to think about the consequences to my actions, I watch as Eddie's eyes drop to my bare legs, just now remembering that I am in my underwear and the T-shirt I wore to the show.

Eddie's T-shirt.

I didn't expect for Eddie to *actually* give it to me, especially because I was just trying to make him blush when I told Mateo he was letting me borrow it, and I definitely didn't expect to have company tonight. I had the T-shirt tucked into my jeans earlier tonight because it is so big on me, but when I was getting ready for bed, I realized how perfectly oversized it was to sleep in, and I didn't fight the urge to put it back on after I showered.

But I wish I put on a pair of fucking pants.

"Eyes up here, buddy," I say, trying to fall back into our usual back-and-forth and faking as though having his eyes on me like that doesn't make me feel I am three seconds away from spontaneously combusting.

Eddie doesn't move; it is like he froze. Eyes stuck on where the hem of the shirt rests at my mid-thigh. The ends of his hair are wet like he just got out of the shower, peeking out from his backwards hat. He is dressed in a black crewneck sweatshirt and gray sweatpants, and my mouth *literally* begins to water.

Stop.

A friend wouldn't drool over another friend in the doorway of a hotel room.

Even when that friend is freshly showered, mysteriously scarred, dressed with the two most universally *hot* things a guy could wear, and can kiss me like his life fucking depends on it.

"Eddie?" I say again, refusing to acknowledge the crack in my voice. I watch as he slowly moves his eyes up my body and, when I see his face, I take back what I said about not wearing pants because what I am greeted with makes my knees go weak.

I have only seen Eddie blush one other time, despite my numerous other attempts, and I forgot what kind of an effect it has on me.

The first time it happened, it was in my kitchen, and I remember thinking that I would never be the same.

If I only knew where we would be the second time it happened.

He clears his throat and coughs into his fist, looking down the hallway as if I wasn't the only one here to catch him in the act.

"How the tables have turned," I tease.

"What do you mean?" He asks.

"It is always *me* getting caught checking *you* out, but today is a different story."

He looks down and laughs before reaching his arms up to grab the doorframe and leaning in closer.

"Just because you don't catch me, doesn't mean it doesn't happen, sunshine."

My mouth dries, and I forget how to speak. I feel my chest heat as he leans in even closer, only a few inches from me. He knows exactly what he is doing, and, like always, I'm not going down without a fight.

But before I can say anything, the air shifts. I can feel as he lets out a breath because he is so close, and my body feels like it is being pulled into him. I watch his eyes flick down to my lips, and my hands, with a mind of their own, find their place on his chest.

Why is it I can think rationally about how to *not* do this when I'm alone, but my brain turns to mush the second Eddie is around?

His breath hitches the moment my palms touch the fabric of his sweatshirt, and I can't help but imagine what it would be like to feel the skin underneath

I close my eyes, ready for what is to come, but then the air shifts again. Eddie drops his arms from the top of the door frame and takes a step back into the hallway.

"No," he says, and I feel a sting of rejection.

"No, what?" Even though I know exactly what he is saying no to.

"Can I come in?" he asks abruptly.

"Are you sure you can handle it?" I try to tease.

"Mia, I'm serious."

I sigh and let out a dramatic groan because I know we can't keep pretending that this *thing* between us is okay.

"Fine," I conclude and turn around to walk into the room. Eddie follows, and I hear the door close behind him.

"Can you, um, put some pants on?" I hear behind me. I turn to see him looking up at the ceiling.

"Why?"

"I can't think straight when you look like *that.*"

"What? You've never seen legs before? It's not like I'm naked."

"Might as well be," he murmurs.

"What was that?" I ask, even though I heard perfectly fine.

Old habits die hard, and messing with Eddie is just too easy.

"I'm having a hard time focusing on anything besides the fact you have nothing on under *my* T-shirt.

"Oh, I'm sorry, raindrop. Did you want it back?" I ask, batting my eyelashes. "Because I can take it off," I say, moving my hands to grab the hem.

"You're going to kill me," he says. "Sit."

I want to say something back, keep playing this game, but his seriousness catches me off guard, and while I want to do the opposite of what he says, there is something in his voice that makes my body listen.

So, I sit.

"Good girl. Now, we need to talk."

He pulls the chair pushed into the desk next to the bed and sits down, arguably further away than he needs to, but I keep my mouth shut.

Something in his voice tells me that playtime is over.

CHAPTER 17
MIA

I LET OUT A SOFT GROAN. In my right mind, I know we have to talk, and I was literally just thinking about how much we have to figure out before he got here. But, now that he is here, ignoring my attempts to distract him, demanding me to sit, and calling me a good girl, half of me wants to be a brat and make this harder for him.

"About what?" I ask, with just a tad of sass.

He sighs. "Well, first. I want to apologize for asking what you were dreaming about. I should've minded my own business."

My knee-jerk reaction is to be a smartass with him, just to drag out this conversation a little longer, but I don't think that will work right now. My next thought is to just tell him not to worry about it and change the subject, but I find myself not wanting to.

I have realized that being with Eddie brings my guard down. My usual barriers crumble when I'm around him, and I have to fight like hell to keep them up.

I don't know if that is a good or bad thing.

"It was just a dream I've had before. Well, actually it is a memory more than a dream."

"You don't have to tell me."

"I want to," I say, and he scoots his chair a little closer to the bed, still leaving a safe distance. I cross my legs, making sure my shirt—Eddie's shirt—isn't too revealing, as I prepare myself for this conversation. I have never talked about my dreams aside from with my therapist, but, for some reason, right now I feel ready.

"Have you ever gone to sleep and felt like, instead of a dream, it was your mind showing you a memory?" I ask.

Eddie's eyes darken in the slightest, but he doesn't say anything. Something unsaid passes between us, like he is telling me "yes" with his eyes, so I continue. "It is kind of like that. Sometimes when I fall asleep, my mind makes me relive the last night I saw Nico." I'm not sure if I ever told Eddie Nico's name, but I can tell he knows who I am talking about.

"Is it a good memory?" Eddie asks, and I am taken aback by the question. Not because it was random or unwarranted, but more because I just recently have been able to think of Nico's memories, the ones with him, as good. But no matter how you spin it, the one we're talking about is anything but good.

"No. We got into an argument that night, and he left angry." I feel tears prick my eyes, but I don't want them to fall.

I am healing.

I don't want to take a step backwards.

"It's okay," Eddie reassures, and, when he says it, I believe it.

I close my eyes and take a deep breath in, filling my lungs to capacity, as a single tear escapes from the corner of my eye. I breathe out and open my eyes to find Eddie watching me. He is leaning forward in his chair, and his hands are tightly wound together in his lap.

"Before I tell you this story, I want you to know I am in therapy and have talked about this night a lot with my therapist. I know what ultimately happened is not my fault, and I have spent years working through my guilt. I also know there were parts of Nico that I couldn't fix, even though I wanted to. That took me a long time to accept."

Eddie nods. "You can tell me whatever you want," he reassures. A small smile graces his lips, pushing them to one side to show a hint of his dimple. The singular light from the lamp makes his green eyes look darker than usual and the sadness in them is on full display tonight. His scar in this light catches my eye, and I don't know why it feels like the right moment to say, "You can tell me whatever you want too," but that is what comes out of my mouth.

He lets out a dry chuckle, making his smile a little wider, and I wish this boy would put away his mask for good and show everyone *all* of him.

"Noted," he says as he stands to take a seat on the bed next to me. His legs are hanging off, and I shift my body to face him. "But tonight is about you."

I take one more deep breath, reminding myself that the past is in the past. Even though it is a part of me, and always will be, I can't let it define me.

"It was my sophomore year of college, and Nico and I were having trouble making time for each other. Me more than him because I was busy with school. He was writing a new song, one for me, and he took his music really seriously. He had come over that night to play the song for me because it was finally finished.

"As he was playing it, I wasn't paying attention. I was trying to finish some stupid paper that wasn't even that big of a deal, and I had heard the song, or versions of it, so many times. He got upset that I wasn't paying attention, and he thought that I didn't care about him or the song, and I just—"

My heart starts beating and my palms feel sweaty as I stop myself from admitting something that I have only ever shared in the confines of my own head. I close my eyes and shake my head as if to shake the thought away, and the rest of tears threatening to fall, feel thick in my eyes.

I open my eyes to find Eddie, waiting.

"I just didn't have it in me that night to fight with him," I admit.

Eddie reaches a hand out to me and then stops, bringing it back to his lap.

"That's understandable," he whispers. "Sometimes we don't have it in us to fight."

He's right, but he doesn't get it—not fully.

"No, it's more complicated than that. Fighting with Nico was also fighting with the demons in his head. The ones that told him that he wasn't enough. The ones that told him to give up." Nico was diagnosed with depression in high school, and he had struggled for years to find the right combination of medication and therapy. He tried and he tried, but he couldn't fight the imbalance in his brain. His parents were supportive, but they didn't see his mental illness for what it was.

I watch as the realization hits Eddie, and that is when I lose the little control I have. My tears begin to fall, but now that I have started, I don't want to stop.

"I knew him leaving angry wasn't good. I knew it, but I didn't stop him. Or, I didn't try hard enough because he left anyway. I went to his house the next morning after not hearing from him the rest of the night. He was renting a place with a few friends who were all out of town that weekend, so I let myself in with the key he gave me. I knocked on his bedroom door, but he didn't answer." The air was crisp and cold that February morning. There were new piles of snow from the night before. The roads were clear of other cars because it was so early when I went to go see him, but I couldn't drive as fast as I wanted because of how slick they were from the snow still falling.

Eddie reaches across me to the bedside table to grab a

tissue from the box there, and he hands it to me. I can't control the sniffles coming from my nose as I wipe my cheeks of the loose tears.

He doesn't say anything, maybe because he doesn't know what to say, or maybe because he knows I have to finish this story.

"I went in, and his bed was untouched," I whisper. "He hadn't been home." I crumple the now-wet tissue in my palm. "My gut told me something was wrong, so I got back in my car to drive to the one place Nico would go when he needed to clear his head. I still had hope that he calmed down after he left and was still there."

"Where did he like to go?" Eddie asks in a whisper, like he is concerned that talking too loud will scare this moment away.

"He liked to go to the beach." North Shore Beach wasn't actually a beach; it is a lake with sand, and as close as you will get to a beach in Milwaukee. "On my way there, I was racking my brain for ways to apologize to Nico, practicing how I was going to apologize for not listening to his song— the song I will never get out of my head—but I never got the chance to tell him."

My heart breaks all over again.

To this day, I will never forget seeing his car wrapped around the telephone pole.

"The police said that it was highly unlikely anyone would have been in the area at the time of night Nico was driving. It was a cold, snowy February night and the roads were icy." I pause and close my eyes. The realization of what happened to Nico never gets easier, and I don't know if it ever will. Nico grew up there, he knew how to drive in the snow. With the speed he was going, along with the evidence they found at the scene, it was concluded that the crash wasn't an accident.

And that makes me cry even harder.

My stomach is in knots, and it feels like the room is spinning. My breath starts to feel like I can't get a hold of it, and my hands begin to shake.

I'm about to have a panic attack.

I can feel it in my chest, suffocating me, spreading to the rest of my body faster than I can control it.

"Mia," I hear, but it sounds like Eddie is underwater.

I'm starting to hyperventilate when I hear, "Mia, breathe. You're okay. I'm here."

No, I'm not.

I'm not okay.

I squeeze my hands into fists to stop them from shaking, my nails digging into my palms grounds me for a moment, but then my heart starts to feel like it is about to explode.

"Mia, you're okay. Breathe, baby. You're okay. Open your eyes."

I can't.

I squeeze them shut even tighter.

"Look at me, Mia."

I feel the bed under me shift, and a presence is closer than it was before. I loosen my fists and rub my palms on my thighs, up and down, focusing on the feeling of my skin on my hands, anything to get out of my head.

"Mia?" I hear one more time before I open my eyes.

It takes me a second to adjust to the light and remember where I am, and then Eddie slowly comes into view. My breathing begins to steady, and I slowly bring my hands up to my face. But, before I can wipe my tears, Eddie reaches for my hands and holds them between his. He puts both of my hands in one of his before using his other hand to slowly swipe his thumb over my cheeks.

He is looking at me, concern all over his face, and I feel like he is looking directly into my soul. He tucks a stray piece of hair from my ponytail behind my ear before bringing his hand back to the other.

"You're bleeding," he whispers as he grabs another tissue

to wipe the broken skin on my palms. "I should have had you squeeze my hand," he says under his breath.

A million and one things run through my head, but all that comes out of my mouth is, "I'm sorry." It comes out as no more than a whisper.

"Don't be. Panic attacks happen."

"I haven't had one in weeks."

"You also have had a crazy day. I'm surprised you're still standing."

Between getting up early to drive here this morning to the busy day of prepping for the show and the emotional roller-coaster that today consisted of, it really is no wonder this didn't happen sooner.

"I didn't freak you out?" I don't know why I ask, but, as I calm down, I can't help but wonder how he is so unbothered. Panic attacks are normal for people like me, and there is nothing wrong with them, but they are not an easy thing to navigate for everyone.

"One of my sisters had panic attacks when we were little."

I want him to say more, but he doesn't.

I don't push my luck.

Instead, I save the small piece of him he shared with me in a special place to revisit later.

I take my hands, now free of blood, back, and I take my ponytail out and run my fingers through my hair.

"I need to go to bed," I say aloud, not to Eddie, just to the room.

"You're right. I should go," Eddie says as he stands up from the bed.

"No," rushes out of my mouth before I can stop it.

He freezes and looks down at where I'm still sitting.

"I mean," I start, but I don't know what to say next. No, I don't want him to leave, but I can't tell him that. "you don't have to go."

"You need rest. I'll see you tomorrow, sunshine." He gives me a smile, but it doesn't reach his eyes.

"Don't do that with me."

"What?"

"Put on the mask."

He laughs, but it is free of humor. "What are you talking about?"

"You don't have to pretend with me. You don't have to act like you're happy all the time."

He turns around and heads to the door, so I get up and follow him. He goes to grab the handle but then stops and turns around, his back to the door.

"I like to make sure everyone around me is happy. The easiest way to do that is to be happy myself."

I cross my arm, ignoring the feel of the t-shirt ride up the side of my legs. "But you're not actually happy, Eddie. You're pretending."

"I'm happy enough," he says. "If it quacks like a duck, it's a duck." He reaches out to me, using his finger to tap my nose.

I want to tell him that the fake-it-till-you-make-it approach doesn't work for the broken ones, but then he turns back to the door, and my arms reach out and grab his on their own. "Wait," I plead. "Stay."

Eddie stays facing the door, "Mia, I can't."

"Just as my friend."

"Sunshine, it isn't a good idea. You're tired, and we still have stuff we need to talk about." I know he is talking about the kiss, but the conversation can wait. As much as I liked kissing Eddie, I can live without it if it means I don't lose him yet.

"Eddie, please. I don't want to be alone right now."

I didn't know it was true until the words left my mouth.

He slowly turns his head to look at me, his body still

facing the door, and his eyes bore into mine. I know he wants to stay, but I also know that he is trying to be the strong one.

The one that keeps the line between us clearly drawn.

"Just for a little while," he answers.

I fall asleep that night to the sound of Eddie humming a tune that sounds oddly familiar, but in my tired state, I don't have the energy to try to figure out what song it is.

CHAPTER 18
EDDIE

WATCHING Mia sleep is my own personal hell. My shirt she is *still* wearing is way too big and rides up every time she moves, and she is quite the mover in her sleep. She also must run hot because she keeps kicking off the blanket every time I try to cover her, exposing her bare legs.

I don't know why I'm still here. I was clear with her that I would stay until she fell asleep on the opposite side of the bed, but I can't bring myself to leave.

When she opened her hotel room door, it was like seeing clearly after walking through fog. After talking to Mateo after our show and letting him know I would be spending the rest of the night at the hotel room, I was moving on autopilot, letting my body go through the motions. I was trying to stay busy until it was late enough to go to sleep, but I couldn't do anything besides think of a certain blonde with lips that were made for me.

Lips that I will never taste again because she will never be mine.

She never can be.

Not when she is my best friend's little sister.

Especially not when I am as broken as they come.

Her panic attack is proof that she is still healing, and the story she told me tonight just proves that the last thing she needs is me, who is falling apart by the second, while she is still putting herself back together.

I can't believe she is still standing after what she went through.

In my experience, *talking* about what broke you is almost as hard as experiencing it.

All I wanted to do tonight was hold her, and kiss the top of her head, and tell her that I will make everything better.

I want to take her into my arms, bring her into my lap, and protect her from anything that has ever and will ever hurt her.

But I can't.

So this is hell.

I can't stop watching her. Her chest slowly rises and falls, soft noises coming from her mouth. The bed is big enough for there to be a few feet between us, but she is the sun with a gravitational pull, and I am the moon, with no choice but to revolve around her.

And never allowed to be close enough to feel her.

I slowly move closer, careful not to wake her, and careful to keep my distance. There is about a foot of the sheet between us, so I lean back against the headboard, one hand behind my head and one resting on my chest, trying to keep my hands to myself.

I turned off the bedside lamp when she fell asleep, but her blonde waves and pink lips are impossible not to see. She looks so calm and at ease, nothing like how she looked when she fell asleep in the car this morning.

I still feel the pull.

My mind doesn't have time to tell my body to stop. I slowly reach my hand out because I can't forget what her cheek feels like against my fingertips. Her skin is warm and soft, and it takes everything in me to not pull her in my arms, so I can feel the skin of her arms, her legs, her neck, all of her, against me.

I tell myself I've had enough—I've pushed my limits far enough at this point—but as I begin to pull my hand away, she stirs.

Still asleep, she flips her body in my direction, quickly crossing the invisible line I put between us. Her leg crosses over her body and falls over my waist, her arm now draping over me, caging me in against her as if answering my selfish prayers. Her head finds its rightful spot on my chest, and I can't do anything but stay where I am.

I was wrong.

Watching Mia sleep was not my own personal hell.

This is.

———

It is safe to say I got no sleep.

Even if I had wanted to, there was no way I trusted myself to fall asleep anywhere in Mia's vicinity. I can barely trust myself when I'm awake. There is no telling what my body would do if I wasn't awake to control it.

It is just my luck that she didn't move from on top of me for the rest of the night except when she flipped over around five in the morning.

I escaped back to my room where Mateo was still sleeping, so I had some time to come up with an excuse for why I didn't come back to the room last night.

I had told him I was going to grab a drink at a bar down the street. I thought he would ask questions or want to come with me, but he was tired from the show. I've learned that Mateo, while coming off as a total extrovert on stage, is a secret introvert. I think he was more than happy to decompress alone and go to bed. He is also a very heavy sleeper.

I take a shower and get dressed, knowing there is no point in trying to get sleep.

Mateo wakes up around seven, and he doesn't question my explanation of coming back to the room when he was already asleep.

Theo and Silas are sharing the room next door, but they are heading out earlier because they have to drop the equipment off at the warehouse before they head home to their place. If I know Theo and Silas, they were out late last night doing who-knows-what, so I knock on their door to make sure they're up.

Even though Mateo is the unofficial leader and dad of the band, it is easy for me to fall into my role of making sure everyone is where they need to be and has what they need. It has always been a habit for me to make sure everyone around me is taken care of before I worry about myself, and that sometimes transfers over to the band.

It takes a few minutes to get one of them to open the door, it doesn't help that neither of them are morning people. Silas is the one to let me in. I only have to take two steps in to see their room looks like it is right out of a music video. There is a random girl in each double-sized bed and empty liquor bottles and beer cans all over the furniture and floor.

I shake my head before turning around and walking straight back out.

"You need to be on the road by eight o'clock," I say over my shoulder.

"Fuck off," Silas mutters before shutting the door behind me.

I laugh to myself as I head back to my room to find Mateo already packed and ready to go. I glance at the clock to see it is only 7:30 a.m., and he told Mia and I to be ready by nine.

"Ready already?" I ask Mateo, sitting down on my still-freshly made bed.

He puts his backpack on and glances at his phone in his

hand. "I'm going to go with Theo and Silas. I have a meeting with the tour manager for next summer's tour this afternoon."

"On a Sunday?" It's rare for a meeting to be on a Sunday, but what I'm really surprised about is that he *actually* landed a meeting. He has been trying to set something up with this tour manager for a few weeks now, but I haven't gotten an update in a while.

Last I heard, this tour manager is close friends with our current tour manager, and we know that if we want to get on next summer's tour, we have to nail these six shows. The show last night went as good as it could have, aside from the issue afterwards, so I can't help but get excited for what this meeting today could potentially hold.

"When Xander Drake wants to meet, you make it work." Mateo took on the role of the band's booking agent when we found out we had this chance in the first place, so it is extremely important that he gets there. "I'm going to need you to get Mia home."

"No problem." The words come out even, but my heart beats slightly faster.

Alone.

With Mia.

In a car.

For four and half hours.

Fuck me.

"I'm going to make sure Theo and Silas are ready to go and then we're going to head out. Can you let Mia know? She can call me if she needs, but I'm going to be prepping for this meeting for the whole ride there. We're meeting at Lenny's at two."

"Yeah, all good. I'll get your sister home."

"Thanks, Eddie. I'll see you later tonight." He heads out of the hotel room, and I'm left alone with my thoughts and the nerves of a teenager going on his first date.

Why I'm nervous to be alone with Mia, I don't know, but it probably has to do with all the lines we crossed in the past twelve hours, and now we have no choice but to talk about them.

I pace back and forth trying to think if I should try to get out of this, but I hear Mateo, Theo, and Silas in the hallway already heading to check out, and I don't want Mateo to think he has anything to worry about. He will see through any excuse I try to feed him about why I can't be alone in a car with Mia all morning, and the last thing I want to do is prove his suspicions from last night right.

I check the time and decide I'll go get Mia in an hour, and then we'll head out right at nine o'clock.

I make sure my wallet is in one back pocket and that my phone is in the other before heading out the hotel door to grab a black coffee and an iced vanilla latte with oat milk.

I tell myself it's just being polite, but it's a lie.

I know her order like I know the chords to our opener, like I know the beats to encore—it's muscle memory, second nature.

It's not just coffee. It's a quiet offering. A peace treaty. A question I'm too much of a coward to ask out loud.

CHAPTER 19
MIA

THERE IS a knock on my door five minutes before 9 a.m. I woke up only an hour ago, surprised by how deeply. I slept. I usually don't sleep well in beds other than my own, but I woke up completely well-rested this morning, better than I was expecting after a day like yesterday.

I like to go on runs for my main workout, but I never go on runs in areas I'm not familiar with, so I opted for the exercise I *actually* prefer: yoga.

It slows me down, gives me the deep breathes I need—the ones my body often forget how to do when my mind begins to race.

And it's exactly what I need after yesterday.

I did a quick flow this morning before showering and getting dressed. I packed up my overnight bag with the unopened bottle of wine and newly-purchased lavender face mask I was hoping to use last night.

Little did I know that I would relax in a completely different way.

Eddie refused to get within three feet of me, but him just being there was comforting.

Would I rather him be near me? *Yes.*

Would that have been the *friend* thing to do? *No.*

I took what I could get, still completely confused on my exact feelings for Eddie, but I know that the amount of time I could spend trying to make sense of the feelings I have is the reason I am in therapy, so I just want to let myself *feel.*

Because I can, and I want to.

And it feels so good to say that.

We didn't talk much, but we didn't need to. He told me about how he felt on stage, and how proud he was of Mateo, Theo, and Silas. I couldn't help but notice how he didn't say himself, but I kept that to myself.

I started to close my eyes when he talked about the small things in some of the songs he wants to change for the next show in three weeks, and that he needed to spend time figuring out the song they want to debut at the last show.

I remember being on the verge of sleep when he asked if I was still awake. I said yes, even though my eyes were closed, and that made him laugh.

His laugh wrapped around me like a blanket, rich and warm, and I remember thinking that he should laugh more.

Just as I was falling asleep, I heard him hum a tune I thought, in my tired state, I knew, but I couldn't remember what it sounded like when I woke up.

Eddie was gone when I woke up, so I'm sure he left soon after that.

I head over to open the door, not even looking through the peephole to see who it is because Mateo told me he would come get me at 9 a.m. to leave.

"Hey, sunshine."

So, not Mateo.

"This is for you," Eddie says, his usual playful demeanor in full effect, handing me a coffee—one that looks exactly like one I would order for myself.

He's dressed in the same black crewneck he had on last night with a pair of black jeans and the same backwards hat. "Where are your bags?" He walks past me and heads over to where I am finishing up packing, waltzing in as if this is his room—no longer needing an invite in.

"Where's Mateo?" I ask, my brain finally catching up to what is happening.

"He left with Theo and Silas. He has a meeting this afternoon."

"With who?" I ask, taking a sip of the coffee Eddie brought me.

"Xander Drake."

"The tour manager?"

"Yeah, sounds like they're talking about next summer's tour."

Mateo told me about the potential meeting a few days ago, but I haven't thought of it since. This meeting could be one step closer to the guys being the openers for the two bands that are set to co-headline the tour next summer, two of the bands they opened for last night. The difference would be that they wouldn't be one of three other openers; they would be the only ones, and that could *definitely* get them on the map.

Eddie sees my opened overnight bag and, with the hand not holding his boring black coffee, he reaches in and grabs the purple container sitting on top.

"What's this?" he asks.

I walk over and look down at the container in his hand. "A face mask."

I'm ready to explain more, but he nods his head once—obviously not caring much about it. "Oh," he says.

I grab the container away from him, wishing I could blame his oversized pores and blemishes on his lack of care in skin care, but I can't.

Because he has none.

And his skin is literally perfect.

Eddie takes a sip of his coffee. "Well anyway, finish packing. We got to hit the road."

It takes me until now to realize that Eddie and I are going to be alone, together, for the next four and a half hours.

"Don't look so glum, sunshine. We have so *much* to talk about." His smile is bright but not enough to hide his feelings from me.

He is nervous. I can tell.

And so am I.

I walk over to the bed and zip up my overnight bag. I pick it up to throw over my arm, but Eddie takes it from me before I can.

"Let's go," he says as he walks to the door, his backpack on, with my bag in one hand and his coffee in the other.

I grab my camera bag where it is hanging on the desk chair and follow him out.

———

The hotel is right off the highway, so we are on the road and driving within a few minutes. We sit in borderline-uncomfortable silence, probably waiting to see what the other is going to say. Breaking the ice first, Eddie asks, "What podcast are we listening to?"

This catches me off guard. "You don't seem like a podcast person," I reply. I'm wearing my white coffee-stained hoodie and matching white joggers. I took my shoes off right when I got in the car, and my feet are up on the dash. Mateo and I have always been road-trip people; I have only been on a plane twice. Growing up, we didn't go on tons of vacations, but we would drive the seven or eight hours to see our closest relatives in Ohio.

With Eddie driving Mateo's car, I didn't waste time getting comfortable.

"You're not a music person," Eddie answers matter-of-factly, and I keep my eyes on the road in front of us. The highway lanes are relatively empty on this Sunday morning, further reminding me that it is just the two of us.

Maybe that is why I answer the way I do.

"I used to be," I say, but now that the words are in the air, I realize that I don't want to say anymore.

"I figured," he says, but he doesn't push. "Why don't you connect your phone? I've been dying to hear what put you to sleep on the way here."

"Ha. Ha. You're hilarious, did you know that?" I deadpan. Mateo's car is old enough to still need a cord to connect to the speakers, so I plug in my phone and press play on the podcast I had planned on listening to *by myself.*

At least we don't have to talk.

The voice of a woman comes on as she teases what the episode will be about, and Eddie and I fall into a more comfortable silence this time. As we listen, I can't help but sneak glances at Eddie as the episode begins. For someone who is usually so adamant with the mask he wears around people, he is actually quite animated. When he isn't worried about putting on his happy face, he wears his emotions openly. He goes from confused to surprised to a *what the fuck* face in seconds, and watching him is more entertaining than the episode.

After about fifteen minutes, he catches my not-so-subtle chuckle when the podcast host describes the crime scene, and his eyes pop out of the sockets.

"Okay, we're done with that," he says, and my chuckle can no longer be hidden. "I can't believe you listen to that shit. For *fun.*"

"I'll turn it off," I laugh. I grab my headphones to connect my phone to them.

"Let's just talk," Eddie says, causing my hands to freeze on the zipper of my bag.

"Or I'll finish the podcast and you can listen to whatever you want."

"No, I'll get bored. Talk to me. Please?" He slightly turns to look at me, stretching out *please* while attempting puppy-dog eyes while also trying to watch the road.

I hate that it works like a charm.

"Fine," I say, sitting back up. "What do you want to talk about?

"What did you think of the show last night?" Eddie asks. He has his left hand on the steering wheel and his other arm is resting on the center console.

This seems like a safe place to start.

"You guys did awesome. The crowd kept growing, and it looked like they really liked the set."

"Really? That's awesome."

"Wait, you didn't notice the crowd?" I know it is hard to see out with the lights, and he has so much to focus on when he is up there, but it seems odd he didn't notice the crowd getting bigger.

"I kept an eye out," he begins, "but I usually get into this zone where it is just me and the guys, just thinking about the music and really feeling the sound. Does that sound stupid?"

"No, not at all," I assure him. "It actually makes a lot of sense." Eddie's love for his music reminds me of Nico's, and I know how easy it is to get wrapped up in the sound. It used to happen to me too, especially when the music is so special, so close to what you are feeling. It is easy to do with songs written by others, so I can't imagine how easy it is when the song is one you wrote.

"How did the show go for you?" he asks. He keeps his eyes forward, but his body is slightly angled toward me with the way he is holding the steering wheel, his arm still resting on the console but a few inches closer than before.

"Better than I thought it would," I reply, which is the truth. I was nervous, but it went well. Better than I could have hoped for, especially taking into consideration where I was this time last year. If you would have told me *this* is what I would be doing with my time, actually looking forward to being in crowded places with music blasting, I would have laughed my ass off. Even a month ago, there was no way I would have even imagined this is where I would be.

Band photography, and photography in general, is something I can see myself doing, which reminds me I need to talk to Mateo about making that website for me.

"You felt okay out there? You know, in the crowd with all the music and people?"

"What do you mean?" I ask. He hit the nail right on the head, but *how*? Am I that easy to read? I haven't told him the whole story about Nico's song and why I don't really listen to music anymore. I don't think I ever even told him I was nervous to be out in the crowd.

"I mean, your brother is in a band, and you're a band photographer, but you have said how you're not a music person," he explains. "You also get punch-y when you're in crowds."

A tiny gasp escapes my lips, "I do not!" I exclaim.

He laughs, and the whole car lights up.

I will never get over Eddie's laugh. It's dangerous how much I love it.

"Yes, you do," he says in between what can only be described as giggles. "When I first met you, you had just punched a grown man."

"First of all," I turn my body as much as my seat belt will allow to face him, "we met before that." Eddie rolls his eyes at my clarification even though it was necessary. We met when I was a teenager and barely knew each other, but we still met before. "Second of all, so do you!"

"That was only because I had to stop *you* from punching him," he retorts, but he does so in a way that is still playful.

"Yeah right, raindrop," I argue. "I can handle myself." He

has yet to tell me to stop with the ridiculous nickname. I started using it as an attempt to make him blush, but it is starting to stick.

"Trust me, I know you can. Doesn't mean I'm going to miss the chance to put a lowlife like that guy in his fucking place." There is an edge to his voice, and I can't help but say what is on my mind.

"Yeah, you were pretty pissed." I guess now is a better time than ever to ask the question I have had in my head. "What was that about?" Eddie's smile is gone now, but he isn't closing himself off. "You could've gotten kicked off the tour," I add.

"I don't care about that," he says quickly and then shakes his head. "No, I mean, I do, but I didn't. Not at that moment. When I saw his arm around you I just—" he squeezes the steering wheel in one hand and fists the other, turning all his knuckles white.

I have the urge to grab hold of his hand resting between us, but I push it down.

"I just don't like seeing grown men take advantage of women. I know you can handle yourself, and I'm sure you would have if I didn't get to you in time. But I couldn't help it."

There is a story behind what he is saying, and I know it has something to do with the anger he buries and the sadness in his eyes. I know it has to do with his need to come across as happy and laid back and why he is always so concerned with everyone around him.

I just don't know the root of it, and I can't make him tell me.

So instead I give in to the urge and grab his hand, warm and rougher than I had imagined, but I pull it into my lap. I feel the tension release as I slowly use my fingers to unwrap his. I steal a glance his way and see his brows are furrowed, and he refuses to turn and look at me. I put my hand in his and interlock my fingers with his. He doesn't reciprocate at first, but, after a moment, his fingers wrap around my hand.

"You don't have to tell me anything you don't want to," I whisper even though it is just us.

"There is nothing to tell, sunshine." He gives my hand a squeeze before letting go, switching what hand is on the steering wheel.

A few moments pass before he says anything else, "Mia," he starts, "we need to talk about us."

I angle my body back to face the front, defiance lining my voice. "There is no *us*. We're friends."

Friends who are only friends because of my brother.

Friends who kissed, who never in a million years can kiss again.

"Are we though?" he asks.

Neither of us take our eyes off the road in front of us, but in my peripheral vision, I see his slight smile.

CHAPTER 20

EDDIE

HER VOICE IS JUST above a whisper, even though it is just us. "You don't have to tell me anything you don't want to." Not only can she see right through me, but she can read me like her fucking favorite book. With her hand in mine, I feel like I could get through anything, like the memories behind me aren't as scary when she is here. Like I could *actually* talk about them without falling apart as long as she is with me.

No.

I can't talk about this with her, no matter how much I want to.

I refuse to put anything more on her.

We can't do this anymore.

"There is nothing to tell, sunshine." I give her hand a squeeze before letting go, and I have to pretend it isn't one of the hardest things I have done. For a moment, before I let go, I pretend our lives are simple enough to hold hands while I drive; simple enough that we can enjoy the time just the two of us, rather than address what both of us have been trying to ignore.

But this isn't simple.

Nothing ever is, especially when it comes to Mia.

I bring my hand to the steering wheel and bring my left arm down to my lap. I try to hide how clenched my fist now is. My hands feel so empty after knowing what it feels like to have her hand in mine.

"Mia," I say, refusing to look anywhere but the road in front of me. "We need to talk about *us*."

She angles her body back to face the front. "There is no *us*," she says. "We're friends."

"Are we though?" I push because we both know there is *something* between us.

It is too strong to just be in my head.

She sighs. "I can't figure you out."

"Come on, Mia. I'm an open book," I try to tease, knowing that there is a hint of truth in the remark when it comes to her.

"Yeah," she scoffs. "With half the pages missing."

"That's what makes it fun," I reply, easily falling back into our comfort zone.

"You're lucky you have me to put the missing pieces together."

And she has no idea how much I wish that was the case, but it can't be.

It is so easy to pretend with her.

To pretend she isn't becoming all I think about.

To pretend that her lips weren't made for me.

To pretend I don't want to hold her so close to me that nothing and no one can get between us.

To pretend that we are good for each other.

To pretend that nothing is wrong, and that we are friends who harmlessly flirt and see who can get closest to the invisible line without crossing, even though we both know that line is miles behind us now.

I shake my head. "No more distracting," I announce, to her and myself. "In case you haven't noticed, you distract me.

You also know exactly how to get what you want from me. Do you know that?"

I don't mean to blurt the words out, or for them to come off as a joke, but she laughs anyway, and some of the tension that was growing dissolves. It is the kind of laugh where you tip your head back, and I only see it out of the corner of my eye, but the sight almost blinds me in the best way possible.

"I'm serious, Mia," I say to the window in front of me. I try to sound stern to let her know I am serious, but I feel my face slightly warm.

"No you're not," she laughs. "I get that we need to talk, but you can't start it off with bullshit."

"It isn't bullshit, Mia. You flirt with me and look at me with those pretty brown eyes, and you distract me from what I'm trying to say. Then, all of a sudden, you walk away, and I find myself dizzy from trying to understand what the fuck just happened. It is literally happening right now."

She continues to laugh, and the words rush out of my mouth. "And then there was the kiss."

The air around us thickens, and her laughter ceases. I let a few moments pass before I continue. "What I'm trying to say is, we can't be doing this, Mia. The lines are too blurred. I want to know you and be your friend, but you're Mateo's *sister*." I regret the last three words the second they leave my mouth.

Fuck.

That wasn't the right thing to say.

Out of the corner of my eye, I see her mouth open slightly as if what I said physically hurt her.

"Mateo's *little* sister," she mutters before letting out a huff. She crosses her arms, and I know I said the wrong thing. "You forgot that part."

I have never been one to word-vomit, but Mia *apparently* brings it out of me. My plan was to explain that, while the kiss was fucking phenomenal (leaving out how much I want to kiss her again), I can't go there, because I want to be her friend.

I wanted to tell her how our growing friendship means a lot to me, and I want to avoid anything messing it up. I also wanted to explain that Mateo wouldn't be happy with her and I being more than friends, which makes sense. Everyone knows that your best friend's sister is off-limits, *especially* Mateo's.

I didn't plan to admit how much she distracts me, especially if she somehow didn't realize it. I wasn't going to accuse her of flirting with me to get what she wants, even though I will gladly fall at her feet, but it all came out.

And now I can't take it back.

Great job, Eddie. Fucking brilliant.

"I just think we need to make sure we are both on the same page," I try to explain one more time.

"Done."

"What?" I turn to look at her. She leans down by her feet to grab her headphones from her bag and I realize I'm losing her.

"We're on the same page now, raindrop. I thought we were friends, but now I see that we are just two people coexisting in my brother's life." The nickname feels like this is a goodbye.

"No, Mia. Please, I didn't mean it like that."

"Please forget anything and everything I ever said." The words are too polite. I'd rather her screaming or yelling at me than the dismissiveness I hear in her voice.

"Mia, wait. Let me explain." It is taking everything in me not to pull the car over on the side of the highway and beg her on my knees to hear me out.

"No, Eddie. I get it. I'm sorry I dumped all my baggage on you last night, and I'm sorry I flirt with you or distract you or whatever."

"It isn't you. It's me and the whole situation. You being Mateo's sister complicates things. You have to know that."

"What makes you think I want to be anything more than friends with you? I mean really, Eddie? You think this is all just a big ploy to get in your pants? You're the one who kissed *me*. You're the one who knocked on my hotel room door last night. I opened up to you last because I thought we were friends. I didn't read into any of this. You did."

I squeeze the steering wheel with both hands as hard as I can to figure out what to say to make this right. "I'm sorry. I just didn't want the kiss or last night to complicate things, but I guess it was all in my head."

"No, I'm sorry," she says as she places her headphones over her head. "Sorry that whoever hurt you made it impossible for you to see that sometimes actions don't have ulterior motives."

I'm left so speechless I couldn't say something even if I wanted to. She takes the opportunity to open her laptop and pretend I'm not even here.

She spends the next hour of the ride with her headphones on and her laptop open on her lap editing last night's pictures. I spend the rest of the ride trying to figure out what I can say, so we can go back to pretending.

We have to stop for gas with about an hour left of the ride, and Mia has yet to even look at me. I get off at an exit with a gas station and a place to grab lunch in case Mia is hungry, and she finally looks up from her screen when she feels the car veer off the highway.

I tap her leg with my finger and then point to the gas station sign, so she knows I'm not trying to kidnap her like the sick freaks in those podcasts she listens to. She looks in my direction and then quickly looks away, and I assume we are still not talking.

It has been three hours not talking to Mia, and she feels so far away even though she is right next to me. I need to let her know that it isn't her. It isn't even Mateo. It's me. I'm the reason we can't be anything more than friends. She made it crystal clear she never wanted anything but friendship with me in the first place, so I'm back to square one of getting my feelings in check.

I park the car next to a gas pump and turn off the car. Mia takes her headphones off, but she still doesn't say anything.

"I'm going to get some gas and then go inside to get some snacks. Do you want anything?"

She shakes her head.

"Do you need to use the restroom?" I try again, more so just to hear her voice.

She shakes her head again.

Damn it.

"Okay, I'll be right back."

I climb out of the car and shut the door, locking the car behind me, and the rush of fresh summer air gives me a second to clear my head. I get the gas pumping before heading inside, looking over my shoulder to see Mia is still in the car. She is leaning her head back on the headrest, and she looks deep in thought.

I would do absolutely anything to read her mind, more now than ever.

Did I read our interactions wrong?

Was I reading into things too much?

Either way, I spent the ride thinking that Mia is in my life to stay. Mateo and I are best friends, so she isn't going anywhere. And I don't want her to. I may want more than friendship with her, but I'm not even in a place to think about that, and it was stupid of me to assume she felt the same way.

It's what I get for wanting something I can't have anyway.

As I walk into the gas station and cruise through the candy aisle, I come to my conclusion. If I can't have Mia the way I want to, I will settle for being her friend.

But, how do I tell her that?

I decide to start with a peace offering. She said she didn't want anything, but on the trip here, Mateo got her a Kit Kat, some kind of sour candy, and a Diet Coke.

And the more I get to know Mia, the more I have learned that the way to get through to her is remembering the little details.

I learned that lesson for the first time by bringing the iced coffee to her apartment, and she *is* my favorite thing to look at, so I keep all my observations about her hidden away to pull out when necessary.

Like today.

I grab the candy bar and a few snacks for me, and then I head to the fridge to get a bottle of Diet Coke. I glance out the window to check on Mia, and then head to the checkout counter to pay for the snacks and the gas when I see she is in the same spot that I left her.

After I pay for everything, I head back to the car, peace offering in hand, and slip back into the driver's seat. Mia is facing the passenger side window, obviously still ignoring me.

Joke is on her.

When I set my mind to something, I don't give up.

"I got you something," I say. Her headphones aren't on anymore, so I know she can hear me. She still doesn't turn my way, but I see a slight shift in her shoulders.

I reach into the plastic bag on my lap, and the shuffling of the plastic grabs her attention and she glances my way before looking back out the window.

"No, thanks," she says, and I feel like I just won the lottery because I just heard her voice.

"C'mon now. You don't even know what I got you." Her body turns away from the window and back to the front, with her feet up on the dash, her arms are still crossed, but that is progress.

Like a predator trying to capture their prey, I'm careful not to scare her away. I lure her in just a little more, hoping she takes the bait. I pull out the bottle of Diet Coke I got her, and I put it in the cup holder on her side. She looks at it, but she doesn't reach for it.

"I'm good," she says.

"You don't think that's all, do you, sunshine?" I take the king-sized Kit Kat out of the bag and hold it up for her to see.

Now I got her.

Her eyes widen in the slightest way, and I refuse to acknowledge how ridiculous this is because I am having way too much fun to care.

"That's too bad," I say with an exaggerated sigh. "I guess I'll eat it."

I can tell she is about to break, so I change tactics and resort to begging. "Please talk to me, sunshine."

She lets out a sigh, and I know I've won. "You're such a dick," she says as she reaches towards me to take the candy bar from my hand.

It's not forgiveness—I know that—but it's the first threat pulling us back together.

She gives me the first smile I have had in hours as I drop the chocolate into her hand.

Is it possible to be addicted to someone's smile?

Because I think I will do anything and everything to see Mia's.

It is a drug, and I need my fix.

And I don't think I'll ever get enough.

"Nope, not until you hear me out."

"Are you really using a Kit Kat to make me have this conversation with you?"

"I most certainly am."

"You're lucky I can't say no to a Kit Kat."

I want to say that I'm the lucky one, that the tension has dissolved enough for her to let me talk to her again, but I don't. Instead, I tell her, "I'm sorry about what I said. About you just being Mateo's little sister. I don't want you to think that is all you are to me."

She nods, so I continue. "You were right. I was the one reading into all of this, so I don't want you to think you did anything wrong because you didn't." I was the one who caught feelings where I shouldn't have, and I am going to be the one who has to suffer in silence, settling for a friendship that is going to take all of me to uphold. Not because it is hard to be friends with Mia, but because it is hard to not want more. "I really want us to be friends. You get me in a way no one else does, and I feel like you see me for more than just the guy who is always smiling or making sure everyone is having a good time."

I have to stop myself from admitting that she is the first person to see *me* in I don't know how long, and it is so fucking confusing. I don't know why I want to tell her everything I've kept hidden or why she makes me want to feel everything I've buried.

But what I want doesn't matter.

What matters is keeping Mia the only way I can.

"So, what do you say? Friends?" I hand her the Kit Kat, and she takes it. A few moments pass, and she seems to be very interested in the wrapper of the candy bar. She doesn't open it, but she looks at the packaging as if it holds the world's secrets.

"Are you going to tell me why you feel the need to always be the one no one has to worry about? The one who everyone can always count on to be in a good mood?"

I think about this for a second because I *could* tell her. She trusted me with something so raw and real to her, maybe I can do the same. I feel the words on the tip of my tongue. I don't know why it feels easy, almost natural, to tell her, but I don't want to read too much into it.

Not after what I almost completely fucked up.

"It has always been the role I took on. My dad, he isn't—wasn't—a good guy. I had to get them away from him, my mom and my sisters. I needed to be the one who took care of them, and I didn't want to ever be a burden for them, not with what they were dealing with."

"What about what *you* were dealing with?" she asks, the candy bar now forgotten in her lap. We are still parked next to the gas pump, but the car is off. I had every intention of getting back on the road after executing my plan to get Mia to talk to me, but now?

Now, we are at the point of no return.

The point where everything is on the verge of coming out, and I don't know what to say.

Being there for my mom, Lucia, Carmen, and Isa was second nature to me. I didn't even hesitate that night when I saw an opportunity to get them away from my dad once and for all. I was finally big enough to take him, and I had begged my mom to leave him so many times before. She refused every time, and I couldn't blame her for it. I know I will *never* understand what a woman goes through when she is in an abusive relationship.

What I did know is I had to take matters into my own hands.

I will never forget sitting down for dinner, like we did every night, pretending we were a big, happy family. From the outside, we fit the picture. But if you looked closely, you would see my mom's timid movements, not sitting down until my dad had his plate of food in front of him and his drink in hand. She painted a smile on her face, and maybe that is where I learned to *put on my mask,* as Mia calls it. My sisters refused to look anywhere but their plates, trying their best to fade into the background in their own fucking house. Me, I was just waiting for my chance to wring the man's neck.

In my gut, I knew that night was the night. The night that

I wouldn't let us all go to bed just for my sisters, now old enough to know what was going on with my parents, to come running into my bedroom, so scared for my mom but also so scared for themselves and each other.

"I don't know if it was because he was such a fucking pussy or because he got off on hurting women, but I never felt like I was the one in any danger." I let out a humorless laugh. "My dad actually pretended that he and I were the greatest son and father duo out there. Like we were on the same team. The way he would talk to me, the looks he'd give me when some sexist, vile shit came out of his mouth. He pretended we were one and the same." I shake my head, thinking about all the times he would flip a switch, one minute he was seconds away from backhanding my mom for not having his drink refilled soon enough, the next, he was trying to talk to me about football tryouts or asking me if I had a girlfriend. "I always felt like I was the one who had to protect them because I was the only one who could."

"How old were you?"

"When?"

"When it started." I shouldn't be surprised she is putting all the pieces together. I wasn't exactly subtle just now or when Annie made the comment about how our friend group doesn't do well with parents at the bar a few weeks ago, and I have no power over how well Mia can read me.

"I was eight the first time I saw him hit her. I was eighteen when I was finally big enough to be the one to hit him back." A weight is lifted off my shoulders with just those two sentences, and it is a weight that I have been carrying with me since that night.

All it took was him telling my mom to get him another drink, and years of holding back my utter hatred towards him came out that night. I stood up and told my oldest sister, Isa, who was fourteen at the time, to get Lucia and Carmen out of the room. She did so without a word, and that's when I told my father to stand up.

I didn't want them to see what was going to happen, especially not Lucia who started having panic attacks almost daily when she got old enough to realize what was happening to her mom. And that the perpetrator was her dad.

I had a couple inches on my father, having grown a little since starting college in the fall. I came home as much as I could, but tonight was the last night before things with the band were starting. Mateo, who was my roommate at the time, asked me to join, and it was going to take up a lot of my free time starting when we came back from winter break.

It had been long enough of pretending not to see what hid underneath my mom's makeup and her long sleeve shirts. I let all the anger in me that had been building for years all out that night. Starting with a punch but not stopping until Mateo, Theo, and Silas pulled me off my dad's unconscious body.

Good ol' dad got a few good hits in, and I wasn't surprised when he played dirty, reaching for anything he could to hit me with. He ended up grabbing a fallen glass, leaving me with a six-inch scar running from my forehead, across my eye, and down my cheek.

My mom had called Mateo when I threw the first punch, knowing that she wouldn't be able to stop me. Mateo had met my mom a few times over the past few months of freshman year, and she had his number for emergencies. The emergencies she had in mind were needing to get ahold of me and my phone being dead. She wasn't supposed to have to call him for help with stopping me from killing my own father.

My dad didn't die that night.

He died a few years later, long after waking up on the dining room floor later that night, with my mom, sisters, and me gone. Our bags packed and never looking back.

He never pressed charges, but I wouldn't have cared if he did.

"Your brother was the one who pulled me off him. My mom had called him because she didn't know who else to call. She had lost all her friends and her only sister was hours away. My dad made sure that my mom had no one besides him."

"Mateo never told me that," she whispers.

"It isn't something I talk about often. We barely talked about it after the fact." Silas and Theo helped my mom pack up everything she needed, and Mateo helped my sisters. The three of them helped us out of there that night, and I never saw my dad again.

It wasn't until the next morning, waking up in my dorm, a bandage over one side of my face, and learning from Mateo that my mom and sisters were staying with my aunt that I realized I could never let something like that happen again.

I will never forgive myself for what I made the guys do for me, and I owe my life to them for helping us get out of there.

"That was the last time I saw him. He died a few years later from a heart attack."

"I'm sorry that happened to you, Eddie," she says, but I don't deserve her sympathy.

"The past is in the past," I say. "We can't change it."

"That's true," she sighs, "but we can learn to live with it, rather than let it take hold of us." She grabs the Kit Kat from where it is sitting on her seat, and she unwraps the red packaging. I watch as she takes out the four chocolate covered rods and breaks the rectangle in half.

Learn to live with it.

Isn't that what I'm doing?

Living with it buried deep inside me, every day.

Feeling a constant dull pain in my chest, every day.

Scared to death I may lose something else that means something to me, every day.

I am living with it.

But it feels like it could kill me.

Mia holds out half of the Kit Kat to me, reaching across the center console. My body is aching to pull her from her side of the car over to mine, bringing her into my lap and holding her close. I'm longing for her to be in my grasp, feeling like she could disappear any second even though she is right here.

I settle for taking the Kit Kat from her, letting my fingers graze against hers, knowing the stolen touches are all I am going to get from now on.

"You're going to share with me?"

"Only because you bared your deepest, darkest secrets with me." There is a playfulness to her voice, one I've been missing. I watch her as she breaks her pieces into two, and I do the same. "Thanks for telling me," she adds.

"Thanks for listening." I take a bit out of my share of the chocolate bar. "You know, there are better gas station orders than Kit Kats and Diet Coke?" I finish one of my Kit Kat sticks and lick the melted chocolate on my fingers. I can't help but notice Mia watching as my tongue touches my thumb.

"Careful, sunshine. You can't be looking at me like that." No matter how much I like it, I want to add. There is a heat in her eyes I haven't seen before, a heat not used to look at a friend, but I keep that to myself.

"As if," she laughs, quickly recovering, and I know the skin on her chest is heating up. I don't need to see it to know the redness is there.

She doesn't miss a beat, changing the subject. "What's your gas station order?" To think the two of us can go from talking about childhood trauma to our go-to snacks when at a gas station is enough to give me whiplash, but it also proves what I said earlier about Mia getting me in a way no one else does. It is why I can't lose her, and why I wish I could have *all* of her.

I pop the rest of my share of the Kit Kat in my mouth

before reaching into the plastic bag still on my lap. I pull out a Sprite and a Twix bar, opening the packaging and giving her one of the two sticks

"The *second* best candy bar," she says, swiping her half of my Twix bar and taking a bite.

We get back on the road, and we only have the last end of the ride left. We should be back at Mia's by noon, and we fall into comfortable conversation. We talk about our favorite movies, books, and TV shows, agreeing to disagree on who has better taste. She asks me why I decided to join Cross My Heart, and I tell her how I didn't know it at the time, but I was dying to feel part of something. I'm realizing now that it was a way for me to just feel *something*.

"Where do you get your inspiration for your songs?" She asks, taking another sip of *my* Sprite. I choose to ignore the opportunity to point out that I *obviously* have the better gas station order.

"My own life mostly." Cross My Heart's songs have a strong beat with the presence of rock instruments like the electric guitar and electric bass giving us that "rock" sound.

Our lyrics have more of a grunge rock influence due to the more heavy, darker lyrics, but we also make sure to have a healthy balance of punk and pop to create a sound that can reach a wide variety of people.

"As someone who has always appreciated all types of music for their uniqueness and individual purpose, our sound and lyrics have been cultivated over the years to be something we hope everyone can connect to. I try to write about things that everyone can understand, like losing someone, finding someone, looking for someone."

I go on to explain that I like writing music that all types of music-listeners can appreciate, whether you enjoy songs for their lyrics or for their beat. It isn't until I get to the end of my long-winded response that I realize I don't even know how long I've been talking.

"Sorry," I run a hand through my hair, my hat forgotten and thrown in the back seat from when I needed to do something with my hands when Mia was still ignoring me. "That was probably not the answer you were looking for."

I take my eyes off the road for a second to see Mia watching me, as if what I had to say was the most interesting thing she has ever heard.

Which is odd because I know Mia isn't a music person like me, so I can't imagine anything I just said is that interesting to her.

"What?" I ask as I turn back to the road. I let out a little chuckle as I ask to hopefully distract from the flush spreading across my cheeks. I didn't mean to go off on a tangent, but I can go on and on when it comes to talking about my music or just music in general.

"Nothing," she answers, turning her head back to face the front windshield. She shakes her head, but she has a soft smile on her face, like she is holding in a secret that she wants to share but thinks she shouldn't.

CHAPTER 21

MIA

LISTENING to Eddie talk about his music is like turning on a light in the attic, where all your memories, stored and forgotten, are. It has been years since I could talk about music with someone who sees it the same way I do, like a way to feel your feelings through someone else's words.

"So," I start. "What kind of music do you listen to?"

"I listen to a little bit of everything, but a *lot* of the good stuff." He gives me a smirk. His eyes are on the road, but I know the smirk is for me. Like he knows something I don't know.

"And what's the good stuff?" I ask, unsure what answer I'm going to get. It has been years since I have opened Spotify or turned the radio on. I don't even know what songs are popular these days.

"You tell me, sunshine."

How do I tell him music reminds me of everything I've lost?

And how do I tell him that he makes me want to listen to music again?

"I used to listen to a little bit of everything." I pause, not sure how much to say.

"Not *anymore*?"

"Ever since Nico died, music has never sounded the same." It is the easiest way to explain something so complicated. I know how crazy it sounds that I drive myself insane trying to find Nico's song in music that isn't his, but I can't help it.

"You said he was writing you a song before he died, right?" Eddie asks.

"Yeah, why?" I turn to look at him, almost seeing the wheels turning in his head. But, for once, I have no idea what he is thinking.

"Just wondering," he answers. "Music has a way of pulling up feelings we try to keep down, almost like the lyrics find a way to speak to us, even when we don't want to listen."

I let out a sigh, "Wow." That is all I can say. I know exactly what Eddie means, but it sounds so meaningful, so finite, when he says it. Like there is no other explanation for why music triggers memories that are so painful to remember.

I finally realize something in this moment.

Music isn't the trigger to my anxiety or panic attacks.

It is the memories that come with it.

I wonder, since I feel like I have come so far with being able to think of Nico without feeling like my heart is being ripped out of my chest, maybe music won't feel as painful either.

I pull my phone out from the pocket of my hoodie, plugging it back into the AUX cord. I tap on the Spotify app that hasn't been touched in years, and I log into my account.

Once I'm in my account, so many memories—more than just of Nico—come flooding back as I scroll through the playlists I used to listen to on rotation.

There is a playlist for every mood I could ever be in, and one to fit any time of day. I smile to myself as I scroll through, seeing the playlist I would always listen to while I showered or the one I would blast in the car. I see the playlist I made for Nico, and the one we made together to see how aligned our music taste is—*was.*

I feel like I'm floating between wishing I never opened the app and wishing I did it sooner. My eyes sting at the memory, but I can't help but let out a breath of fresh air at the fact that I am in control. My mind isn't taking over, tricking me into thinking that I'm not.

A hand on my leg grounds me, and I look down to see Eddie's hand lightly gripping my thigh. Our eyes meet for a moment before he has to look back on the road, and something passes between us.

It's like he is telling me he's here.

Here for me.

If I need him.

And I do.

I place my hand on his as I tap on my playlist titled "Songs to Scream in the Car" and the opening notes of "When I'm Alone" by Post Malone start. One of my favorite songs.

]The song my brother picked for Cross My Heart to cover at their shows.

I take my hand off Eddie's to turn up the volume of the car speakers before taking his hand in mine, interlocking our fingers, and squeezing tight.

Then, I sing.

I sing at the top of my lungs, not caring how bad it sounds.

Tears run down my cheeks, but I haven't felt this much like myself, this *alive,* in months, and I never want to lose the feeling again.

The next song plays—"She Looks So Perfect" by 5 Seconds of Summer, and I sing even louder. I feel like I'm on top of the world as Eddie rolls the windows down, and warm summer air rushes in. I set my phone on my lap to reach my other arm out the window, and I turn to see Eddie, and the smile on his face makes my stomach jump because it is the same smile I see him with on stage.

His *real* smile.

The one where the skin next to his eyes crinkles and the green of his irises shines a little brighter, his one dimple on full display, causing the scar on his face to fade.

When Eddie talked about his dad, I knew that the night my brother, Theo, and Silas had to pull him off his father was the same night he got his scar.

The thought of Eddie having to carry a reminder of that night with him, everywhere he went, left me feeling like I couldn't breathe. We all have scars from the shitty things that happened to us, but we can often hide them because they're on the inside.

No wonder he feels like he always needs to be smiling, distracting others from the one thing he couldn't get away from that night.

The memory.

Right there on his face.

Every time he looks in the mirror.

The song fades out, the beginning notes of "The Tide" by Niall Horan fading in, and the atmosphere in the car changes. The beat of the music is a little slower, the lyrics having more truth behind them than I'd like to admit.

With the lull in the music, Eddie uses it as an excuse to ask, "How does it feel?"

I don't need to clarify the *it* he is asking about.

"Amazing," I breathe. I look down, and our hands are still interlocked on my lap and then back at him. "You know that feeling of finding a song that perfectly matches your mood, and the lyrics somehow say exactly what you're feeling, and you don't have to think about it."

Eddie turns to me, but he doesn't say anything.

"Forget it." I shake my head. I didn't realize how stupid that sounded until I said it. "That probably doesn't make any sense."

Eddie just smiles then looks back at the road.

"I know exactly what you mean. Like you can just listen to the music and *feel*." He lets out a laugh.

"What?" I ask.

"Nothing, it's just—" he starts but shakes his head, laughing to himself again. "That's actually the exact reason I wanted to write songs. To write lyrics people could connect with, so they could be happy or sad, in love or lonely, angry at the world or just one person, and feel like they aren't alone."

There is so much I want to say, but I don't know how to say it.

So instead, I just squeeze Eddie's hand, and he squeezes mine back. We listen to music for the rest of the ride, and, for the first time in three years, that is all I do.

I settle in bed after an afternoon of cleaning up my apartment, unpacking from the weekend, and an evening of reality TV show reruns, white wine, and laundry.

Eddie dropped me off at home around one in the afternoon, and I felt like a new person walking into my place.

Not a new person as in *brand* new, different than I was before.

But new as in the old me. The version of myself I've been missing and fighting like hell to get back.

I feel light on my feet, like the weight I have been carrying isn't as heavy now that I was able to share some of the load.

Talking with Eddie about Nico felt like the start of something I don't really know if I completely understand. We established that we were friends, and that the kiss was a mistake, but I can't ignore the sliver of disappointment at the thought.

My bed feels small after spending the night in a king-size hotel bed, but it also feels a little lonely.

I have been alone for years, missing someone who is never going to come back, but this loneliness is different, like it doesn't *have* to be this way.

This weekend was a whirlwind of emotions, between Cross My Heart's first show, what happened afterward, the kiss, Eddie sneaking into my hotel room, and our road trip back to Milwaukee, I'm left with the aftermath of these feelings, knowing that I won't see Eddie until the next show in three weeks.

Not wanting to dwell on the feelings that come with that thought, I grab my laptop from the foot of my bed and decide that I should go back to figuring out what I'm going to do for the next three months.

One show down, five to go.

The last show isn't until the very end of summer and then things will really die down, so that means I need to figure out how to fill my time between now and then.

I revisit the idea of pursuing photography full-time and confirm with myself that it's what I want to do.

I send a text to Mateo, first asking how the meeting with Xander Drake—the tour manager for next year's tour—went, and if he had time to meet up this week to help me with setting up a website for a freelance photography business.

He responds a few minutes later saying the meeting went well, but there's nothing major to report just yet. We plan to meet up and talk about the website later this week, and then he asks how the ride home with Eddie went.

I tell myself I'm not lying to my brother. I'm just keeping what happened between Eddie and me to myself, like I would with any other friendship. I ignore the pit in my stomach, convincing myself it isn't guilt, and I send off a text saying it went fine.

Eddie and I are friends.

Nothing more.

It is all we can be, all we ever will be.

So why won't this pit in my stomach go away?

CHAPTER 22
MIA

THE NEXT THREE months fly by in a blur but in the best way possible.

The week after the first show, a video of Cross My Heart's opening song, one of their newer originals, went viral. Their following on all platforms quadrupled in a matter of days.

The crowd at their second show was noticeably larger, and the crowds kept growing following every show from there. By the fifth show, the headlining band and the tour managers were so impressed, that they were in the process of negotiating the final contract with Mateo that would make Cross My Heart the sole openers for the Heartbreakers, Burning Down, and The Falling Flames next summer.

Not only that, thanks to the guys' growth in popularity, when Mateo and I launched my freelance website right before their third show, I posted it on Cross My Heart's social media after getting a flood of questions about who manages their social media pages, and I started getting inquiries from other bands looking for social media marketing along with photography for their promos, teasers, and album covers.

The five of us have been so busy, and, because Mateo couldn't handle all the administrative stuff on his own anymore, I took on the role of the band's unofficial manager until they find someone permanent.

My time has been split between growing my own business and helping grow Cross My Heart.

Mateo and I have been spending almost every day together, between my apartment and his, so I haven't even had two minutes alone with Eddie since our road trip after the band's first show.

We chat here and there when I'm with the band or when I'm at Lenny's, but it almost feels like the weekend of the first show was my imagination, like it never happened.

I've also gotten closer with Drew and Annie over these past few months. With Annie usually being at the bar trying to make enough money to cover her tuition for veterinarian school next fall, and Drew being off from school, the three of us have bonded over too many hard seltzers, lots of white wine, our shitty parental situations, and boy problems.

It is truly the perfect combination for making life-long friends.

Tonight, the whole gang is getting together to celebrate the signing of their tour contract. Annie, Drew and I are sitting at a high top table at Lenny's waiting for them to walk in any minute while Emmett and Luke work behind the bar.

"Can you believe how much has happened this summer?" Annie asks, taking a sip of her gin and tonic.

"No," Drew laughs. "I swear, I don't know how much more I can take this year." I recently learned what happened at Drew's school this last year, and I am amazed at the kind of person she is for getting through that. Not only did she survive a school shooting, but the way she talks about how she went back with her only intention of making sure her students felt safe in their classroom made me wish I had her as a teacher growing up.

"Same," I agree. I'm not drinking tonight because I have to be up early to do some work for their social media pages.

After things started picking up after their first show, I started driving myself to shows, so I could head straight to the venue to prepare for the concerts. The other bands for this tour asked if I would do photos for them too, so my work was *really* cut out for me at every show.

I hear the door to Lenny's open, and I turn around to see the men of the hour.

"There they are!" Annie yells, holding up her glass. Drew smiles doing the same with her White Claw, and my eyes go directly to a certain drummer.

All four boys are dressed up, needing to impress at their final meeting to confirm their spot on the tour. Eddie is dressed in black fitted dress pants with a dark green button up, just barely revealing the skin above his chest, his gold chain catching the light from the neon signs in the bar. His dark hair is pushed back as if he just ran his fingers through it, and I feel butterflies in my stomach.

How is it fair for a man to look *that* good?

As always, he catches me staring, but I don't look away. Stolen glances are all I get of Eddie these days.

"How did it go?" I ask my brother as he and Eddie walk over to our table.

Theo and Silas head straight to the bar and sit down in front of Luke and Emmett who both have been looking over here every chance they get, Emmett at Drew and Luke at Annie.

One of those makes sense. The other does too, but only because I have been watching Annie and Luke all summer now, and I am convinced there is more history there than either one of them admits.

"You're looking at the official openers for next year's Heartbreakers tour!" Mateo wraps his arm around Eddie who —no surprise—smiles, all too comfortable fading into the back.

"When's the first show?" Drew asks.

"We have our last show for this tour tomorrow night, and then our first official show as part of a tour is next June, almost exactly a year from the show that got us on the map."

"How poetic," Annie deadpans.

I have become immune to her directness and resting bitch face these past three months, but it was not easy.

I have never met someone who is so hot and so cold at the same time. She flips the switch like nothing, warm and inviting one second, and then plotting how she is going to kill you and make it look like an accident the next.

Mateo looks at her, and I see something pass in my brother's eyes, something I haven't seen before. Mateo has had two serious girlfriends in his adult life, both ending amicably. His excuse for not dating has always been having to balance work and the band, but I think I'm partly to blame too. What I see on his face right now makes me think he is ready to get back out there.

I feel sorry for him though because he isn't the only person to notice how he is looking at Annie right now, and Luke is by her side in a blink of an eye.

"Congrats on the tour, man. Beer?" Luke's demeanor is that of a golden retriever, but I've learned that he isn't afraid to show his edge when it comes to Annie. There is a smile on his face, but the way he comes to stand between her and Mateo is anything but friendly.

"Yeah, thanks. I was going to go sit at the bar with Theo and Silas anyway." Mateo nods to Luke and looks past him at Annie who continues to look at him as if she is completely unfazed. I can't say I'm not surprised.

"Have fun with your yahoos," she calls as Mateo turns to walk to the bar.

"You got the hots for Mia's brother, Annie girl?" Luke asks, resting his elbows on the high-top table, leaning into Annie. It comes off as messing with her, but I know it goes deeper.

I look at Drew with questioning eyes, and she just rolls her eyes. I turn to Eddie who is standing between our chairs, and he gives me a similar response, shrugging his shoulders before following Mateo over to the bar.

"Yep. Been looking for someone to take the edge off. He seems up for the challenge." Annie says as she slowly faces Luke. Her voice is cold, but I feel my chest heat, on full display in my baby pink tank top. Luke is her target, and I'm a bystander. Yet, he doesn't look fazed, and I am the one left flustered by her remark.

"We're going to go get another drink," Drew announces, so I follow her lead and hop off my chair to walk over to the bar.

"Hi, sweetheart," Emmett says, leaning over the bar to kiss Drew. Her cheeks turn the same shade of red as her hair, and I can't get over how cute they are. "Another lovers quarrel?" Emmett asks her.

"Something like that," Drew replies as she sits down on the bar stool.

Emmett comes around the bar to sit next to her, his job being done for the night now that it is just the nine of us—and three of the nine work here. Drew is wrapped up in him as I slide onto the stool beside her.

Eddie is to my left, very interested in the bottle cap of his beer, and Mateo is on his other side turned towards Theo and Silas.

Everyone is coupled off, except for us.

"How did it go tonight?" I ask him.

"Good," he answers.

"That's good."

"Yeah."

Well, this isn't awkward at all.

The last time Eddie and I talked, just the two of us, was almost three whole months ago, but I didn't think talking to him like a normal person would be this difficult.

The last time we talked was the weekend of their first show, and we both opened up to each other in a way I don't think either of us were expecting. There was a comfort with talking to Eddie that I haven't had before, and there was a sense of safety I felt with him that I have been longing to feel again.

That weekend feels so long ago yet so recent at the same time, and I find myself wondering, when I can't fall asleep at night, if it could have gone differently.

And if it did, where would Eddie and I be now?

While the past three months have been busy, they have also been so incredibly healing. I found a worth in myself that I had been missing, and I no longer feel like I am on the verge of falling apart.

I haven't had a panic attack since the night in the hotel room with Eddie, and my therapist has moved me to monthly sessions starting next month because of how much progress she has seen. September will be the first month where I have one session rather than three or four, and I'm proud of where I am.

Music has become my third favorite thing, following photography and being part of Cross My Heart, but I guess all three of those things are bundled together for me.

I still think of Nico, every single day, but I think of the happy memories. The memories that warm my soul like the sun, and I wake up every morning being able to keep my dreams in my head where they belong, rather than wishing they would come true.

"Are you ready to debut the new song tomorrow?" Tomorrow is the last of these six shows. The one they've all been waiting for. Now that Cross My Heart is already signed on for next year's tour, the guys can just enjoy this last show. No pressure, no worries, and they have been planning to debut a new single.

These three months have been exhausting when it comes

to booking a whole-ass tour without an agent, manager, or being part of a record label, so those three things are the next steps along with prepping for the Heartbreakers Tour.

"Yeah, we've been practicing the past few weeks. I think it's ready," Eddie says with a soft smile. He finally turned his head to look at me, and I wish he didn't. His elbow is resting on the bar, and he is leaning his head on his fist. I wish I had brought my camera to take a picture because this moment makes me realize how much I miss him.

Our friendship started and ended and then started again in ways that are still so confusing to me, but, regardless of everything, having him in my life is a gift I never knew I wanted.

Something I never knew I *needed*.

"I'm excited to hear it," I reply, facing him and matching his position. The dim lighting of the bar should be unflattering, but it makes him look even more alluring. A new addition to this process we call healing is, now that my mind isn't so occupied with all the things I can't control, I have more room to think, fantasize, and dream about certain green eyes on me in ways that make my chest heat. Looking at Eddie now, the *way* he is looking at me, does not bode well for me when it comes to keeping my dirty thoughts in check.

No, I tell myself. *Not okay.*

Yes, we are healing. Yes, we are in a good place.

But no. We will not be fantasizing about your brother's best friend.

Not anymore.

"I think you'll like it," he smiles and looks down where my feet are hanging off the stool. I wish his eyes were still on me, making me feel a lot of things I shouldn't, but when I notice the hint of pink in his cheeks, I decide that I'd much rather this instead.

CHAPTER 23
EDDIE

EMMETT ALWAYS TALKS about how cute it is that Drew blushes all the time. How he can always tell how she's feeling by the color of her cheeks.

I never thought much about it, usually ignoring him or giving him shit for being so in love, but now I understand why Drew always complains when Emmett points out that she is blushing.

Mia asking me about the song makes me nervous. Like a first-date-as-a-teenager nervous. She has absolutely no idea that for the past three months, I've been listening to her hum a song I never heard before, and that it got stuck in my head.

The only way for me to get it out was to write it.

When she hears this song tomorrow night, there is no telling how she will react.

Will she like it? Hate it? Not even notice it's *hers*?

And what if she notices it's the song she has been humming and thinks I'm a fucking weirdo?

I have barely seen the girl in three months, and I am almost positive that the weekend in her hotel room and our road trip in Mateo's car were a fever dream. I have convinced myself that after I punched the dickhead at the show for touching her, causing a handprint bruise to form on her arm, Mateo then punched me, and I didn't wake up until Monday morning in our apartment.

My obsession with Mia is officially entering unhealthy territory, growing more so every day that she was around at practice or at our place, but I couldn't spend any time with her. Frustrating is an understatement, and whoever said *absence makes the heart grow fonder* didn't mention that a best friend's little sister with pretty brown eyes and a body taken straight from my fantasies will make your heart forget how to function properly.

Don't get me wrong, the work she has done for Cross My Heart has been fucking phenomenal, and I can't thank her and Mateo enough for working their asses off to get us to where we are now, on tour with record labels interested in us.

The selfish part of me is just bitter that we decided to be friends that weekend of the road trip, but I haven't been able to take advantage of that since.

She also has no idea how many songs she inspired, some that may never leave the privacy of my notebook, but others that I have shared with the guys that could potentially be the start of being more than a local, indie rock band. And one that we are debuting tomorrow.

Mia has been posting about our last show all over our social media platforms, hinting at a surprise at the end of the show as a thank you for the support over these last months.

All eyes on us, but the most important eyes, Mia's eyes, on *me*.

"You nervous, raindrop?" she asks, and my stupid blush deepens at the nickname. Something that started off as her smartass way to get under my skin but reminds me that she is the sunshine to my rainy day.

I keep looking at her shoes, afraid that my whole fucking face will turn red if I look at her now. She is wearing light washed jeans with rips that show off the silky skin of her thighs. Her legs haunt my dreams after feeling them near me when she fell asleep in her hotel room and wrapped around me in her sleep.

She still has that T-shirt of mine that she wore that night, and I go to sleep every night hoping that she's wearing it to bed.

Tonight, she's wearing a tiny baby pink tank top that shows off her bronzed skin on her arms and just above the waistband of her jeans. Her blonde hair is in soft waves resting on her shoulders, and she makes my mouth water. The pink of her top perfectly matches the hue of her lips, and my brain short circuited when I saw her staring at me from that high-top table.

Even though I've seen Mia plenty over these past three months, tonight feels different. There are seven other people in this bar, all wrapped up in their own conversations, and I feel like it is just me and her, especially when she looks at me like I'm worth something.

It reminds me of our night in the hotel.

"I just hope you—and everyone—like it." The "everyone" part is a little too delayed, and I want to punch myself in the face.

"Everyone will," she reassures. "Sad we didn't get to have any more road trips."

"I know. Had our Kit Kats and Twix ready to go too." This makes her laugh, and my heart warms at the memory of our first road trip when we shared our gas station snacks with each other.

"Maybe next summer, when you guys are on your big tour. I'll have our true crime podcast ready and downloaded too," she says, and my head whips up to her, not being able to hide the surprise and slight drop of my jaw. Another fucking podcast where I have to hear about the most disgusting excuses of humanity. This girl is lucky I can't say no to her.

"Kidding," she laughs. "My 'Songs to Scream in the Car'"

playlist has been updated and is eagerly awaiting its launch though."

"Now that's more like it," I say, letting out a sigh. Watching Mia sing in the car all those months ago has been on replay in my head. I can't drive and listen to music without wishing I was watching her on the passenger side. Mia is a music person through and through, and I love that side of her. I'll never tell her, but I would have made it my life's mission to make her fall in love with music again. Lucky for me, it was easier than I thought it would be. All she needed was a long car ride with the windows down.

I love that music and our love for it is something we have in common.

Talking to Mia right now makes me realize how much I missed her, and I have a hard time with that because she isn't mine to miss.

She's my friend, and I am thankful for that.

But if I was a better man, I could make sure everyone knew how proud I was to be hers, and I could spend my whole life showing her how much I need her to be mine.

Instead, I'm selfish, knowing I'm no good for her but needing her in my life any way I can.

Before I can say anything else, Annie bounces over to all of us, and I can tell by her face that she has an idea. Luke follows behind her like the puppy he is with her meaning they already kissed and made up—figuratively speaking, as far as I know—and she already has him on board for whatever she is about to say.

"Alright bitches," she says, clapping her hands together. All the attention goes to her, and if I have learned anything in my years of knowing Annie, it's that whatever is about to come out of her mouth is finite because this is her world. We're just living in it. "It's karaoke time."

CHAPTER 24
MIA

AM I surprised that Annie is the type of girl to call all the shots? *No.*

Am I surprised that the only one grumbling is Emmett?

Also no.

I have been with these people almost daily for three months, and I have quickly picked up on the dynamic, finding my space within the group. Annie is a firecracker. She doesn't take shit from anyone, and she's the kind of person who will fight to the death for you.

Drew is more introverted and takes very great care of her social battery, but she is one of the most down-to-earth people I've ever talked to.

Emmett is the grump who actually is just a big teddy bear when you get to know him. Rightfully protective over Drew, and he is never afraid to say what is on his mind, even if it isn't the most polite.

Then there's Luke, the golden boy, always smiling, usually flirting, but always watching Annie.

Theo and Silas are more on the outskirts, friendly with everyone, but they aren't as close to everyone compared to how they are with each other.

Then, there's Eddie who has known Emmett forever, along with my brother, and he is the one no one ever has to worry about. He's never the center of attention, always watching everyone else.

He never fails to be the center of *my* attention though.

So where do I fit in? I'm still trying to figure that out. Annie, Drew, and I are the same age with corresponding interests and personalities that all complement each other, but I don't have the greatest history with girlfriends. I'm hoping this time is different.

Something tells me it is.

There is something about this group that feels *real*. Like we don't have to put on our polite faces and sugar-coat what we want to say. There is this mutual understanding that we all share something in common, whether that is what we have been through or the kind of people we are, but it is something I don't ever want to lose.

Eddie and Luke close everything up at Lenny's, and we all pile into two cars to head downtown to a karaoke bar. Mateo is driving one car with Annie, Theo, and Silas. Emmett is driving the other car with Luke, me, and Eddie and Drew in the front seat.

I didn't think Drew and Emmett would end up coming, but when Drew batted her eyelashes at Emmett telling him that she wanted to celebrate her last Friday of the summer before going back to school next Tuesday for her third year of teaching, he couldn't say no to her.

It is 10 p.m. on a September night. Some rock song Drew and Emmett like is playing on the speakers of Emmett's Jeep, and the windows are down, letting in the warm summer air. I'm sitting between Luke and Eddie, and I can't settle down the buzzing of my skin that is touching Eddie. My jean-covered thigh is resting against his slacks-covered one, even though there is plenty of room in the back seat. Luke is distracted by something on his phone, his face tense in a way

I haven't seen before, and Eddie is looking out the window. The music playing is loud enough that there is no need for conversation as we drive.

The place we are headed to is a few blocks from my apartment, so it will be nice to walk home later tonight.

My hands are resting on my legs, and I feel a pull to my right, where Eddie is sitting. His left hand is relaxed on his thigh, and it looks empty without mine.

With a mind of its own, my hand slowly inches to the edge of my leg resting against Eddie's, and I feel a flip in my stomach like I'm on a first date hoping he holds my hand.

Which is stupid, and I know that. Maybe it is the high I feel being around these people who are beginning to mean so much to me, but I can't help but lean into the feeling.

These three months have been busy, but they have not been distracting enough to make me forget about the *what ifs* when it comes to Eddie.

What if he wasn't my brother's best friend?

What if I told him that day in the car that he wasn't reading too much into everything?

What if we could explore these feelings we have towards each other?

What if I could make him see that he isn't the broken boy he makes himself out to be?

"Careful, sunshine," I hear in my ear. I was too in my thoughts to realize he turned towards me and shifted, so his lips were close enough to my ear. The music is still loud, and there is no way anyone can hear him over the wind rushing in from the windows.

"We don't want the whole car knowing how much I want to put my hands on you."

My chest is on full display tonight, but I am thankful for the minimal light because I feel all the blood rush to my chest. I got a blush out of Eddie today, but he wasn't going to let me be the winner any longer.

His words hold secrets that make my skin tingle, and my body is *painfully* aware of the power his words have over me.

"If it was just us right now, do you know what I would do?" he asks.

I can't respond, lying to myself that it is because I don't want anyone to hear me, but Emmett is cruising on the highway. You can barely hear the music over the wind. I turn to see Luke looking out the window, his phone forgotten on his lap.

I swallow, feeling a shiver down my spine, even though I am far from cold.

Eddie leans in even closer, so close that if he moved his lips, I would feel them against my ear.

"If we were alone right now, I would tell you that good girls don't tease. If you want to hold my hand, reach out and grab it." Eddie slips his hand into mine and lets out a small laugh. Not only do I feel a shock through my system at his words, but his laugh is icing on the cake.

I could say something back, teasing him, playing into his hand, or I could just enjoy his hand in mine as we drive.

And I decide to do just that.

We get to the karaoke bar a few minutes later, and Eddie slips his hand from mine before Luke, Emmett, or Drew can notice.

I don't let myself dwell on the emptiness in my palm, or the voice in the back in my head asking what the fuck I'm doing as I slide out of the backseat onto the sidewalk.

Mateo's car pulls up right before Eddie's Jeep, and we have a few blocks to walk.

Emmett and Drew start walking, holding hands and making everyone around them jealous of how cute they are.

Annie, Mateo, Theo, and Silas are in a heated discussion

about who gets to sing first, so Luke, Eddie, and I walk behind the foursome as we head to the Karaoke MKE.

"Who do you think is going to win?" Luke asks, breaking the silence between the three of us as we walk. It is no surprise how hyper fixated he is on Annie, and I have noticed a pattern when it comes to Luke's dips in demeanor, and it usually happens when Annie's attention isn't on him.

"Definitely Mateo," I answer as we fall in step with each other. My brother is an oldest child, through and through, completely used to calling the shots and getting to go first. Annie definitely doesn't seem like the type to back down though.

"I don't know," Luke playfully says, "I think my Annie girl is going to give him a run for his money,"

"Want to make it interesting?" I ask Luke.

"You know it. If Mateo sings first, your drinks come out of my paycheck for the next month."

"Deal," I answer. Annie convinced Emmett to give our group what she calls the 'Fam Bam' discount on our drinks at Lenny's, but I spend a lot of time there, so free drinks for a month is definitely worth the risk.

"If Annie sings first, you have to tell me what's going on between you and my boy here," Luke lifts his eyes to Eddie, giving him a wink.

"Fuck off, Luke," Eddie says, adding to the conversation for the first time since we started walking.

Luke laughs. "Don't even try to pretend you weren't eye-fucking Mia at the bar or whispering sweet nothings in her ear in the backseat."

What do I have to do right now for the ground to swallow me whole?

This is what I get for seeking the thrill of sneaking around with Eddie for no good goddamn reason other than needing to complicate my life when things are going well.

My therapist and I are going to have so much fun talking about my new-found ability to self-sabotage in September.

To my surprise, Eddie laughs along, playing into his laid-back, carefree self, and I am seeing first-hand how well it works for him.

"I *wish*. Mia would never settle for a guy like me." Eddie smiles despite the self-deprecation in his words, and I don't think he's joking.

This makes Luke laugh even harder, and I continue to act as though I am not in the middle—or the center—of this conversation.

"You're right, Ramirez. What the hell was I thinking? Our Mia deserves the best," he says, before filling the gap between him and Annie. He rushes up next to her, bumping Mateo from where he is walking next to her, and puts an arm around her shoulder. It lasts all of about two seconds before she shoves him away and picks up her pace.

"Why did you say that?" I ask Eddie, now that is just the two of us. We have two more blocks until our destination, and it is back to just him and I.

"Say what?"

"That I would never settle for a guy like you?"

Eddie runs his fingers through his hair before putting both hands in the pocket of his slacks. I can tell he wants to do something with his hands because he taps his back pocket before realizing his drumsticks aren't there.

"Come on, Mia. I had to set him straight. It's not like anything is going on between us anyway. We're friends, *right*?" His voice slightly cracks when he says "right" so I know he is still trying to put on his happy face.

My turn to turn the tables.

"So," I start. "You weren't *actually* thinking of all the things you would tell me if we were alone?" I look up with him making sure my eyes lock him in like I know they always do. "Because *I* was."

"Don't you dare, sunshine. I know what you're doing, and you need to stop. I'm hanging on by a thread right now as it is." His voice is playful yet serious at the same time, and ust like always, the line between us is blurring. This is turning into a game of who is going to back down first, and I refuse to lose. "You need a friend, here I am. You know I can't be anything more."

"Do I?" I ask, and it flies out of my mouth before I can think of a better response. I'm not sure who is in control right now, and I don't know what part of this is the stupid little game we play, but I couldn't be more serious when I say, "Because this," I gesture between us, "doesn't feel like any friendship I've had."

"That's because it's ours, and I'm nothing like you've ever had before."

I trip over my own foot, clearly affected by what he just said. Eddie reaches out to grab my arm. Without it, I would have fallen flat on my face, but the touch is electric, sending tiny vibrations throughout my entire body.

"You guys coming?" I whip my head up in the direction we're walking, and I see Drew holding the door for Eddie and I at Karaoke MKE. Eddie lets go of my arm as we close the gap and pauses to let me into the door first before grabbing it to hold open for Drew.

Doesn't look like we are finishing that conversation anytime soon.

CHAPTER 25
EDDIE

TONIGHT DID NOT GO how I thought it would, but why am I even surprised? I thought seeing Mia tonight would be like any other day I've seen her this summer since our first show. We would keep things polite and friendly, and I would continue to keep some healthy distance between us.

What just happened between us, in the car and the walk here, further proves how much of a fucking idiot I am because it took me less than an hour with her to resort back to putting myself right into the palm of her hand.

We weren't alone, but we sure as hell could have been. It felt all the same. It didn't matter that there were people around us. When she's in my sight, all my attention is on her and nothing else matters.

Maybe it is the high of making the Heartbreakers Tour official.

Maybe it is because the swell of gratitude in my chest for seeing how perfectly Mia fits into this fucked up crew of my most favorite people.

Maybe it is her stupid pink top and her stupid lush lips and her stupid brown eyes, but I am back to where I was three months ago.

Wishing that I could have her.

Wishing that I was enough for her.

Wishing she wasn't my best friend's little sister.

My brain completely forgot how to act like a normal human being tonight, and my selfish tendencies when it comes to Mia came back in full force.

We're supposed to be friends. That is what we agreed on.

That is what *she* wanted.

Right?

I am right back to where I started.

But why does it have to feel so fucking good?

"I'm first!" Annie announces when we are taken to our karaoke room. She heads straight for the binder of songs.

Karaoke MKE is one of the places where you rent a room with friends, and you can drink and sing to your heart's content.

"No, *we're* first," Mateo interjects, and it looks like the bet between Luke and Mia is void.

Mateo and Annie choose "Breaking Free" from *High School Musical*, but, because it's Annie, she wants to sing Troy's part. Their rendition is entertaining, but it is also actually good, which is to be expected by the lead singer of a band and a retired theater kid. Annie is a hidden gem when it comes to talents, being one of those people that is good at so many things, singing being one of them.

Theo and Silas each sing a Bruno Mars song, "Locked Out of Heaven" for Theo and "Runaway Baby" for Silas. Drew and Annie convince Mia to sing "679" by Fetty Wap, Monty, and Remy Boyz.

Mia had recently got back into her music scene, so I was a little nervous about how tonight was going to go for her. I shouldn't be surprised that she is completely fine, holding her own, as always. She couldn't be cuter on stage, the dim lights of the private room not completely hiding the feelings she wears on her chest.

I find it so interesting that her and Mateo are so different when it comes to music, Mateo being so creative when it comes to making it; Mia being so receptive and appreciative when it comes to enjoying it.

I watch as she shyly holds the microphone to her mouth as the song starts, and as the lyrics run across the screen in front of her, I watch her confidence grow. Mia, Drew, and Annie all scream the lyrics at the top of their lungs by the time they are at the first chorus, jumping around and singing to each other, and me and the guys watch with pure enjoyment on our faces.

The three of them together is like nothing I've ever seen before, complimenting each other in ways that make each of them their best selves when together, and I'm so happy Mia found that.

You don't get that close in three months without a true connection, and these three have it.

"Your turn!" Mia says, handing me the microphone when her song finishes.

"Only if you sing with me," I argue. I didn't think those would be the words out of my mouth, but, once they're out, I don't want to take them back.

She narrows her eyes at me because she has a way of reading me, knowing that I probably have some ulterior motive.

And she's right.

I want to see her up there again, smiling, singing, and having fun.

"I get to pick the song."

"Fine by me," I reply, walking over to the makeshift stage. The private room is dark, lit by the screen that shows the lyrics. The stage is about a foot higher than the floor, but it does the job.

Claps from our audience sound, and I have no idea what she is going to play.

After a few seconds, the opening beat of "(You Drive Me) Crazy" by Britney Spears starts, and I laugh out loud.

Mia starts singing with the lyrics, and she was expecting me to back down. What she doesn't know is that those three sisters of mine never let me pick the music we listened to, so this song is one I have in my back pocket.

When it is my turn to sing, I don't hold back, I sing my heart out to the chorus, and Mia's jaw drops. Her eyes go wide, and her mouth curves into a smile that makes me want to fall to my knees and beg her to never stop smiling at me like that. Fired up from Mia's reaction and the whoops and claps from our friends cheering me on, I sing at the top of my lungs, making a mental note to text Lucia, Carmen, and Isa that suffering through their love for Britney Spears just gave me the greatest reward ever.

My vocals are strong, but I only occasionally do back up, preferring to write the music and hold the beat rather than sing it. Mateo was made to be our lead singer, perfectly supported by Theo and Silas' vocals.

"I didn't know you had it in you, raindrop," Mia says as the song finishes.

"I have three sisters." It is enough of an answer to make sense to her.

"Ahh, so it's in you against your will," she replies.

"It was bound to happen whether I liked it or not, I'm just happy it paid off."

"I never thought 90's music would be your thing."

"I told you, sunshine. I listen to everything."

She laughs, but I don't want this to end. "Who's next?" She asks our audience.

"I don't think so," I tell her, and she turns to me. "It's my turn to pick our next song."

She shakes her head. "I don't want to hog the mic," she says, gesturing to everyone.

"Go right ahead, girly pop," Annie says, giving Mia a wink and me a knowing glance.

"All you," Drew adds from her seat next to Annie.

Emmett grunts his agreement while Theo and Silas hold up their drinks to us. Mateo and Luke are both playing DJ, and I plan on taking full advantage of this.

"All *us*," I say, grabbing Mia lightly by the arm to lead her back to the center of the stage. "Stay," I tell her, holding up my hands. She crosses her arms and sticks her tongue out at me, but I know she will listen. I walk over to Luke and Mateo, "You picked a song from the 90's, so I get the next decade," I say over my shoulder. The speakers are in the back of the room, but the room itself isn't too big.

"Who said this was a game?" she yells to me, and I can tell by her voice she is trying to hide her smile.

"Eddie did," Annie playfully yells. "Now, get ready for your song."

"You sure about this one?" Luke asks, after I pointed to my choice in the binder of songs.

"Of all the songs you could pick, that's the one you pick?" Mateo asks before I can give Luke my answer.

My song choice is bound to be a crowd-pleaser, and it is my turn.

So yes, I am sure.

"Fuck off, both of you," I laugh. "I'll give you each fifty bucks if you can go the whole song without singing along."

"You're on," they both say, but I know my pockets won't be getting any lighter.

I hop back onto the stage where my singing partner and our crowd are patiently awaiting what we will be singing next.

"You ready, sunshine?" I ask Mia.

"I'm always ready." One of her hips is sticking out with her arms still crossed. She has to look up at me to meet my eyes, and the blue hue of the karaoke room somehow makes her even more beautiful. Her lips are pouted, and, if I look too long, I'll become a puddle at her feet.

Instead, I muster up all my strength and tap the tip of her nose with my finger. "We'll see about that." What I want to do is drop this stupid microphone and grab her face in both of my hands and kiss that sexy pout of hers away.

"Ready?" I hear Mateo yell.

"Ready!" Mia and I both answer at the same time.

She drops her jaw, and a laugh escapes my throat when she hears the beginning of the song and the knock. The dialogue between Shaggy and RikRok plays, and any second now the beat is going to drop, and I am going to sing my heart out for the sole purpose of seeing Mia's reaction.

"It Wasn't Me," can only be described as my early 2000's guilty pleasure, and it is one of those songs that everyone knows.

"Alright," I sing before I, and everyone else in the room, sings along. Annie and Drew stand up and come up to stand in front of the stage, and Mia sings with me even though it isn't her turn. Theo and Silas hold their drinks up, and no one is standing still. Even Emmett is standing behind Drew, a hand on her hip, as they move to the beat.

I glance to the back of the room and see Luke and Mateo aren't going to be fifty dollars richer today.

"It Wasn't Me" is also the song I know every single word to, even the Shaggy part that doesn't get as much love as it should.

For the chorus, I gesture to Mia who sings to the audience in front of her before holding the mic to them to repeat that *it wasn't me* echo, and I pull my phone out to take a picture. Mia is literally glowing. She is beaming, and I am sure my face reflects the same. Her eyes are bright, and her cheeks are pink from how much she is laughing.

She keeps singing but noticed I was just watching her

now, so she walks over to me and grabs my hand just in time for me to sing the next Shaggy part. I try my best to sound just like him which awards me with more of Mia's laughs.

By the second chorus, Annie and Drew have joined Mia, and I use it as my escape to watch with the rest of the guys in the crowd.

The three of them sing the rest of the song, and Mateo, Luke, Emmett, Theo, Silas, and I cheer as loud as we can when the song finishes.

Mia, Annie, and Drew take their bows before Mia hops off the stage and runs towards me.

"You!" she says poking me in the chest. "You ditched me!"

"You see me on stage all the time. It was about time you returned the favor," I joke.

"You're the musician, not me," she laughs.

"I beg to differ. You belong up there, baby."

Mia's smile softens and her eyes slightly widen as she looks up at me, and I realize what just slipped out of my mouth. I want to kick myself in the balls because Mia and I are friends who call each other stupid, sarcastic nicknames. Nothing more.

No terms of endearment.

That is not allowed.

An apology is on the tip of my tongue, but Mia doesn't skip a beat. Her smile returns even bigger than before. "Anything for my fans," she says, before she winks at me, and turns to walk away.

She just winked.

At me.

That was *not* fair.

My cheeks flush, but no one can tell with how dark it is. To everyone else, we were just two friends laughing about what we just did up there—sang along to a stupid song, smiling, laughing, having fun. This whole night is just a celebration of what next year will bring for the band.

But to me, tonight was so much more than that.
I am right back to where I started.
Crushing over my best friend's sister.
The one and only girl who is off-limits.
Fuck me.

CHAPTER 26
MIA

GETTING ready for tonight's show is bittersweet, and it's impossible to ignore how much has changed in these three months. Not just what I'm doing and how I'm feeling, but who I am. Three months ago, I was in a constant fight or flight, always on edge and refusing to let myself heal. Three months ago, I punched a guy in the face, and my brother took matters into his own hands, upending my entire life.

Looking back on that night, I don't even recognize myself. There were pieces of me fighting to stay at the surface, but I buried every part of me in hopes that it would help me forget what got me to that place to begin with.

It wasn't until I realized that burying Nico meant burying myself too.

Losing yourself, little by little, is the most heartbreaking thing someone can go through, especially when you don't even realize it was happening.

One day, something terrible happens to you, and you know you will never be the same. The next day, you cry and curse the world, and you wish it was you instead of him. The next day, you do it all again until it is three years later, and you don't even remember letting yourself disappear.

Nothing will ever compare to being with Nico, loving Nico, *losing* Nico.

No one will ever replace him.

And getting myself back doesn't mean forgetting him.

It just means that I will carry him with me wherever I go. I will live because I am here to do it, and I can do it for the both of us.

Three months ago, I finally made the choice to move on. That choice comes with guilt, sadness, anger, and frustration, but it means that I will no longer live in the past.

Three months ago, I never would have told you that I could wake up with a smile on my face after dreaming about the first night Nico showed me the song he was writing for me. The song I wish I could remember, but I can't. The song I will always cherish, and it will always be somewhere in my head along with the memories of Nico.

The smile on my face was also residual from last night.

Three months ago, I didn't have a group of people who make me feel like I am on top of the world. People who fill me up in ways I didn't know possible. People who love and care for one another enough for them to forget the people who don't.

I realized last night that the universe works in mysterious ways, and I am insanely lucky to have walked the path I have walked because it led me to being part of something I never knew I needed.

If you told me back in June that, by September, I would be reminiscing on a night spent singing my heart out in a karaoke bar with seven people who would soon become so important to me, I would have laughed my ass off.

Yet here I am, feeling a lightness to me because I'm not just going through the motions anymore.

I am *enjoying* life again.

Three months ago, that felt impossible.

After finishing our song last night, Eddie and I needed

some space. Not because he did something or because something happened. It was because I was two seconds away from saying fuck the consequences and jumping into his arms and never letting him let me go.

The time I spent with Eddie last night felt like those moments in my hotel room and on our road trip.

Raw.

Real.

Addictive.

Last night showed me that having him as a friend is harder than not having him at all.

But I don't care.

I will keep my feelings in check if it means getting bits and pieces of what it would be like if I was his. I don't know if I could handle having all of him anyway, not because I don't want him but because I just got myself back.

He doesn't deserve someone who can't give him everything.

Walking away from him was for both of our benefits.

I can be strong enough for both of us.

I can keep this line drawn.

As long as it means that I don't have to completely let him go.

The rest of last night, I tried to keep a healthy distance while also subjecting myself to a *healthy* number of glimpses and glances Eddie's way. I didn't even care if he caught me because I was drunk off the night, high on the feeling of knowing that he feels the same way about me, even though we can't do anything about it.

He doesn't have to tell me.

I would actually rather he didn't because I wouldn't be able to hold my ground if I heard the words come from his beautiful lips.

But I know.

I know he feels for me the same way I feel for him.

But he is off-limits.

We all said our goodbyes around midnight, and I walked home on my own. All the non-band members agreed to meet at Lenny's before the show tomorrow, the last one being close enough for everyone to be able to attend. Mateo even said I could leave my camera at home which meant my only job for the show was to enjoy it.

The walk home was quick and easy, only being a few blocks away from Karaoke MKE, and my cheeks were sore from smiling, my voice scratchy from singing, and my heart was full.

I'm hoping tonight is the same.

I take an Uber to Lenny's, not wanting to have to worry about my car tonight. The show tonight is walkable from Lenny's, and the forecast is clear and warm for tonight.

Luke is working behind the bar tonight, but Emmett is closing early tonight so everyone can go to the show.

"Hi, Mia," Luke says, as he makes a drink for one of the men sitting at the bar. Coming to Lenny's so much this summer, I learned who the regulars are relatively quickly. I also learned that the clientele for this bar is the widest spectrum I have ever seen, ranging from just over twenty-one to old enough to be my grandpa, but it works. Emmett has created such a great place here.

"Are Annie and Drew here?" I ask him as I look around the bar. The high-top tables are more occupied than usual, probably because of the bar's distance to tonight's concert venue and because of the weather.

"Not yet," he answers, pouring a Tequila Sunrise for me. It is an inside joke between us because one of the nights I was here when he was working, he asked what my drink of choice was. I was editing photos for one of the other bands I worked with this summer while the band was practicing next store, but I needed a change of scenery. I told him I didn't have one, always opting for a White Claw or whatever white wine is on the menu.

He told me those were boring and spent his shift making different drinks for me until I told him which one I liked best.

Apparently, I'm a tequila girl.

Luke sets the drink down on the coaster he set for me. "Just wait here until they get here," he says.

I look around to see if our usual high-top table is open, but there is a group of girls there. The table way in back is open, probably because it is dark and in one of the corners where Emmett doesn't have a neon sign. "I'll just wait at the table back there."

"Where?" Luke asks before he matches my gaze to find where I'm looking. "No," he denies.

"No?" I take a sip of my drink, instantly feeling the tequila warm my throat as I swallow the alcohol coated with the perfect amount of citrus and sweetness.

"I can't see you from there. Just wait here for them, okay?"

Does this bar have a *you need to be overly protective to work here* clause?

Between Luke, Emmett, and Eddie, you would think us girls were made of glass.

Luke must see my slight discomfort over what he said so he adds, "Eddie would murder me if I let you out of my sight when he isn't here to watch you, and I know how that sounds. Trust me, Annie's catch phrase is 'Fuck off, I can take care of myself', but please? It'll make me feel better." He brings his hand together when he says "please" and throws me one of his million dollar smiles, and I can't say no to him.

"Fine," I conclude and sip my drink as I wait for the girls. Everyone knows my brother is overprotective, but Luke didn't mention him. He mentioned *Eddie* who, I guess, is protective. I have seen his protectiveness come out with him and now knowing what happened with his mom and dad when he was young, but Luke wasn't at the concert to see what happened when that guy grabbed me, and Eddie and Luke don't seem like the type to trade childhood trauma stories.

But what do I know?

I don't have much time to dwell on it because burgundy hair and black skinny jeans appear in the corner of my eye, and Drew comes into focus next to me. She has on a black, cropped Cross My Heart t-shirt.

She hops up on the chair next to mine, and there is a lime White Claw open and in front of her before she even can say, "Hello,"

I turn to see Luke shrug his shoulders before adding, "Boss's orders."

Drew rolls her eyes. "Emmett can calm down. You don't need to drop everything to get me a drink," she tells Luke. "But, thank you."

"Anytime," he says, giving her one of his signature smiles and going back to chatting with the regulars and flirting with the girls coming up to the bar for drinks.

"Annie should be here any minute," Drew says to me. "I hope you weren't waiting long."

"Not at all, just talking to Luke." I stir my drink, mixing the grenadine with the orange juice. My face must still have the confusion from what Luke said about Eddie on it because Drew doesn't hesitate to ask what we talked about.

"It was obviously *something*," she says when I try to tell her it was nothing important. "You can tell me, Mia. If it was something rude, Emmett showed me how to punch."

This makes me giggle because Drew punching someone seems so out of character. "Mateo told me if I punch someone, I have to put a dollar in what he calls the Punching Jar."

Drew lets out a laugh. "I forgot you punched some guy! That was the first thing I learned about you. I knew you were going to fit right in."

Tension releases from my shoulders. Drew has a way of

making you feel like she would never judge you for something. Like how it is with Eddie, I feel like I can tell her anything.

"Luke said something about Eddie," I sigh. "And I don't know how to feel about it."

I turn to see Drew looking at me, not saying anything but silently telling me to continue when I'm ready.

I tell her how about wanting to go sit at a table, but Luke didn't want me out of his sight because of Eddie. I'm ready for her to say something along the lines of Luke being way off with thinking Eddie would care, or how weird it is that he would say Eddie instead of Mateo.

Instead, what she says surprises me even more.

"Luke knows Eddie well. Eddie would never want someone he cares about left alone if they didn't need to be."

"What do you mean?" I ask. Eddie's childhood instantly comes to my mind, wanting to protect his mom and little sisters from his dad, and taking matters into his own hands at eighteen.

"Did Eddie tell you what happened with his parents?"

I nod.

"Well, he carries that with him. *Everywhere.* I've only known Eddie less than a year, but I know what trauma does to someone, both first-hand and as a professional." I know she is talking about the shooting, and I can't help but admire how candidly she talks about it. It truly does reveal how strong she is. "A perceived lack of control over people and events makes someone like Eddie struggle to stay calm. The underlying belief that if they release control, horrible things may happen." She sounds like she is talking from experience, and I can whole-heartedly identify with what she says. As someone who struggles with anxiety, I know what it feels like to not have a sense of control. It sends me into a panic attack, and it can have a different effect on others. It isn't my place to try to diagnose Eddie or project my anxiety onto him, but it might be something worth exploring for him, when he is ready to heal.

"A perceived or real threat to someone he cares about," Drew continues, "it affects him because of what he went through."

"I know how that feels," I say, but it is more of a whisper.

"Me too," Drew adds, and she grabs my hand resting on my leg. "If you ever want to talk, I'm here." She squeezes my hand, and my eyes feel prickly.

"Thank you," I say. "You have no idea how much that means to me."

"I know how hard it can be to do everything alone. Sometimes you need to remember there are people for you to lean on or to lend you strength when you need."

Her words go straight to my heart. "You're right. It can be hard to do it all alone." Not only do I say this for me, but I can't help but think of a specific drummer with green eyes who would also benefit from this lesson.

Drew pulls me in for a hug, and I breathe out a sigh of relief. It feels so good to have a friend.

I feel another pair of arms wrap around us, so we pull back to see Annie between us.

"What?" she asks. "I wanted a hug too." She is wearing jean shorts with a cropped, red Cross My Heart T-shirt. We all agreed we would each wear a different color tonight. Drew has a black one, Annie has a red one, and I'm wearing a pink one.

We all laugh as she sits down on the other side of me. Before her ass even meets the chair, Luke appears in front of her with a gin and tonic, with a bendy straw that he keeps behind the bar just for her.

"Luke," she says.

"Annie," he replies, in the same curt tone as hers. "Still mad at me?" He asks.

"Always," she deadpans.

Obviously, *something* happened between now and last night at the karaoke bar where they were totally fine, but it is getting hard to keep up.

He walks away, and she just shakes her head as if to say *it's not even worth explaining.*

"So," she starts, "obviously, I missed something," she says.

"Oh you know, just your standard Saturday evening trauma-dumping," I joke, even though it is nothing but the truth.

"Without me?!" Annie gasps. "Not okay, girly pops. Start over, from the beginning."

Drew and I laugh at how dramatic Annie is before explaining to her what Luke said to me about Eddie, and she came to the same conclusion as Drew, that he cares about me and he can't help but be overprotective because of what happened to him.

"So, Eddie is open about what happened to him?" I ask.

"No," Annie and Drew say at the same time.

"Not at all," Drew adds. "You saw how he got the one time he overheard Annie and I telling you about our track record with parents. He refuses to talk about it."

"Then how do you guys know?"

"Emmett," Drew answers.

"Luke," Annie answers.

"Makes sense."

"In our defense," Annie adds, "everyone knows that what you tell Luke and Emmett is fair game to us. While Eddie has never opened up about it to us, he knows we know."

"Yeah, we all have had our share of shit, so we all have the shared understanding that we know what each other went through and are there if they need."

"That's beautiful, in a really tragic way," I conclude.

Drew smiles. "The universe sucks, and it always reminds us, but at least it gives us the people we need to get through what it throws at us."

Drew's words stick with me for the rest of the night, along with what she said about Eddie and what happened to him. The more I think about it, the more I hope Eddie knows that nothing is his fault, and that he deserves to heal. He doesn't always have to hold it together for everyone else, he has people who will hold him up when he needs to.

And one of those people is *me*.

We finish our first round of drinks as Luke tells the other patrons that it is last call because Lenny's is closing early. With the heavy crowd, Annie has to step in to help, mostly because she was getting annoyed with the way Luke was running things on his own, so she stepped in to show him how to do everything the "right way." Drew and I do one more round before Annie and Luke get everyone out.

We do a third round and the alcohol makes my face feel fuzzy. Drinks are more expensive at the concert venue, so I don't feel bad heading there with a good buzz because it will wear off by the time Cross My Heart gets on stage.

Emmett meets us at the show having got there early to help the guys with their equipment. They needed an extra set of hands after cutting it close on time with their last-minute practice. They're debuting their surprise song tonight, and they wanted to make sure it was absolutely ready to perform for the first time. I have been hyping it up on their social media, and it got a lot of traction. Fans are excited, and there is a strong sense of anticipation in the air when we get in.

Comparing this crowd with the crowd of the first show is night and day. I would say the number of people here for Cross My Heart specifically has doubled, and the guys couldn't have done a better song creating a setlist that perfectly aligns with the other bands on this tour, helping them dip into those fan bases.

"Have you heard this new song?" Annie asks me over the buzz of the crowd. The guys are supposed to be on any minute.

"No. I don't go to many of their practices anymore, so I haven't had a chance to hear it."

"Should be good. Eddie always kills it," Luke adds over Annie's shoulder. She tips her head the opposite way of his face, but she lets him put his hands in the front pocket of her jean shorts, so I guess they made up.

"Not talking to you," she says, stepping forward to be in line with Drew and Emmett who are standing in front of us.

Guess not.

"Eddie mentioned this song may be a little different compared to their other stuff," Luke tells me. He crosses his arm, and his eyes are on the long brown hair in front of us.

"He did?" He didn't say anything about it to me.

Not that he would seeing that we talked the most time last night than we have in months, and we were most certainly *not* talking about the band.

"Said he had different inspiration for this one," Luke shrugs. "Not that I can talk much on that, I am not musically-inclined."

"Yeah, we saw that last night with your rendition of 'Girls Just Wanna Have Fun' last night," Annie says, turning over her shoulder.

She is good at pretending to be uninterested, but she pays as much attention to Luke as he does to her.

He rolls his eyes and steps forward to stand on the other side of Emmett who is standing next to Drew with one hand in her back pocket. I step forward to fit between Drew and Annie who are talking about how cute the three of us look in our Cross My Heart T-shirts.

Before I can add anything to the conversation, the lights fade and the crowd cheers as Mateo, Theo, Silas, and Eddie walk on stage.

CHAPTER 27
MIA

THE LIGHTS COME up and as the guys get into their positions, I feel my stomach do somersaults. They all have on a black Cross My Heart T-shirt, but each one has their own style with it.

All four guys look fired up, like they're moments away from jumping out of their skin.

My eyes go directly to the drummer.

Eddie is a sight for sore eyes, his bright smile and dark hair perfectly contrasting his tan skin. He has the short sleeves of his t-shirt rolled, showing off his corded arms, and my mouth waters. He grabs his drumsticks from his back pocket before he sits down. I watch his green eyes scan the crowd, not sure what he is looking for, until they lock with mine, and he points at me with one of his drumsticks before giving me a wink.

The world around me spins, and I feel like my movie-moment of locking eyes with the band's heartthrob just came true, and I can now die happy.

"He knows what he's doing tonight," Annie yells to Drew across from me.

"Exactly what he is doing," Drew yells back.

"Excuse me, I'm right here!"

"Are you?" Annie asks me. "Pretty sure you'll need both of us to help you pick your jaw up off the floor." Drew laughs as Annie hits my hip with hers, and we go back to clapping and cheering with the crowd.

Eddie hits his drumsticks together three times, and they start their first song. This is the first time I can listen to the songs without worrying about getting the shot or moving throughout the crowd, and I let myself enjoy it.

Being a part of Cross My Heart has helped me rediscover how important music is to me. I spent so long refusing to let myself enjoy music in fear of what it would bring up. But that is the beauty of it. Music allows you to be taken to the different times of your life, bringing out memories and feelings that you tucked away, and it gives you a space to remind you that you aren't alone. Music reminds me that while the world can feel like it's crashing and burning around me at least I'm still here to watch it all go down.

Annie, Drew, and I cheer on the guys, singing along to every song. I see Luke and Emmett nodding their heads to the beat, cheering every time Mateo says, "Thank you," when they finish a song.

My eyes find Eddie whenever they can, cheering extra loud when I know his eyes are on me. His shirt, as always, comes off before the third song, and sweat flicks off his hair every time he bangs his head down with the beat. His gold chain catches the stage lights, and his arms flex with every move he makes.

He is like a work of art.

Their fifth song tonight is the rock cover of "When I'm Alone" by Post Malone, and I scream the lyrics as loud as I can, not caring that my throat is still sore from singing karaoke last night.

The song ends, and Mateo thanks the crowd. We cheer as

loud as we can, not because of how amazing they sounded, but because we all know what is coming next.

"Okay, this last song," Mateo says into the microphone, "is a new one."

He gestures to Eddie, calling him up to the front of the stage.

Eddie stands up, and the crowd cheers as he comes up to grab Mateo's microphone.

"This next song is a special one. To me, to *us*." He gestures to Mateo, Theo, and Silas. "I wrote it with a certain person in mind, so this one is for her." Mateo scans the crowd until he finds me, putting one hand to his heart and pointing at me with the other, mouthing *thank you*.

Theo walks to his microphone. "Without our girl, we wouldn't be where we are, debuting this song for all of you."

"She made all of you finding us possible, making us look good and putting us out there, showing the world our sound," Silas adds into his.

Mateo takes the mic back from Eddie, "To my little sister, our photographer, social media manager, band manager, tour manager, personal assistant, and anything else we ever need, thank you. We couldn't do this without you."

People in the crowd turn to me, making the tears forming in my eyes even more embarrassing.

This cannot be happening.

Their debut song is for *me*? From all of them?

I clasp my hands together bringing them to my lips because I don't know what to say. I feel Annie's arm wrap around my shoulders, and Drew wraps her arm around my waist.

Eddie takes the microphone from Mateo one last time. "If you have someone in your life," Eddie says, "who brings sunshine even on those rainy days," he pauses, finding me in the crowd again. His eyes lock with mine, and the whole crowd disappears. There is no one besides him and I. "I want you to think of them while you listen to this song, and I want you to tell them how much they mean to you when you see them."

I see Annie and Drew exchange a glance out of the corners of my eyes, but I don't care because my world just stopped, and I will never be the same.

Why does that dedication feel different than the other?

He calls me sunshine, told me how every rainy day needs one.

But there is no way he wrote this song for *me*.

Eddie hands the mic back to Mateo and goes back to the drums. He doesn't look at me again, but I never take my eyes off him. He hits his drumsticks together three times and the next song starts.

And my heart stops.

Annie and Drew are still holding on to me, and I'll have to remember to thank them later because without their support I think I would have fallen to the ground.

I hear Eddie's drumming, and Theo and Silas come in with their guitar and bass. I recognize the song within the first three seconds.

Not because I've heard them play it before, but because it is the song Eddie hummed to me in my hotel room when I asked him to stay with me.

I fell asleep to him humming it to me.

And it is the song that has been stuck in my head.

The song that halts my dreams and haunts my nightmares.

The song I heard in every song I listened to.

The song Nico wrote for me.

Mateo's vocals start, but I can't focus on what he is singing. All I can focus on is trying to breathe as tears stream down my face.

I feel a weight on my chest lift, and the song wraps around me, injecting itself into my bloodstream.

I am in complete and utter disbelief, hearing the song I have been looking for for three years, the song I let go of, thinking I'd never hear it again.

Yet here it is.

And *Eddie* found it.

Giving me the greatest gift I could ever receive.

A piece of Nico I thought I'd never get back.

I hear bits and pieces of what Mateo is singing, lyrics about putting your arms around a ghost and having to close the door on the only love you thought you deserved. He's singing words taken directly from my head, even though I've never shared them. Feeling left to wander alone, stuck wishing you could say goodbye but feeling like they never truly went away.

He gets to the end of the second chorus, holding a note that gives me goosebumps before saying to Theo, "Hit 'em with the riff." Theo comes in with a guitar solo that pumps the crowd up, and then the music stops, and Mateo's vocals are isolated as he sings, *you're still right here with me. I'm stuck in place, can't say goodbye and walk away. I need to let you go.* The instruments start back up again, all building to the final chorus, speaking words that I feel so deep in my skin that they will etch themselves in my bones.

The song ends, and the crowd is silent. A few moments pass before the whole venue erupts in chaos, screaming, cheering, clapping. The air vibrates with all the noise coming from the crowd.

I've never seen anything like it.

Mateo thanks the crowd, and Theo, Silas and Eddie join him at the front, putting their arms around each other and taking a bow. The cheers don't stop even when they are off stage, and it takes me a second to unwrap myself from Drew and Annie who look at me with concern.

I don't have time to reassure them because my one and only priority is finding Eddie.

Every single show after the first one, Eddie always went straight to the merch booth after making me promise before the second show that I would be there when they came out. I'm not working tonight's show, but I still make my way through the crowd to get to the booth.

I don't know what I'm going to say to Eddie, how do you thank someone who gave you something so priceless?

How do you explain to someone that they took the words directly from your head and put them into a song?

How do you tell someone they are the reason you wanted to listen to music again?

I get to the booth, looking everywhere for Eddie. I watch the door that leads to the back, and I wait for what feels like eternity.

My stomach jumps when I see it open, but it's just my brother, Theo and Silas following closely. I make my way over to them, and Mateo's face brightens when he sees me. He pulls me in for a hug, and I forget about finding Eddie for a second and focus on Mateo.

"You were amazing," I say against his chest. He is sweaty and gross, but I don't care. "You guys were amazing! That last song *literally* made the crowd speechless." He pulls back to look at me, and he uses his thumb to wipe a tear from my cheek. His face quickly shifts to concern.

Turning to Theo and Silas, he orders, "You two, go start selling shit."

"No hug for me?" Theo asks.

"Or me?" Silas adds, and I let out a huff of a laugh, and I give them a soft smile, thanking them for being their usual flirty selves with my eyes.

"Now," Mateo grits through his teeth.

They head over to the booth, and Mateo pulls me back through the door he came from. There is random equipment and people all around, so he grabs my hand and leads me to their green room.

"Why are you crying?" He asks when he closes the door to the green room. I look around, seeing an empty couch and chairs surrounding a table with a TV. I thought—hoped— Eddie would be in here, but I don't see him. "Mia?" Mateo prompts, bringing my attention back to him, but I think he already knows the answer to his earlier question by the way he pulls me back in for a hug.

"You weren't supposed to cry," he says into my hair.

"You weren't supposed to dedicate a whole-ass song to me," I argue, and he laughs.

"Mia, you deserve way more than a song." He pulls back and gestures for me to sit on one of the couches. "I never thought making you be my band's photographer would turn into this, and we meant what we said out there. We couldn't have gotten to where we are without you."

"I've never thanked you for hiring me against my will," I say. "I wouldn't be where I am right now without you," I add, alluding to how much has changed since June.

"*You* put yourself together, Mia. Don't let me take credit for that. You did it all on your own, and you should be so fucking proud," Mateo says, and my eyes cloud again. This night was nothing like I thought it would be, from the bar with Drew and Annie, to hearing the guys play Nico's song, to this.

It's all too much for my heart.

"It feels good to be whole again," I say, wiping my eyes, not wanting anymore tears to fall. My makeup is too expensive to be crying it all off.

A few moments pass, and I can't help but ask. "Where's Eddie?"

Mateo looks at me, and I wish I didn't say anything. "Why?"

"I want to thank him," I explain. "For the song. The song you *all* dedicated to me." It's the truth, they did *all* dedicate it to me.

I may have just noticed more weight in a certain drummer's dedication.

"Sure you do," Mateo says, sounding suspicious. "You guys are *just* friends, right? You and Eddie."

"Yes." At least we're supposed to be, but I keep that part to myself.

"Keep it that way," he says in his dad-voice, and I don't argue.

"What did I say about not wanting to bone your friends?"

Mateo groans. "No. No, we are not doing this again."

"What do you mean?" I tease. "You said no talk of 'banging', not boning."

"Stop. He's getting some air outside, I'm sure he'll be back here any minute." He shakes his head, but I know he is trying to keep in a laugh. "I'm going to go help Theo and Silas, so you can wait for him here." He stands up and heads to the door.

He turns around before he opens the door. "No, funny business, Camila."

"Don't call me that. You only call me that when you're mad."

"I am mad," he answers, even though he is totally not and trying to pretend. "Mad that you brought up banging my friends again."

"No, I did not. I brought up *boning*."

"Yeah, yeah, I don't want to hear it. Meet us by the bar in the back, we're all going to watch the rest of the show." He opens the door to the green room and takes a step out.

"Mateo?" He looks over his shoulder. "You know I can take care of myself, right?"

He laughs because I have asked him this before, back when I first started coming around the Cross My Heart's practices before the tour even started. "I know you can," he says. Then he adds, "You are the priority, Mia. I just don't want anyone getting in the way of you taking care of *yourself.*"

I don't get a chance to ask him what he means because he turns back out the door to find Eddie on his way in, muttering "Speak of the Devil," as he steps to the side to let Eddie through.

"Am I interrupting?" Eddie asks Mateo. He spots me, looking surprised to see me back here. "Is everything okay?"

"All good," Mateo says, slapping Eddie on the back of the shoulder, letting him in through the door. When Mateo is out of the door, I hear him call to me, "*Anyone*, Mia."

Eddie closes the door once Mateo is gone, and I pretend to not notice he locks the door.

CHAPTER 28

MIA

I STAND up from where I am sitting, and I walk over to him. Eddie's back is towards me and I stop a few feet away from him.

"Eddie?" He slowly turns to me, and his face says it all. In this moment, I realize why his cheeks turned red when I asked him about the song last night, why he admitted that he wanted me to like it.

The song he was writing was always for me, since the beginning, when they talked about debuting one, the song has always been for me.

There is so much I want to say to him at this moment, but opening my mouth to let the words out feels like crossing a line that we both know needs to stay intact because I know the words will lead to a place of no return.

"Did you like it?" He asks.

I nod.

"You got to give me more than that, sunshine."

"So it's 'sunshine' today? What happened to 'baby'?" I tease. It will always be easy to fall back into where it is comfortable with Eddie, but I know I can't stay in the comfort zone long.

"Sunshine, baby, *mi sol*, which one do you want? Please just tell me what you thought," he begs.

I shake my head.

Can't we stay in this in-between a little longer? Can't we stay in this place we both agreed on? It feels like I'm on a cliff, seconds away from falling, knowing how scary the fall will feel but how long I've been waiting to jump.

"How did you do it?" I ask.

"Do what?"

"How did you take a song from my head? How did you write a song that I have been trying to remember for years? How did you write lyrics as if you read my deepest, darkest thoughts?" I take a step closer to him. "How did you do it?"

"Mia, the second I saw you in the hallway of your apartment, I knew that I would never not be able to look at you again. That's how I did it. I can't help but watch you because you are my favorite thing to look at.

"When you're happy, your smile is so big that you squint those pretty brown eyes in the cutest way known to man. When you find something funny, you tilt your head back and let out a laugh that makes my world go 'round. When you're flustered, your chest turns red, which makes you wearing anything that covers it absolutely infuriating because I love seeing the effect I have on you. When you're focused, you bite your bottom lip and hum a tune that has gotten stuck in my head, and the only way to get it out was to write it.

"You are my biggest distraction and pain in my ass because you have me wrapped around your finger and begging on my knees all at the same time. I know we agreed to be friends, and I know everything coming out of my mouth makes what should be simple very complicated, but these past months, you have become my inspiration, my muse, and you have shown me what it means to go to hell and come back stronger. And now that you're in my life, I never want to know what life is without you."

My brain short circuits because there is so much Eddie just said, and I don't know how to process it. Starting with how he wrote the song, to having him begging on his knees, and everything in between.

There are a million and one thoughts running through my head, and I want to tell him every single one, but my one and only priority right now is crossing that line between us and free-falling past the point of no return.

I grab Eddie's T-shirt that he, *unfortunately*, put back on after the show, and I pull him into me, needing to feel his lips on mine. I hear a catch in his breath as my lips crash into his, and it is nothing like our first kiss.

It is desperate and passionate, like neither of us can get enough. Eddie's hands grip my hips like he is holding on for dear life. His mouth moves against mine, finding a rhythm that makes my legs feel like they are about to give out. His tongue swipes across my bottom lip, asking for access, and I impatiently grant it.

My tongue tangles with his, and a pressure in my lower stomach builds.

I need more of him.

I snake my hands up his chest to find his neck, and I feel his fingers dig into my hips hard enough to leave a mark. My fingers wrap themselves in his hair, and a groan escapes his throat, heeding as my only warning before he lifts me up off the floor. My legs instinctively wrap around his waist, and he turns us so I'm pressed against the door. His body pressing against me is the perfect pressure, and I never want this moment to cease.

His teeth bite down on my lower lip before his lips meet my jaw, leaving kisses along my jawline and down my neck where his teeth lightly graze the sensitive skin before his tongue smooths over. I'm in the middle of a sensory overload, basking in the feeling that Eddie can't get enough of me as much as I can't get enough of him.

His lips are back on mine as he sets me down, my back against the door now, and if he wasn't so close there is no way I would be able to stand. His hands move down my backside, pulling me into him again.

"More," I moan against his lips, not even entirely sure what I mean but knowing that this isn't enough.

His mouth moves from my lips, back to my neck. "More what, sunshine?" I hear in my ear. He squeezes my ass between his palms. "Be a good girl and use your words."

"I want *you*," I half-whisper and half-whine, again, not entirely sure what I mean, but too blind by lust to further explain or care that I'm moments away from begging this man for more.

"What do you want from me?" He asks between the kisses he leaves all over my neck, and I can't hold back a moan as his hands slip from my ass, one lining the skin just above my pants, and the other hand pressing against the door just above my head.

"Touch me," I beg. My hands are on his chest, fisting the fabric of his shirt.

"I think you need to be a little more specific, sunshine." I hear in my ear. "Should I keep touching you here?" His finger continues to trace the skin of my stomach peeking out from my shirt as he kisses my neck, his tongue against the sensitive skin making me go mad.

"Lower," I whine.

"Here?" He asks as his fingers dip into the front of my jeans. He uses one hand to undo the button, moving so slow that I'm tempted to do it myself.

I let go of his shirt and go to unzip my pants, but Eddie stops and grabs my wrists, holding my hands between us.

"What do you think you're doing?"

"You're being a tease," I say, my chest hot, my head dizzy, my heart racing, my skin so sensitive it is almost painful.

"Says the biggest tease of all" he argues, still gently

holding my wrists with enough strength for me to not be able to easily move them but not enough to hurt. "I have waited *months* for this," he adds. "I plan on taking my time with you."

I don't know what to say, so I just stare at him, his green eyes, his swollen lips, the flush in his cheeks.

"Are you going to rush me?"

I shake my head.

"Are you going to let me take my time?"

I nod.

"Good girl. Now, I'm going to let go of your wrists because I'm dying for you to touch me again, but no more trying to take your pants off." He brings his face just inches away from mine. "That is *my* job."

I want to punch him and kiss him and beg him to just shut up and fuck me all at the same time. My mind is spinning. Before I can respond, he brings my hands to rest on his shoulders. He places a hand on my hip and his other hand on the zipper of my unbuttoned jeans and slowly pulls the zipper down.

His lips are against my ear, the warmth of his breath sending goosebumps down my spine. "Are you wet for me, sunshine?" he asks.

"Eddie," I moan. "Please."

"Please what?"

"*Please* touch me."

I feel his smile against my ear. "Only because you said 'please'."

He slides his hand down the front of my jeans, his fingers sliding over my underwear down to the spot between my legs that is begging for his touch.

A groan escapes his throat as his fingers touch me through my underwear, feeling how wet I am. He circles his fingers over the cotton, sending a shockwave through my system, applying a perfect amount of pressure.

Eddie's lips are back on mine, his mouth capturing the noises I make as his fingers slowly bring me closer and closer to the edge, and he hasn't even *fully* touched me.

"More," I say against his lips, and his lips curl upward as he slips his hand into my underwear, finding my clit again.

"You're being such a good girl," he says before he slides a finger inside me, and I suck in a breath. I'm tip-toeing the edge, having not been touched like this in years, and Eddie is making me think I'll never be the same after this. "Now, I want you to ride my fingers until you come," he whispers. "Can you do that for me?"

He doesn't wait for me to respond, starting off slow, the stretching sensation almost being too much. He moves his finger in and out of me before adding a second finger, and my hips begin to move on their own, my body chasing the release it so desperately needs.

"Fuck," I say, a little too loud, so Eddie leans in capturing my lips in his, biting down on my lower lip as I get closer and closer to my orgasm.

He pulls back, and I see his wicked grin and darkened eyes through my partially closed eyes, clouded with need. "Shh, you have to be quiet, baby," he coos. "This is our secret, right?"

I nod and close my mouth, trying to keep quiet. Eddie continues to watch me as I rock my hips against his palm as his fingers glide in and out of me.

"Fuck, you look so good fucking my fingers. Come for me."

His words send me over the edge, and my climax completely takes hold of me, hitting me so hard I see stars. I'm taken to another world, feeling my mouth open, losing control within the pleasure, but Eddie's hand covers my mouth with his other hand muffling my moans as I come undone.

When I come back to reality, Eddie carefully slides his

fingers out of me, and I immediately feel empty. He drops his hand from my mouth, and clarity hits me like a bus as I open my eyes and find him staring back at me.

I hear a knock on the door I'm still pressed against, and it all comes back to me.

The green room.

The show.

The song.

Mateo telling me to focus on myself, not to get involved with Eddie.

And now there is someone at the door.

I quickly unwrap my arms from Eddie's shoulders, realizing now my fingernails were digging so hard into his back that I'm sure I left imprints in his skin.

The knock on the door helped clear the cloudiness in my vision, and Eddie looks exactly like someone still drunk with lust, and I'm sure I look no better. His hair looks exactly how you would picture after having fingers running through it, and his cheeks are flushed.

He runs a hand through his hair, smoothing it down. His lips gather to one side, curling into a smirk. Whoever knocked is probably still there, waiting, and here I am having an existential crisis over what the hell just happened and what the hell I can do to make sure it happens over and over again.

And Eddie is looking at me like he just saw me come.

Because he *did*.

He leans down to whisper in my ear. "Be a good girl, and stay quiet."

My mouth opens slightly, and he doesn't have to worry about a thing because I am left utterly speechless.

Eddie unlocks the door and cracks it to see who it is.

He turns to me and says, "False alarm," before opening it wide and walking right out.

What the fuck did I just do?

PART TWO

CHAPTER 29

EDDIE

A LOT CAN HAPPEN in a year. So much that your life, in some ways, looks the same. Then, in other ways, it does not look even remotely like how it did before. You can go from being a part-time bartender/part-time drummer for a small local rock band to a part-time bartender/full-time drummer for a newly-signed rock band going on their first US tour in less than four months.

You can go from not having the time or energy to worry about anything other than work or the band to worrying about your best friend finding out about you and his sister.

A year ago, I barely even knew Mia. I knew her as Mateo's little sister, and now she occupies my brain in ways I never thought possible.

"You ready to go?" Mateo asks me.

We are getting ready to head to Lenny's to do a small show to kick off the summer and a certain celebration for something taking place as we speak.

Cross My Heart has four months before we go on our first official tour. Before then, we have a handful of local shows to do, and we have a busy-ass schedule with recording and PR responsibilities now that we signed with Thousand Suns Records.

Thanks to all the work Mateo and Mia did last summer, Xander Drake, the tour manager for our upcoming Heart-breakers Tour, introduced us to a few connections he had. Once again, Mateo and Mia worked their asses off, and we signed with Thousand Suns Records this past spring.

"Ready," I call from my bedroom before grabbing my drumsticks and sliding them into my back pocket.

We're headed to Lenny's with our usual crowd plus a few more because we are surprising Drew, who will be newly-engaged by the time we see her tonight, before we play a few songs.

Emmett figured that tonight would be a perfect night to propose just the two of them at their apartment, using the elevator they met in for the proposal spot. Earlier today, I helped him put up a bunch of pictures from their relation-ship all over the inside, and Drew's friend, Lacey, is at their apartment complex making sure everyone takes the stairs for the next hour while Emmett gets Drew into the elevator.

Mateo is worried about being late to the surprise, but I know for a fact that Emmett will be in no rush to get to Lenny's with a bunch of people after Drew puts that engage-ment ring on her finger.

We get to Lenny's with plenty of time before the guests of honor, and we all spend time placing bets on what time they will *actually* be here.

Theo and Silas already set up all our equipment, not that they had to move it far, so we are ready to start the show in an hour. We are still using Emmett's warehouse next door as our rehearsal space, but it is more for old time's sake rather than the need for it.

Now that we signed with Thousand Suns, we have time in a recording studio, but the four of us made a pact when we signed with the record label that we wouldn't forget our roots, and that warehouse is part of our roots.

Annie and Luke are working behind the bar tonight, and they're busy talking with Tyler and Calvin. Tyler is Lacey's partner, and Calvin is Drew's brother. His girlfriend, Emma, is with them too. Tyler, Lacey, Calvin, and Emma join our crew every once in a while, but they don't frequent Lenny's as much as the rest of us.

I look around the bar for the one face I haven't seen yet, the one I look for in any room I walk into.

"She isn't here yet," I hear, and I turn back to the bar to see Annie in front of me.

"Who?" I ask, even though I know exactly who she is talking about.

"Don't play dumb, Ed. You look like a lost puppy anytime she isn't with you."

"You're mixing me up with Luke, and the way he follows you around."

"Good one. Have you been planning that one for a while?"

"I don't know what you're talking about, Ann."

She fakes a gasp. "You don't?" She then smirks at me as she cleans a glass and puts it back behind the bar. "You may be fooling him," Annie nods her head towards Mateo who is standing over by the band's equipment with Theo and Silas. "But, you're not fooling anyone else."

"Mia and I are friends, everyone knows that."

"Do they?" Annie asks before leaving me to tend to a customer.

They should know.

Mia and I are friends.

Friends who have kissed.

Twice.

Friends who have enough sexual tension that makes the room feel like it is about to explode.

Both times, Mia and I have let adrenaline or the heat of the moment get the best of us, and we have made stupid decisions that led us to do stupid things that make things between us even more complicated.

These past ten months, since the night in the green room, Mia and I have been on our absolute best behavior.

We agreed, after she followed me out of the green room that night, that what happened in there would stay in there, and we wouldn't let it happen again.

We blamed the euphoria from the show and the new song, and everything other than our own feelings for each other, and we left it at that.

Now, ten months later, a day doesn't go by that I don't wish I told her I didn't want to be her friend. That I wanted to be more.

But I couldn't do that to her.

I know she would let me be more than a friend. I know she wants it too, but we both know it can't happen. Not only is she Mateo's sister, who has been off-limits since I met her, but I'm also in no shape to be the man she deserves.

I'm the friend she can flirt with and play with because it means I get a few stolen moments where her attention is focused on me and me alone.

How it should be.

No.

But how I want it to be.

It doesn't matter anyway.

I'm busy with the band, and she is busy with her photography business.

We see each other when we can, always with our other friends.

We haven't had a moment alone since that night.

And it is for the best.

Right?

Now that Cross My Heart signed, a photographer from the record label started doing most of our shoots, but Mia is making it big time as an indie band photographer, so it isn't like she has much time for us anyway. She is basically helping other bands do what she helped us do—revamp social media, get them on the map, and then letting them do the rest.

But, she will be coming on tour with us because Mateo convinced our new manager that she is the best person for the job.

Lucky for the band, but not so lucky for me.

Mia, late night road trips, hotel rooms, and songs I poured my heart and soul into.

The perfect mix where nothing could *possibly* go wrong.

A gust of warm air hits my back, meaning the door just opened, and someone is here. I don't hear the "Congratulations" that we all planned to say when Drew and Emmett walk in, and I don't even need to see Annie's raised eyebrows when she shoots a look my way.

I know it is Mia, the scent of lavender and coconut filling the air, before I even turn around.

And this time, like every time before, the moment she is near, my body aches to be near her. She is a constant magnetic pull, her sunshine always making my rain go away, but I bury the feelings down, like I know how to do all too well, and I put on my mask.

My *friend* mask.

And her and I both pretend she can't see right through it.

"Hey, raindrop," she says as she hangs her camera bag on the chair next to mine. The stupid nickname makes my heart skip a beat, and if that isn't pathetic, I don't know what is. I make sure not to show it on my face, and I turn to greet her as she sits. Annie sets a tequila sunrise down for her.

Why does it make sense her favorite drink is as sweet as she is?

The name doesn't escape me either.

"Hey, sunshine," I reply. "Ready for the surprise?"

"Of course," she says, shrugging off her cardigan to reveal the silky, smooth skin of her arms. Her hair is in waves, half tied back and half down. She has two pieces of hair that frame her face perfectly, accentuating her full, pink lips that have a gloss to them today.

That's new.

And not good for my nervous system.

She's wearing the same leather skirt as the first night I saw her at her apartment after Mateo rushed us over there when he found out she punched a guy in the face. The night that started this whole mess I can't seem to shake.

"I'm so excited for Drew and Emmett! I can't believe tonight is finally the night." Mia goes on to explain that Drew has had an inkling about Emmett proposing, but she and Annie convinced her otherwise.

"Didn't know you could be such a good liar," I laugh as she finishes the story about her and Annie making up a customer horror story to tell Drew to explain why Emmett was acting so grumpy and standoff-ish earlier this week. For anyone besides Drew, Emmett being angry at the world is perfectly in-character, so I wouldn't have thought anything of it. But Drew, she was suspicious and knew something had to be up because his usual demeanor is *I hate everyone but Drew.*

The real reason Emmett was extra grumpy that day was because he was nervous Drew wouldn't like the ring he picked out. He decided to not go with a traditional diamond, going with a black onyx stone instead. We all told him it was perfect for Drew, but he only cares what she thinks.

"There is a lot you don't know about me, raindrop. One of those being that, when I want to, I can make you believe whatever I want."

"Is that right?"

"Mmhmm," she nods and smiles, so proud of herself. "I'm

also an excellent secret-keeper," she adds, taking another sip of her drink.

"I'll keep that in mind," I tease. I'm hoping this is one of those moments she can't see right through me because the thought of her keeping all my secrets pleases me in ways it shouldn't.

And I don't need to be thinking of the dirty little secrets I want to keep with Mia.

I cough into my fist, hoping to distract from the heat settling in my cheeks. Annie saves the day, coming over to us to announce that Lacey just texted her saying Drew and Emmett are on the way over here.

Excitement fills the air as we wait for them to open the door. Mia pulls her camera out of her bag ready to capture all the moments of tonight.

The couple of honor walks in. Drew's face is priceless. Her jaw drops to the floor as she turns to look at Emmett who is holding the door open for her. He has a smile on his face that only comes out when Drew is around.

There is a pinch in my chest seeing my best friend so happy, especially after all the two of them went through. Drew and Emmett's story is one that only happens to the best people out there. The people who deserve it.

I know I'll never be one of those people.

We all clap and cheer as the two of them make their rounds, giving hugs and handshakes. When they get to me, I give Drew a hug and shake Emmett's hand. Drew shows her new engagement ring off, and she is glowing. Emmett's eyes are on her like she is the center of his universe, and all eyes are on the two of them.

Except for mine.

I can't take my eyes off the person capturing every moment.

Mia has her camera to her face getting every shot imaginable. She knows exactly how to find the perfect moment to freeze, so it can always stay a memory.

One of my favorite things about watching Mia behind the camera is how she smiles with every photo she takes.

It is at that moment I decide that even the photographer deserves to have her moments captured for memories.

CHAPTER 30
MIA

A LOT CAN CHANGE in a year. In more ways than one, my life isn't even recognizable compared to where it was last June. As Cross My Heart plays the song that permanently altered my brain chemistry in a place that has become a second home with the people who make it feel like one, I can't help but think of how much has changed.

The song Eddie wrote for me still sends shivers down my spine, even though I've heard it more times than I can count. After hearing it plenty over the course of the past ten months, I have honed in on my reactions to it, but there is still always the risk of a stray tear falling whenever I hear Mateo sing the lyrics that are so close to my heart.

The song means more to me than anything anyone has ever given me, and it healed me in ways I didn't even know I needed.

And I owe it all to Eddie.

The man who thinks he is so broken yet knew exactly how to put a piece of me back together.

If I could, I would show all the ways he isn't as broken as he thinks he is.

The night in the green room felt so right and so wrong in

ways that are still confusing to me. Eddie and I are drawn to each other, like moths to a flame, even when we know we are no good together.

But how can something that feels so good be bad?

This spiral of thoughts has become a daily occurrence because we haven't had a moment alone together since that night. We have spent time together, as friends and with our friends, but there is always tension between us.

Not only are we keeping secrets from our friends, and my brother, but we are also lying to ourselves, pretending that we don't have *something* between us, no matter how right or wrong it is.

"You okay?" I hear Drew ask me over the music. Her and I are standing at a high-top table watching Cross My Heart perform. Lenny's is packed tonight, here to support a local band on their way of making it to the big leagues. Drew and I are at the back of the crowd while Annie and Luke man the bar and Emmett sticks to Drew like glue, more so than usual.

"Yeah, I'm all good." My spiraling thoughts showing on my face. I have to talk louder than usual, so Drew can hear me. "Tonight is about you, don't worry about me."

"You looked like you were deep in thought," she says. "Care to share with the class?" She jokes, gesturing to her and Emmett, never missing the opportunity to put her teacher hat on.

I laugh, and for a moment want to tell Drew all about Eddie. The thought of being able to share what is going on, not having to keep it all in my head, is so tempting. But then I remember she is about to marry one of Eddie's best friends. "Not today," I answer, glancing at Emmett.

Drew gives me a questioning look before turning to Emmett. "Hey, handsome. Can you get me another drink?"

Emmett seems reluctant to go but gives her a kiss on the top of her head before grabbing the empty White Claw can she is holding and heading to the bar. Once he walks behind the bar towards the cooler, Drew turns to me. "Spill it."

I glance to see Luke intercept Emmett, so I know I have about two minutes before Emmett tells Luke to fuck off, and he comes back over.

Cross My Heart is still playing, so I lean into Drew, talking right into her ear, and I give her the quickest synopsis of Eddie and I, starting the night him and Mateo came over after I called Mateo at the bar, ending with what happened in the green room and how we decided that we let the moment get the best of us, and it would never happen again. I tell her about the night in the hotel room and the road trip, and I explain how we both opened up to each other about the most broken parts of us, not going into detail about *what* exactly was said.

Drew doesn't get a word in until I finish. I lean away from her ear, meeting her gaze, and her emerald eyes are widened, and her mouth is slightly open.

"Say something," I say as I see Emmett heading back over.

"I figured there was something going on, but I thought it was just a little crush or maybe just physical. I didn't think it was so," she shakes her head looking for the word, "*intense*."

She pauses and lets out a sigh. "Eddie is complicated, and I'm sure you know that. And I know you know what it is like to not want to heal."

I nod, thinking of where I was this time last year. It took me a few months, but I opened up to Drew and Annie about Nico and what happened. I haven't told them about the song and how Eddie wrote it because he heard me hum it. I didn't even realize I was humming while I was deep in thought or working, and I don't think Eddie has told Mateo, Theo, or Silas about where his inspiration came from. Everyone knows the song was dedicated to me, but I don't think anyone, aside from me and Eddie, knows *how* the song was written for me.

Drew continues, "I think that is where Eddie is. He needs someone who gets that."

"What are you saying?"

Before she can answer, Emmett comes back over with Drew's new lime White Claw, and she pulls him down by the arm, so she can whisper in her ear. I can't hear what she is saying over the music, but I see the skin peeking out of the collar of the shirt Emmett is wearing turn a few shades redder than usual, and I instantly feel like I shouldn't interrupt.

Drew gives him a kiss on the cheek before grabbing my arm and leading me through the Employees Only door.

Drew pulls me into Emmett's office and shuts the door behind us.

"What I'm saying is," she continues as if I didn't just watch her flirt her ass off to get her future-husband to agree to let us use his office, "Eddie *needs* you. You guys are *good* for each other."

I laugh, not knowing what else to do.

"What's so funny?" Drew asks, crossing her arm and leaning back on Emmett's desk. His office is small with a desk in the middle of the room, a small couch in the corner, and a whiteboard hanging on the wall with magnets holding the bar schedule, what I assume is stuff for inventory, and some other stuff I can't read. It is minimal and so perfectly Emmett, with no personal touches aside from a note from Drew written on the whiteboard and a photo of them on his desk.

"Hmm, I don't know. Maybe that you *actually* think Eddie and I would work."

"You would. You both have had a shitty hand dealt to you, yet you both are always the first to put a smile on your face."

"Just because you smile doesn't mean you aren't seconds away from falling apart." The words ring true not only for me, and for Eddie, but I know that hit Drew too. Her face softens, and she reaches out to grab my hand.

"We're all seconds away from falling apart, Mia, but that

is why we have people who help hold us together. It doesn't make us any less strong or any less broken, but it makes us less alone."

She squeezes my hand, and my eyes sting.

I want to be that person for Eddie, and the more I talk about us with Drew, the more I feel like it isn't as bad of an idea as I thought.

But, then I remember my brother and how he warned me against getting distracted by anything other than myself, and I have been doing good. It has been months with no panic attacks, helpful therapy sessions, time with friends, doing work I love, and reconnecting with my brother.

I don't want to ruin that.

Mateo has also alluded to Eddie not being good for me, but I can't help but think that is *just* the older brother-protectiveness speaking.

"Drew, I can't."

"Why? Because your older brother said so? If I have learned anything this past year, it is not to let anyone or anything get in the way of being with who you love, even if that person is yourself."

"He's Mateo's best friend."

"Remember what you told me about what your therapist said? To not hyper-analyze every single scenario? Every little decision?" I smile because Drew and I love to compare notes from our therapy sessions, and we are always trying to convince everyone in our friend group that therapy is a godsend. "Here's your chance. I'm not saying Eddie is your soulmate, but you'll never know if you just keep pretending he is just a friend."

I wipe the tear threatening to fall with my free hand, and Drew pulls me in with the hand she is still holding. Her arms wrap around me, as if telling me everything is going to be okay.

"Can I tell you something?" She says into my hair.

"Anything," I answer, and I mean it whole-heartedly.

"I haven't known Eddie as long as Emmett or your brother has, but I have spent a lot of time with him the past year and half." She pulls back, and we drop our arms to our sides. "But I have never seen him look at someone the way he looks at you."

I don't know what to say and I don't think Drew was looking for a response because she hooks her arm in mine and leads us back out to our table where Emmett is waiting for her.

"All good?" he asks, and it takes me a moment to register he is asking me.

"All good."

He gives me a nod before looking at Drew.

"So was that promise a right-now thing or a later-thing?"

"Emmett!" Drew's cheeks flush to match her hair. "Of course it was a later thing."

I can't help but laugh at the two of them, so perfect in so many ways, and I feel so lucky to have been a part of tonight, celebrating them.

Not only that, as Mateo thanks the crowd as they finish their last song, my eyes fall to the drummer who occupies my mind in ways unimaginable, and I am grateful I got the chance to talk to Drew tonight.

Eddie and I are friends.

But I'm ready for us to be *more*.

———

Lenny's has cleared out, so it is just Drew, Emmett, Luke, Annie, Eddie, and me. Mateo went home, and Theo and Silas were meeting up with some friends. I got the chance to meet Tyler and Lacey before they left, and Calvin, Drew's brother, and his girlfriend, Emma. It makes sense for someone like Drew to have such warm, kind people in her life.

The six of us have been spending more and more time together these past few months, especially because four out of the six of us work at the bar.

"Great show," Luke says to Eddie. We are seated at the bar with Luke and Emmett behind the bar. Eddie is to my left, Annie is to my right, and Drew is next to her.

"Thanks," Eddie says, taking a sip of his beer. "And congrats to you two," he holds his bottle up in Drew and Emmett's direction. "The guys and I were honored to play here on your special night."

"Yeah, yeah, yeah. Cross My Heart is amazing. We're so happy for you two. Now, can we talk about the wedding?"

Drew laughs as Emmett answers, "We just got engaged tonight, Ann."

"When are you thinking?" Annie asks Drew, ignoring Emmett.

"I would love an October wedding, small, just close friends and my brother. I don't really want anything big."

"Would your parents come up?" Luke asks Emmett.

Emmett shrugs his shoulders, and I think back to one of the first times I met Annie and Drew, and they told me how this crew doesn't do too well with parents.

"I doubt it. They'll already be in Florida by October, and they don't like to fly more than they need to," Emmett explains. I've gathered that Emmett isn't too close with his parents ever since his sister died, and they are only in Wisconsin for the summer months, or so they say. Drew told me they haven't come home for the past few years.

"Parents complicate things anyway," Annie announces. "Who needs them?"

Luke, Drew, and I can't help but laugh, and Eddie, and even Emmett, crack a smile.

"I could do the photography," I offer.

"Really?" Drew asks. "That would be amazing."

"Of course," I reply. "I would be happy to."

"You got your live music too," Annie adds, gesturing to Eddie who is just following the conversation from the background.

All eyes go to him, and he smiles and nods. "If you want us, we're there," he answers for himself and the rest of Cross My Heart. I know if my brother was here, he would absolutely agree.

"You got your open bar too," Luke says, slapping a hand on Emmett's shoulder. Emmett slowly turns to look at Luke's hand still resting there, and Luke takes his hand off as if Emmett's glare set it on fire.

Annie claps her hands together. "See? It is all coming together!"

Drew looks at Emmett. "What do you think?"

"Whatever you want, sweetheart. I'd marry you right here, right now if I could," Emmett answers. I swoon internally as Annie rolls her eyes.

"You know," Drew begins, looking back towards Annie and me, "we could do this October before Eddie and Mia have to sail off on tour for the year. That is, if you two are willing to use your last summer of freedom to help me plan a whole-ass wedding."

Drew has the summer off, while Annie is starting school to become a veterinarian in the fall. I go on tour with the guys around the same time, so we really do have an open summer. Annie was planning on working the bar as much as she could, but we all spend so much of our time here anyway. I have a few gigs to attend for some of the bands I am working with, but, other than that, I wasn't too sure how I was going to spend my time now that Cross My Heart has a band manager to help with all the administrative stuff I started doing last year.

Annie and I look at each other and shrug.

"I'm in," she says, turning back to Drew.

"Same," I answer.

"We got ourselves a wedding to plan!" Luke shouts, and we all burst out laughing. Luke is always just happy to be involved.

I turn to see Eddie looking at me, and I want to melt into him.

Not only do I have a wedding to plan, but I also have to figure out how to get Eddie alone to tell him that this "just friends" thing isn't working out for me anymore.

CHAPTER 31
EDDIE

TONIGHT IS one of those nights where the smile I have on my face doesn't feel pasted on. Between one of my best friends getting engaged, playing an awesome show, and sitting next to Mia while she talks with Annie and Drew about wedding plans, I feel at ease.

Happy even.

Mia catches me looking at her, and, for a moment, it is just me and her. I reach my arm to rest on the back of her chair at the bar, ignoring the questioning looks from our friends. She turns back towards Annie to continue plotting their summer of wedding planning with Drew, and I just feel *happy* to be here.

Sitting around the bar, Mia by my side, I can forget about all the reasons I'm no good for her. I can forget about her being my best friend's sister, and I can forget that I would risk everything to be with her, if given the chance.

Right now, being friends with her is enough.

"Eddie?" I hear Luke say and I snap back to reality.

"Yeah?"

"I asked if you want another beer."

I glance down at my bottle to see it is empty, and I didn't

even notice I had finished it. The biggest distraction in the world is sitting so close to me, so it is no wonder I have been holding an empty bottle for who knows how long.

"I'm good," I answer. Because I am. I glance at Mia, and I notice her body has leaned more towards me. We're not touching, but I feel her presence all the same.

I'm good right here.

The next hour, Luke, Emmett, and I barely get a word in, and we just listen to our girls as they chat about bridesmaid dresses, catering, and possible venues.

I notice Mia starts talking less and less, and she is yawning more and more.

Her body has relaxed more into me, her shoulder falling into the crook of my arm that is hanging on the back of her chair. I've been careful to let her come to me, not wanting to blur any more lines with her.

But my self-control isn't strong enough to not want *her* to blur those damn lines.

Her ear is a few inches from my mouth, so I close the space and whisper, "Tired, sunshine?"

She nods and yawns again.

"Let me take you home," I reply. She mentioned she took an Uber here, and I hate the idea of her getting into a stranger's car this close to midnight. Luke and Annie moved into a heated discussion about what color looks best against Annie's hair color, which sounds silly but somehow makes sense for them. They can literally argue about anything. Drew, as always, is trying to keep the peace, and Emmett looks about ready to kick us out, so Mia is the only one to hear me.

Too tired to argue, she nods again as she sits up straight causing my chest to physically hurt that she is no longer touching me.

"I'm going to take Mia home," I announce to everyone. My intent wasn't to halt the lively conversation taking place, but that's exactly what happens. Once again, ignoring the looks the four of them give me as I grab Mia's camera bag from behind her chair and loop it over my shoulder.

"Get home safely," Drew says as she and Annie wrap their arms around Mia for the group hug they do anytime they leave each other.

Mia's eyes look like they are seconds away from closing for good as she gives Luke and Emmett a soft smile and wave.

I place my hand on her lower back to lead her outside to my truck, opening the door up for her. She hops up into the passenger seat, and I close the door once she is inside.

"I didn't take you for a truck guy," she says to me as I get into the driver's seat.

"I'm full of surprises," I tease.

"I'm sure you are," she answers, leaning her head back against the seat.

It is a short drive back to her apartment, only about twenty minutes, and the silence is comforting. The radio is playing low, and I have the windows open to let in the summer night air.

When I pull up to her complex, I have half a mind to walk her in, but I know it isn't a good idea. For *either* of us.

So, I don't offer.

"Thanks for the ride," she says as she unbuckles her seatbelt but makes no move to get out of the car.

"Anytime."

She grabs her camera bag from where I set it down by her feet and pulls it onto her lap.

Still in no rush to leave.

"Everything okay?" I ask. It almost feels like she is working up the nerve to say something. Her blonde hair shines even in the darkness of my truck, and all traces of the tiredness I saw at Lenny's is gone.

Suddenly wide awake and looking like she is trying to keep track of all the thoughts circling in her head.

"Yes and no," she answers, and I'm confused.

"Do you want to talk about it?" I ask.

"That's the thing," she starts. "If I talk about it, right here, right now, everything will change."

"Okay," I say, stretching out the word. Even more confused now. Everything will change? For her? For us?

What the hell is she talking about?

She finally says, "I don't want to be your friend." My heart cracks in half. I finally have part of her to myself, and now she doesn't even want that. I want to slam my head into my steering wheel because it would be less painful than this.

I can't let her know the war happening inside of me right now, so I do what I do best.

Pretend that nothing can get me down, the happy-go-lucky part I've gotten so good at playing.

Hopefully good enough that it works on Mia too.

"No worries," is all I manage to say, adding a small smile. I squeeze the steering wheel, hoping she doesn't notice my knuckles turning white.

"You're not going to ask why?" She asks.

"Are you going to tell me?" I argue.

"If you want to know," she answers.

I let go of the steering wheel to run a hand through my hair, just now realizing I didn't put my drumsticks in my back pocket after tonight's show.

"I figured it was just because you like keeping me guessing, sunshine," I try to add a lightness to my voice, even though a heaviness has come over me.

She doesn't play along, so I know she is serious. A few moments pass, and I feel the silence that was comfortable five minutes ago now feels suffocating.

My voice is quiet but sounds so loud in the silent car. "Why don't you want to be my friend, sunshine?"

"It isn't *enough*," she answers. My world stops. "I can't be the only one feeling like there is something more here. Something worth exploring."

There is a voice in my head telling me to shut this down. The same voice that never stops reminding me that I am no good for someone like Mia, someone who is all sunshine. She doesn't need me to spread the gray dreariness of a rainy day on to her. I'm too broken, broken beyond repair.

But there is a louder voice saying this is everything I have been dreaming of for almost a year. A voice that screams so loud it makes my head spin, that we can't keep ignoring how good it feels.

Me and her.

The broken parts of us not feeling so broken when we're together.

"Mia, I'm going to need you to tell me *exactly* what you want because I can't read you as well as you read me."

"Eddie," she says. "I don't just want a friendship with you. I want *all* of you. All the pieces, even the parts you think aren't enough." Her words cascade through the air, making it hard for me to breathe, but in the best way. I want her to say the words over and over again, I want them branded on my skin like the scar I wear across my face because she is everything I don't deserve yet everything I need.

"Say it again."

"Eddie, all those pieces are enough and I want to be the person who shows you that if you'll let me."

"Mia, baby, be careful with what you're asking for right now, because you're making all my dreams come true and I don't know if I'll be able to handle it if this is just you messing with me."

She doesn't answer me. Instead, she brings her legs in and sits up on her knees. I watch as she climbs over the center console until one of each of her legs is resting outside each of mine, and my hands naturally find the tops of her thighs as she locks her arms around my neck. The leather skirt she's wearing rides up, mixing all of these feelings of longing for her in more ways than one hard to keep straight. The bare skin under my palms ignites something inside of me, and I don't think it will ever burn out.

What I do know is I can officially die a happy man now that I know what it feels like to have Mia in my lap.

"No more messing, no more teasing, and no more pretending. I'm in if you're in, raindrop."

I bring a hand up to cup her cheek, and I lean my forehead into hers. There is more I want to say, questions that threaten to ruin this moment, but I decide to save them for another day. "I'm in."

"You sure?" she asks. I know she is thinking the same thing as me. How are we going to make this work? She is Mateo's little sister. He is my best friend. She is off-limits to everyone, especially me.

Despite it all, she is worth the risk. Let it all crash and burn, as long as she is right there with me. "Sunshine, I don't think I've ever been more sure of anything in my life."

CHAPTER 32
MIA

DID I plan on opening this door when Eddie offered to drive me home tonight? *No.*

Am I sure it was the right time? *Also no.*

Would I take it back? *Absolutely not.*

Not in a million years, even though I know the safety I feel in Eddie's parked truck, just me and him in the middle of the night, won't last.

I want him. All of him. Not just the friendship.

But right now, being this close to him, feeling his hands on me and his breath on my lips, I know there is no part of me that doesn't want this.

The questions running in circles in my head threaten to ruin this moment, but I remember what I talked about with Drew, about what my therapist says. I don't have to think of every possible scenario, leading me to the worst-case. I don't have to run through every single way something could end in an attempt to prepare myself for when it goes wrong.

For once, I want to act on impulse.

For once, I want to say fuck the consequences.

For once, I want to believe that things will all work out, even against all odds.

"Sunshine, I don't think I've ever been more sure of anything in my life," Eddie says, and I resist the urge to kiss him with everything I have.

Instead, I slowly move my hands up his neck, feeling the cool, smooth material of his gold chain, knowing he always has it on but not knowing the reason. My hands run up his neck, finding the sides of his face, and I know in my heart that I have never seen a more beautiful man.

A beautiful man who can't hide all of his scars.

Wearing the one that hurts the most on his face.

He doesn't take his eyes off me, his green eyes burning into me, seeing parts of me only he can understand.

I lightly move one of my hands across his cheek, feeling him lean into my touch. His eyes briefly close, and we stay like this for a moment.

My finger, almost instinctively, finds the tip of his scar, starting just below his hairline, the skin lightened and slightly raised. When I move my finger down the scar, his grip on my thighs tightens, and his brows knit together, and I freeze. My hand threatens to pull away, but, just before I do, his eyes open and find mine, watching me.

Allowing me permission to see him, all of him.

And I don't hesitate.

I slowly move my finger down, tracing the raised skin. My finger grazes over his eyebrow and just above his eye. His eyes close for a second as I trace over his eyelid and down his cheek, opening them and finding mine again. Emotion floods me, reflecting what I see in Eddie's eyes. There is hurt, anger, frustration, and sadness, and I feel it all.

"I'm sorry," I whisper, my voice shaking with emotion. I apologize even though it isn't my fault.

"No," he whispers back, shaking his head slowly. His forehead falls to mine. "Don't do that."

"I wish I could take it all away." I close my eyes. Someone like Eddie doesn't deserve to carry the weight he does.

"Don't," he says again. "You're not going to feel sorry for me. You're not going to take on the impossible job of putting me back together. I'm yours, baby, but you gotta take me as I am. There is no fixing someone like me."

"It isn't an impossible job," I answer. I lean back a little, so I can see him more clearly, my hands still holding his face in my palms. "You don't need fixing because you aren't broken."

"Mia, I'm not going to be a burden to you. I refuse to be the person who brings you down. I can't do that to you."

"Eddie," I whisper. This boy has no idea what he is doing to me, and he has no idea how fucking special he is. I want to spend my days showing him how amazing he is, showing him how much the world needs more people like him.

So selfless, so kind, so strong.

We're all broken, in one way or another, but I want to be the person who holds him together because he deserves to see himself the way we all do.

I bring his face to mine, making sure he can see nothing but the truth in my eyes. "You deserve to be taken care of too."

His mouth opens as if to say something more, but nothing comes out. Instead, he tightens his grip on my thighs before moving them up to rest on my hips.

"Let me take care of you," I whisper, and I mean it with everything I have in every way possible. Last time we let ourselves give in to each other, he was calling the shots. And while it was incredibly hot, and the memories are ones I revisit often when I'm feeling rather lonely with no one but my vibrator to turn to, I want my turn to be in control.

His lips are on mine in an instant, one hand finding the side of my neck, the other on my back, both pulling me closer. Eddie's lips against mine feel right. His kiss says the words he couldn't find, and I know there is no going back.

The movement of his lips on mine reignites the fire I felt

all those months ago in the green room, my stomach flipping at the memories. It confirms that these terrifying feelings I have for him are not going anywhere, and it is more than just my body's reaction to him.

I am both scared and exhilarated at the thought.

Our kiss deepens, and the first touch of his tongue on mine makes me feel ready to combust. He pulls me in by the hips, the only thing separating us is the fabric of his jeans and my underwear.

And right now, that is way too much.

Crawling onto his lap in a skirt did not have any ulterior motives, and it did a relatively good job covering me when we were talking. Now, that the talking has ceased, I can see that it may not have been my brightest moment.

I don't have room to care because I feel the need Eddie has for me, and it is the same need I have for him. Pressure blooms in my lower stomach, and the distance between us, no matter how little it is, is too much.

My fingers run up Eddie's neck, eliciting a groan from his throat, and I grab handfuls of his dark locks, in an attempt to pull him closer. My hips move on their own accord, attempting to relieve the pressure budding in any way possible, my composure disintegrating with every swipe of his tongue on mine.

"Mia," Eddie whispers against my lips. "Sunshine, you're killing me."

"Good," I whisper back, feeling his smile against my own. I pull his lips back to mine, rocking my hips against him. I'm rewarded with another groan, and I can't help but love watching him slowly lose control.

For someone who puts on the act that they are all together, so laid back and carefree all the time, having him underneath me, allowing me to be the one in control does something to not only my body but to my heart.

My lips touch his again, and I gently take his bottom lip

between my teeth, and he lets out a tiny gasp as his hips start matching my pace. I kiss his lips one more time before feathering kisses down his jaw, making my way to his neck and loving the reactions I'm pulling from him. Wanting all of them, all at once.

"It's taking everything in me to take this slow with you, but, if you keep doing that, all bets are off."

"Who said we're taking things slow this time?" I challenge, alluding to when he made me come with just his fingers in the green room.

It isn't like we just met. We've known each other for a year.

Tension has been building for months with no talk of what we are or what we want to be until tonight.

I'm done waiting.

Eddie laughs against my lips, sending a shiver down my spine right down to between my legs. He pulls me in, kissing me harder this time, taking my breath away. His hands find my ass, no longer letting me control the rhythm of my hips. He pulls me into him, and I gasp as the perfect amount of pressure hits me in the perfect spot.

I feel his lips curve before he kisses me again, repeating the same move, and I don't even care that we are dry-humping in the front seat of his car.

I have no shame.

He pulls his lips away but his grip on my ass tightens.

"What are you doing to me?" he asks.

"Walk me to my apartment?" I breathe. A minute ago, I was sure I was the one calling the shots, but now? I can't even catch my breath.

"Only to the door."

What?

I lean back to see him more clearly because there is no way he just said that.

"What do you mean 'to the door?'" I ask.

"We can't do this until we talk about how we're going to make this work. Trust me, baby, it is taking all my strength to be the one to say this right now, but you know I'm right."

I do, but that doesn't mean I have to like it.

"Plus, I'm 99 percent sure I'm going to wake up tomorrow morning, and this will have all been a dream," he adds as his fingers graze my cheek, gently tucking a piece of my hair behind my ear.

I want to scream and pull my hair out and kiss every inch of his body all at the same time because he is right.

We do have things we need to talk about before we move forward. But he also never misses a chance to knock himself down a peg.

"I'm the one living the dream, raindrop. You know how many girls fantasize about hooking up with their brother's hot, off-limits best friend. There are books written about this right here." I gesture between the two of us.

"Oh yeah?" He smiles, his hands settling back on the tops of my thighs, which are now completely exposed from my skirt that is basically resting where a belt should be. I should be embarrassed, but I'm not. Being with Eddie is as comfortable as being home.

"Yeah," I reply. "I'm the lucky one, really." I grab his face between my palms and pepper kisses all over his face, adding extra along his scar and on the dimple that made an appearance as his smile widened.

"Plus," I add, "last time you made me come in about five minutes. Think of what you can do with more than just your fingers." I do my best Eddie-wink before I climb off him, demonstrating a not-so-graceful transition back to the passenger seat, and situate my skirt before grabbing my camera bag.

I glance to my left seeing I rendered him speechless, which was my very intention, and the blush on his cheeks is so pink, I can see it in the dark.

Before I can reach for the door handle, Eddie comes back to earth and uses his Edward Cullen vampire-like speed to have my door open and his hand out to help me out of his truck before I can even pull the door handle.

I grab his hand as I step down, but I don't let go as we walk into my apartment lobby. We wave at the security guard in the front lobby and turn the corner to walk to my unit.

The stark difference between the first time we were both here to now is apparent, and I can't help but giggle at the memory of seeing Eddie leaned against my door that night while Mateo was ready to kill me for punching that guy.

"You know," Eddie starts as we pause at the door, letting go of my hand so I can grab my keys. "You were wearing that skirt that night when you came home from the bar." Eddie's mind was right where mine was.

"You remember?"

"How could I forget?"

"That was almost a year ago," I argue. "There is no way you remember what I was wearing. I don't even remember." There was so much going on that night, I can barely remember walking home. Not from alcohol but because my mind blocked it out. I was in a constant stage of fight or flight up until the weeks following that night. There are so many foggy memories from those years. The only clear ones being from the past ten months.

"You looked hot with your leather skirt and your bruised hand." We laugh at the memory, and it feels good. Healing. To be laughing at a moment that is arguably my rock bottom, the straw that broke the camel's back, just shows how far I've come.

"I remember *everything* about you," Eddie adds. He leans his body against the door frame as I open the door to my apartment and step inside. "You like iced vanilla lattes with oat milk, the color pink, you don't like to wear shoes." He lists off these facts about me, holding up a finger with each one as if to show me he could go on and on.

"Wow. So observant, raindrop," I applaud. "You deserve a gold star, you really do," I tease, also ignoring the fact he said the last fact about me as I kicked off my shoes.

I turn to see he is still standing in the hallway, now leaned against the inside of the door frame. "You're really not coming in?" I ask as I unloop my camera bag from his shoulder.

"Nope," he replies, emphasizing the "p" sound. "The things I want to do to you right about now are clouding my judgment, and it is taking everything in me not to come in and rip your clothes off," he explains so matter-of-factly, and my chest reddens at the thought of what those things may be and how they involve me naked. I have the urge to ask him to elaborate, but he continues before I can interject. "I can't do any of those things until we talk about us."

Us.

The fact that there is an us, and hearing Eddie say it, gives me goosebumps, causing me to forget the dirty thoughts that evaded my mind just seconds ago.

Finally, Eddie and me.

Us.

"I would like to set the record straight that we have done *some* of those things already, so what's the harm now?" I ask, crossing my arms. I know I'm being difficult, but he always seems to bring it out of me. Challenging him, teasing him, flirting with him, this is how this whole mess began.

It is also what blurred the lines.

He chuckles, clearly seeing that I'm just being a brat. "Let me rephrase then, sunshine," he says. "We will not be doing any of those things *again* until we have talked about *us.* Got it?"

"Got it," I conclude, rolling my eyes. I set my camera bag on the counter of my kitchen, smiling at that word again.

Us.

But is it too good to be true?

There is a lot we have to talk about.

For one, how the hell are we going to make it work?

I knew leaving the truck would cause reality to set in, and that is why I didn't want to get out.

Mateo has made one thing very clear, and that is he isn't okay with me being anything more than friends with Eddie, but I can't help but think there is more to it.

There is no one more loyal than Eddie, and I know he would never want Mateo to feel uncomfortable or betrayed if Eddie and I are together. I would never want Eddie to prioritize me over my brother, but how will he balance the two?

And what if we don't work out? What if this is all just a big mess that will ruin not only my friendship with Eddie, but Mateo's too?

Mateo is all I have, and I can't risk losing him, but I also don't want him to lose Eddie or Eddie to lose him.

Eddie has become so important to me, and he knows me in ways no one else does.

Plus, what about our other friends? Annie, Luke, Drew, Emmett . . . we can't make them choose sides if we don't work out.

And the band? My work with Cross My Heart? Mateo might hate me and fire me, and I'm not going to make Eddie choose between me and the band.

Eddie and I don't even know what *we* are.

Am I even ready for this? My last relationship ended against my will in the worst-possible way and I barely recovered.

If I try the whole relationship thing again and it doesn't work out, will *I* be okay?

I know I will fall for Eddie. Hard.

Because I already have.

"Whoa, whoa. I see the wheels turning, sunshine. Come back to me," he says.

"What?" Eddie is now right in front of me, using his vampire-speed again because I didn't even notice he closed the space between us until I felt his hands on my cheeks.

He gently angles my head up towards him so I'm no longer looking at his chest.

"I can tell when your mind starts racing, you go quiet, and I can almost see the thoughts spinning around in your head. Tell me what you're thinking?"

I sigh, letting out a humorless laugh because *of course* Eddie can tell when I'm spiraling. He is full of shit when he says he can't read me as well as I can read him.

"I think we should keep things between us. For now. Until we figure out what *we* are."

Eddie ponders for a moment, his brows knitting together, repeating my words in his head. Realization must hit him as to why I think we should keep things a secret for now because after a second or two, his face relaxes, and he gives me a soft smile, and he drops his hands from my face.

"You don't want Mateo to find out?"

I let out another sigh, bigger this time. That is part of it. A *big* part of it. "I just don't want to cause issues between you two or between me and him or us and our friends. Mateo's the only family I have and you guys are best friends. If we keep things between us there is no risk of anyone having to pick sides." I don't tell him about my thoughts about Nico. I think of Nico often; I always will. But bringing that up now will only complicate this already-complicated situation.

Eddie nods, and I can tell his wheels are turning too, but I know him well enough that he will keep it to himself.

Something we definitely need to work on.

"Whatever you want, sunshine," he finally says. "But, I want you to know, I'm all in. I told you before, you saying you wanted me made all my dreams come true. I'm yours, and I want nothing more than to shout it to the world, but if you want to keep things a secret for now, I'll do it." He wraps his arms around my waist, pulling me into him and taking my breath away. "You'll just have to let me know when you're ready."

I nod, forgetting how to form words at his admission.

"The last thing I want is to come between you and your brother or you and your friends. I told you, I'm not going to be a burden to you. You're taking a chance on me, and I'm going to work my ass off to show you that it wasn't wasted."

"Eddie," I start. I want to tell him that I don't see him the way he sees himself. The picture he paints of himself, the one he convinces himself that is the *real* him, is a construed version built from years of unresolved trauma and unfinished healing and putting everyone before himself.

Something else we need to work on.

But none of it leaves my head because he continues before I can say a word.

"And one more thing, while we're 'figuring things out,'" he adds. "Even if I can't show it, you are *mine*. No one else's." He pulls me in for a kiss that makes my head spin. His lips moving against mine reignites the *need* for him that sparked in his truck, and honestly way before that, but he pulls away before I can wrap my arms around his neck and bring him to my bed. "And don't test me, sunshine."

"What?" My lips feel tingly with the aftermath of that kiss, and I don't even know what he is talking about.

"If I see someone's else's hands on you, or even their eyes on you for too long, no matter where we are, I don't care who sees. I will make it known that you are *mine*."

He smirks and taps me on the nose with his finger before turning to leave me standing in the middle of the apartment, speechless.

CHAPTER 33
EDDIE

ASK me how I feel about keeping Mia a secret and I can't say that I'm in love with the idea. While I get the intention, her wanting to figure out what we are before we possibly cause Mateo to go into cardiac arrest, I don't like it.

I've waited for Mia for months, wishing she were mine since I realized how well she fits into this mess I call my life, and when she said she wanted me. *All of me.* I was done for.

No more telling myself I can't have her because I *can*.

She's *mine*.

Even if I don't deserve her, I've been saying for months now that I am too selfish of a man to deny myself of her for any longer.

Her perfect lips, her insane legs, her heart-stopping hips. I need her, and a part of me regrets stopping things between us in my truck.

I know it was the right thing to do, but she has the power to turn me into a mess of a man.

With the tour not starting until mid-October, we have the next three and a half months to prepare. With only a handful of shows and some PR stuff for the label, my schedule is wide open.

I plan on filling it with as much of Mia as possible.

Over the next week, I fall into my new routine. Working at Lenny's during the week for most of the day shifts and band practice four nights a week. I don't have time to sneak over to Mia's until the following weekend, and I'm headed over there late, having just closed Lenny's because Annie and Luke are fighting again, so I took her shift with Luke tonight.

Initially, Mia wanted to go to a movie, her love for movie theaters being a fun fact I recently learned about her. All week she was sending me texts teasing how it felt like we were going on a first date.

It was innocent and fun until I asked her if we could make-out in the back row.

But since I had to close tonight, we decided to recreate the movie theater feel at her apartment tonight instead.

As I walk up to her complex, I can't ignore the nerves bubbling in my stomach. This is the first time Mia and I will be alone in her apartment since deciding being friends wasn't enough.

In my mind, we're together. I have no doubts.

In my mind, she is mine. My girlfriend. My better half.

But I know she is still "figuring things out."

I'm just hoping she doesn't change her mind about me being enough for her.

I know I'm not and I know I never will be.

To be honest, I know it is just a matter of time before she comes to her senses, so that is why I plan on taking every advantage of seeing her, spending time with her, being with her as much as I can, because I know it won't last no matter how much I want it to.

I knock on her door and I'm greeted with Mia's freshly-washed face and her silky pajama set that barely covers the parts of her I am dying to have my hands on. She just got out of the shower, and I know because her usual scent of lavender and coconut is much more intense than usual.

I love it.

I can't help but wonder which is her body wash and which is her body lotion.

And the fact this thought is going through my brain shows what this girl has done to me.

Even though Mia lives alone, and Mateo is probably asleep or out with his work friends—not to mention I am an adult who can do whatever the fuck I want—I still feel like I'm resorting back to my teenage years and sneaking into a girl's house when her parents are sleeping.

There is this feeling of excitement of sneaking around with Mia, but also a lot of guilt that comes with it. Guilt over lying to Mateo but also that Mia is more than a dirty little secret.

I want to be hers more than I want her to be mine. I want everyone to know how fucking amazing that makes me feel, letting me forget for a second the piece of shit I am. I want her enough that I'll do whatever she wants when it comes to telling everyone about us.

"Hi, raindrop," she says as I walk into her place. Knowing it is just her and me, and our time together has an expiration date, I don't waste any time. Pulling her into my arms, wrapping my arms around her waist, bending down to nuzzle my face in the crook of her neck and shoulder, I feel any negative emotion fade away, the guilt, the worry, and the anger that is always just below my skin. All tension evaporates, and having her in my arms is incredibly addicting.

Her hair is piled on the top of her head, exposing her neck, and I can't help myself.

"Hi," I say before my lips meet her neck, eliciting a hum from her that goes straight to my dick. The door has barely closed behind me, yet I already feel my body warm and my head go to last weekend in my truck when I was seconds away from flipping her over the center console and fucking her right there.

The way she runs her hands up my arms, wrapping

around my neck, the way she runs her teeth over her bottom lip, I think she's right there with me.

"I missed you," she says.

"I missed you too," I reply, settling my hands on her waist. "If I had known how hard it was going to be to find time to see you, I would have forced you to take a chance on me last summer." The amount of time we spent together last year is astronomical compared to now. Last year, Mia was there for all the practices and shows, and everything in between. So many nights alone in a hotel room *wasted* when I could have been sneaking into her room.

I snuck into her room that first night, and the scene was far more PG than the scenes I'm visualizing now, but I wouldn't trade that night for the world because she opened herself up to me. It got us to where we are now.

Mia rises onto her tiptoes to place her lips on mine. Her lips fit mine like they were made for me, and I don't know how anyone else will ever compare.

She pulls back, too soon, and my gaze drops to her chest, reddening by the second.

"You wear your emotions on your chest. That's not fair."

She looks down before rolling her eyes at me and turning around to head to the couch. "Life's not fair, raindrop. Plus, I love seeing you blush."

My eyes are on her ass as she walks away from me, peeking out from the bottom of those silk pajama shorts.

She's as distracting as ever.

Of course, she likes when I blush, she's usually the reason for it. She gets the advantage seeing the reaction she pulls from me. She gets to hide hers with a T-shirt or hoodie.

Instead of sitting down on the couch, she sits down in front of it. The lights of her living room turned off, candles lit, and blankets and pillows on the floor. I was so focused on her when I walked in, I hadn't even noticed.

She turns to me, tapping the space next to her.

"What movie are we watching?"

"Well, I figured we could decide together," she says, grabbing the remote to turn on the TV.

"You're going to let me have a say?" I feign surprise. "That's a first."

"As long as it is one of the *Twilight* movies," she adds.

"Never seen any," I admit.

Mia looks at me as if I just admitted to committing murder.

"What?" I say. How did I already fuck something up with her?

"You've never seen *any* of the *Twilight* movies? Don't you have sisters?" My sisters liked the movies, and I remember driving them to the midnight premieres when they were in middle school, but I always just dropped them off and picked them up after.

"Yeah, but I still have never seen them. I've heard you and Drew talk about them though." Drew and Mia immediately bonded over their love for the *Twilight* movies early on in their friendship. One of the nights I was bartending last summer, the girls were there catching each other up on their weeks, and I had to listen to Mia, Drew, and Annie argue which of the five movies is the best. Drew said the last one; Annie said the first one; Mia said the third one.

"That is about to change. What time is it?" She taps her phone sitting on the ground next to her. "Okay, the run time of all of them is probably just under ten hours, and it is 10 p.m. now, which means we won't have time to do all of them in one night, so we will do the first two, maybe three tonight, and then you'll come over tomorrow night and we will watch the last two."

I try to suppress my smile, but I don't do a very good job.

"What?"

"Nothing," I reply. "I didn't know you took your movie-watching so seriously."

"I don't. I take *you* watching my favorite book-to-movie franchise seriously." This time, I don't try to hide the grin on my face because this makes me happy.

And I don't know why.

Maybe it is because it means she wants to let me know her more, and that is all I want. What Mia doesn't know is that I take *everything* seriously when it comes to her.

"We better get started then."

Mia smiles, turning on the movie, and pulling the blankets on top of us. We spend the next six hours watching the first three movies, one after another, and I can't say these films are ones I would pick as my favorites, but then again, I would watch her favorite movies with her over and over again as long as it made her happy.

I'm lean back against the couch and Mia is leaning on my chest. If I look down, I can see her, watching so intently, and I find myself focusing more on her than the TV.

What I learn about Mia through watching these movies is she likes to talk about what other work the actors in the movies have done, and she likes to share what is different compared to the book and the movie.

Watching movies with her may be my new favorite pastime because she *feels* everything. She laughs out loud at the funny parts and cries at the sad ones. Her brow furrows, she bites her lip along with the characters when they're stressed or confused, and, even though she has seen the movies dozens of times, she watches as if it is her first time.

There is something about it that is refreshing, seeing her so *in* the moment rather than so *in* her head. It is similar to when she is taking photos.

Her mind isn't racing. She isn't trying to catch up to her thoughts.

We get to the end of the third movie and I don't want the night to end, even though it is late and I have to be at Lenny's early tomorrow to help Emmett go through some job applications. Since Annie starts veterinarian school in the fall, we have to find someone to replace her by the end of the summer.

The thought of leaving right now though, leaving the comfort of the cozy blanket and having Mia wrapped around me. Sometime towards the end of the second movie, she shifted from sitting up and leaning back against me, to resting her head on my chest and hooking her leg around mine. My arm is resting on her back, and her arm rests across my stomach.

"This is my favorite part," Mia whispers, just as the characters on the screen have their final interaction. The last scene ends, and Mia lets out a gasp as if never seeing it coming, even though she told me when *Eclipse* started that it is her favorite movie of the series.

The credits begin to roll, and I feel Mia begin to press herself up from my chest, but I use my arm around her to keep her close. The air around us thickens, knowing that our night together is over, that it is time for me to go, but it feels like I just got here.

CHAPTER 34

EDDIE

NERVOUSNESS BLOOMS in my belly at the thought of *how* to end tonight, what could be considered as our first official date.

As the credits fade out and the TV goes back to the home screen for the streaming service, Mia turns her body, so her head is resting on my lap, and she is looking up at me.

"Tired, sunshine?" I ask, already knowing the answer. While she looks tired, that look in her pretty brown eyes says otherwise.

She slowly shakes her head, her blonde hair contrasting against my black joggers. My white hoodie feels suffocating all of a sudden, my body heating at the way she is looking at me.

"What did we say about using our words?" I tease.

"No," she says, sitting up. I watch as she slowly moves in her stupidly silky pajamas. She sits up on her knees, never taking her eyes off me, and I feel like she is the predator and I'm the prey. Her movement is so slow, almost calculated, as she straddles me, my hands naturally finding her hips and hers find the back of my neck.

She leans in, and I'm dying to have her lips on mine, but

when I close my eyes, my lips remain untouched. Instead, she leans in further, pressing her soft, pink lips to my forehead, making my chest tighten at the affection. I close my eyes, and she kisses me again, this time more towards the top of my scar, and I have to stop myself from flinching.

The scarred skin doesn't hurt, the pain of how I got it hurting much more than the actual injury, but it is always the reminder that it is there that stings.

I sit still, trying not to tighten my grip on her hips too much, not wanting to hurt her, but a lot of emotions are coming up for me, faster than I can keep track of. The same thing happened that night in my truck.

She lightly kisses the lid of my eye before she leaves a kiss on my cheek, and I let myself let go of a breath I didn't even realize I was holding on to. As the exhale leaves my lips, so do those feelings of discomfort. My mind clears, and I remember that I'm not back at that night, the night that everything for my family changed. The night my anger took control of me, and I almost let it kill my father.

I remember that I'm with Mia, in her apartment, with her in my lap, giving me all her attention, and I don't ever want to take advantage of the time I have with her, especially because I know it is limited.

She kisses my cheek until she gets to my lips, placing a feather-light press to my lips before she continues her journey down my jaw, finding my neck. Her intent changes the moment her lips are on my neck, swiping her tongue against my skin, and I instantly feel like something inside me comes alive.

Something strong.

Strong enough that it might be able to pull all the broken pieces of me back together.

I take in a sharp inhale as she leaves a warm trail of kisses up my neck so hypnotically slow that my head starts to spin, the mix of emotion and pleasure beginning to take over my thoughts, and now all I can focus on is the growing need to have her. All of her. Now.

Mia twists her fingers in my hair, using her grip to gently pull my head to one side, giving her more access to my neck. I slide my hands from her hips to her ass, pulling her into me.

I want her to *feel* what she is doing to me.

Her lips make their way to my ear, whispering in a way that somehow makes me harder than I already am

"Are you going to let me take care of you tonight?" she asks.

Both my dick and my heart are no match against her.

She has no idea how crazy she is capable of making me.

I want to say yes to her, so badly, and it would be so easy to.

Not only do I know that I will forever give her whatever she asks of me, but she is the only one who has ever made me feel like it is okay to not have it all together, despite the voice in my head telling me that I have no other choice.

Mia on my lap, her lips on my skin.

I want nothing more than to forget that *I'm* the one who is supposed to take care of her, the one who isn't supposed to be a burden or someone for her to worry about.

At least just for tonight.

"Baby, my place in this world is underneath you," I say, my eyes still closed but still solely focused on her. "I'm all yours."

I feel her lips curve into a smile against my ear. "That's exactly what I like to hear." I tighten my grip on her ass, the silk bottoms leaving nothing up to the imagination. "Take off your hoodie," she demands, rocking her hips into me.

"What's the magic word?" I manage to say, most of my attention on the way her hips always seem to move as if they were made for me.

She should know by now that I like to hear what she wants, for more reasons than one. The first, and most important, is I care, never wanting to do anything she doesn't want me to. Second, and the more selfish reason, is it is part of me to want to be in control, to take charge, and be the one calling the shots. That is the case for all aspects of my life.

It is what I know, it's how I function. I don't know any other way.

"Now," she says in my ear and my world changes forever. Expecting "please" to come out of her mouth was my first mistake with Mia. It is what I thought I wanted to hear.

But, no.

This girl. *My girl.*

Infuriating. Frustrating. Devastating.

In all the best ways.

Ways that ruin me and rebuild me all at the same time.

I can't help but let out a huff of laughter. "Excuse me?"

"You heard me, raindrop. Take your hoodie off. Now."

Maybe being in control isn't all that great after all.

"Your wish is my command, sunshine." She leans back, so I can take my hoodie off over my head. I let the shirt I have underneath it come off too, throwing both off to the side.

I lean back against the couch, and I can't stop my hands from finding the bottom of her pajama top that is just *begging* me to take it off. I slide my hands to feel her smooth skin against my calloused palms, slowly sliding her top off. "Your turn," I say.

She shakes her head. "I don't think so."

She grabs my hands and sets them back down on the tops of her thighs.

"But that's not fair." Her brown eyes somehow glowing in the darkness of her living room. The candles lit accentuating the specks of caramel, like stars in the night sky.

"Patience, Eddie," she teases, leaning in to leave a line of kisses across my chest, and I feel myself losing control with every one, my grip tightening on her thighs.

"I'm a patient man," I explain. I waited for her for a year, but that patience is gone now knowing I can finally have her. "But, if you keep doing that, and you're going to be bent over this couch with those stupid little shorts ripped to shreds."

Her teeth scrape against the skin, and a shiver runs through me. "Promise?"

She is going to kill me.

She kisses her way up to my lips before finally placing her lips on mine, kissing away the anticipation and confirming that no amount of time with her will ever be enough.

Our kiss deepens, her tongue dancing with mine, fighting for the control I'm finding that I will easily give up to her. Her hands move up my bare chest, and wrap around my neck.

She pulls me in, but it isn't close enough.

My hands find the bottom of her top again, but this time, she lets me lift it off her, breaking our kiss to pull the top over her head, throwing it to my pile of clothes and adding some green to my all-white pile.

I take a second to take in my view. It is one that will be hard to top. Mia's swollen lips, the beautiful mess of her hair, confidence radiating from her as she sits on my lap, her body on display just for me.

Her chest has a pink hue to it, and I feel like I won the lottery seeing the slight flush in her cheeks too.

"You're so fucking beautiful, Mia." My throat feels dry as I get the words out, but it is just a reflection of how bad I have it for this girl. She has the power to take the breath right out of me.

No.

It is more than that.

Because I would willingly give her my ability to breathe if she wanted it.

My hand wraps around the back of her neck, and my lips find the skin just under her jaw. I return the favor of lining her neck with open-mouth kisses, feeling a surge go through me with every moan she makes.

I kiss my way down her neck to her chest, feeling the warmth of her skin elicits a groan from my throat as I use my tongue to draw feathery light lines.

"How do you taste so good?"

She hums, no words leaving her lips. I lift my eyes to see hers are heavy-lidded, watching with an intensity that is so strong, so intimate.

My hands find her tits, perfectly fitting in the palm of my hand, and the rocking of her hips is deeper, the fabric of her shorts and my joggers being too much of a barrier.

I move my hands from her breasts, down her tight stomach, finding the top of her bottoms, and I line my fingers under the elastic.

"I think it's time to take these off."

"You first," she demands.

Her hands find the tie on my pants, and she makes quick work of it, a new sense of urgency in her movements.

When her fingers glide under the waistband of my boxers, I lift my hips to let her take them off me, knowing there is no stopping, no going back now.

Tonight, Mia is showing me I'm *hers* and it is the only thing I ever want to be.

Mia lifts on her knees, breaking the connection for a moment, and helps me slip my pants and boxers off. I kick them off, and I am completely exposed to her.

The only thing I have on is my gold chain that I never take off, and Mia is still partially clothed. The feeling of being completely at her mercy is the freest I have felt in years.

Her eyes on mine, that intense gaze, fills me with anticipation, and it takes everything in me not to rush this.

She wanted control, and she is the only person I have ever given it up to willingly.

Her hands find my erection, and I watch as she looks down to watch herself work. Her hand moves up and down, and I am already seconds away from *really* embarrassing myself.

She still has her bottoms on, and her ass is resting on my thighs as she works me up and down.

A hiss escapes my lips as she swipes the bead of pre-cum with her thumb against the tip, and I can't keep my head from leaning back against the couch, closing my eyes and feeling her every move.

I feel her shift in my lap, and in seconds, she replaces her hand with her mouth, switching positions seamlessly as she nudges my legs open, finding her space between them.

It is almost too much.

"Goddamn, sunshine." I can't stop my hips from lifting to meet her with her every move, and she hums with pride as I slowly melt beneath her.

I bring my head up, opening my eyes because this is a view I *never* want to forget. Mia is on her knees, bent in front of me in a way I have only dreamed of. Her blonde hair is splayed across my lap, and I gather it all in one hand to get a better view.

"You look so good, baby." Her pink lips wrapped around my cock is enough to send me into a frenzy, pleasure clouding my vision as I pump my hips to meet her every move, matching the rhythm she determines. My grip in her hair tightens, and she moans around my cock, sending a vibration that threatens to push me over the edge.

Her tongue swirls on the sensitive skin on the underside of my shaft, and she takes me so deep that I worry about hurting her. I try to slow my hips, shallowing my thrusts, but she doesn't let me.

For a moment, I'm worried my loss of control will be too much for her until I see her other hand is hidden in her pajama shorts, and I lose it right there.

My hips pump into her mouth, growing in speed, and my

girl meets me every step of the way. She moans against my cock, and her loving this does something to me.

"You're such a good girl, Mia. Taking all of my cock." She hums in response, and I use my grip in her hair to allow myself to take over. She set the tone, but I can't help but take over the rhythm. "You're loving this, aren't you, sunshine? Is that pussy of yours dripping while I fuck your pretty little mouth?"

Her hum of agreement hits me hard and I come undone.

"Fuck," escapes my lips as I chase my release, shamelessly pumping in Mia's mouth. My heavy-lidded eyes catch her moving the hand hidden in her pajama shorts moving faster and faster, sending aftershocks of pleasure through my system.

She moans around my cock as she sucks me dry, and I use my grip to pull her up, bringing her to me. Her lips are on mine, and my possessiveness rips through me with the taste of me on her.

I kiss her hard, reaching down to rip her pajama bottoms down, with the intent to replace my hand with hers.

"You loved sucking my cock so much that you couldn't help touching yourself? Baby, I don't think you know what that does to me."

"I think I do," she says, smirking against my lips. "I think I have a *very* good idea of how much you liked it."

"You want to know what I think? I think it's time I finish the job. You've done such a good job taking care of me tonight, but it is my turn to take care of you."

Her skin against mine is enough to wake my dick up, and I know it won't take long until it is ready to go again.

What is it about this girl that has me completely insatiable?

I switch our positions, sitting her down where I just was and sit back on my knees.

I didn't know what I was talking about before.

This is my favorite view.

Mia is sitting with her back against the couch. I never thought our cozy movie spot would turn into the place where my dirtiest fantasies would come alive.

Her hair is a mess from having my hands all over it, and her lips are swollen. Her cheeks are the softest pink, and her eyes are on me as I take her all in.

Her perfect tits are on full display for me, and I can't help but lean in. My lips find her nipples, swirling my tongue over the sensitive skin. Mia moans, grabbing one of my hands and bringing it to the spot I have carelessly neglected until now.

"Please," she whines, and I realize she is already so close, and I've barely even had the chance to touch her.

I nip, lick, and suck on the skin of her breasts, leaving marks in places only *I* get to see.

I slide my finger down, and she jolts when I lightly touch her clit, slowly circling the spot as I take her other nipple in my mouth. I groan at how wet she already is, and one of her hands finds the back of my head, her fingers knotting into my hair.

"Eddie," she whispers, and I can tell by how she moves her hips and presses my head against her that she is closer than I thought.

"Not yet, sunshine," I say against her sweet skin. My breath eliciting goosebumps across her chest. "Let me taste you first."

She lets out a sigh as I settle between her legs, looping my arms under her thighs, opening her up for me, and making sure she stays put.

"I've been dying to know how you taste, sunshine," I say against her inner thigh, leaving light kisses until I'm at the spot she wants me most.

My girl does a good job of letting me take my time, but I give her what she wants as she whines my name again followed by a plea.

"Okay, but only because you said, 'please.'"

Giving her what she wants is what I was made for, so I dive right in. My tongue finding her clit, circling slowly but growing in speed. I lightly suck the sensitive skin, before lapping her up like a man dying of thirst. She writhes beneath me, fighting for control, but I hold her hips in place, not letting her rock them against me just yet.

"You taste better than I ever could have imagined, Mia. God, how the hell do you taste this sweet?" I swirl my tongue around her clit before letting go of one of her thighs to push a finger inside of her. With me not holding her in place now, her hips begin rocking, riding my finger as my tongue circles around her clit. It only takes a few seconds for her to scream my name, her movements getting sloppy as her orgasm takes over. I stick my tongue out, letting her ride my face until her movements slow, and she lets out a sigh.

"You're too good to be true," she says to me as I find a spot next to her, her back against my front, pulling her into me.

Her words go straight to my heart, even though they don't ring true.

I don't let my mind go to the place that it's threatening to go. There is nothing good enough about me. Not when it comes to her.

And when she figures that out, my borrowed time with her will be up.

Silence takes over before I hear her breathing get heavy. While I want to stay with her, fall asleep alongside her, and stay here in our movie night forever, I know that I should probably get home.

On the bright side, she did say she wanted to do this again tomorrow, so we can finish the rest of our marathon. That is what gives me the courage to unwrap myself from around her, ignoring my dick that doesn't understand that its job is done. For tonight.

Mia looks so peaceful as she sleeps, and I wonder if she still has dreams, like the one she had on the road trip to our first show last summer. I wonder if she healed. If she isn't haunted by the past.

If she can do it. Can *I*?

No. What am I talking about?

I'm too far gone.

"Where are you going?" I hear as I'm putting my pants on. I look down to see Mia, her eyelids threatening to close but she sits up on her elbow.

"Go back to sleep. It's late. I didn't mean to wake you."

"You're not allowed to leave when I'm sleeping."

"What?"

"You heard me." She is so fucking cute. I can't handle it. She is pouting, trying to show me she is mad, but it is the cutest damn thing I have ever seen.

"I got to go, baby."

"You can go," she says, sitting up. "But you can't leave without saying goodbye. *Ever.*"

Something flashes in her eyes. There is a sadness threatening to take over the stars I see in them, and I hate that I was the cause. Then, it's gone. Almost convincing me that I imagined it.

She stands up, wrapping her arms around me. Her bare chest against mine is a warmth I've never known. We stay like this until I feel the goosebumps on her skin, so I reach down to our pile of clothes and put my white hoodie over her head.

"Oh, I will *definitely* be keeping this," she says as I put the hood on her head and tie the drawstrings in a bow.

Good, I think to myself.

The sight of her in my clothes will never get old.

"Never got the coffee stain out of mine," she adds.

Oh, how times have changed since that day in her kitchen and I thank all that is good in the world that it has.

CHAPTER 35

EDDIE

BEING HERE, at Lenny's, in Emmett's office, is the last place I want to be. I *should* be waking up next to Mia, maybe in her bed, maybe on the blankets and pillows scattered across her living room floor. I regret leaving last night, but I knew Mateo would find it odd for me to not have come home.

Not that I owe him an explanation.

I just want to avoid how often I need to lie to him.

"Eddie!"

I shake my head as if shaking the thoughts away. "What?"

"Did you not get enough sleep last night, dumbass? I need your help," Emmett barks. He is on another level today, pissed that he had to come in but more pissed that these applications for Annie's replacement are all young college girls who he thinks will bring in even more of a college crowd than we already have.

"I'm too old for these kids. All they do is get piss-drunk and fight over stupid shit, trying to impress girls who think they are way cooler than they are."

"Okay, gramps. Calm down. We're in our early thirties, I think we have a while until we're considered *too old*." Emmett has always been a grump, ever since I met him in college, but more so before he found Drew. Before Drew, Emmett was in a relationship with a woman who thought she was too good for the life he wanted, thinking the bar he was so proud of, the one he renamed after his late sister, wasn't good enough for her.

"I'm too old to have a nineteen-year-old bartender."

"Annie was nineteen when you hired her three years ago."

"Yeah, but I knew she could handle herself. I've known Ann since she was a kid, and I know she doesn't take shit. I think most of the guys who come in here like how mean she is to them."

"We could always have Annie train whoever you hire."

"No, I'm having Luke do it. I don't want her to have to worry about not being able to get all of her tips for her last few weeks of shifts."

We continue to go back and forth on the best hire, narrowing down to a few girls who Emmett will interview before Annie's last shift at the end of September.

I'm bummed Annie won't be working at Lenny's anymore, but I know I will still be seeing her plenty. Lenny's isn't only a place of work for us, but it has become our unofficial hangout spot.

Once we finish for the morning, and head from Emmett's office to the bar, Luke is already in for his 10 a.m. opening shift, getting ready to open in half an hour.

"Can I leave early today?" Luke asks Emmett, and I internally flinch. I don't know if it is because Luke spends so much time being a target to Annie's perpetual meanness, but he is anything but intimidated by Emmett who can be even meaner.

Luke started working here last year, and I was surprised when Emmett hired him. It wasn't until a few months of getting to know Luke that I realized he is almost impossible not to like.

Being in his mid-twenties, younger than Emmett and me and closer in age to Annie, Mia, and Drew, Luke isn't someone you would expect to be in line to take over his father's law firm, having passed the bar to be a practicing lawyer but choosing to bartend for a living instead.

"No," Emmett says.

"Please?" Luke replies.

"Do you want to get punched in the face?"

"You sound like Annie," Luke laughs, "who is actually the reason I need to leave by four this afternoon. She's volunteering at an animal shelter, helping the practicing vet give rescue dogs their shots as part of her veterinarian program."

"I don't care," Emmett says, rounding the bar to leave. He is supposed to be back at six to take over the evening shift because I'm off today.

"Please, please, please. I'll work a double tomorrow, so you can have a night with Drew." Luke knows exactly how to play Emmett.

Emmett stops before he opens the door to leave. "Fine. See you at four," he says, not even turning around. He pushes the door to Lenny's open and leaves without another word.

"Why are you going to something Annie is volunteering at?" I ask. Luke doesn't even have a dog, or an interest in getting a dog as far as I know. I do know he has a strong interest in Annie though, so I guess I didn't really have to ask.

"You mean, why are *we* going?" Luke smirks at me, crossing his arms and leaning back against the bar.

"I'm not going. I have plans tonight." Mia and I have our second movie date, which I have been thinking about *literally* since I took one step out of her apartment last night.

"I know. Annie told me you and Mia are watching those vampire movies."

"You and Annie obviously don't have much to talk about if you talk about Mia and I," I say, giving him a hard time.

Annie's his soft spot, just like Drew is Emmett's and Mia is mine.

"Fine. If that's how you want to play it, I won't tell you what *else* Annie told me about what Mia said."

"I'm going to kill you."

"Get in line." It doesn't take a rocket scientist to figure out who is first in that line.

"Whatever. I'll go. What did Mia tell Annie?"

"You didn't tell me best friend's little sisters were your thing, Ramirez. I mean, I had a feeling, but I thought it was just *your* little crush."

"She told Annie about us?

"And Drew apparently."

"Emmett didn't say anything." I was with him all morning, and aside from the stupid comment about not sleeping, he didn't say anything about Drew telling him, which I'm sure she did.

"You think Emmett gives a shit about your love life?"

"Watch it. It's not love. We're just seeing if this could actually go anywhere." The complete lie gracefully escapes my lips, and I hate how easy it is. "Plus," I add, "it is only a matter of time before she realizes I'm not worth the risk."

"I'm not so sure about that," Luke says, grabbing a towel to wipe down the bar.

"What do you mean?" I ask, more desperately than I'd care to admit. "Did Annie say anything else?"

"Nope," he says, and he is full of shit, but I leave it alone.

"Please don't tell Mateo. He'll rip my dick off if he finds out."

"Your secret is safe with me," Luke says, stupidly pretending to lock his lips with an invisible key and going back to wiping down the bar. "Oh, but I *did* forget to mention. Annie said Mia might stop by the shelter this afternoon."

My heart skips a beat. "You could've led with that, idiot."

I head to the door. "I'll see you at four." I push the door open, and hear Luke yell behind me.

"See you then, lover boy!"

Asshole.

———

We get to the shelter, and it is a sight. There are dogs everywhere, with different stations and people holding up signs to cars passing by. Volunteers are manning stations for baths, selling homemade dog treats and toys, and Annie is helping at the station where dogs can get fifteen-minute check-ups and any vaccines they need.

There are people and dogs everywhere, making this way more of an event than Luke explained.

"You didn't say this was a whole thing," I say as I park on the street across from the shelter's parking lot where all the commotion is. I look around for a certain blonde, but I come up empty. "I thought you said Mia would be here."

"Annie said she might stop by. We can ask her."

We cross the street and enter the parking lot, immediately greeted with every kind of dog you can imagine. Laughter and barking fill the air as we make our way to Annie who has two golden retrievers on her table.

"Hey, Annie girl," Luke says, as we approach her booth. One of the goldens, not a puppy but not full-grown either, pounces on him as he stops in front of her table.

"I see you've met Rosie," she says as the golden—Rosie— licks Luke all over his face. The other golden stays seated on the table, not at all interested in joining the lovefest.

I'm instantly drawn to her. I like that she can seem so unbothered, so calm, surrounded by all the commotion. Just sitting and looking at me.

"And this is Daisy," Annie says. She has a white coat on with her veterinary assistant badge. "These sisters are waiting to be checked by the vet, so I'm just hanging with them while they wait."

Daisy looks up at me, and I look at her. Her tongue is hanging out of her mouth as she pants in the heat of the summer afternoon. Rosie, on the other hand, now has her paws on Luke's shoulders, standing on the table on her hind legs.

"You are just the cutest," Luke says in a puppy voice as Rosie continues to lick his face.

"She's looking for a home too," Annie says, reaching out to pet Rosie's head.

"Don't tempt me," Luke says between Rosie's kisses.

"She is such a lovebug. I'd take her if I could, both actually, but not with vet school starting."

"I won't take a lot of convincing, so please stop talking."

"Wait, these dogs are rescues?" I ask Annie. Daisy is still looking at me, tail wagging, but staying calm. Such a contrast to her sister. I reach out and pet her head, and she leans into my touch.

"Yeah, some guy dropped them off here yesterday after getting both from a breeder. Said they were too much work, and the rescue's manager freaked out on him, saying you can't get a dog and expect it to be no work, let alone *two*."

"What a fucking idiot," I say, instantly feeling sorry for these two pups.

"You didn't deserve that, Ro-Ro. No. No, you did not. Do you want to come home with me?" Luke's dog voice is in full force, and it is a laughable sight, seeing the two together.

The human and dog versions of golden retrievers.

"But, I can't take one and not the other," Luke says. "They're sisters. They deserve to stay together."

Annie looks at me, and smiles. "What do you say, Ed? Daisy seems to like you. This is the first time her tail has wagged all day."

I look back at Daisy and her puppy-dog eyes are a close second to Mia's.

"I really would, but I can't with the tour coming up."

"Luke can watch her during the tour. It will give the sisters time together," Annie argues.

"I don't know, Ann," I let out a sigh, feeling myself folding the more Daisy stares up at me. "I have to make sure it is okay with Mateo. He said he didn't care if I got a dog when I first moved in, but I really should make sure it is still okay."

"He won't care," Annie says. "Come on, just look at her. You want Eddie to take you home, don't you Daisy?" Annie's dog voice is as bad as Luke's.

Daisy lets out a small bark, turning to lick my hand patting her head.

I guess it's decided.

Daisy is coming home with me.

CHAPTER 36
MIA

LAST NIGHT HAS BEEN PLAYING over and over in my head since Eddie left, and I missed him the second my door closed behind him.

I woke up with a smile on my face, walking from my bedroom into my living room to see the mess of the blankets and pillows I set up for our movie night, a flip in my stomach at the thought of how it got that way.

Head over heels doesn't even begin to explain how quickly and deeply I've fallen for Eddie. I think I've been falling since the second I saw him leaning against the door to my apartment with Mateo.

The night we decided to see where things could go between us, I had full intention of not diving in head first. But now?

I find myself repeating what Eddie told me.

I'm all in.

But is this going to work?

We have to tell Mateo.

I already spilled to Drew and Annie, and I'm sure that means Luke and Emmett know. The girls agreed to keep things between the six of us, but it isn't fair to make them keep the secret from Mateo, who is their friend too.

I go about my day, with the memories of last night in the back of my mind, often pushing their way to the front, making me blush, as I work on a few social media posts for bands I'm working with at the moment.

I remind myself that keeping things a secret is only temporary.

I'll tell Mateo.

Soon.

Being self-employed, working as a freelance photographer, was the best decision I ever made. I was so lucky to find my niche working for indie bands, and I hope to branch out with other opportunities starting with Drew and Emmett's wedding in October.

I was supposed to meet Annie at the animal shelter she was volunteering at, but I got so buried in work that I didn't even look up from my computer until it was time for me to leave.

I send her a quick text, that I won't be coming, and she responds with a picture that makes my heart stop.

Eddie and Luke are holding two golden retrievers that look to be about six months old.

I text back my reaction in the form of emojis before I go back to work. I want my full attention to be on Eddie tonight, so I need to get the work done.

Being a chronic worrier, diagnosed with depression and anxiety four years ago, I have found that emptying my brain is easier said than done.

Finishing my work is essential for being able to fully be present with Eddie, and that is something that took me years to figure out about myself.

In more ways than one.

I spent so much time worrying about what was coming

next or thinking through any and all possibilities rather than being in the moment.

There are so many memories I wish I could look back on and see more clearly, but they are clouded due to me not being able to have fully enjoy them.

There is a knock on my door just as I close my laptop for the night, and I glance at my oven clock from where I am sitting at my kitchen island to see Eddie is right on time.

I thought I would have time to shower and change, but I had more work to do than I thought.

I look down at Eddie's white hoodie and my black yoga pants, and I guess this is my attire for my second official date with Eddie Ramirez.

"Hi, raindrop," I say as I open my door. The nickname coming out of my mouth so naturally now—more of a term of endearment rather than a smartass retort.

He leans in to kiss me on the cheek, a sweet gesture that is ruined when he whispers in my ear, "I don't think you know what seeing you in my clothes does to me, sunshine." I can't control the grin on my face hearing his nickname for me. Out of everything he calls me, I think it is my favorite. And I can't control the heat rushing to my chest at the seductive tone of his voice, reminding me of that dirty mouth of his.

He steps inside my apartment as if he didn't just make me melt, and I notice the plastic bag in his hand.

"What do you have there?" I manage to ask, feeling a little dizzy at how fast he can flip the switch of sexy to sweet. At least this switch, both sides are the *real* him.

He sets the bag down next to my laptop on the kitchen island.

"Movie snacks," Eddie answers as if saying *duh*.

I open the bag and see a king-sized Twix and a king-sized Kit Kat, reminding me of our road trip together. My favorite and his, along with something else.

A dog toy.

"And this?" I ask, pulling out the knotted pink rope. Realization hits me. "Wait, you got a dog?!" I thought the picture Annie sent me was just posed, not a *hey look at the two hooligans who just adopted dogs.*

"Her name is Daisy. Your brother is having a bonding session with her as we speak. Luke adopted her sister, Rosie."

"Her name is Daisy?" I can't help but smile, looking at Eddie's grin as he pulls out his phone to show me all the pictures he took of her in the past few hours. Her in the bed he picked up for her on the way home. Mateo holding her. Eddie kneeling down next to her, hugging her.

Oh my god, my ovaries can't take it.

"She is the most laid back, calm puppy I have ever met. You're going to love her." The pride in his voice when he talks about her makes me emotional. I have this sudden urge to cry happy tears at how happy Eddie looks right now.

"Of course I will. I can't wait to meet her!"

"You can come over to meet her, if you want. Mateo hasn't been home much. I think he is seeing someone."

"Seeing someone?" My brother is *dating*? This is news to me. Mateo and I talk on an almost-daily basis about random shit, whether it is catching up, sending each other stupid sibling memes, or discussing Cross My Heart stuff.

"Yeah, we're not doing this. You want to know, you ask him."

My annoyance at the line Eddie draws only lasts a second because I know he is right.

This is one of those boundaries that we have to set.

He can't be telling me things my brother may not want me to know, and it isn't fair for me to put him in the middle.

"Anyways," Eddie says, taking the toy from me and putting it back in the bag. "I came prepared for our second *Twilight* marathon." He pulls out the two candy bars, and I smile at the memory of how we split the both of them, which I definitely plan on making him do tonight. "Oh, which reminds me. You told Annie about us?" There is no hint of accusation, just questioning. "Luke knows too. I thought you wanted to keep things a secret."

"About that," I start. "I wanted to talk to you about that, but I need to shower first."

"I could help you shower," Eddie teases, my favorite smirk on his face.

I roll my eyes and turn to walk into the living room and pull out the blankets from the basket next to my couch. "No. You're in charge of setting up our space and getting the fourth movie set up."

He comes up behind me, snaking his arms around my waist, leaning into my neck, shocking my system. "Are you *sure* you don't need help? I think I could be much more productive in the shower. With you."

It is concerning how quickly he fills me with need.

I almost give in until I remember that I haven't showered today.

"Not that kind of shower, raindrop." I turn in his arms and loop my arms around his neck, popping up on my tiptoes to kiss him on the nose. I head to my bathroom, turning to him and saying, "Maybe next time," before I close the door.

I leave Eddie in my living room to take a quick shower, changing into my purple silk pajama set, knowing how much he liked my green one last night.

I shave my legs and lather my body in my coconut lotion, halfway convinced that Eddie doing this would have been a big help.

No.

No fooling around until we talk about us. I thought I needed time to realize what Eddie could mean to me, but I was stupid to think he already didn't mean the world.

A knock on the bathroom door brings me back to the moment, and Eddie peaks his head in.

"So it's the lotion," he says, and he walks into my bathroom. He stands behind me, but I meet his gaze through the mirror I am standing in front of.

"What's the lotion?" I ask.

"You always smell like coconut and lavender. I wondered which scent came from where." He slides my shower curtain, looking for something, and then closes it. "The lavender is the body wash. The coconut is your lotion." He explains it as if I didn't already know, being the one who bought them and uses them every day.

Before I can give him a sassy comment, joking about how he is so obsessed with me, his eyes spot the basket on my bathroom counter with all of my face masks.

"What are these?" He asks, picking up the wire basket and grabbing the tube on top.

"Face masks," I say.

"What are they for?"

"Um, your face."

He looks at me and raises an eyebrow. "No shit, sunshine. I remember you telling me that when I saw this in your bag at the hotel room last year. I mean what do they do?"

I laugh and take the basket from him. "They help your skin. I have some for acne, anti-aging, purifying, balancing, you name it." I grab the purple container in his hand, and I see it is a lavender mud mask for relaxation. "Please don't tell me you are one of those men who uses a five-in-one shampoo and body wash on everything, including your face."

"Excuse me," Eddie says, plucking the tube from my hand. "I take good care of my skin, thank you very much. I just never use these."

"Get ready to live, raindrop."

We are fifteen minutes into *Breaking Dawn: Part One*, and I look over to my man in his purple face mask and a hair tie holding back his hair, and my heart is so full.

He brings his half of my—our—Kit Kat, already finishing his half of his—our—Twix, to his lips, and turns to look at me. "What?"

"You're so fucking cute, I can't," I say from my spot on the couch. Eddie wanted to make the couch cozy tonight rather than the floor, and he even lit the candles and everything.

My face matches his, covered with the purple face mask.

I put his mask on, and he put on mine, and you can tell with how well I smoothed the purple mud mask over his face and how he clumsily smeared it all over mine.

"Time to wash them off," I say, pausing the movie and grabbing Eddie's hand. We walk hand-in-hand to the bathroom, making a purple mess at my sink, before starting the movie again, all wrapped in each other.

Tonight has proven to me that this is more than a physical connection. While I know my body aches to be with his, my heart aches for his just the same.

Maybe more.

CHAPTER 37
EDDIE

WHEN WE'RE with our friends, it is easy to fall back into mine and Mia's flirty, harmless friendship, but it is impossibly hard to keep my hands to myself. Whenever I can, I make sure I'm near her and my eyes are always on her.

How can they not be? She is the most beautiful woman I have ever seen. Her smile is blinding and her laugh beckons me like Daisy and her favorite peanut butter treats.

Mia is so damn tempting, but the time with others makes our alone time so much more special.

The nights I can get to her place, the tension is usually so high that I can barely get through the door without ripping her clothes off. We have yet to have sex, but we make good use of our time doing everything in between.

But seeing her. Being with her. It is so much more than the physical stuff.

We also talk about everything and anything, and she truly is the sunshine to my rainy day. Every time she laughs, cries, smiles, or moans, it further proves to me that I was meant to be hers.

Lying to Mateo, putting on a show in front of our friends, that has been starting to weigh on me.

I also have the guilt of keeping Mia a secret, when she is so much more than that. Even though Annie, Drew, Luke, and Emmett know about us, it is always the elephant in the room. None of us talk about it. None of us address it.

The morning after our first *Twilight* movie marathon, almost three weeks ago, I couldn't shake the feeling of heaviness. It wasn't bad. It wasn't like feeling weighed down. It was more like I was no longer missing parts of me anymore. Like the parts I lost all those years ago were somehow back where they were supposed to be.

I felt more myself than I have in ages. Like I didn't have to go through the motions, numb and disconnected.

I was grounded. I could feel my feet on the floor.

When I saw the flash of sadness in Mia's eyes when she told me I couldn't leave without saying goodbye, I realized something.

That night that changed everything for her, she never got to say goodbye to Nico. He left angry at her, at the world, and it took so long for her to forgive the fault she found in herself.

Seeing the sadness cloud the stars in her eyes, and then disappear without a trace showed me that it is possible to not always feel this way. Like you could break down at any moment, whether from sadness or anger, or the combination of both.

I want that.

And Mia makes me feel like I might *actually* deserve it.

The morning after our second *Twilight* marathon, it solidified in my brain that I wanted that for myself but also so I could be the man Mia deserved.

I decided to start seeing a therapist.

I made the appointment and everything.

The first session came around, and I got to the parking lot and everything.

But I didn't go in.

I didn't tell Mia either, that she indirectly helped me take this first step even though it ended up being a step backwards.

I rescheduled for next week.

And I'll make it to the office this time.

I hope.

I'll keep trying until I don't have to be someone that needs someone holding them together because I refuse to be a burden.

The night after our second movie marathon was also when we decided that it was time to tell Mateo about us. She told me she was like me, all in.

The fact that Mia doesn't see us with an expiration date turned out to be enough to convince me.

It was also enough to convince me that the time to heal is now.

It isn't too late.

Not if I wanted to put the pieces of me back together, so I could show Mia that I don't need her putting me back together.

I would be whole enough for her.

And I couldn't help but kiss her all over, telling her I would never stop proving to her she didn't make a mistake giving me a chance, until I made her come on my face.

Twice.

But *soon* actually didn't end up being that soon because of how damn busy the man is.

I see Mateo at home on the off-chance we are there at the same time, and I see him at our band practices, but other than that, he is severely preoccupied.

I can't help but feel a little relieved every time he is too busy to hang out with all of us or declines Mia's invitations for lunch or coffee.

There is no telling how Mateo will react, and the last thing I want to do is have to choose between him and Mia.

• • •

Tonight, we have a show downtown, and Drew, Emmett, Annie, and Luke are coming. It's our first show in about a month, having no shows in June, except for the one at Lenny's, or July because of so much recording in the studio.

It is the first weekend in August, and we're meeting up after the show to grab some drinks near the venue. Theo and Silas will most likely bow out for an offer that will end in sex, but there is a fifty-fifty shot on whether or not Mateo will come, possibly having plans with the girl he pretends to not be spending all his free time with.

I hate that I'm hopeful that he does have plans because it means I get more of Mia to myself.

We let our guards down more when Mateo isn't around.

Mateo and I head to the venue, driving in comfortable silence, until he asks, "Are you seeing someone?"

I turn from where I am sitting in the passenger seat to look at him. "What?"

Does he *know*?

"You seem busier than usual."

Between balancing my time at home with Daisy, bartending, band practices, and Mia, I'm so tired at the end of the day that I am passed out by the time my head hits the pillow.

Mateo was a little on the fence about Daisy at first, but over these past few weeks, he has warmed up to her. She is the calmest dog I ever met, super smart too. She was potty-trained in less than two days, and she switches between sleeping in her bed in my bedroom and her bed in Mateo's.

I haven't had a chance to invite Mia over to meet Daisy yet, whether it is because one of us is busy or Mateo is home, but I can't wait to have my two girls together.

"No, I'm not seeing anyone." The lie feels sour on my lips. I change the subject. "Are you?"

Mateo nods his head, and he has a boyish grin. "Yeah, it's new. I'm waiting to introduce her to everyone. Don't tell Mia, okay?"

"Secrets safe with me," I manage to say. Keeping secrets with the Lane siblings is apparently my favorite pastime.

We fall back into silence, only this time it isn't comfortable for me.

———

There is no feeling like being up on stage. The electrifying energy of the crowd washes over you, and the rush is unexplainable. Each beat of my drum forms this connection with the music and it surrounds me. Time feels like it stops and nothing else matters.

When we end the song, the applause from the people there supporting us brings me back to earth before it starts all over again when I hit my drumsticks three times. Theo's guitar riffs surge through the air, and Silas's bass grounds us. Mateo's vocals hit hard, lyrics meaning something different to each of us.

I wasn't able to see Mia in the crowd, assuming that she stayed towards the back. I'm anxious when I can't see her, but I know Luke and Emmett will keep an eye on her.

The show ends, Mateo thanks the crowd like he always does, and we all take a bow. The screams and cheers never get old, and my smile always feels bigger on stage.

"We killed it!" Theo exclaims as we get backstage. He slaps his hands down on Silas's shoulders.

"We really did," I laugh as I twirl one of my drumsticks between my fingers. I'm itching to go find Mia in the crowd, but I don't want to seem too eager.

Theo and Silas have been on my case about Mia since day one. Lucky for me, they collectively have the attention span of a gnat, so they lost interest in if Mia and I were a thing.

"You coming tonight?" I ask Mateo as we head to the merch booth. We always like to spend some time at the booth, selling T-shirts and hoodies to our fans. It is fun to meet the people who make it possible for us to do what we love.

"Where?" he asks.

"To Cityscape?" Annie, Drew, and Mia wanted to try out a new rooftop bar near the part of downtown Milwaukee we're in, but I figured Mia would have let Mateo know.

"Oh yeah, Mia mentioned you all were going out later. No, I'm good."

I feel a rush of excitement surge through me, and it is almost immediately replaced with guilt.

"You sure?" I ask him as we walk over to the booth. The volume around us rises with the increase of people in the crowd versus backstage.

"Yeah," he says over the noise. "I have plans."

I stop in my tracks.

"Wait, you're saying you have friends other than *us*?" I ask, gesturing to me and Theo and Silas who are already flirting away with some girls buying Cross My Heart T-shirts.

Mateo laughs. "If by 'us' you mean these two yahoos and the Lenny's crew? Yes, in fact, I do."

The Lenny's crew.

I like it.

"I've been spending time with a few people I work with." Since Mateo works from home during the week, it makes sense he has to make plans to see them since they don't have an office to go into. "I'm actually going to head out now. Can you tell Mia bye for me?"

"Yeah, no problem."

"Thanks, man. You're the best. See you later." He gives me a wave before he leaves, and I walk over to the booth, the guilt in my stomach not residing.

"Where's he going?" Silas asks when I start checking out the few people in line next to where he and Theo are supposed to be selling t-shirts rather than making plans to meet up with this group of girls.

"He had other plans," I explain.

"You get Mia all to yourself then, huh?"

I turn to look at him as the crowd around our booth slowly fades as another band begins to play.

"Excuse me?" I say.

Silas laughs, "Do you guys really think you're hiding anything? You can tell you two are fucking from a mile away."

"Hey," I say, a little louder than I meant to, getting Theo's attention as he says bye to the group of girls. I take a step towards Silas, and I see Theo's face harden. "Don't *ever* let me hear the words 'Mia' and 'fucking' come out of your mouth in the same sentence again. Got it?"

Theo and Silas both know my track record when it comes to losing my cool, both having been there when I lost it on my dad over a decade ago, and a few other times over the years.

"Chill, man. It was just a joke," Silas says. His voice is even and calm, but I can't help but feel the anger under my skin begin to bubble.

Maybe it's the guilt about lying to Mateo or because Silas caught me off guard, but I feel myself heading the opposite way of "chill."

"Eddie," Theo says, and my eyes dart to him. I watch as his eyes widen, and he nods his head to the right. I turn to see the Lenny's crowd, Annie, Luke, Drew, Emmett, and Mia, talking and heading this way.

Whatever is bubbling inside, I tamper it down, refusing to lose my cool in front of Mia again.

Seeing her makes me momentarily forget about the guilt, or Silas's stupid comment, but a different kind of tension in me builds.

Her tan legs are peaking out of black denim shorts that

have rips lining her upper thighs. She is wearing my black Cross My Heart T-shirt that she has yet to return from last summer, but I can't say I'm mad about it. It is tied just under her tits, showing off her toned stomach, and her blonde hair is in a high ponytail, showing off a mark on her neck that she said she would tell everyone was a burn from her curling iron.

The way she looks tonight makes me want to fall to my knees and worship that body, but I can't.

Yet.

As she walks over to us with the rest of our friends, I watch as she unties the knot she has at the front of her shirt, and she begins to pull it off over her head.

What the hell is she doing?

Not taking her shirt off in front of all these people, I'll tell you that.

Before I can think about it, I'm pushing past Theo and Silas to round the booth, heading over to her with full intention to stop her from showing this whole fucking place what is *mine* and *only mine*.

But I'm too late.

She pulls the T-shirt over her head, and I'm still a good five feet away from her.

"Mia," I yell to her, but the rest of my words get caught in my throat.

Under her T-shirt is a pink, lace top that accentuates her jaw-dropping frame. It is flattering, feminine, and literally makes my mouth water. Her arms on display, one thin strap falling off her shoulder.

How much I wish it was just me and her right now is unhealthy, and that top and those shorts are already turning heads as people walk past her.

Cityscape is a nicer place, so I get why she doesn't want to wear my old band T-shirt there, but the way she looks tonight, the amount of attention she is bound to get…

Yeah, I'm going to jail tonight.

She sees me, and the smile on her face is the nail in my coffin because she is drop dead gorgeous. There is a flush to her cheeks, gloss on her lips, and, if we were alone, I would ask her to leave pink kisses all over me. "Hey, raindrop," she beams as I walk up to the group.

"Great show, Ed," I hear Annie say, but I don't see her. All I see are those pretty brown eyes that make my world go 'round, and I want to spend the rest of my life counting the stars in them, getting lost in them.

Mia holds power over me that no one else does.

I had anger clouding my vision before I saw her, and I feel it all slowly fade away. I can't shake the feeling of tension in my shoulders, left over from before and now with the anticipation of knocking people out who look at her a little too long, but being near her calms me down.

"Ready to go?" Mia asks, hanging my T-shirt over her arm.

"You were wearing my T-shirt," I announce as if it was apparent.

"Well, you are my favorite," she teases, calling back to last summer when she announced to Theo and Silas that I was her favorite instead of them.

"Atta girl," I say, forgetting the act we're supposed to be putting on. I put my arm over her shoulder and lead her to the exit, the wide eyes and smiles of our friends behind us.

I'm already going to hell.

Might as well enjoy it.

CHAPTER 38
MIA

CITYSCAPE JUST TOOK the spot of my new favorite place. Not counting Lenny's and my apartment, of course, but obsessed is an understatement. While I love our usual spot, I have been itching to go out ever since our karaoke night, and this is the first night since then we could all get together.

The rooftop bar looks over the city, pulsating with energy below. The warm, gentle breeze of the August night brushes against my skin. Twinkling lights lining the space, casting an intimate ambiance over the comfortable lounge seating we're at.

Around us, you can hear the mingling, the laughing, and clinking of drinks, and the horizon is filled with a tapestry of illuminated skyscrapers, the lake, and the mesmerizing starlit horizon.

I take a moment to let it all sink in, taking a page from Eddie's book, and following the conversation around me.

Drew and Annie are updating Luke and Eddie on the wedding plans for Drew and Emmett's wedding so far, talking about the colors Drew picked for Annie, Lacey, Emma, and I to wear, and I still can't believe I get to be a part of not only the planning process but her special day.

Drew isn't having her bridesmaids or Emmett's groomsmen stand up with them for the ceremony, so I'll still be able to do the pictures for the ceremony.

They chose a venue not too far from where we are downtown right now, a hall with a small stage and a dance floor, and we are all staying at the hotel next door to the venue to get ready for the day and to stay at for the night.

"So girls will be in black, surprise, and guys will have black suits with a white dress shirt," Annie explains.

Spending so much time with her and Drew to plan, I like that the three of us couldn't be more different. Our styles, our upbringings, our interests, even our music tastes are all so different, yet when I'm with them, there is no need for me to recharge my social battery.

While I know Annie's aesthetic for a wedding wouldn't be like Drew's, this planning process has shown how perceptive Annie is. She was vocal about not loving the black, gold, and forest green Drew picked, but she was also the one to put together a vision board that was somehow exactly what Drew was picturing in her head.

Getting to know Annie, I have learned that her hard, unapproachable exterior is only for people she doesn't trust. She has opened up about what happened to her in high school, the bullying having a lasting impact on her on top of her family issues, but it truly explains why she holds people at arms-length until they prove to her she can trust them.

Once she trusts them, she is your ride-or-die for life.

Drew goes on to explain how the ceremony will be just the wedding party, and the reception will be everyone else when Eddie reaches his arm over the two-seater lounge chair we're in.

Since we left the concert, he has been *touchier* than we have agreed on. Yes, we do care a little less about the PDA with our friends, but I won't be free of my guilt until we get the chance to talk to my brother.

"Emmett, did you decide on your groomsmen?" Annie asks him. She is wearing a blue corset top with white jeans and her long brown hair is glistening under the twinkly lights hanging above us.

"Yes," Emmett grunts, taking a sip of his drink. He has his arm around Drew who has her red wine hair twisted in a clip with a black tank and jeans.

"Care to share with the class?" She retorts, using one of Drew's lines, so unaffected by what could be perceived as a bad attitude if you didn't know Emmett well enough. In all reality, he cares more about marrying Drew than planning the wedding, but he wants her to have whatever wedding she wants.

"Eddie, Luke, Cal, and Mateo."

"See? That wasn't so hard." Annie reaches over at pats Emmett on the knee, ignoring his death stare. Drew leans back and laughs, and Eddie chuckles in my ear, somehow closer than he was a few moments ago.

"Wait, *I'm* going to be a groomsman?" Luke exclaims. He is seated next to Annie, his thigh touching hers.

"Guess it's your lucky day, Lukey-poo," Annie says, turning to him. She swipes the condensation on her glass and flicks the droplets of water at him.

"Okay, calm down, kids," Drew says. "Eddie, did you talk to the guys about playing at the wedding?"

"Yeah, we're all set to play for your guys' first dance and a few songs at the reception." His attention is on Drew, his usual smile in place, but I feel his arm behind me move, bringing it to rest on my thigh. "The wedding is a week before we leave for tour, so it works out great."

I feel my body heat, Eddie's hand on me in front of everyone, and I don't know how to respond.

"It'll be a fun night," Annie says, her eyes finding mine with a raise of one eyebrow. I turn to see Drew and her eyes flicker to Eddie's hand on my thigh.

"Tons of fun," Luke echoes, taking a sip of his drink. I see him and Annie exchange a glance, and I instantly feel like I'm on display.

"So," I start, needing to shift the conversation, so we aren't all focused on the elephant in the room. The attention goes to me, but I don't know what to say.

"How did the pictures turn out for that shoot you did with that all-girl band?" Drew swoops in and saves the day, and I thank her with my eyes.

"Good! It was a nice change of pace doing an all-girl shoot versus the usual all guys."

"What band?" Annie asks.

"Pink Roses. They're a folk-pop band based out of Chicago. They were up here for a show, so we did a cute shoot to promote their new single."

"How cute! I want to see," Annie replies.

"Do you guys want to come to my apartment? We can head there before you guys go home. It isn't too far from here."

"Works for me," Annie says, looking at Luke who nods.

"Yeah, I want to see too!" Drew says, which means Emmett will be coming too.

I turn to look at Eddie who has had his eyes on me this whole time, I could feel his gaze as I talked, blood rushing to my chest trying to stay calm.

"Wouldn't miss it," he says, his lips curved to one side, his dimple on full display. And I want to kiss his smirk right off his face.

I only live a few blocks from where we are, but the rest of the crew drove here. Mateo and Eddie drove to the show together, but Mateo got a ride to wherever he was going. Drew, Emmett, Luke, and Annie are finishing their drink while Eddie and I hop in his truck to head back to my place. I told them not to rush because I wanted to make sure the apartment was ready for company. They will probably be about half an hour behind us

"I want to clean up a little bit before they all come over," I tell Eddie as we walk to where his truck is parked. Annie and Drew have each been to my place before, but it is the first time I've hosted all the Lenny's crew.

"I can help," he says, grabbing my hand and bringing it up to his lips.

We walk in comfortable silence, and I use the few seconds to take a breath, feeling the weight of our friend's eyes on us lift. Putting on our act is getting harder and harder these days; the more I fall for Eddie, the harder it is to pretend he is just a friend.

Now that we're alone, a surge runs through me. There are pods of people in their own worlds, standing outside the bars, enjoying the nightlife of downtown. To everyone else, we are just a couple walking to our car. Holding hands. Falling for each other more and more.

I have had to push down all of my feelings, put on an act, but it all melts away when it is just the two of us.

Is this how Eddie always feels?

I've been doing it for a few months. Eddie has been doing it for years. Burying his true feelings just to make everyone around him more comfortable. Not wanting to worry them.

And now I'm making him do the same for me.

Hiding him away like a dirty little secret even though he is so much more than that.

"Mia?" I hear, and I turn to look up at Eddie's concerned eyes.

"We have to tell Mateo."

The concern fades, but it is replaced with confusion.

"Something on your mind, sunshine?"

"Is this how you always feel?"

"You're going to have to give me a little more than that."

We get to his truck, and I lean back against the passenger side door.

"Pretending, putting on a fake face, wearing a mask in front of your friends. This is exhausting. I don't want to have to wait until we're in the car to hold your hand or kiss you. I want to be able to do it whenever I want."

Eddie holds my hand in one of his and reaches to cup my cheek with the other, leaning down to press his forehead against mine. "You make me feel like I don't have to wear this mask anymore. I told you once, and I will tell you again. I'm ready to show the world that I'm yours. I'm done pretending."

His lips crash into mine, and I know that this is it.

He may be happy being mine, but I am so proud to be his.

The breath from my lungs is gone, butterflies filling every inch of my soul.

When he kisses me, nothing else matters.

We aren't kissing against his truck at ten o'clock at night. We aren't standing in some random parking lot. We aren't supposed to be cleaning my apartment so it is ready for our friends.

It is just us, and our need to be each other's.

"I need you," Eddie says against my lips. "*Now*." I need him too. So badly. More now than ever, now that I know I am moments away from falling in love with this man.

"I don't know if we want our first time to end in an arrest for public indecency, raindrop."

"Then you better sit in that seat like a good girl, so I can focus on driving and getting us back to your place before I fuck you right here against my truck."

The ride home is a blur because my focus was on resisting the urge to tell Eddie to pull the truck over. We stumble into my apartment, shutting the door behind us. We don't even make it to the couch or the bed, ending up at the kitchen island. The same place we were when this whole mess started.

Eddie's lips are on mine, and he makes quick work of my jean shorts, unbuttoning them with one hand, the other gripping my neck to keep my lips on his. My hands go straight to his belt buckle, shamelessly fumbling with it because I can't work quickly enough.

"We don't have a lot of time," I say, as my jean shorts fall to the floor. Left in only my underwear and top that doesn't cover much. We have already had the talk of birth control and how both of us are clean, having been a while since our last sexual encounters before each other.

The anticipation is killing me and, quite frankly, has been for weeks now.

Eddie's lips find my neck, his tongue swirling on the sensitive skin as he loops an arm around my waist to hold me in place as his other hand finds the hem of my underwear.

"You're wet for me, aren't you? Have you been thinking about this all night, sunshine?" His words elicit a pressure in my stomach, and my underwear is soaked. His fingers feel me through the cotton before slipping his hand into my underwear, a groan escaping his mouth as he continues kissing up my neck until he finds my lips again.

"You're going to ride my fingers until your sweet, little pussy is ready for my cock," he demands as his finger slowly circles my clit, making me moan into his mouth.

I'm already so close, his words having an intense effect on me. He is in control tonight, and I don't care. There is no use fighting when it feels so good to give in to him.

His finger finds my entrance, pushing into me in a slow thrust, and I almost lose it right there. "Good girl," he coos as he adds a second finger, stretching me so I am ready for him.

My back is against the kitchen island, my hands holding onto the cool granite as he pushes into me. I'm too lost in his touch, my kisses become sloppy, so Eddie moves his lips on my neck, my chest, and the tops of my breasts. The movement of his fingers along with the feel of his lips all over my body is pushing me closer and closer to the edge.

He slowly retracts his fingers before using his arm around my waist to turn me around, pressing my front into the counter, and slightly pulling me back by the hips.

"What a gorgeous sight, sunshine," he says into my ear, my back against his front. "You're almost ready," he says as he pushes two fingers inside of me from the back, faster this time, a sense of urgency as he pumps into me.

"Now," I moan. "Please. I'm so close."

"I love it when you beg. Your wish is my command." I hear the shuffling of his pants behind as he lowers his jeans down enough to release himself. I look over my shoulder to see him fist his cock.

"Hold on to the counter, baby." I lean forward, holding myself in place against the kitchen island as he aligns his erection with my center. He begins to push into me before retreating, then going back in a little more, repeating this as I adjust to his size.

"It's a lot," I say, not knowing if I can take it.

"We'll make it fit."

Then he thrusts into me and I feel all of him. I let out a gasp as he lets out a moan, and I'm ruined.

Eddie Ramirez has officially ruined me.

"Fuck, Mia. Look at you, taking all my cock. Keep holding onto the counter." He pumps into me, grabbing my hips in his hands, hitting me in the perfect spot, and I feel my release growing closer and closer. I'm seconds away from falling apart.

"Eddie," I beg, not sure what for.

"I wish I could fuck you all night, but we have company on the way, so I'm going to need you to come on my cock like a good girl."

His words are what I need to fall over the edge, my release coming so hard I see stars behind my closed-lids.

"There you go, sunshine," he says through his teeth. "Fuck, it is like you were made for me. Let it all out." His hips keep rocking into me, harder and harder as I come back to reality. His movements get sloppy as he chases his own release.

"Your turn, raindrop," I tease. "Give it to me."

"Fuck," he grits out and his hips still behind me. His grip on my waist tightens, and I know I'll have bruises tomorrow. I feel him release inside of me, his upper body going limp over mine resting on the counter.

He leaves a line of kisses on the back of my shoulder, but we don't have time to enjoy these post-coitus moments because there is a knock on my apartment door, and our friends are here.

"Get your pants on." Eddie says against my skin. He stands up straight, so I can too. Eddie's pants didn't even make it all the way off, so he tucks himself back in and buckles his jeans. Me, on the other hand, my underwear is nowhere to be found on my kitchen floor, so I quickly put my shorts on as Eddie turns on the light, and I pretend that I've been picking up the living room this whole time.

I hear Eddie open the front door, and voices fill my entry way as our friends make their way in.

We go about our night, showing everyone my pictures from the band shoot I did, sneaking glances at my man who has a pink to his cheeks for the rest of the night and a slight mess to his hair.

His eyes hold the same secrets as mine, and my stomach flips at the thought of them.

Drew and Emmett head out after about an hour, and Annie and Luke stay for a little longer. The four of us shoot the shit about random stuff, Luke and Eddie comparing stories on what it is like to be dog owners of two sister golden retrievers.

It isn't until I walk the three of them to the door, giving a hug to both Luke and Eddie, Eddie's lingering just a bit longer, that I see Annie snatch something from Eddie's pocket. He doesn't notice and keeps walking with Luke looking over his shoulder to wave goodbye to me, not missing his chance to make my heart stop with a wink.

"I assume *these* are yours," Annie says before she hands me my pair of underwear that was nowhere to be found two hours ago. She smacks me on the ass before kissing me on the check. "I'm expecting a full report tomorrow at lunch with Drew."

With that, she is running to catch up with Luke and Eddie leaving me flustered, embarrassed, and like I was just officially caught in the act.

CHAPTER 39

MIA

LUNCH WITH DREW and Annie is spent planning the final details for the wedding now that we are officially two months out from their October date.

I tried to keep the conversation surrounding Drew, but Annie did not let me out of that full report she mentioned last night. I spared all the dirty details, but I did admit to Drew and Annie that this thing between Eddie and me is real. Realer than anything else I've known, and I want it to be, which means telling my brother.

They both were supportive, agreeing to keep my secret until I told Mateo, which leaves me feeling conflicted. While I have definitely grown closer to them this past year, Mateo is still their friend too. I can't ignore the guilt of making them keep a secret from their friend just because he is my brother.

I head home to work on my website, calling Mateo on the way because he has been helping me with the updates. The more bands I work with, the more my name gets thrown to other bands, widening my network, and allowing me to add more to my online portfolio.

I'm still planning on going on tour with Cross My Heart the week after the wedding, even though their label has a photographer for them. I was happy Mateo wanted me for this first official tour, and it will probably be my last one with them as their photographer.

"Yeah, I can do that." Mateo says as we talk on the phone. I'm on my couch with my laptop in my lap, discussing the changes I need him to make to my website, but I find myself moving the conversation in a different direction.

"Great. Also, there was something I wanted to ask you."

"And what is that?"

"Anything new with you?"

Silence.

"Mateo?"

"Did Eddie tell you?" There is accusation in his voice, and my attempt to begin a conversation to catch up, maybe open the door to talk about my dating life ends up doing the exact opposite.

He is on edge.

Does he know?

Did Eddie tell him?

"What? No. Tell me what? What are you talking about?"

"Well, he is the only one I told, and I specifically asked him not to tell you. Glad to see I can't trust my best friend with my fucking sister."

"Whoa, where is this anger coming from? I don't even know what you're talking about."

I hear him sigh, but he doesn't say anything.

"Mateo, he didn't tell me anything. I just noticed you've been busy. I was just trying to make conversation, catch up, see what was new with you."

"Sorry, I didn't mean to blow up. I just—" He sighs again. "I'm just feeling a little stressed with the tour starting soon, and work is really busy, and I um . . . I am seeing someone, but it's still new. I told Eddie about it, and I know you guys hang out a lot, so I thought maybe he told you."

A lot to unpack here, starting with my brother seeing

someone, and how I am so happy for him. Also, I can't ignore that he knows Eddie and I are getting closer, but it seems like the possibility of us getting together isn't on the forefront of his mind anymore. He obviously just sees us as friends.

The last thing I want to do is stress Mateo out any more, so now would not be a good time to unpack any of these things with him, and I don't want him to be worried about me or his best friend.

I can't tell him.

Maybe after the tour starts.

But for now, no. I'm not going to stress him out more.

"I get it. No worries," I say. I take my phone out to check the notification I just got, a text from Eddie, and my stomach drops, for more reasons than one.

"No, I'm sorry. I didn't mean to take it out on you."

"So… What's her name?" I ask, trying to ease the tension.

"Camila. Don't."

"Fine, fine. Don't be mad at me."

"Don't piss me off," he says, but I can hear the smile in his voice.

We end our conversation, and I let him know that I am here for him if he needs anything, hoping the stress of tour, work, and his new girlfriend isn't too much. And I tell myself that there will be no stressing him out any more than he already is, not if I can help it.

CHAPTER 40
EDDIE

MIA IS on her way over to meet Daisy, and I am so excited to have my two favorite girls together.

It has been a few weeks since our rendezvous after Cityscape, and Annie and Luke teased me the whole way to my truck about how I look like a love-sick teenager whenever Mia is in the vicinity, so I'm hoping Mia also has an update on when we can tell Mateo about us, so we can stop all this hiding.

I also have something to talk to her about.

Mia texts me that she is here, and I let her know the door is open. Mateo is gone now and won't be back later tonight, so it is just me and Daisy. I take the few minutes I have before Mia is here to prepare Daisy for who she is about to meet.

Daisy is lying in her bed that sits on the floor next to mine. She is already bigger than when I got her back in July, growing a good amount in just about a month.

"Okay, Dais. You're about to meet my girl. Her name is Mia, but I call her sunshine."

Daisy's tail wags, but she keeps her head down on her bed, her eyes looking up at me from where I'm standing.

"Why do I call her 'sunshine'? I'm glad you asked. You'll

see why when you meet her. She lights up every room she walks into. She's the sun on my rainy day, and I think I love her, Dais."

There is a knock on the door, and then I hear it open and close.

I bend down next to Daisy. "She's here," I whisper to her, kissing her on the top of the head.

"Hello?" I hear from the entryway. Our apartment is a two-bedroom, two-bathroom, with a kitchen and a living room, big enough for Mateo and I to have our own space.

"In here," I yell back to her.

"Hey, raindrop," she says from the doorway of my bedroom. She has been to this place dozens of times but never has she been in my bedroom.

Her eyes go from me to Daisy way too quickly, and I'm suddenly jealous of my dog for stealing all the attention. "Oh my goodness, who is this beautiful girl?" Mia goes straight to kneel by Daisy, her puppy voice being much cuter than Luke's or Annie's. Daisy rolls over on her back, her tongue hanging out as Mia rubs her belly.

"Daisy has been waiting to meet you." I kneel down with my girls, and the smile on my face is so big that it hurts. There is nothing forced about it. Being with Mia has allowed me to forget to put on the mask, remembering that there is no need to pretend around her.

Mia talks to Daisy, telling her how cute she is, and Daisy is as calm, cool, and collected as always, tail slightly wagging as she takes in all the love.

It is moments like these that remind me that I am capable of being whole again. I am capable of putting the pieces back together.

I clear my throat. "Uh, Mia."

She looks up at me with those pretty brown eyes, and I know I love her. I also know I'm not ready to tell her yet.

"I wanted to talk to you about something."

"Okay," she says, stretching out the word. She goes from kneeling to sitting down next to Daisy's bed, slowly petting Daisy's head. I can tell her mind is spinning with what I'm about to say, so I don't make her suffer.

"I started therapy."

Her face goes from worried to surprise in seconds, and then a huge smile blooms on her face.

"What? That's great!"

That is what I love about Mia. Her first question wasn't why, like my sisters asked when I told them. Instead, she just said more than I could have ever asked for. Her reaction is what I needed, telling me it is a good thing. A *great* thing. Because I am *not* broken beyond repair.

"Yeah, I went because I wanted to prove to myself that I could be the man you deserved, but the first session came and went. I couldn't even make it to the door. The second one, I just sat there. I didn't say a word the whole time. The woman probably thought I was insane.

"It wasn't until the third session that I felt like talking. Starting with why I wanted to come, ending with telling her that I didn't want to feel so broken anymore. It wasn't until the fourth session that I realized therapy wouldn't work if I went to prove something to you. While I want you to see me as someone strong enough to take care of you, I realized that I wanted to see myself as someone strong enough to be worthy of you."

"Eddie," she says, and I see her eyes cloud. "You have always been worthy. I've always known it, but I've been waiting for you to see it too." She reaches out to cup my cheek in her hand. "I am *so* proud of you. For taking the step to heal. It's not easy, but I'm here for you."

She leans in, taking her hand from Daisy to cup my other cheek. She pulls me in, and I see a tear stray from those eyes that have been on my brain since that night last summer. "Someone once told me that we all are seconds away from falling apart, but that is why we have people who help hold us together. It doesn't make us any less capable or any less strong, but it makes us much less alone."

"Thank you, sunshine. I couldn't have done it without you. You have shown me, time and time again, what it means to live. You've reminded me how good it feels to just *feel*, and I don't want to lose that."

My lips gently touch hers, leaving a kiss before I drop another bomb on her. "Also, are you busy tomorrow night?"

She slightly tilts her head, backing away enough for me to see the confusion all over her face. "Why?"

"I want you to meet my mom. My sisters too."

There is that smile again. The one that makes my heart stop.

"Eddie, of course! I would love to."

"I'll pick you up tomorrow night after I'm done with band practice. My mom is making dinner and my sisters will be there too."

"I can't wait," she says, leaning in to leave another kiss on my lips. "This is a big step, raindrop. Meeting the family."

"You make me want to take all these big steps. Remember, I'm all in."

"Me too," she says.

It takes longer than I thought to unravel myself from Mia on my bedroom floor, but I can still taste her lips on mine as we take Daisy for a walk. We stop at the dog park near my place, but there is mud everywhere from the rain we got early this morning.

Daisy is well-behaved, and she is usually very calm. This is the first time I've taken her to the dog park and she hates it. She refuses to leave my side, even when I take her leash off to run.

Mia tries to get her to play fetch with the tennis ball we brought, but it is no use.

"It's okay, Daisy," Mia says as she clips her leash back on.

"The dog park isn't for everyone. I would always rather be home too."

We start walking towards the entrance when we hear a loud bellow behind us, someone calling for their dogs.

"Come back here!"

We turn around just in time to meet the two dogs who, apparently, were on the run. Two huge labs, one black and one brown, covered in mud, are running our way, and we have no time to react. By the time we realize what is about to happen, the two dogs jump on us.

Friendly, excited, but also muddy and wet.

The two dogs don't stay with us for long, moving on to their next victims as their owner shouts an apology our way.

Mia and I look down at our clothes, now covered in mud, and then down at Daisy who is looking at us like we're crazy from where she is sitting.

We can't help but burst out laughing at the complete madness of the situation. Mia has muddy paw prints all over her legs and t-shirt, and she somehow got mud on her face too.

I'm sure I look no better, with matching muddy paw prints all over my T-shirt and jeans.

"See, Daisy," Mia says. "*This* is why we stay home."

CHAPTER 41
MIA

AFTER THE DOG PARK FIASCO, we make it back to Eddie's place laughing the whole way there.

"I swear, it was like a movie seeing the two of them charging us," Eddie laughs as he opens the door to his and Mateo's apartment. They live about twenty minutes from me, closer to the part of Milwaukee that Drew and Emmett live. Their complex is older, with a rickety elevator that makes you want to take the stairs. The place is relatively big, fitting both of them nicely. Their living room is filled with a record player, various records, Mateo's bass guitar, and I'm sure I've already spotted six drumsticks just laying around.

"Did you want to clean up?"

"Yes, please." I was supposed to meet Annie and Drew again tonight for dinner at Annie's place, but I will definitely need to make a pit stop home before heading over there.

We walk into Eddie's bedroom, and Daisy plops into her bed. Eddie's room is exactly what I would picture for him. Dark with pockets of light. The walls are dark and covered in posters—Metallica, The Weeknd, Hozier, and Post Malone—just to name a few, showing how he really does listen to everything.

There are personal touches everywhere, and the room feels *lived* in. He has a sweatshirt hanging over his desk chair, one I definitely wouldn't mind adding to my collection of *Eddie's clothes I won't be giving back,* with a picture of him and four other women who slightly resemble him. The same dark hair, striking green eyes, tan skin, and sharp, yet soft, features. The five people in the photo are wearing the same smiles, ones that don't look like they are just for the camera. One of the women has the same dimples he does.

"Those are my sisters: Isa, Lucia, and Carmen. Isa's the oldest," he says, pointing to where she is standing next to Eddie in the photo. "That's Lucia," he adds, pointing to the woman with his same dimples, on the other side of him. "And that's Carmen, the youngest."

In the photo, Eddie and his three sisters are standing behind a chair where an older woman is sitting with a cake in front of her.

"And that's your mom?" I ask.

There is a gleam in Eddie's eyes as he takes the framed photo from the desk, bringing it close. He nods, emotion flooding the space around us. The mud on our skin and clothes and cleaning up long forgotten.

"You look like her," I say, wrapping an arm around his, leaning my head against his shoulder. "All four of you do."

Eddie's mother exudes a timeless grace, her lines of wisdom and hardships etched gently across her face. Her dark hair has lines of gray, her eyes warm, and her smile radiating the love she has surrounded by her children.

"I'm excited for you to meet her," Eddie says. A blush forms across his cheeks as he puts the photo back on his desk. "I've um . . . told her a lot about you."

"Eddie Ramirez, are *you* a mama's boy?" I tease, knowing the lightness of the conversation has a deeper edge, remembering what Eddie told me about his mom, and how he was the one that got her out of the house with his abusive father.

I know Eddie is a protector. It is laced in his blood. This healing journey of his will be so good for him. I hope it helps him see that he can be protective of the ones he loves, but he can also allow them to protect him too.

Eddie laughs at my remark. "You could say that. I definitely can do no wrong in my mom's eyes. My sisters and I always joke how that aspect of our mother falls head first into the Mexican mother stereotype."

This makes me smile, seeing the way Eddie's features soften as he thinks about his mom.

"Did you like growing up with sisters?" I ask, turning towards him and sitting on the edge of his bed. "I mean I know they made you listen to Britany Spears and take them to midnight premieres of *Twilight*, but other than that."

Eddie laughs at the small details I remember him telling me about having sisters. "I really did," he says. "Being the oldest, and the only boy, I did my fair share of running to my mom and playing the *your favorite* card, but I think my sisters really helped turn me into the man I am today. They're excited to meet you too."

"Tell me about them."

"Well, Isa is the oldest. She is four years younger than me. She's a teacher, like Drew. Lucia is two years younger than her, and she lives with her boyfriend in Chicago. She works for a marketing agency. Then, there is Carmen. She's your age. She works for a fashion company, hoping to land a spot as a designer." He continues telling me about their lives and how they all make time, once a month, to visit their mom all together.

"They all sound so successful. I'm sure you're proud of them." Hearing Eddie talk about his sisters makes my whole body feel warm, like his words are wrapping around me in a big hug. His subtle smile, his bright eyes, how fast he's talking, how he is so quick to show me pictures of them and talk about their hard work. I can see the pride Eddie has in being their brother, how much he loves them.

This is one of the many beautiful parts of himself that I wish he would see and acknowledge.

"They're going to love you," he says, sitting down on his bed next to me, nuzzling into my neck.

"I always forget how old you are. Your youngest sister is my age," I tease. "Grandpa."

He nips me in the neck as he gently knocks me over onto his bed, crawling on top of me.

"Watch it," he says into my neck, digging his fingers into my sides. It tickles so much I start to move my limbs uncontrollably.

It isn't until I am gasping for air from my laughter that Eddie finally lets up, but he takes my breath away in a different way.

All traces of laughter are gone as Eddie's lips land on mine, the smell of rain lingering in the air from the mud still on our clothes.

"What happened to cleaning up?" I say as his teeth find my lower lip.

"I think you're about to ruin showers for me, sunshine. I'll never be able to take one alone again." He kisses along my jaw, sending shivers down my spine.

"Who said we were going to clean up *together*?" He presses up on his elbows that are resting on the bed on either side of my head.

"My shower. My rules."

I let out a sigh, feigning defeat. "Well, if those are the rules." As if I haven't thought of Eddie every time I've showered alone.

With the hot water raining down on us, the glass door closing us in, it is like we're in our own little world.

Eddie looks good enough to eat as he reaches above his

head to get his hair wet. His biceps flex and the water drips down his tan skin. He's in nothing but that gold chain he never takes off, and I can't help but lean forward to run my tongue up his chest, feeling like I could lick every part of him.

Eddie opens one of his eyes through the water coming down on his face, and he pours body wash in his hands, his eyes on me.

Without a word, he begins to lather up the soap in his hands, and a rush of excitement shoots through me at the thought of smelling like Eddie, hopefully in more ways than one, by the time I leave here today.

He takes ample care, running his soapy hands down my arms, turning me so my back is against his front as he slides his hands down my waist and up my stomach, palming my breasts. I look down at the erotic sight, seeing his large hands cupping me, as he leans into my neck and grazes his tongue up my neck. I lean back into his shoulder, not even caring about how loud I am as I let out a moan.

Feeling his hands on me, feeling his body against mine, it is almost too much, filling me with the need to have him inside of me.

"Eddie," I moan, louder than I'd care to admit.

I've never been vocal in the bedroom, but being with Eddie has brought out a side of me that I never knew was there. Not only does he demand my voice be prevalent whenever we have sex, but I like the feeling of acting on instinct, doing what feels right in the moment, not caring about the consequences.

Until I hear a door slam and someone else shout Eddie's name.

Someone who sounds very similar to my *brother*.

Who wasn't supposed to be home for another few hours.

And I'm in the *shower*.

With his *best friend*.

Naked.

Eddie doesn't seem to notice, or care, moving as if my brother didn't just come home. The bathroom is in Eddie's bedroom, and I'm sure they have boundaries like not barging into each other's shower, but I can't shake the feeling that we are about to blow our cover, and give my brother just one more thing to stress about.

One of Eddie's hands slides down from my breasts, down my stomach, finding the spot between my legs. The spot that is aching for him, even when it shouldn't be.

"Eddie," I whisper through a moan as his finger finds the most sensitive part of me, circling mesmerizingly slow yet perfect at the same time, making me forget how to speak.

"Eddie," I say again, trying to see through this cloud of pleasure. "We have to stop or he'll hear us."

His fingers move further towards my entrance while his free hand over up my chest to my neck, stopping for a moment. "Or you can be a good girl and stay quiet."

He presses two fingers into me, swiftly and easily, wet from the shower and from the moments before. At the same moment he covers my mouth with the hand that was on my neck just in time to smother the moan that escapes me, seconds before he picks up speed, and I come undone.

CHAPTER 42

MIA

WE'RE on the way to Eddie's mother's house, and saying that I am nervous would be an understatement because I have so many feelings floating through me right now. I can't keep them straight.

After sneaking out of Eddie's apartment yesterday, making sure my brother didn't realize I was there, I headed home to get ready for dinner with Drew and Annie, and I was *dying* to tell someone what happened by the time I got there. I was barely inside Annie's apartment before completely unloading what the hell happened.

"Your brother caught you guys?!" Annie exclaimed, freezing mid-wine pour.

"In the shower?!" Drew added, her glass frozen a few inches from her mouth.

"No!" I clarified for them the events that took place from the mud at the dog park to him telling me about his mom and sisters to how we eventually ended up in the shower.

"You guys need to get your shit together," Annie said, sliding the very-filled glass of wine over to me.

"Yeah, maybe fooling around in the shower of the same

apartment your brother lives in was not the best idea," Drew said with a shrug.

"I know. Never again," I concluded.

I felt better after talking to them, feeling a little guilty to pile on the secrets they are also keeping from Mateo, but I *needed* to tell someone.

The subject changed to me meeting Eddie's family, and I told them that I was more excited than nervous. They both smiled saying that the nerves would come, but I left Annie's apartment that night feeling much lighter than when I got there.

Friends like Annie and Drew have that effect.

But now, on the way to Eddie's mother's house, there are nerves, just like Annie and Drew said there would be.

Who wouldn't be nervous to meet their boyfriend's mom?

Boyfriend? Is he my boyfriend? One more thing to think about right now.

Aside from the nerves, my mind is swirling with the possibilities of how tonight could go. What if they hate me? What if I don't live up to their expectations? What if they find me annoying and too chatty or weird and too quiet? What if I tell a stupid joke or make a dumb comment? The questions are endless, and when I think of one, it sparks another.

There is also this odd feeling in my chest, like a weight that makes my breathing come in shallow. I don't know where it's coming from, but it won't go away.

I feel a hand squeeze my thigh. "Come back to me, baby."

I turn to see Eddie, one hand on the steering wheel and one on my leg. His hair is slightly wet, making my stomach flip at the thought of our stolen moment in the shower yesterday.

He has on a black bomber jacket over a white t-shirt, his gold chain peeking out, unintentionally matching my black long sleeve tucked into a pair of white jeans.

It is unusually cool for an August night, the wind coming in from the window making the end of my ponytail whip against my neck.

"Sorry," I mutter. "Just a little nervous."

"I told you. They're going to love you. I'd tell you that you have nothing to worry about, but I know that beautiful brain of yours loves to worry." I turn my head and match the smile he is giving me with one of my own. He knows me so well. "So, I'll just hold your hand," he adds.

The rest of the ride, we listen to my "On Repeat" playlist on Spotify, and I can't help but smile at the fact that I have one, meaning I've been actually using my Spotify enough for it to curate a playlist based on all the random music I've been listening to.

Music was something I tried so hard to remove from all aspects of my life after Nico died, only for it to become an even bigger part of my life when I needed it most.

Cross My Heart, my brother, Eddie, my Lenny's crew, I never would have had them without what happened.

So why can't I get rid of this weight on my chest?

Seeing Eddie with his mom makes my heart feel like it is literally about to burst. On top of that, the way that he dotes on her, making sure her glass of wine is always filled, that her plate is refreshed, that she has everything she needs.

It is almost too much.

Not to mention the way that he does the same for his sisters, being the one to get up from the table to grab them something or clear their plates when they finish their dinner.

It *is* too much.

When we got here, walking through the front door felt like walking on stage, not knowing the words to the song you are supposed to sing.

Eddie squeezed my hand as he announced, *"Estamos aquí."*

One more thing that isn't good for my heart: hearing this man speak Spanish.

Having parents who immigrated from Mexico before the four kids were born, Eddie and his sisters grew up speaking Spanish at home and English at school.

Eddie mentioned they switch off between Spanish and English at home, his mother having learned English when she moved here with Eddie's father, which was something else that made me a little nervous being the only one who didn't speak Spanish.

Luckily, all worries subsided when we walked into the lively kitchen, his three sisters sitting at the kitchen counter, his mom at the stove. Glasses of wine in everyone's hands, smiles on everyone's faces.

"*Mi niño guapo.* My handsome boy," Eddie's mom, Cecilia, bellowed as she stirred up a big pot of what I now know is *pozole*, a brothy, Mexican soup made with hominy and meat. "*Dame un beso, mijito.*"

Eddie walked us over to her, giving her a kiss on the cheek before holding out his hand to me. "Ma, this is Mia. *Es mi novia.*"

Novia?

"Mia, it is so nice to meet you." She reached out and grabbed my hand that Eddie had just let go of. She brought me in for a hug like it was the most natural thing to do. "*Mi* Eduardo has talked so much about you." Her voice is thick with an accent, words warm in my ear.

"Thank you for inviting me to your family dinner. It's so nice to meet you." She pulled back, her hands on my shoulders, and took a look at me for a moment before looking back at Eddie.

"*Es muy bonita.*"

I watched Eddie's cheeks go pink before he coughed into his fist and placed his hand on my lower back to lead me over to the kitchen counter.

Meeting Isa, Lucia, and Carmen was like reacquainting with people you knew in a different life. Right away, we bonded over how white wine was superior to red as Isa poured me a glass of what they were drinking.

Eddie talked with his mom, helping her prep the soup as I chatted with his three sisters about my time with the band.

His family is so supportive of Cross My Heart having been to a few of the shows over the last three years. They talk about Eddie with such high regards, so proud that his band is going places.

Isa and Carmen asked a lot of questions about Theo and Silas, being the two single ones out of the Ramirez siblings, and I couldn't ignore Eddie's head whip in our direction when Isa said how Theo was the hotter of the two.

"Don't even go there," he said to her.

"You have no room to talk," Isa responded in the same way I've talked to Mateo before during one of his protective lectures.

It looked like she had more to say, but instead Lucia chimed in, eyes dropping to Eddie's neck. "You still wear *abuelo's* chain?" Lucia asked.

Eddie brought his hand to his neck, lightly touching the chain before rubbing his palm against the back of his neck, a flush in his cheeks.

"Yeah, ever since mom gave it to me after graduation."

"Better you than *him*," Lucia replied. Something passes between Eddie and his middle sister, and I realize who they are talking about.

After the most amazing meal, Eddie already clearing the plates and starting the dishes in the kitchen with his sisters, I'm left with just Cecilia.

"Are you sure I can't help clean up?" I ask her.

"No, no," she says, waving her hand. "*Mis hijos* can do it. You are the guest. Besides," she says, taking a sip of her wine, "I wanted to talk with you."

The nerves are back.

What could she want to talk about?

Did I already fuck this up somehow?

I thought it was going well.

Isa and Carmen seemed to like me.

Lucia too, but she seems a little harder to impress. By dinner, I think she warmed up to me.

"Of course," I say, trying to hide the uneasiness in my voice.

"Are you serious about *mi* Eduardo?"

I feel my chest heat at the question, at the thought of how we promised each other we were all in.

Tonight has been a lot. A lot of new feelings, new emotions, new people. The worry subsided, leaving me with such a full heart, but I still have this discomfort I can't shake.

Is it because I'm not all in like I thought I was?

This is a big step. Meeting Eddie's family.

My only family is Mateo and some extended family we barely hear from, and I haven't even told Mateo about Eddie and me yet.

The only other family I ever knew—felt like I was a part of —was . . .

Nico's.

I bury the thought, not wanting these thoughts to come up now, of all times. I've been fine. Monthly therapy sessions keep me grounded. I haven't had a panic attack since that night in the hotel room, being able to manage them before they become out of control.

I only think of Nico in a positive light, only getting teary-eyed when his favorite song comes on or I see his guitar case in my closet, no longer hidden under my bed.

I can't think of him right now. Not with Eddie's mom here, asking me how serious I am about her son.

I am serious about Eddie. So much so that it scares me, diving into feelings I have never felt before.

So I push it down.

Nico, the thoughts, the feelings, the memories, all of it.

"I am," I answer. "We were friends at first, but I realized it was more than that."

"He did too, I am guessing. I see the way he looks at you."

"What way is that?" I ask.

"Like he's been waiting for you his whole life."

I'm left speechless.

I've known this woman for two hours. She has known Eddie his whole life. Her words hit me right in the chest making it even harder to breathe than before, adding to the weight that is already pressing down.

"I'm sure you know that my son has been through a lot. We all have. Without him, well," she pauses, setting her elbow down on the table and resting her head in her hand. "I do not know where we would be."

"I'm sorry for what you all have been through. You are all so strong. I can't even begin to understand."

"Thank you, *mi cariña. Pero*, Eduardo, he took it all the hardest. I did not think I would ever see him with a real smile on his face again. And I have seen it more tonight than I have since he was young. I cannot help but think you are the reason."

She reaches a hand across the table, grabbing my hand resting next to my wine glass. She squeezes, and I feel my eyes dampen. So many things running through my head, but I tamp them all down to focus on the woman in front of me.

I squeeze her hand. "I think he'll be okay." The words seem small compared to the words she just said, but I know she knows what I mean when I see her eyes cloud too. Not only will Eddie be okay, but he *wants* to be. Knows he *deserves* to be. And he knows he has people who are there for him even when he's not.

The night wraps up with a promise for the two of us to be at the next family dinner in September. I exchange numbers with Isa, Lucia, and Carmen, starting a group chat to talk about the *Love Island* season they are each watching, one I am rewatching but still would love to enjoy their commentary about.

"What did I tell you, sunshine? They loved you." Eddie puts his hand on my thigh as we drive back to my apartment. "My mom even said she's keeping you if we ever break up."

I let out a small chuckle. The comment is funny, but I don't feel like I'm in the mood to laugh.

I'm also not in the mood to ruin Eddie's good mood, so happy we all hit it off. But I can't shake these feelings, these thoughts, that maybe I'm not 100 percent *in*, not like I thought I was.

It isn't just that we haven't told Mateo, but that is part of it.

Tonight reminded me that I'm moving on.

Like I should be.

But I still feel so damn guilty.

"Mia?" Eddie turns to look at me at the red light we are stopped at. "What's the matter? You don't think it went well?"

"No, no. That's not it at all. I love your mom and your sisters, and I've had such a nice time tonight."

"Then what is it?"

This isn't the kind of conversation to have at a red light.

"Nothing."

The light turns green, but Eddie doesn't move the car.

"The light is green, Eddie."

"Don't do that."

"Do what?"

"Don't go back to pretending everything is fine. We don't do that. Not anymore."

I sigh, loving yet hating how much this man knows me, how he can see right through me, more now than when we first met.

The car behind us honks and drives around us to make the light.

"Go. We'll talk when you drop me off."

The rest of the ride is filled with silence, loaded silence. There is tension in the air. Both our minds spiral with thoughts faster than we can keep track of them.

How am I supposed to tell the man I am falling in love with that I can't give him all of my love?

The more I think about what is holding me back, it isn't Mateo, it isn't seeing Eddie's family, it isn't even what happened.

It's that a part of me will always love *Nico*. A part that I can never give to Eddie. And how is it fair to ask Eddie to give all of himself to me, no hidden memories, no masks, no fake feelings, but I can't give all of myself to him?

He parks in the lot outside my apartment complex, and we walk to my apartment, hand-in-hand but still not letting the other one know what is on our minds.

It isn't until we are on my couch that I let the tears I've been holding in all night, both happy and sad, stream down my face.

"No, baby. Please. Please don't cry. Whatever it is, I'll fix it. Please, just don't cry." Eddie pulls me into his lap, and I lean my head against his chest, letting out a sob as I begin to feel everything I pushed down earlier.

It takes me a few minutes to catch my breath, the tears subsiding after giving them a chance to fall.

"I can't," is all I can say.

"Can't what? Please, Mia. Tell me what's wrong."

I take a breath, sliding off his lap, crossing my legs underneath me and facing my body towards him.

"I'm in love with you, Eddie."

His eyes light up and his mouth slightly opens. He grabs me by the face, bringing me in, kissing me hard.

He pulls away, leaving his forehead resting against mine.

"Then why are you crying, sunshine? Because you just made me the happiest man on this fucking planet."

"Eddie, I want to love you. So badly, with *all* my heart, with *all* my soul, but I can't. I just can't."

"I love you too, baby. So much. More than I thought I was capable of. Please don't say you can't. I know you can." He leans back, taking my hands in his and bringing both to his lips, leaving kisses on all of my knuckles. The gesture is so sweet that it makes my vision even blurrier.

I try to continue, not wanting us to fall victim to the miscommunication tropes Drew is always talking about in the romance books she reads.

I want to tell him what I'm feeling, in hopes that he can help me figure it out. "There is a part of me that will always belong to someone else, and I can't give it to you. It isn't fair for me to ask for all of you when I can't give you all of myself."

He lets go of one of my hands to bring his up to my cheek, grazing the warm, damp skin, as he wipes a stray tear with his thumb.

"Mia, Nico meant the world to you." More tears fall. "You grew up together. He changed you. He taught you things about yourself. Those same things I love about you. You will always love him. I would *never* ask you to give me the part of you that will always be with him." I let out a small breath, trying to get air moving in my lungs. "Baby, he was your first love, but I intend to be your *last*."

CHAPTER 43
EDDIE

IT'S OFFICIALLY WEDDING WEEKEND, and I can't believe we are finally here. Drew and Emmett chose the first weekend of October, which is perfect since we leave for tour next Friday.

Mia, Annie, and Drew did all the planning, bringing in me, Luke, and Emmett when they needed us. In the end, we all pulled in together, and it is going to be one hell of a weekend.

The wedding is tomorrow, so we are using our Friday night for the rehearsal dinner at the hotel near their venue. We are headed back to Cityscape after we rehearse the small ceremony, and then we are up bright and early to do all the wedding stuff tomorrow.

The end of August and all of September flew by. Between band practices, picking up more shifts at Lenny's with Annie officially gone as of the last weekend, waiting for Emmett to fill her spot, balancing time with Mia, friends, and family. October came out of nowhere.

Our record label, Thousands Sun Records, is also on my ass about getting a few more songs for them for the EP we are supposed to release at the end of the year. Luckily, songwriting has never been easier than it is now, having inspiration at my fingertips, *literally*.

Mia intertwined herself into my life so seamlessly, I forgot what it was like without her.

And I hope I never have to know.

We still haven't told Mateo about us, so the guilt of not only fooling around with his little sister, but falling in love with her is still heavy in my stomach.

What I do know is, I never want to let her go.

Having her meet my mom, Isa, Lucia, and Carmen, that night, has forever changed me. I saw a future, and, for the first time in my life, I didn't feel the past pulling me down. Going to the September monthly dinner solidified that even more.

When I took Mia home that night in August, and she opened up about how she was feeling about loving me, I can't say I hadn't thought it was a possibility myself.

It was actually something I talked about with my therapist.

My weekly sessions have been going well, and I used a few of our past sessions to voice my concerns about Mia loving me. My feelings of feeling undeserving of her love but also knowing it wasn't going to be easy for her to give her love away freely again. Not after what happened to her.

When she told me she loved me, my knee-jerk response was to tell myself that she didn't. Even as she said the words, I was tempted to not believe them because I have been conditioned to learn that I am not lovable unless I am putting on this face that everything is okay. That I am whole. That I'm not broken.

In reality, Mia loves me despite my broken pieces, and she has helped me put myself back together.

We're supposed to dress-up tonight, so I have on black, tapered slacks and a black, long-sleeved dress shirt. To make it more casual, I have the first few buttons undone, my gold chain on display.

The gold chain was my grandfather's, but my mom had given it to my dad. He never wore it, always kept it in the drawer of his bedside table, and it was the *one* thing, she later told me, that she refused to leave at that house the night we left.

My phone buzzes on my hotel room's bed. I'm not exactly sure what the room situations are, aside from me sharing a room with Mateo. Theo and Silas both didn't get a room, only coming for our show at the reception and then to stick around for the celebration of Drew and Emmett finally tying the knot tomorrow.

I think Mia and Annie are sharing a room, and Luke got his own. Drew and Emmett don't care about the superstition of not seeing each other before the wedding, so they have their own room too.

When I walk out of my hotel room, the door closing behind me, the door two down from mine closes at the same time. I turn to my left to see Mia, who I was just on my way to go see before heading down to the lobby.

My heart stops when my eyes find her. Her blonde waves are curled, flowing behind her shoulders. She has a black dress that stops just above her knees, and the cut of the top drops low, making me salivate. The sleeves are long, her long bronzed legs and the glow of her chest being what all my attention will be on tonight..

"Hey, raindrop," she says as she closes the space between us. My feet are glued to the ground because she damn near took all the breath from my lungs, and I'm so glad she is the one to do it.

I see her glance past me and look over her shoulder before grabbing me by the shirt and pulling me in for a kiss. She has red heels that match the color of her lips, so I don't have to bend down too far.

Her kisses always send me to another dimension, but this one might kill me.

She pulls back and smiles, using her thumb to wipe my bottom lip.

"Sorry, forgot I had lipstick on."

I want to tell her never to be sorry because the thought of her mark on me, for everyone to see, excites me in ways it shouldn't.

Especially if those marks are on my neck, my chest, around my—

I cough into my fist. "No worries. You look beautiful."

"You clean up well too. It's going to be hard to keep my hands to myself tonight."

"Then maybe you shouldn't try," I say too fast, still light-headed from the kiss and forgetting that she wants to wait until *after* the wedding to tell Mateo.

She said that telling him on tour would be too late, but before the wedding would make the day about us rather than Drew and Emmett.

Since Mia is still set to go on tour with us, it is a big gamble to tell Mateo *before* we go, but Mia is as ready as I am to be rid of this guilt.

I think we have to sit down and explain to Mateo that things just happened, and we aren't just messing around. That what we have is real, and I have never been so sure about something, or someone, in my entire life.

I want to tell Mateo that I'm all in with Mia, that I always will be. I know if we can explain everything to him, he may be mad at first that we kept it a secret, but he will understand.

"We just have to get through this weekend," she says, grabbing my hand and leading us to the elevator. She has her camera bag around her shoulder, so I grab it and sling it over mine. The bag is worn and on the verge of falling apart, and it looks out of place next to her pretty dress.

"How am I supposed to keep my hands to myself when

you look like *that*?" I push the down button on the wall between the two elevators.

"I've heard something like that before," she teases, squeezing my hand as I feel my cheeks burn.

I will never forget when she opened the door to her hotel room after our first show last year, and all she had on was my t-shirt. I admitted to her what a distraction she was to me that night, practically begging her to put on a pair of pants.

"You're still as distracting as ever." I bring her hand up to my lips, leaving a light kiss on the back of her hand as we wait for the elevator to stop on our floor.

She glances at the elevator. "Can we take the stairs? I hate elevators."

"Scared? Don't be. I only know *two* people who have ever gotten stuck in an elevator before."

"Two?!"

I knew she didn't like elevators, but I didn't know she was actually scared of them.

"You'll be fine, sunshine. I can be a good distraction too."

The elevator dings, and my stomach flips when I see it's empty. Stolen moments with Mia are always giving me butterflies.

I pull her into the elevator, my back against the right side. I push the Lobby button before letting go of her hand and grabbing her by the hips. My hands fit so perfectly as I pull her into me. I want her to feel how much I need her already while also kissing her neck the way she likes so she regrets making me wait.

"You look gorgeous in this dress especially because I know how gorgeous you are *underneath*," I whisper into her ear as we move down the nine floors to the lobby.

"That was good. Have you been practicing?" She reaches between us to rub my cock through my dress pants, which are tight enough to not leave too much up to the imagination.

"Careful, sunshine. We don't want everyone to know you

were feeling me up in the elevator." She kisses me, moving with the rhythm we have perfected over our months together, her tongue tangling with mine.

"It's that pickup line, raindrop. It got me so hot and bothered," she says against my lips, and I can't help but grin, laughing at not only her sassy comment but how the banter between us has only strengthened with time.

It used to be our way of distracting ourselves, distancing ourselves from the terrifying feelings the other made us feel. Now, it is the fun, flirty teasing that we always pretended it was.

The elevator dings, signaling that the doors are about to open to the lobby, so we part like two teenagers coming out from under the bleachers. Mia uses her thumb and her middle finger to make sure her lipstick isn't smudged around her lips, and I wipe my mouth on the back of the hand, my cock coming more to life when I see the smudge of her lipstick.

Before the elevator doors open I look at her, wishing I could have her body back on mine.

She returns my gaze, before the doors open, and she asks, "What two people do you know who got stuck on the elevator?"

"The two people who are getting married tomorrow."

CHAPTER 44
MIA

THE REHEARSAL GOES SMOOTHLY. I didn't realize how easy weddings are when there are no overbearing mothers or other family members trying to make it about themselves.

Drew's friend, Lacey, takes charge, cueing Drew's bridesmaids when it is our turn to walk down after Emmett and his groomsmen make their way.

Drew and Emmett aren't having any of us stand up with them and the officiant, Lacey's boyfriend Tyler, so we all just practice walking down the aisle and then standing in front of where we will sit during the ceremony until Drew gets to her spot in front of Emmett.

Theo and Silas are there manning the music in charge of playing the song we will all walk down to, "A Thousand Years" by Christina Perri.

"Okay, all good!" Lacey exclaims after we finish our fourth practice, finally living up to her expectations. Lacey looks gorgeous in her lavender dress, her blonde hair a little darker for the fall season. She dotes over Drew like an older sister, and I can tell how happy she is to be part of Drew's special day.

Eddie and I barely get a chance to talk after our *distracting* elevator ride, but my eyes always find him.

The way he looks tonight is straight out of a wet dream, and it took a hell of a lot of willpower to not push him into his hotel room when I saw him earlier tonight.

"It's a little chilly, but Cityscape is only a five minute walk. We ready to go?" Annie asks the crowd. After some chatting, it is decided that the Lenny's crew will be heading to Cityscape, but Mateo is meeting his girlfriend who can't come to the wedding tomorrow night due to a work trip.

Theo and Silas have dates, so they head out, and Lacey and Tyler are staying back at the hotel because Lacey wants to make sure everything is ready for tomorrow.

"You sure you don't want to come with us to Cityscape?" I ask Mateo. "You can bring your girlfriend." He hasn't even told me her name, but I am hoping he introduces us all to her soon.

"No, not tonight," he replies.

Drew, Emmett, Luke, Annie, and Eddie have started making their way to the door, but I stay behind to ask Mateo one more time. "Are you sure? We would all love to meet her." I can't hide the disappointment of feeling like Mateo doesn't want to let me in on this part of his life.

He must be able to tell because he reaches out to put a hand on my shoulder. "It's not a you thing, Mia. It's a me thing. I just want to make sure this thing between us is in a good spot before she meets you."

"Mateo, it's not like you're my dad, introducing me to a new flavor of the month. We're adults."

"I know that, but still. It is my first real relationship in years, and I want to do things a certain way. Seriously, it isn't you." I can't lie. It does hurt my feelings that he doesn't want me to meet her yet, but I get what he is saying.

"Fine." I cross my arms.

"Don't be mad." Mateo shakes my shoulder, getting a small smile out of me.

"You're the worst," I say, lightly punching him in the chest.

He brings his hand to it, leaning back as if I actually had put power behind the punch. It makes me laugh.

Bastard. I'm trying to be mad at him.

"Do you want me to bring your camera back up to your room?"

I glance at my shoulder, realizing I still had it. "Oh, yeah." I hand it to him after grabbing my wallet from the front pocket. I never carry a purse because I usually have my camera bag.

"Room key?" Mateo asks.

"Oh, duh." I grab one of the two room keys I got when I checked in. Keeping one for me and giving the other to my brother.

"Don't lose your wallet."

"Okay, *Dad*."

"Camila."

I laugh. "You're so easy to piss off."

The six of us head over to Cityscape to celebrate the kickoff to the weekend, already a slight buzz from some drinks we had during the rehearsal.

Cityscape is a little different tonight than it was in the summer, the same string lights setting the perfect ambiance on the now-heated rooftop. The night is clear with a cool breeze but the blanket of a few glasses of wine and a Tequila Sunrise helps keep me warm.

The alcohol and Eddie at my side.

I let go of all my better judgment tonight, forgetting what I said earlier about keeping our hands to ourselves.

With his hands on me, I can't think straight. The only thoughts I can manage to string together are how to not completely melt into his hands.

We are seated at a table on the rooftop, all six of us surrounding a low table while sharing a two-seater lounge chair with our other.

Drew and Emmett.

Annie and Luke.

Eddie and I.

Why does this feel so perfect?

My cheeks hurt from the amount I have smiled, my throat hoarse from how much I've laughed.

I sit back, and finish the last sip of what will be my last drink tonight if I don't want to wake up hungover tomorrow for the wedding day. I look around at the five people who have come to mean so much to me, all in their own ways.

Drew, with her appreciation for love and life, always wanting everyone around her to be happy.

Annie, with her sass and her spunk, always making me feel like I have a ride-or-die at my side.

Even Luke and Emmett, getting closer with them to learn more of who they are behind the golden retriever smile of Luke and the gruff and tattoos of Emmett.

Then there is Eddie.

My rainy day.

My broken boy.

My drummer with the sad eyes.

The eyes that aren't so sad anymore.

Eddie leans in, pressing a kiss to my temple as we listen to Annie talk about how vet school is picking up as the second month starts. Luke gives her a hard time, telling her to come back to Lenny's because Emmett still hasn't hired her replacement yet.

Emmett rolls his eyes, and Drew laughs at her future-husband's look of annoyance at his bartender who knows exactly how to push his buttons.

I turn to Eddie. "I'm going to go get some water."

"I'll get it for you."

"No, no. You stay. I'll be right over there." I point over my shoulder to the bar not even ten feet away. "I'll be fine, Eddie." I lean in, knowing our friends can see but not caring anymore, pressing my lips against his. Feeling the warmness of his full lips, making me forget we aren't the only one's on the rooftop.

"There it is," I hear Annie yell. My exposed chest reddens as our friends hoot and holler.

"About time," Emmett says under his breath as he takes a sip of his whiskey.

"You guys are stupid," I say as I stand up.

"Not stupid enough to know you guys have been falling for each other for over a year now. About time you stopped your silly hiding," Annie replies, slapping me on the butt as I scoot past the lounger she and Luke are sitting in.

"Watch it, Ann." I hear Eddie say. "There's still one more person to tell." With that, I walk over to the bar, a smile on my face at the fact that our friends were so happy for us to come out with our relationship, even though all of them have known about it.

It is nice to feel like Eddie and I are finally out in the open, after being a secret for so long.

"Can I get a water, please?" I ask the bartender. I have a pleasant buzz, and one more drink will take me over the edge.

"You got it," the bartender says, as he grabs a plastic cup to fill with ice.

I set my elbows on the bar, waiting for my water. I'm tempted to turn around, knowing Eddie's eyes are one me. I can feel them like a handprint on my heart, always looking out for me, the protective man that he is.

"Hey," a voice says. I turn to my left to see a guy about my age. He is cute but nothing special, no striking green eyes, no mysterious scar, no calloused hands that fit perfectly around my hips.

"Hi," I say, to be polite. I look back at the bartender who left the cup with ice unattended as he took other orders. My water long forgotten.

"I like your dress," the guy to my left says.

"Thanks," I say. He isn't being too forward or rude, but I still feel my skin prickle at how he seems to inch into my space with every second that passes.

"Can I buy you a drink?" he asks, and he no longer keeps his hands to himself, his shoulder now against mine as he copies my position against the bar.

"I'm good," I politely decline, moving my upper body a few inches the opposite way.

I glance over my shoulder, but I don't see Eddie where I left him. I turn back to the bar, contemplating just forgetting about my water like the bartender did.

"Hey," the guy says, but he is looking over my shoulder, and I feel the familiar presence before I even have to look. "Back off, she's mine," the guy says, a new edge to his voice, no longer playing the nice guy.

"Sorry, man. I'm *already* hers." Eddie loops his arm around my waist, pulling me into him. My skin no longer prickling at the unwanted attention of some stranger but instead heating at Eddie's choice of words.

I know Eddie is protective, possessive even. I've seen him lose control before, the anger he buries boiling over in a matter of seconds. But not today.

Granted, no one was threatening me or refusing to let go of me, but I can't help the smile on my face and the heat swirling in my belly at his calm and cool demeanor, simply stating that he is mine.

I look up at him, leaning my back against his front, focusing on him and him alone.

"I love you, raindrop."

He looks down, pressing his lips to my forehead, my chest aching from the tenderness of the act.

"I love you, sunshine."

CHAPTER 45

MIA

THE SUMMER of planning we had talked about four months ago has come and gone, and tonight is the last night before Drew and Emmett become husband and wife.

Even though I stopped drinking, my buzz is still strong, hitting me harder as Eddie walks me to my hotel room.

After joining our friends again, sitting in the lounge chair, leaning into the crook of his shoulder, his arm around me, the drinks from earlier in the night caught up to me, and it wasn't until we stood up to leave that it all hit me.

"No more white wine or tequila for you, huh?"

"Shut up. I can handle my liquor," I say, proving myself wrong when I touch my dress where pockets would be. My stomach drops, and I slap a hand to my forehead. "I lost my wallet."

Eddie laughs as he reaches into his pocket, pulling out my pink card holder. "You gave it to me on our walk to Cityscape, remember?"

Nope, but I don't tell him that.

Instead, I snatch it from him, pulling out my one room key.

It takes me more times than I would like to admit to open

up the door, somehow not timing the swipe of the card with the turning of the door handle. Eddie tries to hide his chuckling, but he doesn't do a good job.

I finally stumble inside, but Eddie stays in the doorway.

"You're not coming in?"

"My room is two doors down, and I don't want your brother to wonder where I am."

"He's out with what's-her-face," I reply, still a little bitter he doesn't want to introduce me to his girlfriend, even though I have no room to be bitter. I haven't introduced him to my boyfriend.

Not that they need much of an introduction.

I cross my arms, pouting and shamelessly resorting to guilt-tripping.

Eddie laughs, looking up at the ceiling of the hotel hallway before taking a few steps towards me, not yet closing the space like I would like him too.

"You need sleep. I'll see you tomorrow in your bridesmaid dress."

"I want to sleep with *you*," I say, uncrossing my arms.

"It's not a good idea. We don't want to get caught *this* weekend, of all weekends." He is trying to stay strong, but I can tell his willpower is wavering the more I beg him to stay.

I know he is right, but in this moment, the combination of seeing his flushed cheeks and buttoned dress shirt, revealing the tan skin of his chest. His internal struggle of wanting to take me to bed but also be the responsible one and not risk my brother catching us and ruining the wedding weekend.

I blame the alcohol in my system for making me want to be selfish and not think about the consequences to our actions, but I know it's not. It is Eddie. The only part of my life I have ever been selfish about is him. Not overthinking every downfall, not worrying about every conclusion, not thinking myself into a panic attack at the thought of what could happen if we don't work out.

With Eddie, it is easy to be in the moment.

He makes me forget all the thoughts constantly spiraling in my head.

I close the space between us, reaching out to grab his hand, pulling it to rest around my waist. I snake my arms around his neck, pulling his lips down to mine. "Stay," I whisper against his lips.

"You don't know what you're asking for, sunshine."

But I think I do. He kisses me, and it sets me on fire. I push him back until he needs to reach behind himself with the arm not holding onto me to slam my hotel room door shut before I press him against it.

I can't get enough of the taste of him, his tongue dancing with mine.

I will never get sick of it.

My lips find his jaw, kissing the hard yet soft line, making my way to his neck, his skin warm under my lips, as I reach a hand between our flushed bodies.

"Mia," he moans, leaning his head back against the door, and I smile against the skin of his chest at the thought of our position flipped in that green room. How it feels like it was a lifetime ago.

The memory makes my stomach flip, the thought of Eddie's attention all on me during that stolen moment.

Two can play at that game.

I make quick work of his belt, before I kiss down on his exposed chest. Eddie's grip goes from my hips to my ass, his fingers digging into the material of my dress before he lifts it up, the cotton of my underwear being the only barrier between us.

"I need you naked. Now," he growls, his control slipping with every kiss of my lips on his skin.

"No," I say.

"What have I told you about telling me 'no?'" he asks, his eyes open, but I'm already on my knees.

Before he can say anything else about me being a brat or how good girls use their words, I slide his boxer briefs down, freeing his erection.

I look up at him, green eyes dark, his scar making him look almost dangerous at this angle, but I know I'm the one holding all the power.

His eyes slightly widen as I bring my hand to my mouth, licking my palm before using it to fist his cock, a groan escaping his lips as I move my hand up and down.

"Fuck," escapes his lips, his head leaning back against the door again, his eyes shutting as his hips slowly begin to move with the rhythm of my hand.

I bring my mouth forward, sticking out my tongue to swirl against the tip.

"I'll give you three seconds to get your mouth on my cock, sunshine, or I'm taking back control."

You wish, I think to myself before taking him all into my mouth, a mix of my name and a moan coming from Eddie's mouth.

His hands find my hair, pulling it all into one hand, but he holds onto his control, letting me set the pace as I adjust to his size, opening my throat to get as much of him as I can.

"That's my fucking girl."

His grip on my hair makes my scalp slightly sting, but it makes the pressure between my legs almost unbearable. It is as if Eddie knows, understanding my body better than I do myself, because he pulls himself out of my mouth, before pulling me up from my knees and throwing my body over his shoulder as if I weigh nothing.

"My turn," he growls as he throws me down on the bed, laying me on my back and having my dress lifted in a matter of seconds.

"Impatient today, are we?" I tease, as he hooks his fingers under the elastic of my underwear, yanking them down and spreading my legs.

"Always am when it comes to tasting you." His breath against my sensitive flesh, almost making me come undone by his words alone.

His tongue swipes up, opening me up for him, before he finds my clit, circling his tongue around the bundle of nerves in the way he knows drives me crazy.

I reach between my legs, gripping his hair like he did mine, begging for more pressure as he devours me. Licking, sucking, nipping, until I am a complete and utter mess, writhing beneath him like he didn't just break me apart and put me all back together.

Eddie climbs up my body, using his elbows around my head to support his weight, pressing his lips to mine and kissing me with all he has. The taste of myself on his lips makes the fire in my belly ignite once more. "Stay," I say, but this time, I know he will.

"You're lucky I can't say no to those pretty brown eyes," he says, looking down at me with a lazy smile on his face before he thrusts into me, and we spend the rest of the night falling apart with each other over and over again, not caring about how tired we will be in the morning, not wasting a moment of our stolen time together.

CHAPTER 46
EDDIE

A KNOCK on the door wakes me up, but Mia doesn't even stir. Her ass is pressed up against my dick, covered by only my boxer briefs, her back covered by my shirt from last night flush against my naked chest.

I've learned over our months together that Mia is a heavy sleeper, just like her brother, but only when she is in my arms. She is convinced she is a light sleeper, always waking up in the middle of the night at her apartment whether from one of her recurring dreams or a creak of the old building.

In reality, she doesn't ever take into account that I can kiss my way all the way between her legs before she'll wake up.

Wait.

I never went back to my place last night.

I'm still in bed with Mia.

She convinced me to stay.

And the door to her hotel room is opening.

Right now.

"What the fuck?!" I hear, and so does Mia because the white sheets around us ruffle before being thrown to the end of the bed.

Mia and I look at each other for a second, and it is the last second before everything changes.

"Mateo," she says. "What are you doing here?"

"Really? That's the question you're going to go with? I brought you a fucking coffee along with the key you gave me, wanting to apologize for blowing you off last night." He sets the coffee down on the dresser before throwing the room key down on the bed. His attention turns to me. "What the hell are you doing in bed with my sister?" He steps forward, and I think for a second he is going to rush me, but I put my hands out.

I look to Mia to see if she wants me to explain, but her eyes are on Mateo as she stands up and rounds the bed.

"This isn't how I wanted you to find out."

Mateo runs a hand through his hair, and he is pacing back and forth, in the way he does when he is trying to stay calm and losing against his anger, but he stops when she says this.

"Find out what? It is pretty clear what you guys are up to," he spits.

"No," Mia says. "It wasn't just a hookup, we—me and Eddie—we've been," she pauses, looks at me, and I give her a nod.

"We're toge–"

"No," Mateo interjects, and the harshness of the word makes Mia take a step back from him. "Don't say it. Don't you dare tell me the two of you have been doing *this*," he gestures to the mess of the bed and the two of us half naked, "behind my back for more than just last night."

"Mateo, I wanted to tell you," Mia pleads, tears clouding her eyes. "You were just so stressed, and I didn't want to stress you out more." Tears escape from her eyes as she continues. "We were just friends at first, but we developed feelings. It wasn't until earlier this summer where I—"

"Months?! You have waited *months* to tell me you were fucking my best friend. And you," he says, turning his attention to me. "What did I tell you about leaving her alone? I told you she didn't have the time or energy to put up with your sorry ass. Now, here you are, making her think that she can what? Fix you? I can't believe you!" His voice raises, but I've known Mateo my whole adult life, and I have never heard it get this loud. The only times close to this either being on stage or that night at Mia's over a year ago.

"I didn't mean for it to happen, Mateo. I'm sorry we didn't tell you."

He looks between me and his sister. "Who else has been keeping this little secret of yours?" He asks, and, when neither of us answer, he shakes his head. "Unbelievable." He wipes a hand across his mouth before he lets out a humorless laugh. "This is great. Just great."

"Seriously, man. We were going to tell you. We were just waiting for the right time," I try to explain, grabbing my pants from the floor and putting them on.

"No, you know what? You're out."

I freeze. "What?"

"You're out of the fucking band." The words hang in the air. I blink, unsure if I even heard him correctly.

"Mateo, stop," Mia pleads, but he puts out a hand to her.

"I'm serious. I'm telling the label we need a fill-in for the tour. I'm fucking done with you."

"Mateo, come on. The tour is next week. Let's just talk about this. You can't kick me out of the band."

Mateo takes a step closer to me, and says in a voice scarier than his voice raising. "Watch me."

He turns to leave, but Mia grabs his arm. "Mateo, wait. Please. Just let us explain. This isn't just a fling or fooling around. This is real. We wanted to tell you, share it with you, but I wanted to wait until your work stuff died down and the stress with the tour subsided. Please, just talk to us."

"No, I'm done. Done with this. Done with *him*. Done with

you. Don't bother coming on tour either. I'll have the label's photographer come. I'm done, Mia."

Mia looks like his words slapped her across the face.

"Camila," is all she says, and both Mateo and I look at her. I know that is her full-name, but I also know she doesn't use it. She says Mateo only uses it when…

Oh. Realization hits me hard, and my heart breaks in half for her. Knowing these two so well, watching what is about to happen is like when you watch two cars crash. Knowing it is coming, but you can't do anything about it.

"You call me 'Camila' when you're mad."

"I'm not mad at you, Mia." The words *I'm disappointed* are left unsaid, but Mia hears them loud and clear.

Her head falls, and I have to fight against my own body to resist the urge to go to her, to bring her in my arms, to protect her from all of this.

But I can't.

We knew this could happen.

I think that is why we lied to ourselves, telling ourselves, and each other, that we were waiting for Mateo's benefit. But that wasn't the case.

I know that now.

And I think Mia does too.

"You have to get ready," Mateo says as he walks towards the door. "We're not going to ruin Emmett and Drew's day. Put a smile on your face and pretend. You're good at that," he says to both of us, but I know who the comment was for.

He walks out without another word, and Mia falls to her knees by the foot of the bed, her sobs start coming out hard, like she can't catch her breath.

She is having a panic attack.

"Mia, baby," I say, my feet moving as fast as they can, bending down to her and bringing her to my chest. She's hyperventilating, her eyes closed, her chest moving up and down way too fast. There is no way her lungs are filling.

My sister, Lucia, used to have panic attacks. They started the night that I finally stood up to my dad. That's how I know that Mia needs to breathe, come back down from where her mind is holding her captive, and breathe.

"Come back to me, sunshine. There you go. Take a deep breath in for me." I take a deep breath in myself and let it out. I take in another, exhale, and she breathes in with me this time.

"That's my girl. One more for me, okay?" We take a deep breath in together before we exhale it out. Her eyes slowly open, the redness around those pretty brown eyes ripping me to shreds.

"It wasn't supposed to happen like that," she whispers, more to herself than me. I hug her closely, kissing the top of her head.

"I know," I whisper into her hair. "I know."

CHAPTER 47

MIA

I HATE myself for letting this happen. I hate how I disappointed Mateo, how I got between him and Eddie, and how this had to happen today of all days.

The last thing I would ever want is to make today about me, or Eddie, or Mateo. Not when it is supposed to be about Drew and Emmett.

After Eddie picked me up off the floor, *literally*, we decided it would be best to focus on the wedding, being there for Drew and Emmett, and not letting on to anyone what happened this morning.

Not ideal.

Not the most healthy.

But it is our best option.

Eddie kissed me before I left, and it made my eyes sting all over again because, for some reason, it felt like it would be the last time.

How did I ever think we were going to make this work?

How did I ever convince myself, and Eddie, that we were doing the right thing?

How the hell are we going to fix this?

We can't.

But I don't have time to dwell on it, swallowing the feelings and the thoughts and the questions even though I know my therapist would tell me to do otherwise.

I take a few moments to myself when Eddie leaves, not having the energy to worry about whether or not he and Mateo are going to have to navigate their shared space when getting ready today. Especially because they are both groomsmen.

Drew, Annie, and the other bridesmaids are expecting me down the hall in Drew's hotel room in less than twenty minutes. Annie and I were technically sharing a room, but we all ignored the fact that she ended up in Luke's.

Pretending seems to be the theme of the day.

Fake smiles, fake peace, fake being okay.

I take a quick shower in an attempt to wash away the headache from my slight hangover and the aftermath of the first panic attack I have had in *months*.

I grab my dress, covered on a hanger, and my duffle bag packed with everything I need to get ready before hooking my camera over my shoulder, and heading down to the end of the hall to Drew's hotel room.

I don't even have time to take a breath, putting myself into autopilot, and pasting a smile on my face like I've seen Eddie do so many times before.

"There you are," Annie says as she opens the door.

"Looks like we're just waiting for Lacey," Drew says as she brings me in for a hug. She is in her white silk robe that says "'Til Death" on the back with a skeleton hand holding up the ring finger. Her red hair is in soft waves, clipped back so Annie can do her makeup.

Annie's two hobbies are makeup and baking, both having come in handy as she is helping us all get ready *and* she baked the cake for the reception.

Drew was so happy to have all of us using our hobbies

and talents for her day, and I think it made it all the more special to her.

She only wants photos of the ceremony because she is like me and doesn't love having her picture taken, and, with everything else going on, I'm thankful I don't have to worry about capturing the entire night on top of balancing the bridesmaid duties with also trying not to let on the war going on in my head.

It is easy to forget everything going on with my brother and Eddie while I'm with the girls. I find myself not even having to pretend to be having fun or putting a smile on my face. It comes naturally when I'm with them. Laughing, drinking mimosas, and enjoying our time with Drew was exactly what I needed.

At one point, Annie asked if everything was okay, her sixth sense of being able to sense the smallest change in someone's demeanor. I was able to convince her I was fine, but I think she knew something was up.

"You'll fill me in later?" She whispers, as she lightly brushes a soft pink blush onto my cheeks.

"Nothing to worry about," I whisper back, widening my eyes slightly so she knows I don't want to make anything about me.

She nods as she puts the blush and brush down and hands me a lipstick and grabs a handheld mirror, but her wheels are turning. She eyes me as she holds up the mirror for me to put the red lipstick on my lips. "I saw Mateo on his way to your room this morning."

I try not to show any reaction on my face, but I'm sure Annie clocked the millisecond it took me to recover from hearing what she said. I rub my lips together, evenly spreading the red across my lips before closing the lipstick and handing it back to Annie.

I look into her eyes and I know she knows.

"Was Eddie still there?" She asks, and I don't even have to

say a word. I just stare into her big, chocolate brown eyes. She hears me loud and clear..

"Are you okay?" she whispers, and it makes me want to crumble.

No.

I'm not okay.

I fucked up with the two people who I owe everything too, and I fucked things up for them too.

This is what I get for not thinking things through. This is what I get for being selfish and only thinking about myself. This is what I get for not worrying about what could go wrong in an attempt to avoid hurting two of the most important people in my life.

I smile, but there is no happiness behind it. Instead, it is just lifting the corners of my lips upward in an attempt to stall the tears threatening to escape again. I shake my head no before I turn around to where Lacey and Emma are helping Drew with her hair, adding tiny braids in the midst of her red curls with little butterflies clipped to the ends.

I widen the smile on my face, hoping that if I pretend long enough, the smile will become a real one.

I spend the rest of the morning trying to stay in the moment, rather than get trapped in my mind. I keep trying until everything with Eddie and Mateo falls into the back of my mind, admiring Drew as Lacey and Emma finish her hair, as Annie adds the finishing touches on her makeup, and as I pretend that my heart isn't currently sitting at the bottom of my stomach, shattered into pieces too small to ever put back together.

CHAPTER 48
MIA

WHEN IT IS my turn to walk down the aisle, holding my bouquet of red roses, my black silk dress dragging on the floor behind me, it takes everything in me not to glance at Eddie, or Mateo, knowing I'll lose it if I look directly at either of them. They are standing in front of the first row of chairs, facing the aisle, but I keep my gaze forward as I follow Lacey and Annie to the first row on the opposite side.

I'm saving the rest of my tears today for Drew and Emmett.

The music changes after Emma gets to her spot next to me, and I reach down under my chair—where I put my camera earlier—to start getting photos of the ceremony

There isn't a dry eye in sight when Drew walks down the aisle, her eyes cloudy, staring at Emmett who is looking at her like she is his whole world.

She is wearing a long-sleeved white dress that hugs her figure, the silk material accentuating every curve. The neckline is high, but her back is on full display as the material hangs low, adding an edge to the otherwise simple, yet beautiful.

She is holding a bouquet of red and black roses as she

slowly walks towards Emmett who is sporting an all-black fit, a black velvet suit that hugs his massive frame, all his hair pulled back in a bun, his smile shining behind his beard.

I get shots of them both as they make their way to each other, and it is so easy to capture the love they have for one another.

My job feels almost too easy when the people I'm taking photos of forget I'm there, focusing on what they're doing, letting me freeze the beautiful moments in time for them to cherish forever.

Drew and Emmett are so focused on one another, I wouldn't be surprised if they forgot about me—and everyone else in this whole hall.

The venue is basically a big warehouse, with greenery and string lights lining the walls and ceiling, black and gold accents speckled about. There are chairs lined with the twenty or so people here for the ceremony with a big wooden bar lining the back. It is right next door to the hotel we were all staying at and it will be flipped to hold the reception when the ceremony finishes.

Emmett reaches up to wipe a stray tear from his eye as Drew walks herself down the aisle. Tyler, the officiant, does an amazing job relaying to the small crowd of loved ones how Emmett and Drew found each other when they both least expected it. A beautifully tragic love story where the two of them helped each other heal and learn to love not only each other, but themselves too.

I'm trying not to focus on Eddie, but it takes every ounce of effort I have left. I also have to actively avoid looking at my brother, worried that him dismissing my gaze, refusing to look at me altogether, may send me into another panic attack.

Eddie is seated with the other groomsmen in the first row on the right. He is the first one off the aisle with Drew's brother, Calvin next to him, and Mateo is on the other side of Cal. I'm watching the ceremony from behind the camera, thankful for the distraction of being able to focus on getting all the perfect shots of Drew and Emmett rather than having to sit in the heat of Eddie's green eyes.

Reminding myself that this is a moment I don't want to forget, I, once again, push all the thoughts of Eddie and Mateo to the back of my mind, the pit in my stomach the only reminder of the shit show I put myself in.

I focus on the intensity in Emmett's eyes as he looks down at the love of his life. I focus on the soft smile on Drew's face as she slides the black ring on to Emmett's ring finger. I focus on the way Emmett squeezes her hand as he says, "I do."

"Emmett, you may kiss your bride. Drew, you may kiss your groom," Tyler says, and I brace myself for the tears threatening to blur my vision as I forget the world around me to get the photo I've been waiting for since I offered to take these pictures.

Emmett brings a hand to Drew's cheek, leaning down slightly because of their massive height difference, even in Drew's heels, and presses his lips to hers.

I take as many photos as I can, clicking the button in hopes to capture the perfect shot, and it isn't until Emmett pulls back do I let go of my camera to hang around my neck and clap and cheer with the rest of the small crowd.

"Congratulations, you guys," I say as I wrap my arms around both of them, needing the hug more than I'd like to admit. "I'm so happy for you two." The wedding party followed Drew and Emmett to a private room while the venue employees set up the hall for the reception, the small crowd of guests surrounding the bar while the tables get set up around the dance floor.

I don't have time to chat more with them as they make the rounds to the other bridesmaids and groomsmen, one of those groomsmen who gives them their congratulations and starts to make his way over to me.

I glance to my right to see Annie chatting with my brother,

but I still don't think it is a good idea for Eddie and I to be anywhere near each other.

I'm about to turn to Emma and Cal to avoid Eddie, but my feet glue to the floor when I take a second to look at him. I've been avoiding it all afternoon, but now that he is walking towards me, I take him in, and there is no going back.

His brown hair is more tame than usual, but I know that he has been running his fingers through it. His black velvet suit matches the one Emmett is wearing, but the white dress shirt underneath Eddie's accentuates the tan skin peeking out of his collar. He has a black tie that I have the urge to reach out and grab, so I can pull him closer to me, and his green eyes bore into me, and I never want to look away.

"Hey, sunshine," he says as he puts his hands in his pockets. If I know my raindrop, I know he is resisting the urge to reach for me, the same way I am as I close my hands into fists at my sides.

"Hi," I reply, my eyes roaming around his face, looking at it like I don't have every line, every freckle, every angle memorized. His lips curve, a small smile angling to one side of his face, revealing the dimple that I still believe doesn't belong on a face with a jaw so sharp.

"You okay?" He asks, even though I know he knows the answer. There are conversations buzzing around us, and I know no one but Mateo—and Annie—know the act we're putting on.

"Not really," I say because I promised him I wouldn't pretend. The same as he promised me.

"Me either," he answers. There is a discomfort in this conversation, which makes my chest ache. Conversations have never felt forced with Eddie, confirming my fears that things will never be the same.

"We shouldn't do this right now."

"I know," he replies.

"We can't make today about us."

"I know," he says again.

I turn to see Mateo and Annie still talking, now joined by Luke, and Mateo must sense me looking at him because his eyes meet mine for a brief second before he looks away, and I knew that him dismissing me would be the nail in the fucking coffin.

I feel my breathing go shallow, but I can't do this here.

I don't want to remind everyone, now of all times, that I betrayed the one person who has been a constant in my life. The one person who was there for me when my life completely fell apart, more than once, and I didn't know how to put the pieces back together.

I feel Eddie's hand on my back, and I use it as my lifeline, reminding me that I need to breathe, but I can't get my lungs to take in air.

I close my eyes, trying to stop the inevitable, but I can't stop my mind from racing. I can't calm the thoughts telling me that I fucked everything up. That I deserve to be alone because I'm selfish. It's why Nico left angry that night. It's why Eddie and Mateo won't be friends anymore. It's why I'm such a fucking disappointment to the only family I have.

"I got her," I hear, but it feels like I'm underwater. Mateo has appeared at my side, staring daggers at Eddie. I don't even have time to register what is happening as Mateo walks me out of the private room until he leads me outside and the gust of the fall wind helps me catch my breath.

The wedding ceremony started at 5 p.m., and the dinner and reception is set to start at 6:30 p.m. It must be almost time for the rest of the guests to arrive because the sky is getting dark.

"What did I say about making today about you, Mia?" Mateo says, his voice stern. I thought he brought me out here to help, but it just confirms how much of a fuck-up I am.

I don't know what to say to him. Knowing now is not the time to hash this out but also knowing that I don't think I can make it through the rest of the night if I keep letting my mind run wild.

"Mateo," I start. He is leaning back on the brick wall of the venue. We're out on a vacant patio that is used for summer weddings, the patio furniture covered with plastic tarps. "I'm sorry. About not telling you about Eddie."

"Mia, no. We aren't doing this right now." He makes a move to head back inside, but I grab his arm.

"No, Mateo. You need to listen to me. I never meant for this to happen. It just did!" My voice is raising, but I can't help it.

He turns to face me, pulling his arm out of my grip. "I told you. I told you to focus on yourself. To not let yourself get distracted with someone, let alone my best friend."

"I am focusing on myself. I'm not the broken girl going around punching guys at the bars or refusing to let go of the past anymore. I'm moving on. I'm healing," I reply, needing my brother to see that I am not the same person I was two summers ago.

Mateo scoffs. "You're doing it again, you know. Trying to fix someone who is broken. You tried it with Nico; you're doing it now with Eddie. I need you to focus on you!" His voice raises slightly before he begins to pace.

Eddie's possessiveness must have rubbed off on me because my instinct to protect him overpowers the apology I was ready to spout.

Mateo is stooping low, and I've learned that he uses that tactic when he's mad.

But mad is good. I can work with mad.

Anything but disappointment.

"I'll apologize for not telling you, but I will not apologize for loving Eddie." All day, I have been battling thoughts that I haven't had about myself in months because of how shitty I felt for lying to my brother. I've been telling myself for hours now that I ruined everything. That Eddie and I will never be able to get over this. That I got between my brother and Eddie, but I don't think that's the case. "You have no right to speak about Eddie that way. He is not broken, and I never thought he needed fixing. And shame on you for throwing Nico at me." My voice has an edge that I barely ever take with Mateo.

"You don't get to talk to me about Eddie. He's my best friend. I've known him for a decade. You've known him for a year." He is trying to hit me where it hurts, but I can take it.

"I didn't mean to come between you guys, but you're acting as if he is someone who is going to ruin me. You're wrong, Mateo."

"I told you to stay away from him and you went behind my back. You lied to me for months and so did my friends."

"I'm not saying it was the right thing to do, but I can't take it back now."

"I thought I could trust you. I thought I could trust my best friend. You took that from me, Mia."

I take a step towards my brother, and tears fill my eyes. This isn't about me and Eddie. This is about how we lied to him. This is about how he feels he misplaced his trust, and it makes me feel even worse.

"Mateo," I say, and I watch as the hurt writes itself all over his face. The sky keeps getting darker, the air getting cooler, but I don't care. I ignore the goosebumps on my arms, my exposed skin freezing to the touch. "We didn't want to hurt you." My voice cracks, and I am struggling to keep all the thoughts and emotions straight.

He looks down at his feet, and I watch as he inhales and lets out a shaky exhale.

"You could have told me," he says, but his voice is just above a whisper. "You didn't have to hide it from me."

"I thought it was for the best. Initially, I didn't know what was going to happen between us. Then, I was scared. I was scared you would be mad, and I never wanted to come between you two."

"You love him?" The question seems random, but I know how my brother's brain works. He is trying to see things clearly, trying to get all the facts so he can make a decision on how to move forward. I don't know if he thought we were just fooling around, but I know Mateo wants what is best for me and for Eddie. I knew I just needed to be able to explain that we are what is good for each other.

"More than anything," I say. "I didn't think it was possible to love someone again, but this is different. Eddie, every day, reminds me that life doesn't have to be about what you lost."

Mateo shakes his head. "I don't know about this," he says but more to himself than to me.

I take a step towards him, and I wrap my arms around his waist. "I'm sorry," I say, knowing my makeup is ruined with the amount of tears that have slid down my cheeks.

It takes him a second, but he returns my gesture, wrapping his arms around my shoulders. "I've always just wanted what was best for you, Mia. I know you think I'm overprotective, but I never wanted you to think you couldn't come to me about anything. I never wanted you to think you had to hide something like this from me."

"I should've come to you," I say into his chest. "I just didn't want you to be mad, especially because you made me so off-limits to any guy who even glanced at me."

"I was just trying to look out for you."

"But I've told you I can take care of myself."

"I've seen you do it too. Starting your photography business. Getting those clients. I don't tell you this enough, but I am so proud of you."

"Does this mean you'll let me back on the tour?"

"Don't push it. I've barely forgiven you."

"So you're saying I'm forgiven," I tease.

"What I'm saying is," he pauses before saying, "I should trust you to take care of yourself."

"You *can* trust me."

"You're right. I'm just having a hard time accepting it, I guess. When I told Talia the story about you punching that guy last year and me getting pissed at you, she told me I was overreacting. She thinks I'm too overprotective of you."

I lean back and look up at him. "*Talia*?"

It is dark now, the only light being some string lights on the vacant patio. His lips threaten to curve upward, but I know he is trying to be serious and probably stay mad at me.

"My girlfriend," he responds.

"You talk about me with your girlfriend?" I step out of his embrace but immediately regret it with how cold it is getting.

"I was actually on my way to invite you to dinner with us tomorrow when I found you boning my best friend."

My jaw drops, and my eyes widen. "I was *not* boning your best friend. I did bang him last night though," I say and stick my tongue out at the same moment Mateo groans and shakes his head.

"No, nope. We are not doing this. Boning my friends—banging my friends," he pauses to exaggerate a shiver, "it is still an off-limits topic. I'm pretending that you never said that."

I laugh, and it feels good after a day like today, having to pretend and hold everything in.

Mateo smiles at me, and I know that I didn't lose him.

I know I never will.

"So, I get to meet your girlfriend tomorrow?"

"I was hoping. She wants to meet you too." Mateo slips his hands in his pockets and his features have a boyish glint to them, almost like he's embarrassed.

"Can my *boyfriend* come?"

Mateo sighs. I'm worried I pushed him too far, but he surprises me when he says, "Let me talk to him first."

"I'll go get him," I say all too quickly, but I run past him and open the door leading back inside before he can change his mind. "Wait here," I yell over my shoulder. I cannot take another minute of being between these two.

"And tell him tonight doesn't count. He can play with us tonight, but I'm not letting him back in the band. Yet." He tries to sound serious, but it isn't convincing.

I fast-walk back into the private room, but it's empty. I glance at the clock on the wall to see it says 6:34, so I know Drew and Emmett and the rest of the wedding party, Eddie included, probably joined the rest of the guests by the bar while they waited for dinner which is being served at 7:00.

We aren't doing anything special, no DJ announcing the couple or wedding party. Drew just has her phone hooked up to the speakers with a playlist we made over the summer, and she wanted to have time to mingle with guests before dinner. Cross My Heart is still supposed to perform, playing their rendition of "A Thousand Years" for Drew and Emmett's first dance and then a few of their originals to get the dancing started. Luke is supposed to then take over the music with the playlist he made for the dancing after the show.

With all the craziness of today, I don't even think about what the hell was going to happen with Cross My Heart playing, just now realizing that Eddie and Mateo were going to have to play together in the midst of this mess that is slowly getting cleaned up.

I leave the empty room ready to head to the bar, but I run into the chest of exactly the man I was looking for.

"There you are," he says, grabbing me by the arms. Worry lines his handsome features. "Are you okay? Holy shit, you're freezing. Where have you been?"

"Talking to Mateo, who wants to talk to you. Let's go." I grab him by the arm, needing to get the two most important men in my life talking before Mateo changes his mind.

"What happened? Wait, Mia. Stop. You've been crying."

We pause just a few feet from the patio door. "Tell me what happened."

I sigh. "He was upset that we lied to him. I think he was more hurt about us not trusting him enough to tell him than us actually being together." I look down the hallway we're in towards the direction where everyone is out there celebrating the newlyweds. We have already been gone for a while, I don't want Drew and Emmett worried about where we are.

"Don't worry. Annie told everyone that you're helping Mateo and I with our performance tonight," he says, literally reading my mind.

"Are Theo and Silas here?"

"Yeah, setting up now. But wait, are you sure Mateo wants to talk to me? I think I'll be much harder to forgive than you. I don't get to play the *little sister* card with him."

"He wants to talk to you. Regardless of what it is, we owe it to him. You guys need to talk before you play together anyway."

Eddie sighs, grabbing me by the arm and pulling me into his chest. I instantly relaxed in his embrace, tension I didn't know I was still holding releasing every moment he holds me.

Mateo may be on the road to forgiving me, but I know we won't gain his trust back overnight.

I run my hands up Eddie's chest, finding his face between my palms and pulling him down to my lips. I'm wearing the same red heels as I was last night, but he still towers over me. I lightly press my lips to his before pulling back, not having to worry about the lipstick that I'll have to reapply before joining the party.

"You ready?" I ask.

"Are you coming too?"

"It'll probably be better if you two just talk." I drop my hands to my sides. "Go."

CHAPTER 49

EDDIE

I WANT to take Mia's hand and run. Wishing that we could go back to our little bubble of just us. The bubble that we worked so hard to create, only for it to pop in an instant and for reality to spill in.

I shake the thought away, knowing that I didn't work this hard to be the man she deserved to not convince her brother —my best friend—that I am the man who will love her for the rest of my life.

Mateo has seen me at my absolute worst, and I am about to show him that I am at my absolute best, and it's all thanks to his little sister.

I push the door to the patio out, and I see Mateo leaning back against the brick wall of the venue we are at. He turns to look at me as the door closes behind me.

"Mia said you wanted to talk," I say. I figured it would be best to let him lead the conversation, knowing that this morning he wanted nothing to do with me.

"She told me you guys were serious about each other. Is it true?"

"Yes." I barely let the question leave his mouth before I answer. "I'm in love with her."

Mateo shakes his head, but it isn't out of disappointment. It kind of seems like he's at a loss. This is my best friend. Someone I know like the back of my hand. I know he doesn't lose his cool. I know he thinks of every single possible outcome, so he can be prepared. He is just like his sister in that way.

I also know that he likes solutions. He likes clear-cut ways to solve problems.

He doesn't like losing his cool. He doesn't like conflict.

So, I'll make it easy for him.

"Mateo, I love her in a way I didn't know I was capable of. I thought I was broken, too broken to even bother fixing. I grew up thinking my only job was to make sure everyone around me was okay. Protected and safe. I never wanted anyone to have to worry about me.

"It was Mia who helped me realize I was capable of more, that I deserved more. She helped me see these parts of me weren't so broken to begin with. I just buried them so deep that I forgot they were there." I pause. Mateo's eyes are glued to mine as he takes in every word. "She made life worth living again, Mateo."

A few silent moments pass before Mateo lets out an exhale. "I will never forget that night with your dad." We have never talked about this. Ever. One of the things we both leave unsaid.

"I've never thanked you for that."

"You didn't have to. I'd do anything for you, you know that. That's what I'm saying. But that's also why I think I reacted the way I did this morning. I asked you to stay away from Mia, knowing that she had a lot going on, and so do you, and you went behind my back. That's fucked up, man."

"Trust me, I know it was a really shitty thing for us—for me—to do to you. I can't explain to you how guilty I felt, but I also can't explain to you how I was willing to do anything not to lose her. But I should've never let that include lying to you." I reach out to put my hand on his shoulder. "I'm sorry."

"You guys are the real deal? Not just messing around?"

"What I have with her is as real as it gets."

He nods his head, taking in my words. For a second, I worry that he's going to say he doesn't care and kick me in the balls, but then he finally says, "I'm happy for you."

What?

Not what I was expecting him to say, and the confusion must be written all over my face.

"I know the road here hasn't been easy for you. I've noticed a change in you. I just didn't realize it was because of my sister. You seem happy. *Genuinely* happy."

"I am."

"Don't fuck it up."

"I don't plan on it." I pull him in for a hug, feeling a weight on my chest lift, the guilt I've been carrying dissolve.

"Did you guys kiss and make up?" I hear behind me, and I would know the voice—the sass, the spark—anywhere.

"Come here," I say, bringing both my best friend and my girlfriend in, and the three of us don't have to say aloud how much it means to hold one another after thinking we never would again.

"So, am I back in the band?" I ask, and the three of us laugh, and all is right in the world.

"Now, join me in welcoming Drew and Emmett, our beautiful newlyweds, to the dance floor for their first official dance as husband and wife!" Mateo says into the microphone.

After the three of us joined the wedding party, only Annie knowing some of the details of the whirlwind of what just happened, we got some drinks and sat down for dinner, and it was like we never left.

The guests cheer as Emmett and Drew make their way to the dance floor, and I tap my drumsticks together three times to signal Theo and Silas to start our rendition of the song Drew walked down the aisle to.

While the couple is beautiful, lovingly looking into each other's eyes, I can't stop staring at my girl, sitting at our table, watching Drew and Emmett dance.

When I look at her, I see my future.

When I'm with her, I feel like the best version of myself.

When I hold her, I am reminded of everything I have been missing all my life.

Mateo comes in with the vocals, and I didn't realize it when Drew was walking down the aisle, which feels like days ago at this point, but I realize now why she and Emmett chose this song as theirs.

The lyrics Mateo sings portray the feelings I have for Mia. Every word, every phrase perfectly captures how I feel about her. How I have spent my whole life waiting for her, and I will spend the rest of my life loving her.

I watch her until her eyes finally find me, and I give her a wink. Wishing I was close enough to see her chest redden as she smiles at me. I feel like I am capable of anything when she looks at me that way.

As Mateo continues to sing, as we continue to play, Mia's mouth moves with the lyrics, and it feels like she is singing to me, telling me she feels the same way about me as I do her.

Music is something she thought she would never get back, yet here she is enjoying the music and letting herself feel all the feelings she used to run away from.

I'm so fucking proud of her. So fucking proud to be hers.

And when we finished our few songs, I *finally* get the chance to ask Mia to dance with me. With one hand on her hip and one hand holding hers at my chest, I bring my lips to her ear, and I tell her I never want to know what a day feels like without her, and I will spend every moment I am with her showing her that she is the best thing to ever happen to me.

EPILOGUE: THREE MONTHS LATER

EDDIE

WE HAVE to remember for our next tour that having a break for the holidays is non-negotiable. We have played dozens of shows since the weekend after Drew and Emmett's wedding, and we finally have a chance to *chill*.

It is also impossible to get everyone together these days between tour for Mia and I, vet school for Annie, school for Drew, and running Lenny's for Luke and Emmett who have still not hired someone to replace Annie and me.

I'm not technically employed for Lenny's anymore, both Mateo and I decided to quit our day jobs to focus on the band, but I don't think I'll ever make a clean cut from Lenny's. Not with the people who I spend all of my free time with.

It's Christmas Day, and we are supposed to be at Drew and Emmett's new house in twenty minutes, but Mia and I are taking every minute we can to enjoy time in *our* place.

The day after the wedding, Mia and I went to dinner with Mateo and Talia, and I could tell it meant a lot to Mia. It was my first time meeting one of Mateo's girlfriends, so I knew he was pretty serious about her.

He is spending Christmas with Talia's family in Michigan, and he mentioned that he is going to ask her to move in with him when we finish the Heartbreakers Tour in March. I can't help but think that he put a lot of his own life on hold for Mia, and I think he is finally realizing that he doesn't have to anymore.

After the pleasantries at dinner, we laid down some ground rules for navigating this brother's best friend and sister's boyfriend relationship, for all of our sanities.

Mateo was very clear about being newly on board with my relationship with Mia but not wanting it to be in his face all the time. Talia, who was the perfect mediator for the three of us, brought up the idea of me or Mateo getting a new place, but Mia threw me for a loop and made all my dreams come true at the same time then she asked me to move in with her.

It took me less than a second to think it over and agree.

I spent over a year only being able to indulge in stolen moments with her.

And I'm done with it.

"We got to go," I whisper against Mia's skin. My face is nuzzled into her neck, her naked body pressed into mine, her back against my front while we lay in our bed.

"I don't want to," she groans, but she knows we have to. She presses her ass into my lap, and I try to keep my composure; otherwise, we are going to be *really* late.

It ends up taking ten more minutes and one more time making her come on my tongue before we make it out of bed to get ready.

We spent the entire night wrapped up in each other after getting back to our place late last night, but I will never get sick of her.

"Can you grab the bag of presents?" She asks as she puts on her shoes. "And the wine?"

"Done and done," I say as I grab my keys and step into my shoes.

I'm sure I look ridiculous with my sneakers and my pajamas, but when Annie says that Christmas Day is for pajamas, you don't argue.

Mia and I have matching pajama sets, white with Christmas trees dotting the long-sleeve shirt and pants like polka dots, and with the presents and wine in hand, we are ready to go.

"Perfect. We'll call your mom and sisters on the way over to wish them a Merry Christmas. Did they make it to your aunt's okay?"

"Yep, all good."

"Good. Daisy?" Mia calls. Our dog, now full-grown still as calm, cool, and collected, as ever slowly saunters over and sits at her feet, wagging her tail as Mia gets her into her white sweater with a big Christmas tree on the back that matches the little ones on ours.

"You ready to see your sister, Dais?" Mia asks in her puppy voice as she hooks Daisy to her leash.

Daisy barks once, her tail wagging a little more. Her energy comes out more with any mention of Rosie.

"Okay, let's go."

"Wait," I say, as she opens the door to our apartment.

"What?"

I lean in and kiss her hard because I learned it helps her slow down her mind when it's moving too fast.

"Okay, now I'm ready," I say, giving her a wink as I grab her hand and lead her out the door.

Mia

"You're just jealous, Emmett," Luke bellows. "You wish you were in a reindeer onesie, not just boring plaid pajamas."

"I didn't even say anything," Emmett deadpans.

We are sitting in Drew and Emmett's newly decorated living room. There is a big sectional that takes up most of the room. The TV has one of those videos of a fireplace on a loop, and Christmas music is filling the space not filled by the conversations. There is a Christmas tree in the corner, decorated with black and silver ornaments, a present for each of us under the tree.

The six of us did a Secret Santa this year, but Annie said presents had to wait until after the brunch Emmett made and after her signature hot chocolate. And what Annie says goes.

Luke is on one side of the couch, picking a fight with Emmett who is sitting on the floor with Drew in his lap, both in black and white plaid pajama sets.

"Luke, don't make fun of the plaid pajamas, or Emmett won't let you have the extra waffles when you get hungry later," Drew says, and I see a twitch of Emmett's lips.

Eddie and I are sitting on the couch, my back leaning against his front as we just let Luke go off about how the reindeer onesie he has on and Annie's snowman onesie are the best pajamas out of all six of us.

Rosie and Daisy got all their energy out when they first saw each other, running around in Drew and Emmett's backyard. Luke put Rosie in reindeer antlers that stayed on her for about three minutes, but my girl Daisy is still rocking her Christmas tree sweater.

Annie comes in from the kitchen, a tray of hot chocolate with RumChata in her hand, handing one to each of us before adding her two cents to the conversation. "The onesie is much better than the Britany Spears costume he wore for Halloween this year."

"Hey!" Luke exclaims as we all laugh about the memory of the Halloween party Eddie and I hosted a few months ago when Cross My Heart had the weekend off from shows. Luke showed up with pink pom poms in his hair and a schoolgirl outfit, and he kept queuing "...Baby One More Time" to the point I think we listened to it fifteen times. "It was better than Emmett's usual black attire with the addition of the Jason Halloween mask. Boring!"

"It wasn't a competition," I say in between laughter, as Emmett looks at Luke like he is a bug about to be squashed. The memory of how the two of them looked next to each other in our kitchen will forever be burned into my brain.

"You're just saying that because you *won*. Just wait until next year," Luke says to me. "I'm already thinking about how I'm going to top it. You and Eddie may be reigning champs with your Rocky and Apollo costumes, but I will win next year."

"Relax, Rudolph," Annie says as she sits next to him on the couch with her mug of hot chocolate. "Are we ready for presents?" She asks the rest of us.

"Let's do it," Eddie says from behind me, excited to give Emmett his gift. We picked names out of a hat when we celebrated Thanksgiving at Annie's apartment, and Eddie has been planning Emmett's present since we went home that night. Emmett is a big fan of the headliner for the Heartbreakers Tour, so Eddie got him some merch and had the band sign a record for him to give to Emmett.

The smile on Emmett's face, the one that shows all his teeth—and is usually only directed at Drew—came out when he opened it, and he knew it was from Eddie right away.

"They're excited to meet you too. I invited them to Lenny's after the show we have in Milwaukee next month."

"Seriously?" Emmett's eyes widen, and it is the first time his hard, gruff features look have a boyish, fan-girling charm to them. "Thanks, man."

I'm next, and I know when I open the new camera bag, one way more stylish than my gray one that is on the verge of falling apart, that my Secret Santa was Annie.

"Annie! I say, pulling it out and grabbing my old one that I have at the foot of the couch. "It's perfect. Thank you." I grab my camera and turn it on. "I meant to take pictures today, but I always forget when I'm with you guys, which I guess is a good thing—" my voice trails off when I start arrowing through the pictures. I put a memory card in from the night Drew and Emmett got engaged, and it is the same one I kept in there for the whole summer, aside from switching it out for the ones I use for work or the one I used for Drew and Emmett's wedding.

As I arrow through, I see a bunch of pictures of me. Ones I didn't take from various days. Some are at our apartment. Some are out. I usually bring my camera with me, but I thought I was the only one to use it.

I look over at my shoulder to the smirk looking down on me. "What?" Eddie asks, taking a sip of his hot chocolate.

"I'm the photographer," I say. "*I* take the pictures." I'm not fooling anyone with my fake annoyance. In all reality, it makes me feel warm inside. Eddie wanting to take pictures of me, and sneakily doing so. I thought I didn't like having my picture taken, but looking at these pictures of me, Eddie knew how to capture my moments of smiling, laughing, or literally doing nothing.

This man is something else.

Making me feel things like it is the first time.

"I love you," I say, pressing a kiss to his lips. He tastes like chocolate, and I wish we weren't surrounded by our friends right now.

"Okay, okay, lovebirds," Annie interrupts. "Drew, you're next."

Luke got Drew two new books that were released less than three days ago, and Emmett got Annie new stainless steel mixing bowls. I got Luke the new sneakers he's been talking about, and Drew got Eddie new headphones he's been wanting.

This group of people know each other inside and out, and we love each other regardless. It is the family I never knew I needed, but the one that I will always cherish because I know they aren't going anywhere. It is the one that will continue to grow and flourish, and I can't wait to see where we all will go.

With a soreness in my cheeks from smiling, surrounded with the people I love the most, I thank my lucky star, the one who I miss every day, that I have such a life to live for.

EXTENDED EPILOGUE: ONE YEAR LATER

MIA

IT'S the last show of the tour, and I cannot wait to be home with Eddie and Daisy.

The Heartbreakers tour has been life-changing in more ways than one, but I cannot wait to no longer have to live out of a suitcase for weeks at a time.

Cross My Heart is almost done with their setlist, the one I have heard one million times but could hear one million times more, and I am in the zone, getting pictures of the crowd, the guys, and trying not to drool over my boyfriend.

My knees will never *not* go weak watching this man rip off his T-shirt and play his drums with nothing but his black jeans and gold chain on.

Mateo's vocals and Eddie's lyrics fill the humid air around us, the last show of the summer causing a buzz within the venue that every screaming fan can feel.

As the last song—my song—ends, I drop my camera, letting it hang around my neck, and clap my hands above my head with the rest of the crowd, cheering for my brother, Theo, Silas, and Eddie loud enough that my voice will be scratchy tomorrow.

"Thank you, everyone!" my brother says into his microphone, wiping his sweaty hair from his forehead, a wide grin on his face. Theo and Silas walk towards him in the middle of the stage as Eddie rounds his drum set to join them.

"This tour has been a dream come true for us," Mateo continues, "and it wouldn't have been possible without the amazing bands on this tour. Thank you to Burning Down and The Falling Flames for bringing us along on this wild ride, and we can't wait to join them again next year!"

The crowd cheers as the guys clap towards the backstage in their thanks to the co-headliners for the tour along with all the behind-the-scenes team who just recently invited Cross My Heart onto next year's Heartbreakers Round Two tour.

"As always, we want to thank all the people who make this possible. We are so lucky to have such an amazing Cross My Heart team," Mateo says, but I can't tear my eyes away from Eddie who has the genuine smile on his face that sends heat to my lower belly and my skin to tingle. His eyes are on me, and you would think I would be used to being under his gaze, but it will never get old.

We have been *officially* together for over a year now, but it feels so much longer. Eddie is someone I feel like I've known my whole life, someone who gets me on a level that goes deeper than anyone could ever understand. I know the universe helped me find him when I needed him most, when I needed the reminder on how to live. Eddie helped me move on from the past, keeping it close but not letting it take over, and he helped me look forward to the future, a future I thought I lost all those years ago.

"Lastly, Eddie wants to give a special thanks to our photographer, who you all know is the person that we will forever owe everything to. Everyone, please help us in thanking the person who has been with us from the begin-ning, my baby sister, Mia Lane!" The crowd cheers as faces around me turn towards me. "Mia, come up here!"

And just like that, the crowd parts, and I make my way to

join the guys on stage. I can't help but be a little confused as I make my way towards the guys, unsure of what exactly they have planned.

I usually always just meet them by their merch booth to help with their sales after their shows, but this? This is new.

The closer I get, the smirks on Theo and Silas's face become clearer, and my brother is looking at me as if I just found the answer to world peace. Eddie runs a hand through his hair, and I read the nerves on his face like words on my favorite book.

Something is up.

When I'm up on stage, Mateo brings me in for a hug, and I ignore the layer on sweat on his skin as I feel his arms tighten around me. "I love you," he whispers in my ear. I hear the crowd's cheers grow louder, and I have no idea why.

Maybe they are liking the cute brother-sister moment?

Before I can say it back and ask what the hell is going on, Mateo lets go of me and places his hands on my shoulders, turning me around to a sight that instantly knocks the wind out of me, tears forming in my eyes.

"What the actual hell is happening?" I exclaim when I see Eddie down on one knee. His smile is wide, my favorite Eddie smile that causes the skin surrounding his eyes to crinkle, making his green eyes shining brighter. In one hand, a pink ring box. In his other hand is the microphone Mateo must have handed to him when we were mid-hug.

"Hi, baby," he says into his microphone, a slight crack of emotion in his voice. The crowd hoots and hollers before going completely silent. Eddie lets out an exhale, before bringing the mic back up to his mouth. "Mia, you coming into my life was a gift I didn't think I deserved. The light that you have washed over me since the moment I saw you turn the corner in the hallway of your apartment building is something I will spend the rest of my life showing you I am deserving of." I bring my hands to my mouth, tears streaming down my face. "You are the sunshine to my rainy day. I love you with everything I have."

Eddie hands the microphone to Theo who is standing just behind him, the rest of his words being just for us. He opens the pink ring box to reveal a pear-shaped diamond that makes my tears stream even faster because my raindrop knows exactly how to make my heart feel like it is about to explode.

"Sunshine, will you marry me?"

I don't even hesitate because I've known for months that this is the man I want to have by my side for the rest of my life. "Yes!" I exclaim through the tears, my head nodding up and down, not being able to believe this is happening.

Eddie takes the ring out of the box and slips onto my finger. The crowd goes wild, but I can only focus on us. He is off his knees, arms around me in less than a second, his embrace being my favorite place to be—where I belong.

ACKNOWLEDGMENTS

Writing this book was hard, but it was one of the most rewarding accomplishments in my life. *Giving Me Butterflies* was a story I sat on for so long and I thought my writing career started and ended with it. It wasn't until the thought of a drummer with sad eyes who fell in love with his best friend's sister wouldn't leave my mind that I told myself that I *could* do this again.

Crash & Burn has been such an incredible rollercoaster, one that I never thought I'd be on. With this book, I had such an amazing community of family, friends, fellow indie authors, and readers cheering me on from the very beginning, and that community is what made this book possible.

Thank you to my alpha reader, Hannah, for loving this book and these characters as much as me. To have someone in my life for so many years, someone who has grown up with me, it was so amazing to have you on this journey with me.

Thank you to my beta readers. Your comments, reactions, and feedback helped me make Mia and Eddie's story the best it could be.

Thank you to my editor, Caitlin, who never ceases to amaze me with her skills and attention to detail. Working with you makes the daunting task of tearing a book apart to make it better way more fun than it should be.

Thank you to my real-life found family for making it so easy to write about a crew of trauma-bonded friends who love each other through all the hardships that come their way.

To my Elle-Bell, this book is dedicated to the readers who

loved a story about a teacher and a bar owner, and that dedication was written with you on the forefront of my mind. You found me when I thought this whole author thing was a dream that was meant to stay a dream. You loving Drew, Emmett, Mia, Eddie, Annie, Luke, and this world that they exist in is one of the biggest reasons this book is what it is. I don't ever want to know what it's like to write a book that you aren't a part of. Thank you for making me feel like I always have someone in my corner who not only gets me but makes me feel understood in ways no one else does.

As always, the biggest thank you goes to my rock. Max, I am so lucky to have you. You make writing about love so easy because I have the privilege of being loved by you.

Finally, to my readers. Thank you for making my dreams come true. Being able to write these silly little stories about these silly little characters who live rent-free in my brain is the greatest gift I could ever ask for. Your love and support for me makes this all possible. I am forever grateful to you.

So happy you're here.

ABOUT THE AUTHOR

Katy is the indie author based in Milwaukee. Her favorite trope is forced proximity, and she is a firm believer that found families are the best families.

Lover of all things romance, pop punk, tattoos, anime, rainy days, matcha, her husband, and her daughter, Katy's purpose for writing is to remind readers that you are deserving of the love you read about.

When she's not writing, you can find her reading, or adding to her never-ending TBR.

instagram.com/authorkatymichele

tiktok.com/@authorkatymichele

threads.com/@authorkatymichele

goodreads.com/katymichele

amazon.com/author/katymichele

ALSO BY KATY MICHELE

Lenny's Bartenders

Giving Me Butterflies (Drew & Emmett)

Crash & Burn (Mia & Eddie)

Back to You (Annie & Luke)

Hey Honey's Baristas

From the Ashes (Rumi & Jack)

Call You Mine (Ava & Anderson)